KOSTAS KROMMYDAS

# Lake

# of

# Memories

*Based on a true story*

Kostas Krommydas

*With the kind support of*

***REALIZE***

*Via Donizetti 3, 22060 Figino Serenza (Como), Italy*

*Phone: +39 0315481104*

"What's past is prologue."

— William Shakespeare, The Tempest

To Vivi, for the life lessons she taught me while fighting for
her life ...

Kostas Krommydas

# Contents

Kostas Krommydas

# January 28, 1979, Ioannina, Greece

The small red lamp dimly lit two dark figures—a man and a woman—squeezed under a tin roof awning. They were barely visible as they huddled at the entrance of an old house, its walls peeling with dampness. They stood there like marble statues, shivering, bundled up in so many clothes, scarves, and woolly hats that their faces were imperceptible. The howling wind, carrying the musty smell of the nearby lake, whipped their clothes and frosted them with thick white snowflakes.

The nearby houses were dark. A loose wooden shutter on an abandoned house thumped against the window frame, the only artificial sound, a monotonous, repetitive thud against the growling gale. The wind's bellows made it sound like a monster baring its teeth, ready to devour all in its path. It roared and tore into an abandoned Christmas tree lying on a pile of junk, trying to rip off its faded ribbons. With every blast of frigid air, the two figures shifted closer together, trembling, seeking shelter.

The door suddenly burst open and a woman wrapped in a thick coat appeared in the semidarkness. The unbuttoned garment flew open in the gust, revealing her underwear. She gripped it tightly, raising the collar against her neck to shield against the cold. Leaning towards them, she hurriedly said something. Barely had the words left her mouth before she drew back inside and slammed the door shut.

Inside the house, a small hallway ended in a wooden staircase, which led up to an interior balcony surrounded by a wooden railing and a row of open doors. In the meager light of two lackluster oil lamps, two women stood over a blazing wooden stove desperately trying to chase away the cold, the embers casting shadows on their faces. They huddled over a pot of water, waiting for it to boil.

A sudden gust of wind blew the smoke back down the stove's chimney and into the room, where it mingled with the heavy scent of cheap perfume and filled the room with a gray haze. Cheap paintings of naked women lounging provocatively decorated the walls. A skeletal man with sunken eyes lay fast asleep on a wooden bench under a threadbare overcoat, his loud snores accompanying the crackle of burning wood.

The woman, still wrapped in her coat, hurried past them and up the stairs. They looked at her anxiously as she ascended, and then up at one of the open doors on the landing. Loud moans spilled out of that room. In a house such as this, it was not easy to tell whether the sounds were cries of pleasure or pain.

The moans got louder and louder, masking the whistles of the gale. The voice of a man muttering oaths through gritted teeth echoed down the stairway. The woman approached the open door timidly, scared, and slowly entered the room.

The light inside was stronger. A heavyset man was crouched between the open legs of the screaming woman. Behind her, at the head of the bed, another man sat on a pillow and gripped her hands tightly. He wore a knit cap and nervously chewed the end of a damp, unlit cigarette hanging from his lips. The cast-iron rods of the headboard rose threateningly behind him against the cracked wall that supported a roof made of cheap planks.

On the sweat-drenched mattress, the young woman tried to relieve her pain with loud, piercing screams. Her nose and mouth were crusted with dry blood. Her cheek and jaw were purple and swollen. She appeared to be pleading for something between screams and sobs.

The man in the knit cap pulled her hands sharply. The woman in the coat looked at him and said, as gently as she could, "You must let go of her hands. Otherwise, she won't be able to ..."

He cast a glance at the man at the other end of the bed, paying her no heed. One nod from the other man, however, and he sharply released his grip on her wrists. Swiftly, the woman brought her arms down by her sides and gripped the sheet, as if desperate for something to hang onto.

The man at her feet pulled his hand away from between her legs and reached for a knife lying on a nearby table. He gripped it firmly in his hand, as if he was about to plunge it into her flesh. He moved closer to the woman on the bed. Tearfully, she begged him in a mixture of broken Greek and a foreign language to let her go. He brought the knife between her legs and snarled at her that it would soon be over.

Suddenly, he paused. The woman in the coat grabbed a towel and rushed to his side. A scream split the air, a howl that twisted the prostrate girl's face into an ugly grimace as she summoned her last ounce of strength. Then, at last, deathly silence. Everyone stared at her open legs and the bloody hands of the man before her. Even the roaring wind interrupted its frantic lashings.

The tinny sound of a baby crying broke the silence. The woman in the coat hurried to scoop up the child with the towel. For a second, its appearance seemed to stun the two men. Then, waking from his stupor, the heavyset man gripped the umbilical cord and cut it in one sudden, clumsy movement.

The mother's desperate cries as she tried to get up, stretching her arms to try to touch her baby, did not seem to move him. The man in the knit cap spat his cigarette on the dirty floor and pushed her back onto the mattress, hastily tying her hands to the headboard with a red handkerchief. Just then, one of the women who had been standing by the woodstove hurried into the room, holding the steaming pot wrapped in a piece of cloth. She placed it on a table and, assisted by the other woman, began to clean away the blood and birth fluids from the baby that did not stop wailing for a second.

Its eyes were still shut and did not open, except when they tried to clean its face. The two men stood beside them, impatiently waiting for their brief administrations to the defenseless human to come to an end. The mother's heartbreaking sobs as she begged them to hand the baby to her fell on uncaring ears.

Soon, the baby was mostly clean. The women wrapped it up in a sheet and then a blanket, and carefully handed it over to the man in the knit cap. Awkwardly, he held the swaddled infant and glanced at the woman on the bed who was struggling to escape her bonds.

With his free hand, he pulled his knit cap low over his brow to hide his face. Sensing his hesitation, the other man pushed him onto the landing. Needing no further prompting, he obeyed and walked downstairs.

Back inside the room, the two women approached the bed and tried to clean the blood from the sheets and the new mother's body. As if the loss of her baby had sapped her strength, she stopped struggling and faintly called out for help. Her beautiful eyes shone feverishly every time she opened them and looked at the two women. They tried to calm her down under the watchful eye of the man who had just separated mother and child with a single slash of his knife.

The man holding the baby carefully descended the stairs carrying his fragile cargo. An old *rebetiko*[1] song blared out in a crackle of static from an ancient radio beside the stove. As if nothing out of the ordinary was happening, he tunelessly sang along:

---

[1] Translator's Note: Greek urban popular song from the late 19th century to the 1950s, especially popular among the poor.

*Even if he cheated on you,*

*Even if he hurt you,*

*This love makes your eyes glow*

*Like a golden palace ...*

The skeletal man lying on the bench sat up and looked at him. A shriek of delight escaped his lips, and he lay back down again, pulling his overcoat up to his chin to keep warm.

Ignoring him, and still humming discordantly, the man in the knit cap reached the front door and opened it, coming face to face with the two dark figures waiting outside. A ferocious gust of wind forced him back a step, as if it were trying to stop his abduction of the defenseless baby.

Planting his feet firmly on the floorboards, he held out the bundle. The woman carefully cradled the blanket-wrapped baby, trying to shield it from the wind and the cold. The man accompanying her hastily brought out a package wrapped in white cloth and handed it over. The man in the knit cap grabbed it, hastily checked its contents, and then stepped back inside the house, still whistling the tune that had been playing on the radio. Without further delay, the woman's escort turned towards her and pulled her into his arms, shielding her and the baby with his coat.

They set off into the dark night, following the narrow path that led to the town center. Behind them, the shadow of a man who had been watching their every move from the sheltered porch of a nearby ruin stepped onto the path and followed them. He walked with great difficulty, holding a roughly bandaged hand tightly against his ribs. He paused and stared back at the brothel, then swiftly turned towards the couple moving away and followed them as noiselessly as his limping feet would allow.

The baby's loud wails echoed in the night. The woman's voice immediately rose in a tender lullaby as she tried to soothe it. As they walked away, its cries became fainter, swallowed up by the howling wind. Only the strange figure of the man was still faintly visible as he hobbled after them in the dark ...

Kostas Krommydas

# Athens-Present day

I stared at my screen and furiously clicked away, trying to bring some order to the files on my screen. I had to get all the Photoshopped images to the magazine by the evening, before it went to press the following morning. The latest disconcerting events in my life would not let me concentrate, however.

The soulless gazes of the skimpily clad models made my task even more difficult. No matter how hard I had tried in the studio the previous day to get them to show a spark, some feeling, I had failed. Almost all of them bore the usual faux-seductive expression: pouting lips and come-hither eyes filled with promise. Ironically, it had been Mary, the manager of the underwear company, who had encouraged them to project what my lens had captured.

I'd struggled to find angles that would somehow camouflage the evident pretense, but to no avail. Photoshop could work wonders, but it could not bring feeling to an impassive face. In moments like these, I bitterly regretted dropping out of medical school. My only consolation was that I rarely took on such gigs. I only did it for the money, so I could then accept projects I enjoyed for less or no pay—like my next job.

I could not wait for the weekend to come: a trip to Galaxidi, a low-key seaside town in mainland Greece. I would be photographing a famous dancer. Her latest show was a box-office hit and she was the current talk of the town. Tomorrow would be her last performance, and I would be attending so I could meet her and discuss details of the shoot. I would get to watch the notorious dance recital most had loved, and a vocal few had hated.

Absorbed in my screen as I was, I jumped when Ella gently touched my shoulder. I had forgotten she was in my house. She had styled the shoot, and we had returned to my house to grab a bite and pick the photos together.

Her touch made me uncomfortable, and I froze, averting my glance. I could tell she was flirting with me, a prospect that left me cold. I refused to mix business and pleasure, although she clearly had no such qualms.

"I think it's time for a break, Constantine," Ella said, moving closer. "I've settled on the photos I'd like to use, but I think we both need an interlude ... What do you say?"

I had asked her over because I needed help to select the photos, but now I realized that things were taking a direction I did not like. I decided to stop working for a moment and deal with the situation before it got out of hand.

"Yes, let's take a break," I agreed, standing up and moving towards the living room.

"I'd love a glass of wine if you'd join me," she said as she followed me.

I thought about refusing, but did not want to appear rude. She was a good-natured woman who had often helped me out. She worked for an advertising company, was good at her job and well connected.

Walking to the fridge, I removed a bottle of white wine. She asked me if she could put some music on, and I nodded. Inside me, however, I was already forming an escape plan should her moves become more overt. I did not want to give her false hope, nor did I want to hurt her.

She turned my antiquated CD-player on, and grimaced. I could tell she did not appreciate the strains of Chopin that filled the living room. Without asking me, she switched to the radio and found a station that played all the latest club hits. I hated the sound, but did not comment.

I poured the wine and walked towards her, holding out her glass. She shifted on the couch, making space for me to sit beside her, and I silently groaned in dismay. I sat as close to the armrest as I could, clinked her glass, and took a sip.

"I don't think you enjoyed that shoot," she said, gazing up at me through lowered eyelids.

"No, it was fine. I just struggle sometimes to understand what they want the photos to show. It can get confusing. I get one brief from you, a different brief from the client, and then ..."

She smiled as if I had just said something funny and moved closer, determined not to let the moment pass. "The client is always right, isn't that so?" she asked, arching her back and forcing the thin material of her top to stretch dangerously.

Just then, as if someone had heard my prayers, I thought I heard the doorbell ring. I listened carefully, trying to block out the loud music—there it was again. I stood up abruptly, and Ella cast me a perplexed look. "Someone's at the door," I said, just as a loud thump shook the wooden door.

Startled, she placed her glass on the coffee table. The pounding continued, and I heard my father's voice call out, "Constantine, open up! It's me!"

I was rooted to the spot with surprise. What was he doing here, at this hour? Without knowing why, I hurriedly pulled Ella up and led her to the bedroom, for some reason scared that he might see her. She looked stunned by my reaction but did not say a word. I signaled she should stay where she was and keep quiet, then closed the bedroom door.

My father's fists had not stopped hammering the door for a second. I ran to the living room and flung it open.

He was dressed in his police uniform, and he looked furious. "What took you so long?"

My surprise at seeing him was so great that I was at a loss for words. Impatiently, he pushed his way inside, motioning to a policeman standing behind him to wait in the corridor.

I caught a whiff of alcohol as he turned to close the door. It emanated from every pore of his massive frame. I had not spoken to him in a while, and our last conversation had not gone well. Ours had been a relationship of long silences and ferocious conflict. I could count good memories with my father on the fingers of one hand. I was now at a point where I no longer wished to see him, unable to forgive him for what he had put us through. My mother might have put up with him all these years, but I no longer could. Any recent contact with my father had been due to her, although her latest revelation had been the stroke that finally broke my back and shattered any threadbare bonds that may have lingered.

Lost in my own thoughts, I did not see him move farther inside the house. He stood staring at my computer screen. He made me feel like a teenager again, caught doing something I shouldn't be.

Annoyed, I walked over to him. "What do you want?"

"Is this what you photograph? Is this the reason you dropped out of med school? To take pictures of a bunch of sluts?" he asked sarcastically, his gaze fixed on the screen.

I could feel my blood boiling. I switched off the screen, trying to keep my cool. "What I do with my life is none of your business anymore. Now, speak up! What brings you here, uninvited?"

I realized that he was drunk. Not only did his breath stink, but his blurry eyes were having trouble focusing. He looked at me with the scowling grin he always wore whenever he was about to make some serious statement. "I dropped by to see how my son is doing. Is that so bad?"

I swallowed my snarky retort, determined to get rid of him as quickly as I could. "Well, now you have. If you don't mind, I need to get back to work."

He burst out laughing as if I'd said the funniest thing in the world. His loud guffaws turned into a hacking cough, unsurprisingly. The man smoked like a chimney. "Work? Looking at whores is work?"

I was beginning to lose my patience. If he carried on in this vein, I'd kick him out. As if he sensed my mounting anger, his demeanor changed. He sat down at my desk chair and swiveled towards me. He had gained even more weight, and his shirt was straining to contain his bulging stomach. He took on a serious look and pulled out a packet of cigarettes from his shirt pocket. Slowly, he removed one and placed it at the corner of his mouth, a familiar gesture for as long as I could remember. He spoke in a calmer tone, the cigarette bobbing up and down as the words poured out.

"I'm up for promotion these days ... an important post in drug enforcement. As you can understand, your running around with this crowd makes me look like a fool. But that's the least of it, boy ... I received a report yesterday that there was drug trafficking going on at the studio you were in. Drugs and prostitution. The place was under surveillance. I knew you were in there, so I called off the raid." The sardonic grin vanished, and was replaced by a scowl. "If the raid had gone ahead, our name would be all over the papers today. I won't be able to protect you forever, do you understand?"

It had not escaped my notice that such things went on in places I frequented, but I was enraged that he had sent his men to follow me. In any case, I was not involved in the crimes he'd mentioned. I could not even be sure he was telling the truth.

I tried to keep calm as I spoke, but even I could hear the tension in my voice. "I was at the studio only as a photographer. Once the job was done, I packed up and left. Whatever happens in that place when I'm not there has nothing to do with me. Since when do you keep an eye on what I do and where I'm at?"

He opened his mouth to reply, but I did not let him. "I'm asking you nicely. Stay out of my life. I will go wherever I like, work with whomever I want. If that leads to me getting arrested, then so be it."

My father stared at me fixedly, sucking the cigarette filter. He rose with some difficulty and brought his face close to mine. "I came here to tell you to be careful. I can see you don't appreciate it. Maybe you don't understand that your actions don't just affect me, but your mother too ..."

It was too much for me. "Don't you dare speak to me about my mother!" I yelled. "Not after everything you put her through. Where were you when she patiently waited on you? Out with your whores!"

I felt the sting on my cheek before I heard the slap. I pulled back in shock. He had not laid a hand on me in years. He used to hit me frequently when I was a child, but my mother put an end to it when she caught him cheating. Now, he knew that if he struck me, I would retaliate. And I was about to, raising my fist and ready to hit him with all my strength, when Ella burst into the room and grabbed my hand.

She stepped between us, pleading with me to calm down. My father looked at her, his twisted lips mocking her. I spat out words with venom, barely aware of what I was saying. I just wanted him to get out.

Slowly, condescendingly, he began to walk towards the door. The policeman outside had heard us argue and was pounding on the door. My father opened it and gestured at him to calm down, then closed it and turned back to us.

I could faintly hear the worried voices of my neighbors, but the throbbing in my ears drowned them out. Ella's pleading words to calm down brought me back to reality.

I stared at my father like a wild animal ready to pounce on its prey. He had removed the cigarette from his lips and was awkwardly shredding it with his fingers. I hated this gesture—it triggered unpleasant memories of a childhood spent with this man.

He spoke hesitantly, trying to control the hacking cough that threatened to choke him with every word. "I'm just looking out for you, son ..."

"Get out!" I yelled at the top of my lungs before he could say any more.

He froze and stared at me. If he did not move soon, I was determined to kick him out. As if he could sense it, he slowly turned and said, "We'll talk soon," before slamming the door behind him.

My heart was about to burst with anger, and Ella cupped my face, trying to calm me down. I did not think I could feel such hatred for another person: a violent hypocrite, he hid his secrets well behind the façade of devoted family man. All he cared about was climbing up the ranks by sucking up to his superiors.

Something trickled down my nose and touched my top lip. Ella hastily wiped it with delicate fingers, then ran to the bathroom to bring a towel. I tasted blood—possibly not caused by his slap, but the tension that had mounted inside me.

She returned quickly, and carefully pressed the damp facecloth to my face. She led me to the sofa and sat me down. Softly, she tilted my head back to stop the bleeding. I gently touched her hand. "Thank you, Ella. I'm sorry you had to see that ..."

"Don't worry about it," she replied. "Try to forget it. I didn't know things were so bad with your dad; you never said anything." She moved closer, trying to comfort me.

I did not know what else to say. Embarrassed, I slowly stood up and walked to the bathroom to splash some water on my face. I hated that she'd seen me like this, and would rather be left alone. The reality was I felt very uncomfortable that she had witnessed the scene and did not feel like discussing the details of this fraught relationship with her.

Inside the bathroom, I looked in the mirror. A small bloodstain had dried under my nose, and I tried to wash it off. The need to cleanse myself of what had just happened drew me into the shower.

The cold water poured down, gradually putting out the flames of anger raging inside me. Motionless under the frigid stream, I thought of my mother and what she had revealed a short time ago—I had been shocked in the beginning, but then felt relief and an even greater hatred for my father. I could still see her pained expression as she recounted everything. She kept asking for forgiveness, over and over again, as I tried as hard as I could to convince her that I harbored no hard feelings towards her for what she had just disclosed.

I lost track of time as I stood in the shower, letting the water sweep away everything that had happened. When the cold became too much, I stepped out and wrapped a towel around my body. As I walked into the corridor, I found Ella standing there in her jacket and holding her handbag, as if she had sensed my desire to be left alone.

I did wish to be by myself, it's true, but I was nonetheless surprised to see her leaving—in fact, I felt irritated that she did not ask me whether I wanted her to stay a little longer. My needs battled with my ego yet again. I had been ready to reject her barely an hour ago—now, I felt that I needed her support.

I had not asked her to stay, I reminded myself. On the contrary, I had lingered in the shower, and she may have thought that was a subtle hint she should go. I still felt so disoriented that I barely registered her saying something in a soft tone, giving me a fleeting kiss, and then leaving.

As soon as the door closed behind her, I felt calmer. But the sensation that I had been vulnerable before a stranger was still there. The reality was that, after everything that had happened, I no longer knew what I wanted.

I flung the towel on the couch and walked to the bedroom. A photo on the dresser, of me as a child, caught my eye. It had been taken one Christmas long ago. My mother was holding me in front of a nativity scene, a fake camel towering behind us. The joy in our faces was the reason I had enlarged that photo and placed it there, cropping out the figure of my father standing beside us. My mother was the most important person in my life. No matter what the future held, I vowed to do everything in my power to spare her any more pain ...

At the monastery of St. John in the town of Patmos[2], the figure of a man sitting on the ramparts surrounding the courtyard stood out against the darkening sky. The man sat still, his feet dangling over the stone wall above the void. He was gazing at the horizon, where the sun had just set. Like a painting, a burst of nearly every color splattered the surface of the sea and tinted the vaults of heaven. The sky looked like a clear glass stained with the soft tones of the afternoon. The first stars—tiny, bright pinpricks—had just appeared, slow and nonchalant harbingers of the impending darkness.

The air was chilly despite it being early summer. It was still too soon for the island to be overrun by tourists. Occasionally, a car would wind down the road, illuminating the trees and rocks rising on the edge of the asphalt with its headlights.

Skala, the island's port, was visible in the distance. Lights flickered on in succession, lighting homes and shop windows and adding a festive atmosphere to the vista before him. Two fishing boats were leaving the port to gather their nets. The light breeze carried the sounds of

---

[2] TN: Patmos is a small Greek island in the Aegean Sea. It is most famous for being the location of the vision given to the disciple John in the Book of Revelation in the New Testament, and is also where the Book of Revelation was written.

village life to the foothills of the monastery—a baby crying, shushed by the faint lullaby of its mother. The man on the wall seemed to enjoy both the view of the port and the sound of the mother's song. Tears and melody flitted through the rustling leaves and sailed on the southerly wind as it rose to the tall castle walls unimpeded. In a few moments, silence fell, a sign that the child was fast asleep.

The island had largely managed to retain its character despite the growth of tourism in recent years. Here, however, the small homes letting out rooms were gradually giving way to large, luxury hotels. A few tourists visited at this time of year, those who wanted to enjoy their vacation in peace and quiet before the busy summer season began.

Pilgrims still flocked to the island, of course. They wished to visit the monastery and see the grotto where John the Revelator was supposed to have written the Book of Revelation. The energy emanating from the island was unique, a constant source of conversation among both locals and visitors. The myths and stories surrounding the island further accentuated the mystical aura shrouding it.

A voice from inside the castle made the man look over his shoulder. "Michael!" a monk called out again.

The man immediately stood on the wall and beckoned the old monk towards him. The monk hesitated, then carefully climbed the handful of steps that led to the rampart, holding Michael's hand to keep his balance. Without exchanging another word, they sat next to each other and let their eyes wander over the beauty that lay before them.

The monk's face looked troubled under his thick gray beard. His worries seemed to vanish, however, as he took in the view. His eyes drank in the sprawling vista as if encountering it for the first time.

"I have not been up here in months, Michael ... I don't even remember the last time," he said, keeping his eyes fixed ahead.

Michael gently smiled. His eyes were peaceful pools of tranquility. His long hair was tied in a ponytail that sat low on his neck. His thin mustache and goatee stood out next to his unshaven cheeks and made him look like he had just stepped out of a medieval tapestry, a knight from another era. His voice was soft and warm, as if the words he spoke truly came from the depths of his soul. "Peter, my brother, I am glad I was the cause for this return. I was trying to follow your advice. Regain some of the freedom I had lost."

Peter glanced at him approvingly. A mischievous spark lit up the monk's eyes. "We define freedom according to the choices we make. Some claim they find it in the walls of a palace, others by looking at the sun sink into the sea. For you, at this moment, freedom is the steps you took to climb up here ... although I thought the library was your refuge; your harbor, as you often say."

"I feel free there, too, surrounded by all the books, the knowledge that has survived the passage of time to reach our hands. We just need to make sure it reaches those that come after us. That is a kind of freedom, too—the knowledge that nothing belongs to you, that the meaning of life is to leave behind something in a better state than when you were given it. To hold the manuscripts written by enlightened men centuries ago, from every corner of the world. It is as if fate has entrusted us with this privilege ..." Michael replied seriously, as if he had not realized Peter was teasing him.

"And God, Michael ... Do not forget God. Everything begins with Him and ends with Him."

He reached out and gave the monk's arm a reassuring squeeze. "Of course, God too, my brother ... God too ..."

Peter looked at the hand Michael had pressed against his black robe. The thumb was missing, the result of an old injury. He gave the hand a fatherly pat and said, "That is how you won your freedom once, Michael, isn't it? You paid for it with an ounce of flesh..."

A collection of fragmented images passed through Michael's mind, as if his life was passing before his eyes. His face darkened, and he averted his gaze, turning to look out to the sea. The monk took Michael's hand in his palms, as if he wished to protect him. "Confession is a great virtue, my brother. Not to be pardoned, but to pardon those who have hurt you. Do not keep the pain, the burdens, inside you. You have been here for so many years, but you are still not free from the past."

Michael took a deep breath and exhaled with a long shudder, as if he wished to blow away everything that was tormenting him. "You are right. I did earn my freedom once, in exchange for the piece of flesh I left behind. If that was all I had lost, I would have found my salvation. But I left behind something even greater. A piece of myself ... Besides, as you often say, nothing ever truly ends in this life. We all pay our dues in the next one ..."

"This is serious talk, Michael, and I must return to my chores. I only came to remind you that the famous French actress will be visiting tomorrow. They have asked that you guide her around the library and the Cave of the Apocalypse, as you speak French."

"Renée?" Michael bristled. "The truth is I had forgotten. You did well to remind me. I was planning to go down to the port tomorrow for some supplies I need. I think I'm growing forgetful."

"I don't think you are growing forgetful, Michael. I think you are growing selective ... There was some backlash about her visit, you know, but it is rumored she is about to make an important donation to the monastery. Have you heard of her? She is apparently very well known, but she has asked for the visit to be kept a secret."

Michael smiled. "Yes, she is very famous. She was famous in Paris, too. The queen of the movies, they called her. It's wordplay on her name, Renée—Reine meaning queen." His smile evaporated. "I just wish I could avoid this altogether ..."

Without another word, they rose carefully. The walls were high, and a fall could prove devastating. They delicately walked down the steps and stood in the courtyard for a moment.

"I'm going to the library to lock up, and then I will go rest," Michael said. "I have a difficult day ahead of me tomorrow ..."

"God be with you, my child," said the monk, and returned to the buildings at the end of the courtyard.

The sound of applause reverberated backstage. *Bravo!* the Athenian audience cried out, over and over, as the group of seven dancers stood center stage. Among them, standing a step ahead of the other dancers, Persie raised her hand to her heart and took a deep bow before the packed theatre. The main musical theme of the performance that bore her name—Persephone—rang loudly from the speakers. Backstage, the technicians also watched with interest. She took a last bow and, with a light skip, turned to go backstage first. The other dancers followed her, their masks hanging around their necks. Some of the masks looked like the stuff of nightmares.

As they jostled in the wings, the cries and clapping grew louder, calling them back to the stage for another ovation. Unable to believe what was happening, Persie clasped her hand against her open mouth, unsure what to do. The rhythmic claps continued, and she attempted to pull everyone back onstage with her, but they motioned that she should return alone. One of the dancers walked with her to the edge of the stage and gave her a light push, then withdrew into the shadows of the wings.

Persie, alone before her audience, watched as they stood clapping with all their strength. Around three hundred people, more than the theatre was supposed to hold, were there. So many bodies, and the early summer heat made the air warm and stuffy, almost oppressive. That was one of the reasons tomorrow would be her last performance. At least, that was what she had claimed, as the producer of the show.

The show had been running for two months, and the theatre had been full every single night. It had sold out early on, for the entire run. The only blemish had been the reaction of several religious organizations, who considered part of the performance blasphemous and campaigned for it to be censored or cancelled. In the early days they'd picketed the theatre, preventing people from entering. But the notoriety—and the fact that she shared the heroine's name—had worked in the show's favor in the end, giving them greater publicity than they could have ever hoped for.

All of Greece now knew about the performance. How could they not, when everyone raved about the quality of the show, about Persie's stunning interpretation of Persephone, about how expressive, how convincing she had been in the part? For a dancer it meant even more, as the performance allowed them to speak only with their bodies, their movements, and not their words. She not only had to conquer the part, she had to transmit it to the audience according to the dramatic needs of the choreography, the storyline. The masks they used made their task even harder, hiding their expressions and allowing only movement to communicate with the audience.

The critics and the media lauded her and the concert dance. Persie had declared that this would be her last performance as a dancer and that, as of next winter, she would devote herself to teaching and choreographing. Even though it bothered her that the protests had been the reason the wider audience had become aware of her as a dancer, she enjoyed the renown as much as she could. She had turned down all offers for a summer tour, believing that the magic of this enclosed space would be lost and that any artistic heights scaled would quickly diminish before the need for more and more receipts. She also feared the reaction of less urban audiences. They had received quite a few threats from religious fanatics warning them to keep their blasphemous play, as they called it, away from their towns.

But all her plans for the future could wait for another day. Right now, Persie wanted nothing more than to stand on that stage and soak in the audience's applause with every cell in her body. She stood there, lapping up the applause with every cell in her body. A bead of sweat, tinted with makeup, slowly trickled down her cheek to her neck. Deep down, she felt that she needed time to stand still. The greatest joy and pleasure for an artist is the moment the audience rewards them for their work. No words can capture the intensity of emotion an artist feels as they face their audience. Those feelings now flooded her—awe and satisfaction mingled with the emotions the performance had stirred up in a heady mix which she had experienced in the past but could never get enough of. She had received adulation and applause every night of the run, but this evening was different. Evidently moved and affected by everything going on in her life off-stage, she had given one of the best performances of her career.

Her eyes brimmed with tears at the intensity of it all. She lingered a moment longer, then slowly withdrew, keeping her eyes on the stalls. As soon as she could hide in the wings, she bowed her head and let the tears flow freely. The other dancers encircled her and hugged her. With a wave of her hand, she quietly gestured that she wished to be alone for a moment.

The audience was still applauding loudly. Persie raised her head and led her dancers to the edge of the stage, motioning for them to go take a bow. When the last dancer had left the wings, she ran up the stairs to the dressing rooms, letting her colleagues enjoy their moment in the spotlight. As she moved away, the shouting and applause from the stalls began to fade. She quickly entered the dressing room and locked the door behind her.

Flowers, bouquets, and countless notes from admirers were scattered around the room. She rested her hands on the dressing table and looked in the mirror. Her eyes were smudged with the tears that had run down her cheeks, leaving behind dark, moist trails. The show was a success; she should be happy, yet she was anything but. Her personal life was a mess. She picked up her cell phone and once again read the text sent by Steve, her boyfriend and choreographer these past three years.

*It's been a total disaster. I have no reception here. Catching a flight tomorrow. We may need to go on tour. Try to get your hands on any funds you can get. I should be landing in time for the show. See you then.*

Steve was in Thailand, trying to untangle the mess of an investment they had made at the local stock exchange. They had invested a large amount of money, which would not only leave them strapped for cash, but also in debt. He had convinced her to entrust him with all her savings, as well as to mortgage her home. Now, despite losing everything, he was asking for whatever remained of their receipts, which had been earmarked for the salaries of those working on the show.

The quality of Persie's work was finally being recognized by both her audience and her peers, yet she could not savor the moment. She did not know how to handle the matter, the mess into which he had drawn her. She was seriously considering consulting a lawyer. An ex-dancer, Steve appeared on the bill as Choreographer despite Persie having done most of the work. He had drawn the guileless Persie into a series of dubious schemes and taken her down a vortex of needless investments and expenses.

The knock on the door disconcerted her for a moment, but she dried her eyes and unlocked it without asking who it was. Theo, the theatre manager, looked at her with a puzzled frown. He wore a white t-shirt with a deep V-neck that left his tanned, hairless chest exposed. The footsteps of everyone returning to the dressing rooms echoed up the stairs.

"Darling, what's the matter?" he asked, with evident worry. "Why did you run off so abruptly? They would still be applauding you if you hadn't disappeared."

Without replying, she turned away and sank into an armchair. Tears began to flow down her cheeks once again. Theo quickly drew up a chair and sat down beside her. "Did something happen to Steve? Is he okay?"

Everyone had picked up on the fact that relations between the couple were strained, but no one knew any details. Persie had kept the losses to herself, the fact that she now probably faced financial ruin.

She looked at Theo, dried her eyes once again, and summoned all her strength. "I need you to pay everyone tonight. Make the transfers from the receipts account as soon as you get home. You told me yesterday that the funds we currently have would cover a large part of their salaries."

Taken aback, he immediately replied, "But I was going to do it at the end of the month—"

"Tonight," Persie interrupted sternly, in a tone that brokered no argument.

"What about Steve? What if he asks me why?"

"I'll handle him; you just do what I asked. Please, pay everyone, tonight."

Theo was obviously still confused, but he also clearly realized her mind was made up. Rising, he said, "Whatever you want, darling, you know best. People will be coming backstage for autographs any minute now. Do you want me to tell them you are feeling unwell and send them on their way?"

"No, just give me a couple of minutes, then let them in," she replied, and turned to the mirror to fix her makeup.

Theo gave her another look, but apparently decided it was best not to push her. He was halfway to the door when he paused. "We are leaving for Galaxidi the day after tomorrow. The photographer is coming to watch the show tomorrow evening and make arrangements ..."

"I think we should postpone that. I can't go home now. Think of a good excuse and cancel it altogether if possible. Tomorrow will be a tough day and I have no idea how it will end," she said.

"Persie, that's impossible!" he cried out, alarmed. "The photo shoot was booked weeks ago and so many people have worked to make it happen. They are giving you a huge spread. An entire production has been set up around this shoot. Don't even think about cancelling!"

Persie was aware of all it had taken to arrange the shoot. One of biggest, most prestigious magazines in the country would be publishing an article dedicated to her entire career. She was silent for a moment, thinking about it. "I think it's best that you call and cancel, Theo. I'm in no state to go to Galaxidi and pose as if everything is okay ... I can't hide what is going on from those who know me so well. If you can't cancel, at least postpone it for next week."

"Listen, how about I leave you to wind down, and we talk about it over dinner. How about that, eh?"

Theo was an old friend, and the two had worked together many times. He was not the most vocal of men, but he did not miss a thing. He was excellent at his job, and she had kept him by her side for years. She recognized what he was doing now—not pressing her further, believing she would later change her mind—because he'd done it before. He gave her a wide smile and left.

Persie paused for a moment, trying to order her thoughts. So much had happened, she craved some time to think things through. The sound of an incoming text startled her. She was on edge and everything was a source of worry. She gingerly picked up her cell phone, fearing the worst, then grinned with relief when she saw it was from Violet, her childhood friend from Galaxidi.

*Persie, what's this I hear? A night of triumph? Some friends from Galaxidi watched you tonight and are raving about it. Can't wait to see you and properly catch up. I'll call you tomorrow morning! Love you xxx*

She dropped the phone on the dressing table and looked in the mirror with newfound determination. Her features suddenly hardened. Tomorrow, she had to face not only her looming bankruptcy, but Steve too. She had lost her parents years ago, but her family home in Galaxidi still belonged to her. Violet lived there now. She had mortgaged it to bankroll him. Steve had reassured her that he would need the money briefly and return the sum to her three-fold. As if that were not enough, she had convinced Violet to contribute her savings, without telling her the reasons. She would have to, sooner or later, before Violet found out on her own.

The knock on the door brought her back to the present. She quickly lit a candle on her dressing table and inhaled deeply. The scent of vanilla hit her nostrils, reviving her.

Kostas Krommydas

Her face brightened, and her mood lifted as she let her fans in, who had come to get their programs signed and have their photos taken with her.

The rays of the early morning sun lit up the stone walls of the monastery on Patmos. It contrasted sharply with the lower part of the ramparts, which remained in a hazy shade, the dark remnants of the night that was now fading away. Soon, the whole monastery would surrender to light. The higher the sun rose, the further down the golden dividing line sank, highlighting more and more of the building. The monastery seemed to be rising from the bowels of the rock. This land was blessed, if only by the presence of the monastery and the Cave of the Apocalypse. Nature, however, had been generous with it, gracing this piece of land with a unique beauty that married the deep blue of the sea and the small white houses with care and respect for tradition.

At the entrance to the courtyard, Michael patiently awaited the French actress to give her a tour of the library first, and then the grotto. Along with his native Greek, he spoke English and French and was well-versed in the island's and the monastery's history. Every time a visiting dignitary needed a tour, as on this occasion, he was always invited to play the guide. Michael had been a sailor for years and had circled the globe, wandering, collecting images and experiences from the four corners of the world, vowing never to return to his homeland. His love of art and painting put an end to his wanderings. He studied art conservation in France, where he had met a group of people who had helped him get back on his feet and prolong his stay in the city of light.

The death of his grandfather had been the cause of a short trip to Patmos to deal with the bureaucracy surrounding his small inheritance, a tiny home on the beach. When he arrived on the island, he was awed and realized he wished to spend the rest of his life here. It was as if he had finally found his own harbor after a lifetime of dropping and raising anchor in other ports. He loved exploring and conserving the priceless treasures crammed on the shelves of the library and in its small workshop. He spent his free time in imaginary travels painting his canvasses. So, he gladly accepted the post of book conservator. He had decided that Patmos would be his last port of call. He had only left the island once since moving there—to journey to a nearby island and accept old manuscripts donated to the monastery by some Russians.

Distant but unfailingly polite, he enjoyed the respect of not only the few locals he encountered, but the island's entire monastic community. Often, he acted as the link between these two different worlds, his mild nature bridging whatever differences arose. Other than the small house by the sea, his grandfather had bequeathed him the love everyone had had for him.

Michael now stood and waited for the famous visitor. Only a select few knew she was on the island. She had asked for anonymity, staying on a large yacht anchored in a remote bay. A car had collected her and carried her to the monastery.

Suddenly, he noticed a striking figure making her way up the stairs, accompanied by two men. She wore a long black dress that nearly reached the floor. Her long black hair flowed under a pale blue headscarf that covered her head as a sign of respect. A pair of large sunglasses masked her eyes. If you did not know who it was, you would notice an attractive woman without being able to identify her.

Michael stretched out his hand and welcomed her in French as she drew nearer. She seemed impressed by his appearance and halted, examining him. She hid her astonishment quickly, however, and shook his hand. He was simply dressed, but his gray hair, pulled back in a low ponytail, and his tidy moustache gave him a unique appearance. His face was thin, and his cheekbones jutted slightly, forming two tiny, sharp corners as they pressed against his skin.

"My name is Michael. It's a pleasure to have you with us," he said in fluent French, bowing his head slightly.

"Renée. Pleased to meet you. Thank you so much," she replied.

Without wasting a moment, he stepped aside so she could pass under the small dome that led to the monastery courtyard. The soft voice of a monk singing a prayer in his cell reached their ears. It reverberated against the walls, creating a tiny echo, which the soft breeze picked up and carried far away.

They walked on until they came to the steps leading to the library. Michael stopped, and turned to face the group with an expectant expression. Renée caught on quickly, and asked the two men escorting her to wait outside. It had already been agreed that only she would be visiting the library, which was closed to the public.

He gallantly let her lead the way, and followed her down the steps into the library. Before vanishing under the awing that covered the landing, he looked up. Peter, the monk he had been talking with the previous evening on the wall, was silently watching them from a balcony. They exchanged a smile and a brief nod. Then, realizing he had fallen behind, he rushed to catch up.

Michael apologized to Renée as he overtook her and pressed the entry code on the lock so they could enter. That was when she noticed his missing thumb. Her expression remained the same as she patiently waited for the door to open. They had barely exchanged more than a few sentences all this time, sticking to what was strictly necessary.

He held the door open and motioned for her to step inside. All the lights were on, highlighting the books and manuscripts in all their detail as they lay piled up on shelves or sheltered in glass cases. She moved through the room slowly, clearly impressed, and removed her sunglasses so her eyes could drink in everything.

To the left, a row of monastery tables served those who wished to read in the tranquility offered by the room, but also because it was rare for a manuscript to be allowed out of the library. Massive bookshelves with glass doors laden with hundreds of books towered all around them. A red carpet covered most of the floor. Michael said nothing, letting her enjoy the moment. He liked her genuine humility and the fact that her every move spoke of gentility and respectfulness.

A few minutes later, with her gaze still fixed on the books, she said softly, "I have heard so many things about this library, but please enlighten me about some of the things it contains. If it is not too much trouble …"

Michael smiled faintly, showing her that he was at her disposal. He looked her in the eyes for a fleeting moment. Her gaze was clear, and he was impressed by the absence of snobbism so frequently encountered among the rich and famous. He had met many "notable" people during his years at the monastery, and few had her kind of grace. He had often wished he could throw some of the visitors out, feeling that their comportment demeaned the sacredness of the space. He felt very much at ease with this visitor, however, so he began to recount the history of the monastery and the library. "Let's take things from the beginning. Would you like to sit down? It is a rather long story …"

"No, I prefer to look around as I listen, if you don't mind," she replied, giving him a questioning look.

He acquiesced with a nod, and took a deep breath. "The monastery was founded by a monk, John Christodoulos. Some archeological finds indicate that an ancient temple dedicated to the goddess Diana once stood here. During the period when the Arabs dominated the region, Patmos was almost deserted. In 1088, John Christodoulos, an enlightened and educated warrior-monk, asked the Byzantine Emperor Alexios I Komnenos to grant him the island. He wanted to build a monastery here, to honor John the Revelator. He stayed until 1118, when he was forced to abandon the island due to the raids of pirates and the Arabs. His work was continued and completed by other monks in the following centuries. That was the birth of the monastery, the birth of a cultural and spiritual center that has become a reference point not just for Christianity, but humanity in general."

Michael paused to check if all this information was boring her. The look she gave him made it clear that she wished for him to continue, so he did.

"The monastery has been continuously occupied for nine hundred years, which has led to the creation of such a significant library. From the very first books and manuscripts belonging to its founder to the present day, the material in the library and its archives has been ceaselessly enriched. Tens of thousands of old codices, documents, prints ... it is a beacon of spiritual wealth. We are currently trying to photograph and digitize all of it. It will take a long time. A few years ago, the library and the conservation workshop were moved here, where the space complies with conservation requirements."

A corner where books lay wrapped in transparent plastic had caught Renée's attention. Seizing the pause in his narration, she asked, "Why are these books in plastic bags?"

Judging by her tone, she didn't like what she saw. Michael immediately leapt to the library's defense.

"I don't like leaving them like this, but we do it to protect them from insects, especially woodworms. Those bugs may be tiny, but they wreak havoc nonetheless. Our basic weapon in the fight against insects is to deprive them of oxygen. We place the book in a tightly sealed plastic bag. The levels of oxygen drop to about 0.2% and, after twenty days, all the bugs in that environment have been exterminated. It's a method used widely around the world."

"It's just that, when you see them like that, they look like bodies about to be buried."

"You're right. But often, even in life, we sacrifice the image of perfection for the sake of survival ..."

Renée seemed struck by his words, and her eyes drifted towards his injured hand, which had reappeared from under his sleeve. She immediately averted her gaze towards the books, tilting her head sideways, somewhat awkwardly, to read a spine.

The soft ring of the telephone in the other room forced Michael to excuse himself and go answer it. When he came back, he paused to study Renée.

Having found herself alone for a moment, she had noticed the edge of a painting enclosed in a plastic sleeve among all the papers piled up in front of her. She had pushed the other papers aside to pick it up.

A woman's face occupied most of the page. Her deep red hair covered every part of her body like a cloak. Her eyes were tinted bright green. She was holding a blue flower in one hand. Renée focused on the flower, as if the tiny blossom reminded her of something. She examined the sketch with interest, her gaze pausing at the lake surrounded by mountains, barely perceptible in the fog behind the woman. Her tiny frown showed she was struck by the painting's presence in the library, as it had so little to do with its surroundings.

Michael cleared his throat, startling her. He walked up to her and took the painting from her hands. The work was his own and had no business being there.

Renée must have sensed his discomfort. She let him take it from her and place it back on the shelf without saying a word.

For a moment, they both stood in awkward silence. "Would you like to visit the workshop where we treat the books?" Michael asked in the end.

She quickly nodded, and they moved into the room next door. He spent the next half hour explaining the conservation process and adding a few more historical facts. Then they agreed to visit the rest of the monastery before making their way to the Cave of the Apocalypse.

The sight that greeted me when I arrived at the theatre was something I had never seen before. A huge queue of people was waiting to pick up their tickets. Another crowd was desperately trying to get their hands on this magic piece of paper that would grant them entry to the last performance.

The word *Abduction* dominated the marquee in massive letters. On either side of the entrance, banners depicted scenes from the dance concert, none of them showing the faces of the dancers. They either wore masks, or hid their faces in the shadows or with their posture. *Good work,* I thought, examining the photographs with professional interest. Before I could even get to the ticket booth, a woman approached me and anxiously asked me, "Do you have a spare ticket, by any chance?"

I smiled awkwardly and shook my head. An invitation was supposedly waiting for me at the ticket booth, but one look at the line and I realized I would have to find another way in if I wanted to enter the theatre any time soon.

A little further away, a dozen people were clustered holding up hand-made signs. "Shame on you" the nearest one said; the others were too far away to make out clearly. An elderly woman was shouting things through a bullhorn in a stringent voice that sounded more like the crowing of birds than the voice of a human being. Two bored policemen stood before them, not even looking at them. I'd heard that the protests had been more vociferous in the early days, but had calmed down significantly as the show neared the end of its run. It was also rumored that the main dancer had received threats, but it could just be rumors.

I moved closer to the line inching its way towards the booth, and noticed someone raise their hand at the other end of the line, beckoning me to join him. I looked around to make sure he wasn't waving to someone else, then started to jump the queue as discreetly as I could. Some people stared their disapproval; I kept my head down and tried to avoid eye contact.

When I reached the man who had been waving, he stepped forward with a huge smile and shook my hand. "Hello!" he said loudly. "You must be Constantine."

Everyone turned towards us, as if they expected to see someone famous. I felt embarrassed in front of all these people, and lowered my voice. "Yes, that's right. You must be Theo, Persie's assistant. We spoke on the phone?"

"Indeed! Welcome! Follow me, I'll take you inside. It's mayhem today ..."

He had not let go of my hand all this time, and now he pulled me behind him as he wove his way through the crowd. I felt like a little boy being taken for a walk. When the crowd thickened and tried to cut through us, I seized the moment and released my hand from his warm grip.

We entered the foyer to the sounds of a solemn orchestral piece. *Must be part of the performance,* I thought. The music imposed a kind of hushed reverence on the room, compounding the mood already set by the banners at the entrance. It all felt very mystical. My curiosity had been piqued, and I could not wait to watch the show and see its protagonist, who I had never met before and had no idea what she looked like in real life. I could tell from the photos outside that she had an amazing body. Her muscles, visible in most of the images, spoke not only of a well-honed body but also the passion her dynamic movement exuded. None of the pictures showed her face, though.

This is what fascinated me most about photography: for both the photographer and the subject to immortalize the intensity of a moment by capturing in a single click more than just an interesting pose. I must confess that seeing the exceptional photography outside, my expectations for the performance rose, but so did a feeling of jealousy, as well as my stress levels about the shoot in Galaxidi the following day.

Theo had gone to fetch my invite while I looked around. Now, he was making his way back to me, wearing a huge smile that made his face look like a Renaissance theatre mask. Once again, he stood too close for comfort, making me shift uneasily. The formidable, monumental music halted, and a familiar melody followed—softer, but equally arresting.

His voice interrupted my efforts to remember what the piece was. "Well, here is your little invite. Persie will meet you in her changing room at the end of the performance so you can chat about tomorrow. There is a teeny tiny glitch, but I'm sure it will all work out once you guys talk. You have the best seat in the house, just so you know. Well, I must dash, but I hope to see you tomorrow in Galaxidi," he said, and sauntered off, leaving me perplexed.

What did he mean, there was a glitch? Was there a chance the trip would be cancelled? If so, why had they not notified me earlier? The truth was that I felt the pressing need to leave Athens after the scene with my father yesterday. I still felt ashamed that it had all happened in front of Ella, who had of course called me today to see how I was. The argument had frightened her, and I begged her not to tell anyone, fearing how ridiculous it would sound that my father still hit me.

Just then, I realized what we were listening to: Rachmaninoff. I knew a lot about him. He had written this piece inspired by a painting called the Isle of the Dead. My mother had bought a print of the painting, and I still remembered it, so impressed had I been. My father hated it, so she had to put it away. He'd condescendingly informed her that all this "art nonsense" was a waste of time and money, and he certainly did not like seeing such *rubbish* in his house.

I never saw the painting again, and I fear he forced her to get rid of it altogether. But the image had stayed with me. Later, I learned the startling story behind the painting and felt fear, a fear I always felt at the notion of death. No matter how hard I tried, I could not reconcile myself with the dread that at some point my loved ones and I would simply cease to exist.

The painting depicts an isolated and rocky islet in an expanse of dark water. A small rowboat is just arriving, maneuvered by an oarsman from the stern, ceremoniously rowing across the still waters. A white-clad figure stands at the bow, facing the island, and just behind the figure is a coffin. The tiny islet is dominated by a dense grove of tall cypress trees, symbolizing death and mourning, surrounded by precipitous cliffs. Rachmaninoff's symphonic poem begins by suggesting the sound of the oars as they sink into the calm waters. The strange rhythm of the piece alludes to the breathing of the oarsman, who distances the boat from the living as he brings it closer to the land of the dead.

I remembered all those details so well thanks to my mother, who had ensured I received a musical education from a young age. In one of her rare acts of defiance, she had ignored my father's protestations and sent me to a conservatory. My horizons had been forever broadened there, although I'd found some of the stories behind the music both fascinating and frightening.

The doors to the auditorium flung open and spectators began to make their way to their seats, carrying me along with them. The music grew louder, already imposing on us the mood of what we were about to witness. An usher looked at my invite and guided me to the front row, pointing at a particular seat. I failed to understand what made that the best seat in the house. *Probably just formalities,* I thought. With a shrug, I sat where she was pointing. The stalls slowly filled behind me.

A veil covered the entire stage, allowing us to catch only a hazy glimpse of the settings. Center stage, the semi-naked body of a woman was faintly outlined as she lay on a chaise lounge, her open legs turned towards the audience. Her nudity was obstructed by the figure of a man sitting in front of her, holding a large knife at his side. Everything gave an impression of fog, enhanced by the strains of the same music by Rachmaninoff. Movements behind the gauzy veil appeared as if in slow-motion, as if the mystical ritual of a long-gone civilization was taking place.

I glanced at the program to better understand what I was about to watch. Before coming, I'd read that the entire concept was based on the myth of the abduction of Persephone[3]. The program was a single page. A Photoshopped photo of Persephone in the water covered one side. A pair of hands were trying to drag her to the deep, as her body and dress pushed up towards the surface. Once again, the face of the dancer did not appear clearly. Only her large eyes could be discerned, searching for the surface.

I turned the stiff paper over and saw the same picture, only without Persephone. In the woman's place, the text read: *Persephone. An endless journey between light and dark. The eternal struggle between man and death.* Then, a few lines about the musical accompaniment. No information on the dancers or their names. Every detail was being presented in

---

[3] TN: In Greek mythology, Persephone is the daughter of Zeus and Demeter. She becomes the queen of the underworld through her abduction by and subsequent marriage to Hades, the god of the underworld. The myth of her abduction represents her function as the personification of vegetation, which shoots forth in spring and withdraws into the earth after harvest.

such a way that I felt I would soon be participating in some occult practice, wrapped up in the strange ritualistic atmosphere that prevailed. It felt as if we were all members of some cult about to participate in an initiation rite. My interest and curiosity were at their peak.

When the room was overflowing, the lights slowly dimmed, and the music suddenly stopped. A strange silence reigned; unexpected, given the large audience gathered. The only source of light was the dimly lit center of the stage, where the slow movements of the dancers began to depict a ceremonial yet nightmarish birth. The performance had begun.

The curtain slowly disappeared into the wings, and it was as if a gentle breeze had blown the wisps of fog away. The reclining woman began to breathe, slowly at first, then faster and louder, to the point where I was unsure whether I was hearing moans of pleasure or pain. At the same time, softly, the next musical piece began. It sounded familiar, too. I hastily looked at my program and, in the faint glow cast by the stage spotlights, I read, not without difficulty, what we were listening to. It was *Requiem for a Dream* by Clint Mansell. This was a very particular rendition that sounded entirely different from the original piece. The sound of the strings was intentionally tuneless. As the seconds flowed by, passion harmonized with this mix of musical intensity and human pain ... or ecstasy? The man's body prevented any visual contact with the source of the female voice, which alternately sounded like she was in pain or in the throes of all-consuming pleasure. And while the melody and the human sounds synchronized in a nightmarish crescendo, the lights began to dim, until absolute darkness masked the stage ... Silence again.

A small spotlight showered the woman with light as she walked slowly towards the audience, in a straight line towards me. From the roof of the theatre, drops began to fall on her as if a small cloud was following her every step. A narrow, bright corridor lit her path forward.

As she neared me, I noticed that the drops were not water, but something else, a dark fluid that stained her body as she approached us. Four shapes appeared behind her in the darkness. As they neared the spotlight, they became clearer. One looked like a lion, the other like a bull. The next one was human, and the last one looked like a large eagle[4].

The lighting slowly changed, revealing the color of the liquid that had stained her body. It was as red as fresh blood. She moved closer and closer, looking straight ahead. The music from *The Isle of the Dead* could now be heard, ceremoniously imposing its rhythm on her steps. Although she was dimly lit, semi-hidden in the shadows the lights cast on her body, I realized it was *her*. Persie.

It was the first time I was seeing her up close, even in these difficult conditions that did not allow me to make out her features. Her nearly naked body, its every move filled with emotion, was very close to me. She was coming towards me, her eyes fixed to the spot where I sat. Now, I could not only better observe her nightmarish and tense expression, but also see her beautiful features. Beneath the expression

---

[4] Book of Revelation, Chapter 4.

of turmoil that had seized every muscle of her face, I could detect the sweetness of her human dimension. Only a few meters separated us, and her eyes were locked on me, as if I were the reason for this strange ritual. I felt a bead of cold sweat run down my neck, intensifying my suspense.

As the music continued, the four figures following her broke into a frenzied dance. Their bodies were naked from the waist up and they wore frightening masks. She kept moving forward, reaching the end of the stage. Another step, and she would be falling into the void. She stood there, still, eyes on me. I didn't know if she could actually see me against the spotlights, but I hoped she could not, because she would then see the fear that was surely etched on my face. I felt as if she were about to pounce on me and devour me.

Just then, I remembered Theo's words that this was the best seat in the house. So this is what he'd meant! Evidently the choreography led her steps to this very spot.

The dancers approached her and began to cover her body with white fabric. At the end, one of the dancers pulled a mask over her face, depicting an expressionless female face. Even through the eye openings of the mask I could feel her piercing gaze. They lifted her up and placed her body at the center of the stage, where they all danced before the strange male figure. His mask made him look like the devil. From that point onwards, I let myself get carried away by the performance unfolding before me, breathlessly watching the main dancer sweep us into the imposing vortex of her dance recital.

The loud applause woke me up from the dream world of Persephone and the legend I had entered. Enthralled, I awkwardly applauded, unable to tear my eyes away from the stage. All the dancers were lined up holding hands. They stood still for a moment, looking over the stalls, where the audience was rising to its feet with loud cheers. As they slowly moved towards us, I tried to order the maelstrom of feelings and images whirling inside me. There had been no intermission and I had had no sense of almost an hour and a half passing by. She was at the center and, along with everyone else, walked forward. They paused and took a synchronized bow, as if that was the last step of their choreography. I could not stop looking at her.

She shone, as if standing under a cataract of light, unintentionally leaving everyone else in the shadow. As she raised her head from her bow, our eyes met for a fleeting moment, enough for me to realize she had noticed me. This time, the stage direction had not determined the direction of her glance. Captive, our eyes locked as if bound by an invisible thread that ignored space and time. The thread only snapped when she was pulled backstage.

The cheering echoing in the stalls called them back to the stage once again. This time she did not look at me, letting her eyes wander over the audience. I don't know how many times they took a bow as an ensemble before they left her alone to enjoy the acclaim she deserved for her breathtaking performance as Persephone. Her movements, her bow, spoke of a person filled with humility and a gentle nature. I enjoyed watching her so much, I don't remember ever having felt something similar.

The stage lights came down, a sign the dancers would not be returning. As if angered by that move, the audience began to rhythmically clap their hands, wanting to show them that their acclaim was not over. The entire dance troupe lined up on stage, but she was not with them. I was surprised she was absent from their last bow. The others lingered on stage for a while, then withdrew to the wings.

The applause slowly faded away and I was possibly the last man clapping. I knew she was waiting for me, but with so many people crowding to leave the theatre, I decided to remain in my seat for a while. I was as nervous as a teenager before a first date and, admittedly, after what I had just watched, also felt small and insignificant before her. The strength of her performance made her seem even more impressive in my eyes.

I took out my cell phone and checked my emails. A message from the magazine director that had commissioned tomorrow's shoot had arrived moments ago. I clicked on it and waited for it to open; reception in the theatre was poor. In the meantime, however, Theo stepped out from the crowd. He was no longer the cheerful man I had met earlier in the evening. He looked downcast, as if something bad had just happened. He tried to smile as he came nearer, trying to chase the shadows away. "I hope you enjoyed it, Constantine ..."

I was at a loss for words. How could I describe that this was the most amazing thing I had ever seen on stage? The black mood that had come over him perturbed me. "Is everything okay? Did something happen? Did—"

With forced cheer, he interrupted me. "Everything is fine, yes. It's just that we will have to postpone tomorrow's shoot. The magazine will be getting in touch with you shortly."

I was stunned. It was the last thing I had expected to hear. As I watched the performance, I had thought that I would be spending two days in Galaxidi with that woman, and the prospect had filled me with joy.

I tried to hide my surprise. "Why not? Did something happen? Is Persie okay? I noticed she did not return to the stage for the curtain call."

"She is fine; she will fill you in shortly. She just asked whether you minded waiting for a while, until she finishes greeting fans and signing autographs. If you can't, she'll call you tomorrow to explain and maybe set another date for the shoot. But she did ask whether you could wait."

No way was I leaving the theatre without congratulating her, shoot or no shoot. "No, I will wait. I do want to congratulate her and thank her for the invite," I determinedly replied.

Theo smiled at my statement. "I'll have someone call you in a bit. I think you might just be able to change her mind ..."

I thought I'd misheard. Change her mind? How? Before I could ask him what he meant, he vanished in the crowd lining up to visit the dressing rooms, leaving me speechless.

Michael, Renée, and her companions had just arrived at the stairs that led to the Cave of the Apocalypse. The weather was good, and the sun had climbed up high in the sky, evaporating the morning dew. Late spring, with its bright flowers and untamed lush greenery, was still resisting the oncoming summer.

She asked the two men escorting her to wait for her, and they moved to a small gazebo. Michael and Renée carefully descended a handful of steps that led to a large room. There, an elderly man stood behind a counter to serve tourists who wished to purchase souvenirs. Michael was opposed to the sale of such items so close to the grotto, but the strange laws governing land ownership left no room for his views. He was not a religious fanatic, but he believed some boundaries needed to be imposed on this trade taking place in the name of the saints and religion in general. He could never understand how some people believed they would find salvation and atone for their sins through the purchase of prayer beads and icons. There were those who were certain that if they built a chapel or gave a votive offering, they would secure a place in heaven, even if they led a life of sin and greed. They were not solely to blame for that belief; those who encouraged them, even if they belonged to the actual institution of the church, were also to blame.

The old man behind the bench greeted Michael and looked at Renée, who had kept her glasses and headscarf on, covering most of her face. He turned back to his prospective customers, without paying her any more attention.

As if sharing Michael's objections, she cast an indifferent glance at the icons and other merchandise spread on the counter and turned away, waiting for him to lead the way to the grotto. He understood, and instantly pointed towards the stairs that led downward.

Slowly and carefully he led the way, giving her his hand to help her descend the last few steps. They walked to the grotto's entrance together. An old monk was sitting on a chair, hands leaning on a staff he held by his feet. Prayer beads snaked through his fingers. He did not look up at the visitors who had just entered the grotto.

Michael approached him and bowed his head slightly. "Good morning, my brother ..."

Slowly, as if there was no need to ever rush, the monk raised his eyes and gave him a piercing look. "God be with you," he replied in a soft voice, without looking at the woman standing beside Michael.

He lowered his head immediately, as if he wanted nothing to disturb his musings. The way he leaned against the top of his staff, he appeared to be lost in a trance.

Michael showed Renée inside the grotto. The Cave of the Apocalypse was just that—a domed cave nestled inside a rock where a few sparse icons were laid out, along with two wooden benches, a railing that separated a small space, and a few other objects.

A strange silence descended upon them. Only their breathing could be faintly heard, but even the breaths that escaped their chests seemed to be more quiet than usual. Renée slowly covered her shoulders with her shawl, shivering in the sudden chill. It was as if they had crossed a portal into a different reality. Despite being a frequent visitor, Michael always felt a sense of calm numbing his limbs whenever he entered the grotto. She seemed to be feeling it, too.

Immobile, she looked at the murals and the shape of the roof. Without a word, he sat on one of the wooden benches, looking straight ahead. She followed him and sat beside him. For a while, neither uttered a word. Her demeanor impressed him. She spoke little, but soaked up everything she saw and heard.

Michael let her examine the space for a while, and then decided to give her some information on the grotto. "So, if you don't object, I think I should briefly give you a summary about the grotto, and then you can ask me whatever you like ..."

She nodded, and waited with interest for him to begin.

"In 95 AD, John the Revelator was exiled to Patmos by the Roman Emperor Domitian. He began to converse with God, here in this grotto, and received revelations, which he recorded in the 270th and final book of the New Testament. It is said that he leaned there to write whatever God was dictating." Michael pointed to a small cavity in the wall beside them. He then turned to look at the low roof of the cave. "It is also said that the three cracks you see symbolize the Holy Trinity. God's voice could be heard through the cracks dictating the Apocalypse. In any case, according to the New Testament, the book is one of the few places in the world where communication between man and God has been recorded."

She drew a deep breath as if she was suddenly tired. Michael asked her if he should continue, and she encouraged him to do so. "The Revelation is one of the official parts of the Bible, and has been a source of inspiration for religious art throughout the centuries. However, it has also inspired artists of all kinds by being a poetic, symbolic, prophetic, and eschatological text. That is why it has generated so much discussion, as well as reactions. Some claim the time for the fulfillment of the prophecies is already upon us."

Michael glanced behind him at the monk. He still sat in the same position they had found him in, unperturbed. Michael knew that he could hear everything, despite his apparent detachment. Turning back to Renée, he asked, "Have you read the Book of Revelation?"

Her answer came swiftly: "Yes."

He was surprised. All this time she had listened silently, giving him the impression that she knew almost nothing of what he had been narrating. Uncertain for a moment, he decided it was time for them to leave. Nonetheless, before they departed, he added some details about the grotto and their symbolism. When he finished, he noticed her devout expression, a look of veneration in her eyes. So, he rose slowly and said, "I'll wait for you at the entrance. You stay as long as you like."

She smiled. From the corner of his eye he caught her removing her sunglasses. He walked up to the monk. A couple of tourists entered the grotto and greeted them as he stepped aside to let them in. Turning towards the bench where she still sat, he saw her put her sunglasses back on at the arrival of the other visitors.

Michael chatted with the monk, who paused his musings and leaned back in his chair. Within a few minutes, Renée had come to stand beside him and greeted the monk with a swift movement of her head. The monk returned the greeting the same way, as if he were mimicking her. An awkward moment followed where no one said a thing. His piercing glance had come to rest on her sunglasses, as if he could see her eyes behind them. She gave him a stiff little smile and gestured to Michael that she was stepping outside the grotto. He immediately turned to follow her, waving goodbye to the monk. Just before they left the grotto, the voice of the old monk rang out, heavy and imposing, as if calling after them.

*"Je lui ai donné du temps pour faire pénitence, et elle ne veut pas se repentir de son impudicité."*

His words filled the grotto, making her stop in her tracks, dumbstruck. She collected herself almost instantly and, without turning back, walked towards the exit at a faster pace. It was evident she was upset. Michael looked at the monk, trying to understand whether his quote from the

Book of Revelation was addressed to him or the woman he was escorting ...

Most of the audience had departed and only a few stragglers remained in the stalls. I wondered whether I should leave, but I wanted to meet Persie more than anything in the world, even if only for a few moments. My indecision vanished the moment I heard Theo call out from the other end of the aisle, "Constantine, you can go now, Persie is expecting you." He pointed to a door beside the stage that led to the dressing rooms.

I discerned a look of concern in his eyes, and took a deep breath as I walked towards the door. It led to a dimly lit corridor. A group of youngsters was walking towards me, comparing the autographs Persie had just signed. One of the boys was loudly lauding her eyes and her indisputable beauty. Our paths crossed, and I walked on. Almost everyone had left, so I began looking for her dressing room.

I opened a door and congratulated the dancers gathered inside, asking them where I could find her. They told me to walk ahead and take the stairs to the right, which I did. In the tenebrous corridor, I noticed a large poster for the recently discovered mosaic of Amphipolis[5]. I moved closer and saw that it depicted Persephone being snatched by Hades, the god of the underworld. Hermes, the messenger god, and Demeter, her mother, stood to one side. I realized the poster was on a door. Her door.

---

[5] TN: The Amphipolis tomb is an ancient Macedonian tomb discovered in northern Greece in 2012. The mosaic was discovered in the second chamber of the tomb.

It was ajar, and I inched closer to knock. I stretched out my hand, but just before it could brush against the wood, I froze as I saw her move through the crack. Surrounded by the clothes and veils hanging in the middle of the room, she was naked as she rummaged through the hangers, having just dropped a towel at her feet.

I was rooted to the spot, unsure as to what to do. My brain screamed that I should follow decorum and turn around, but my eyes refused to obey. I felt my heart pound as my eyes and body responded to the sight before me. Her wet hair fell below her shoulders and lightly covered her firm breasts. The light that filtered through the red fabric surrounding her cast a dreamy, otherworldly tint on her skin. My eyes thirstily took in her every move. I felt deeply ashamed, yet there I was, a captive of the scene unfolding before me. My feet were nailed to the floor as I watched her dress.

She took a white dress from a hanger, turned her back towards me, and raised it over her head. Before the fabric could slide down her skin, I saw the small tattoo of a pomegranate on her lower back, where her spine ended. I felt a bead of sweat on my forehead, and raised my hand to wipe it away. I was so shaken that I clumsily knocked on the door. Unperturbed, she turned towards it. "Just a moment ..."

As soon as she noticed the tiny crack, she hastily pulled her dress down and turned to the doorway. I had already stepped to one side, unsure whether she had noticed me peeking. I wanted to disappear from the face of the earth, feeling like a stupid fool. She opened the door swiftly and smiled. "Hello," she said, waiting for my reaction.

For a few seconds, I thought I would never be able to utter a word in my confusion. On the one hand, I did not know whether she had spotted me; on the other, there was a beautiful woman standing before me, gazing at me with those magnificent eyes. Her wet hair had drenched her dress, and the water dripped on the floor from her loose hair strands. I finally managed to mumble, "I'm Constantine ... the photographer ..."

"I guessed so, Constantine. Theo described you in *great* detail ... Persie," she said, and stretched out her hand.

I took it, and our palms met in a warm handshake, her grip tight. We looked at each other, swept up in a perplexing mix of intensity and awkwardness. Still holding my hand, she stepped aside to let me pass through. "Come in, sit down. Don't just stand there!"

Only then did our hands slowly part, as if we both wished for the contact to last a little longer.

She pointed to a chair in front of the mirrors in her dressing room. Photos, flowers, and greeting cards were spread everywhere. When I sat, she excused herself for a moment to finish getting ready and hastily moved behind a folding screen. I shifted in my chair and looked the other way to give her some privacy. In reality, of course, I was trying to salvage my reputation in case she had noticed my presence at the door earlier. For now, it appeared that she hadn't, and I felt my courage rise.

"I hope you liked it ..." she called out from behind the screen.

"I think it was one of the best things I've ever seen in my life," I answered with great certainty.

"I'm glad to hear it."

"It's a shame you are stopping now. So many more people would like to see the show. Honestly, amazing work ..." I said, without receiving an immediate reply.

She stepped out from behind the screen, smiled, and sat in the other chair. She had pulled her hair back, and a towel covered her neck. Her dress rose as she sat, revealing her legs. I tried not to look, but I could sense all the naked parts of her toned body out of the corner of my eye.

Before I could share more of my impressions, she said with a sudden change of mood, "All good things must come to an end. I'm glad you liked it. No, really! Every artist likes to hear nice things about their work. When it's an honest opinion and not flattery ..."

I felt her piercing gaze as she silently examined me for a moment.

"Unfortunately," she continued, "we have to postpone tomorrow's shoot. I have notified the magazine. I'm sorry to ruin your plans at the very last minute, but there is something serious I must attend to here in Athens. I hope we'll be able to do it some other time."

I did not know how to respond. If I could speak from the heart, I would tell her how disappointed I felt, but I decided to shelve my own feelings for the moment. Besides, I did not know what was going on in her life, and I didn't want her to feel pressured. "Never mind, Persie, just the chance to watch the show made it all worth it ... and meeting you."

The last three words had escaped my lips involuntarily and, impressed, she gave me a closer look. She was about to say something when a ruckus echoed down the corridor. She jumped up and ran to the door. I followed closely behind. The shouts got louder and, by the time we reached the stalls, I could clearly hear a man swearing at someone in the worst possible way.

Troubled, Persie ran towards the source of the shouting. Through the open corridor door, I saw someone grab Theo and violently shake him as a torrent of obscenities poured from his mouth. Without breaking speed, she flung herself on the man, trying to free Theo. I could not make out what anyone was saying amidst all the shouting. Some others stood farther back, without intervening. Persie was desperately trying to help Theo, but in vain. I did not know how to react. They both obviously knew the assailant in some way. A large tattoo of a dragon spitting flames bulged on his arm.

He still held Theo in a tight grip, and the poor man was cowering to protect himself but unable to break free. Persie tried to pull him away with all her strength, tearing his t-shirt. He turned roughly and gave her a violent push, knocking her to the floor.

I saw red just then, and flung myself on him without a second thought. I grabbed him by the arm, fingers digging into the dragon's mouth, and shouted at him to stop. He was fit and strong, and it was not easy to keep a hold on him. He looked at me with a puzzled frown, shook his hand free with an oath, and then tried to punch me. I barely had time to pull back, and felt his knuckles brush by my chin. As I stepped back, I stumbled and fell on the floor beside Persie, who was trying to get up. We exchanged a brief look of despair and turned back to the raging beast of a man.

He had let go of Theo and looked at us as if he were lost, breathing heavily like an injured animal. I stood up first and helped Persie get back on her feet. She rubbed an injured wrist. I was so shaken up I could not follow what they were arguing about—something about money missing, but it made no sense. Theo's nose was bleeding. I felt Persie's hand lightly touch my shoulder, and her voice telling me it would be best if I left now.

"Will you be okay?" I asked, looking at the man who seemed ready to resume his assault at any moment. She nodded.

Now all of the theatre's employees were watching from afar. A few moments later, the man furiously stormed off towards the dressing room. Persie looked at me, then turned to follow him. I lightly touched her hand and, as soon as our eyes met, whispered, "I don't know what is going on, but do not let anything spoil the beauty you have created here. You were born to do magical things. Do not allow anyone to ruin it for you ..."

She squeezed my hand as her eyes filled with tears, ready to pour down her beautiful face as if what I had said had touched a chord. She turned and slowly walked to the dressing rooms. Just before she closed the corridor door behind her, she turned and cast me an apologetic look.

The other dancers began to disperse, and I was still trying to figure out what had just happened. Turning to Theo, I asked, "What was that all about? Who is this guy?"

"Steve? He is the show's choreographer and Persie's boyfriend ..."

The word "boyfriend" stabbed me like a small defeat. I don't know why, but for a few seconds I had engaged in thoughts where no boyfriend featured in her life.

I stepped closer to Theo and asked in a low voice, "Is there something we can do? Are you sure she will be okay?"

Nothing about him resembled the cheerful young man I had met earlier in the evening. Downcast and visibly exhausted, he was trying to straighten his crumpled clothes. "Everything is under control, Constantine. We appreciate your help, and I apologize you had to see that. I will call you soon, to see if we can ever get around to doing that shoot."

I felt I had to leave. The situation was becoming uncomfortable for everyone, so I said goodbye and made my way to the exit. I stepped onto the street and welcomed the fresh breeze that hit my face.

The few remaining spectators were slowly dispersing into the nearby streets. Someone had hung a banner protesting the show on a wall opposite the theatre, but the protestors were gone. A sense of melancholy overcame me, casting a momentary shadow on the feelings the show had stirred up inside me. Psychologically, I had prepared myself for the trip to Galaxidi, and this sudden turn of events had spoiled my mood. For the second time in twenty-four hours, I had found myself embroiled in conflict. Yesterday with my father, and today with the mad conclusion to this evening.

Instead of driving, I decided to walk to the nearby bar of a friend of mine and have a drink. Sleep would be elusive in any case, so I somehow had to wind down from all the tension that had been building up inside me since the previous day. I had not expected things to take such a turn. I felt bad for Persie, understanding how upset she must have been. What had happened, though? Why was this Steve behaving so deplorably?

Without realizing it, I found myself standing at the bar's entrance, the music and cheerful cries spilling out onto the street. I pushed the door open and stepped inside.

Nearly half an hour had passed, and I was on my second drink as I sat at the bar with a friend, who was now keeping me company. I did not mention the earlier events of the evening, trying to forget. The music was loud, and I only noticed my phone ringing at the last moment. I quickly pulled it out of my pocket, but it was too late. The caller had already hung up.

I stepped outside and dialed the number. A woman's voice answered at the first ring, asking me if I was Constantine. I quickly understood that Persie was at the other end of the line. She started off by apologizing about what had happened. I nearly dropped the phone in surprise as I pushed it harder against my ear, trying to understand if I'd heard right. She told me that, if I was still available, we could make the journey to Galaxidi the following day and do the photo shoot.

Suddenly, all my negative feelings disappeared. I asked her to give me five minutes to contact everyone and see if they were still available. I knew it was late, but, even if I could not reach everyone, I was determined to go anyway. My assistant was in the area and could join us the following day. The clothes were already there. All that was missing was the photographer and the model. We hang up with the promise that I would be contacting her shortly with any news.

I could not understand what had happened to change her mind, but right then I did not care. It was enough that I would be leaving with her tomorrow morning ...

Kostas Krommydas

# Paris, a few days earlier

In the Hôtel Dieu in Paris, Christian climbed the stairs that led to the upper floor. Birdsong drifted in from the luscious garden, flitting through the wide, open windows and echoing strangely down the corridor. Built at the turn of the previous century, the hotel retained much of its original character. The huge building block was defined by the large open space at its center. There, in a beautiful garden, patients and visitors could stroll.

Christian, sneaking looks outside the window as he went, reached the correct corridor and began to search for the room. A nurse approached him and asked what he was looking for. He smiled without hiding his admiration and, after a brief chat, thanked her for her assistance. He managed to steal one last glance in her direction as she walked away. As if sensing his gaze, she gave him a look over her shoulder without breaking her stride. A quick smile and then she turned away, the rubber soles of her shoes leaving a piercing squeak in her wake. Christian moved in the direction indicated, slowing down. The pleasure was evident on his face. He was the kind of man who enjoyed having his charm confirmed, even in the simplest ways. Like a fleeting, flirtatious exchange in a hospital corridor.

Despite nearing fifty, Christian had the aura of a much younger man, with his rich mane of hair and his trim body that he kept in rigorous shape. He looked elegant in his tight suit, and his every move had an air of suaveness. A red pocket square jauntily rested against the gray fabric of his jacket. A white shirt, its top two buttons undone, discreetly showcased his muscled chest.

The phone call he had received three days earlier had startled him. The woman looking for him had disclosed that the two knew each other, but without revealing how or where. What impressed him most was that she had called him by his Greek name. Very few people knew his mother was Greek and that he had been christened on a Greek island.

However, the nature of his job had made him familiar and at ease with mysterious circumstances. A private investigator, he ran one of the most successful agencies in Paris and was not unaccustomed to strange phone calls from clients who needed his help. The unknown woman had insisted that she speak to him personally and, his curiosity piqued, Christian had come to the hospital. He realized she must have known him a long time ago, but could not determine how. Even if her last name meant nothing to him, he was convinced that he had known her. Soon, all his questions would be answered.

Christian stood outside the door with the ward number indicated by the nurse. He gently knocked on the door, and a young woman opened it. He realized immediately that she was not the woman who had called him, and gave her his name. Upon hearing who he was, she opened the door wide and ushered him into a small entry hall. He saw a large couch and two armchairs, on which a dozen beautiful bouquets rested. A collection of vases filled with flowers covered the surface of the coffee table. Their scent had overtaken the room. Upon realizing that he had come empty handed, Christian felt bad that he had neglected to bring something in his haste.

The nurse asked him to wait a moment and entered the main room. From what he could glimpse as she opened the second door, he realized this was no ordinary hospital room, but one of the suites. Filled with curiosity, he lifted the cards attached to the bouquets of red roses and other flowers. In vain, he tried to read a card through its thick white envelope.

The sound of the door opening called him to order. The same woman reappeared, holding a mask and a pair of gloves. She asked him to put them on and, seeing his surprise, explained that it was for the safety of the patient and not him. Even though he felt uncomfortable, he pulled on the mask and gloves and slowly entered the large room.

His eyes immediately zeroed in on the woman lying on the bed. Her head was slightly raised on a pillow, and she wore a red headscarf to cover the loss of her hair. Her face was pale and drawn. Her cheekbones jutted out, pressing against her skin. A plastic tracheotomy tube covered with gauzes pressed against her neck. Her beautiful eyes stood out against her wasted features, still bearing testament to the vivacity that must have once flowed through her veins.

She smiled when she saw him, and tried to push herself up with the help of the nurse who had opened the door for him. Slightly shocked, Christian looked at the man standing beside the bed, who walked around and greeted him with a dry hello as he if was unable to utter another word. The patient looked at him eagerly, and stretched out a frail hand, waiting for him to take it. She squeezed feebly—that was all the strength she could muster. "Welcome, Christian," she said. "You can take the mask off, if you wish. I don't think anything worse could possibly happen to me."

The nurse opened her mouth to speak, but the woman shushed her with a wave of her hand. Christian hesitated, but then saw that she expected him to comply with her wishes. He slowly removed the mask.

The curtains were drawn open, allowing the Seine to be seen through the window as it snaked through the city. Everything was a lush green—the beginning of summer. The sun was setting, and lampposts along the banks of the river glowed bright yellow.

The woman broke the awkward silence by looking at Christian with admiration and saying, "You have not changed much since I last saw you. Any change has been for the better. Time has been generous with you, but did not hold anything good for me ..."

Feeling her piercing gaze, he struggled to remember where they had met. The hue of her voice, though altered, woke a host of muddled, murky memories. Her French was perfect, but the slight hint of a foreign accent betrayed that it was not her mother tongue. His head was about to explode with the effort to remember her identity. A host of thoughts rose like hurdles, blocking him and confusing him even more. A collection of female faces from his past flitted before him as he tried to match her face to one of those images—in vain. Perceiving his confusion, she asked him to sit in the chair by her bed. Then, she introduced him to the other two.

"Marie is my nurse, and Monsieur Pascal is my legal advisor and the manager of my fortune. You will have a chance to talk to him later."

Then she politely asked them for some privacy. Before exiting the room, her lawyer placed a large manila envelope by her bedside table, nodding with meaning. She touched his hand in thanks. As soon as the door closed behind them, Christian, who was still looking at her at a loss, decided to end the mystery. "I'm afraid I still can't tell how we know each other ..."

"I'm not surprised at all, given the state you find me in ... my darling Chris ..."

The sound of those last three words cracked open the vault, dragging up memories long gone.

The expression "my darling Chris" spoken in Greek, the green eyes looking at him nostalgically, stunned him for a moment. It could not be the same woman after all these years! The eyes were the same, but the rest of the face made him stare in disbelief, unable to accept that this was the woman he had met thirty years ago, that this was the same person. It was the desire to remember people as one had known them in better, happier days, not as they lay ravaged by the harsh marks of illness or time. How was it possible ...? Even her name had been different to the one she had used when she had called him.

Kostas Krommydas

His gaze unwittingly turned to a red light blinking far away, in another building. A torrent of memories flooded his mind as everything came back ... A shiver ran down his spine as he realized who the woman was ... All he could do was utter her name through his parched lips ... *Melek.*

The verses from the Book of Revelation that the old monk had spoken in their wake had greatly upset Renée. Michael was still struggling to understand why the monk would speak to her like this. He knew the book by heart, could easily identify the verse spoken in French:

*And I gave her space to repent of her fornication; and she repented not.*

While they walked towards the exit, leaving the sacred grounds behind them, he tried to make some sense of what had just happened. When they arrived at the cars parked outside the monastery, he approached her, trying to lighten the mood. "Would you like to take a drive up the mountain? The view from the chapel of Prophet Elias at the top is said to be magnificent."

She smiled uneasily. "No, thank you, we must head back. But I would like to thank you for the tour. I was not visiting today simply as a tourist. A tenth century manuscript has been in the possession of my family for generations. I plan to send it to you when I return, so it can enter your beautiful library. I think it belongs here, as it speaks of the island. I will make sure it gets to you as soon as I am back."

Michael was astounded. Even though he'd suspected she might be donating, he had had no idea about the manuscript. Most gave money and left convinced that their generosity had purified them of all their previous sins. It was an unexpected and exciting development.

"I don't know what to say. Thank you. I will be sure to inform the monastic community, so they can thank you in turn. There is a certain protocol to be followed in such cases. I would also like to apologize about what happened back at the grotto. I do not know why it was said, but I will find out, and the monk will have to explain himself," he said, stretching out his hand to bid her farewell.

Renée removed her sunglasses and looked at him. Then she took his hand and held it while she spoke. "I want you to promise me you will not make an issue out of it. It is not the first time I've heard it. The words were spoken by an actor playing a monk a long time ago. I played another part in the film—a prostitute—and it provoked intense reactions. There were objections to both the part and my performance."

Michael was shaken at the sound of the word "prostitute," but said nothing and let her continue.

"Those were the exact same words and I will never forget them, because for a long time they were repeated and thrown at me by those who objected to the film. I almost gave up acting as a result. I did not expect anyone to remember after all these years. Especially here ... But please, let us put the matter to rest."

Michael did not respond, trying to absorb all this information. With great effort, he managed to reply. "Even though this puts me in an awkward position right now, I give you my word. I will let the incident go, if this is what you wish."

She smiled, satisfied. "Would you like us to drive you back to the monastery?"

"No, thank you, I will linger awhile and return later. It is not far, and I enjoy the walk there," he said, thinking he would like to have a word with the monk anyway. Not to accuse him of anything, but to see whether the old monk would allude to the incident himself.

"Thank you once again. I had heard so much about this place, and I am glad I got the chance to see everything up close. You painted a very complete picture—not only of the island, but of everything we saw today. I am grateful. And I owe you an apology, too."

Michael gave her a puzzled look.

"I unwittingly saw the painting in your study," she explained. "I thought it had something to do with the library; that is why I picked it up. I then realized it was something personal, and I would like to apologize for my indiscretion."

"You were not indiscreet. The painting should not have been there, so the mistake is not yours, but mine," he said, trying to mask his discomfort.

"In any case, I would like to express my admiration, if you don't mind. You paint in a unique style …"

He could not think of something to say and, feeling ill at ease, opted to put an end to the conversation. "Thank you, I am honored …"

Sensing his awkwardness, she said goodbye. It was evident that, even though the words of the monk had bothered her, she had bypassed the incident by changing the topic and focusing on the sketch. Without any further delay, she hid her eyes behind her sunglasses and stepped into the car, while one of her companions held the door open for her. Michael approached the window without a word.

"Maybe we will talk again soon ..." she said, confusing him further.

They looked at one another as the car pulled away in the direction of the port. The fact that she would be donating such an important relic to the library filled him with enthusiasm. In the upheaval, he had asked for no further explanations. All he knew was that the text she was sending mentioned the island.

Many manuscripts and books lay scattered around the world, stolen or in the hands of collectors, some of whom were deciding to return them where they belonged. Recently, a Russian tycoon had gifted the monastery invaluable icons and manuscripts. It was never verified how they had ended up in his possession. The looting that had taken place not only in Greece but around the world had scattered priceless, important treasures across the globe. Many of them returned or found a new home here. Michael felt immense satisfaction at being part of such significant work that extended beyond the borders of the country. He felt like the protector of all those lost treasures that were either rotting in some basement, or decorating the indifferent bookshelves of a home a continent away.

After a while, he began to walk towards the grotto. He was trying to decide what to do about the monk. He had given Renée his word, and intended to keep it. Relations and politics in the monastery required a delicate approach in such matters anyway. He felt ashamed deep inside him, because her overall comportment had shown a person who was sensitive and noble. But that was not all. Even more intensely, he felt that one of his greatest secrets had been revealed. No one had laid eyes on the sketch of the woman with the flower ever before.

Kostas Krommydas

# Paris

Christian had drawn his chair close to Melek's bed. He was holding her hand, his eyes brimming with tears he desperately struggled to hold back. His arrogant look had disappeared, lost in the emotions that had overwhelmed him as soon as he realized who she was.

His last memory of her dated many years back, when she'd worked at one of Paris's most famous brothels. She was the one who had initiated him into the secrets of lovemaking. In fact, he had fallen in love with her at the time. He found it impossible to accept that illness could ravage her former beauty in such a devastating way. All that was left to remind him of her former self were her emerald eyes. The number of times he had lost himself in those eyes while they made love! Many women had followed her, but Melek was the woman who had marked his existence, even if his time with her had been bought and paid for. Even if he had never managed to meet her, not even once, outside the brothel where she worked. He used to spend every last penny to buy another minute with her. Their "relationship" had lasted one year. When he had to leave to pursue his studies abroad, he had promised to take her far away from that place when he returned. He had tried hard to keep his promise, but had failed.

Returning to Paris two years later, the first thing he did was look for her. She proved impossible to track down. Her former employers told him that Melek had left, and they did not know where she lived. He searched every place she could possibly frequent, to no avail. She had been one of the reasons he had opened the agency. The contacts he had made with people who moved in the shadows led him to this career. He had tried to find some trace of Melek for a long time, but his search proved fruitless. The years passed, and his desire to find her slowly faded away—only the beautiful memory of her still lingered. He assumed she must have left the country, vanishing as suddenly as she did without a trace.

In the space of a few seconds, all the wonderful moments they had shared flashed before his eyes. She always called him "Chris," and had often uttered a few words in Greek, without ever revealing what her connection to the country was.

Sensing his surprise, Melek had allowed him to sit and stare at her for a while without saying a single world, as if she wanted to grant him the space to connect past and present. Finally, she turned her head towards him with great difficulty. "I am glad you are well, Chris. I want you to know that I did think about you all these years. The time we spent together was one of the happiest times of my hard life."

Christian interrupted her with an apologetic tone. "I looked for you, Melek ... I tried to keep my promise. I came back and looked for you for a very long time ..."

She motioned for him to shush, that she did not have the strength to speak loudly enough to interrupt him. "None of that matters any more, my dear. It is best that I tell you some things now, about what happened then, but mostly about why I got in touch with you after all these years. Allow me to start at the end of my story, an end which seems to be rapidly approaching."

Christian, still not quite believing what was happening, just looked at her, dumbfounded, unable to mask his surprise. He sat rock-still, anxiously waiting to hear what she had to say.

Melek picked up a plastic cup and swallowed a sip of water through a straw with difficulty. She leaned back against her pillow with evident relief, and her eyes drifted towards the large windows across the room. "Two years ago, I was diagnosed with an aggressive form of breast cancer. I began treatment at once. Initially, it seemed that my body was responding well, to the point where we all began to believe a miracle had happened. Two months ago, however, everything inside me began to collapse. My *visitor* has now metastasized to almost all my vital organs. I traveled around the world hoping to find treatment, but in the end ... My doctors try to keep my spirits up, telling me there is still hope. But I know that I have very little time left ... That is the reason I looked for you, my darling Chris. Even though I wished to leave you with the picture of how I used to be— alas, circumstances forbid it.

"Now, let's take it from the beginning, if you can call it that. I have started my life from scratch so many times, I no longer know where the starting point really is. I was told I was born in a village in Armenia, close to the Turkish border. At some point we had to flee—we were refugees. When I was older, my father sold me to a Turk. In the beginning I was glad, so desperate was I to leave him. Then, I realized how mistaken I was. No one had ever touched me before, not in that way. The Turk was a middleman, looking to make a good profit from the sale of my body. Virgins were expensive back then ... very expensive."

Melek picked up the cup once again and drank another sip. She struggled more this time, and Christian reached out to steady her hand as she tried to place it on the bedside table. "I would love to hear your story, Melek, but I know this is so hard for you. Maybe it is better to take it slow, come back tomorrow ..." he said.

Her voice came stronger this time, more determined. "There is no time. This might be our only chance. Let me say it now, even if it drains me. I could walk up until yesterday. Today, my legs no longer obey me."

Realizing she would not be dissuaded, he said no more, waiting for her to resume her story. He had never imagined he would see her again, especially in this condition.

Paying no heed to his thoughts, Melek carried on. "A buyer was found for me, and they told me he was Greek. Once again, I was glad, still naïve. I had heard the Greeks were good people. I was hoping they would take pity on me and free me.

"The real nightmare began from the moment I set off on my journey to Greece. A few days later, we arrived at a small town on the northern border—Ioannina. I thought about ending my life so many times. I did not, because I met someone who kept me alive, who breathed life into me. But, even that life they took from me ..."

Melek began to sob uncontrollably. She squeezed Christian's hand, showing him that she wished to carry on, determined to finish what she had started.

"In the beginning, they kept me in a house in the countryside. There, the man who had bought me would come visit. Once he got tired of my body, they brought me to the city. I was now 'ready' to work as a prostitute, alongside the other women. My first day there, I managed to run away. Stupidly, I went to the police. They were all in on it. The policeman I spoke to dragged me back to the brothel.

"I met a young man at the station ... I managed to explain what was happening with the few words of Greek I had picked up. We hid in a closet, but it did not work. They caught me again.

"The young man I met began to come to the brothel and pay to spend time with me, without even touching me. He was only trying to help. At some point, they began to suspect what was happening and threatened to hurt him if he ever came back. He did not give up on me, and we met in secret, at a nearby shed. Whenever he could get his hands on a boat, he would row me across the lake to the small islet at its center. I can still feel the humidity soaking my clothes as we crossed the water. It was the purest, most real thing I have ever experienced. He gave me love ... and paid a dear price for it.

"There is a reason I am telling you all this. I need you to do something for me, so bear with me. We were planning to run away together, but then I fell pregnant. I hid it in the beginning, pretending I was sick, smearing my legs with pig's blood to keep everyone away. If anyone realized what was happening, they would take my baby away. I had heard that if one of the girls fell pregnant, they took her to a doctor who snatched it from her ... You understand what I mean. I wanted to keep it. The only one who knew the truth was that young man, who loved me more than anyone in the world ... 'Forget me not' he would say every time we parted. And I never did. I still carry him with me, in my heart ..."

Christian had barely drawn breath, afraid to disturb the flow of her words. He was astounded to hear her story. He had never learned anything about her past during their acquaintance. He had asked questions, but she always replied vaguely. He felt his chest ache at the thought of how much pain her exotic beauty had been hiding. Curious as to what she could possibly want from him so near her end, he kept his mouth shut.

"When I was too far gone to be able to hide the pregnancy any longer, they let me keep it for some reason, but kept me a prisoner inside the brothel. I realized why a few months later.

"As my birth date came due, we tried to run away once again, but they caught us. They beat him up savagely, right in front of my eyes. Then they told me he'd jumped into the lake to escape, and drowned. I never saw him again. I could not believe that I had ended up being the cause of his death. They kept me tied to my bed for the next few days, waiting for me to go into labor. I kept trying to postpone the inevitable, to keep the baby inside me, afraid they were planning to kill it. They had other plans. And so, they waited.

"My water broke one evening, and I realized I could no longer postpone the arrival of new life that wanted to surge into this cruel world ... They snatched it from me as soon as it was born, before I could even see whether it was a boy or a girl. That bastard of a policeman, the one who had returned me to the brothel after I ran away, was there too. One gang, the lot of them. Animals, exploiting everyone, numb to human pain. I later found out they sold the prostitutes' babies, forging birth certificates with the names of the 'new' parents. I never found out if my baby was alive, or who raised it.

"A couple of weeks later, I was pushed back into work, before I had even recovered from the birth. I swore to take revenge. One night, when they were all asleep in a drunken stupor, I set fire to the house. I wanted to destroy them for what they had done to me ...

"I managed to get out. I later found out that they assumed I had died in the blaze. They never suspected I was the one behind it. They found the remains of women's bodies and thought mine was one of them. One of the women who died had been good to me and had tried to help me as best as she could, as best as those animals would allow. Her death torments me to this day, and will haunt whatever little time

I have left. I condemned them to the flames, but what good did that do ..."

She swallowed hard and shook her head, as if trying to chase a nightmare away. "I can't even talk about it with you. It is all written there, in that envelope ..."

Christian nodded that he understood, and she ploughed on. "I managed to hide in a shed with some gypsies. They hid me for a few days. I was grieving for everything I had lost, and I wanted to die. Then I followed them to a port, hiding inside their caravan. From there, I managed to cross over to Italy ... always using my body as currency. It kept me alive. From then on, everything that happened led me to Paris and the brothel where you met me.

"I must have been on a trip abroad working as an escort when you looked for me upon your return. I never stayed in one place for long. About ten years ago, I married a man who fell in love with me and I stopped working. We moved to his house in Neuilly. I changed my name to erase my former life, and started to live like a normal person for the first time, with him. He treated me with respect, as if I had never been a prostitute. He was killed in a car accident four years ago. Once again I was alone, but no longer powerless. I inherited his fortune. Until the reading of the will, I had had no idea he was so wealthy.

"In that moment, I decided to look for the child I'd never met. I had thought about looking for the baby in the past, but I always stopped when I imagined how he or she would react upon hearing their mother was a prostitute. I did not even know if the poor lamb knew they were adopted. But, at that moment, I decided to go for it without caring about the consequences. Deep inside me, I felt that if I did not do it, the gaping void in my soul would follow me to my last breath. The disease got the better of me before I could act, and I kept postponing the search until I recovered. As you can see, that never happened."

She looked at him intently, summoning her last ounce of strength. Her voice cracked with emotion. "Christian, I am asking you to find that child and, if it is alive, deliver the letter inside the envelope. It is sealed, and I want you to swear that you will deliver it to my child only. If that cannot be, then destroy the letter. If it comes to pass, I would like my child to know the story of the woman who gave birth to it. I wish for the letter to be read where its life began—in Ioannina, by the lake ... I think it will make understanding what happened easier. Make sure you stress how important it is that the letter be read by its rightful recipient. It contains all that remains from that time ..."

A sob racked her chest, but she bit her lip and continued. "There is so much more that I have not told you, but it is inside the envelope. Information, names, everything I managed to uncover whenever I dabbled in a search before abandoning the idea; things I remember from back then. Now, it is all a blur in my mind, so study the contents carefully. You will discuss details with my lawyer. He is fully informed. So even if I ..." She looked tearfully at the darkening sky outside the window. "There is a small envelope in the drawer. Please take it out and open it."

Christian reached into the drawer and picked up the envelope. It was not sealed, so he easily removed the check. He brought it close to his eyes, convinced that there had been some error with the numbers. Melek noticed and asked him, confused, "Is it not enough?"

Christian smiled rather uncomfortably. "It is enough to search for many, many children, not just your own."

Relieved that all seemed to be well, that he appeared to accept the mission, she said, "I don't care how much it costs; I want the child to be found. It is the only way I will be able to rest. As I said, my lawyer has my will, which accounts for every eventuality. I know this is a lot to take in, but there is no time to lose. If you don't want to, or can't ..."

Christian spoke firmly. "Melek, you have just entrusted me with something so important. It's not the money ... it's what you ask of me, and that you are the one asking. I will move earth and high heaven to find the child you lost."

She looked at him, her eyes still moist. "All these years, I learned to read people ... little things. Your soul remains as pure as the day I met you, Christian. I did not choose you by chance. I always thought I had plenty of time, yet my stay on this Earth shall be brief. No one believes they will ever get sick, no matter what they see happening to others around them."

Christian pushed the check back inside the envelope and tucked it in the inside pocket of his jacket. "I promise you I will do everything I can. In two days at most, I will travel to Greece and begin my search ..."

Her face lit up, and for a fleeting second he saw the woman of long ago before him, all red hair and jade eyes, smothering him with kisses and caresses. It was as if someone had just breathed new life in her. She rose up with a vitality that startled Christian. Her words came easily, joyfully.

"All the details of what I want you to do, how I want you to proceed if you find the child, are in the envelope. I must warn you to be very, very careful. Many people were involved in that racket. Many well-connected people. Our clients at the brothel were family men and upstanding citizens. Some of them might be powerful men today. Be careful. They think I'm dead, but the child's existence is proof of the crimes they committed. When they find out that I am alive—" She paused and swallowed hard, trying to maintain her composure. "When they find out that I lived, they will want to erase anything that ties them to that time ... Please find the child ... to read my letter ... If it is still alive ..."

Christian had met all kinds of unsavory characters in his line of business, but not men like Melek had described. He had heard a lot about gangs trading not only women, but small children too, who they sold to childless families— they did not all have a happy end. Now, he felt driven, determined to help. He could see for himself that her days were numbered.

A persistent, loud beeping sound snapped him out of his trance and back into the room. It sounded like an alarm, coming from her bedside. He saw that her eyes were shut, as if she had just fainted. It had all happened in the blink of an eye.

The nurse ran into the room, closely followed by the lawyer. Christian stepped aside so she could approach the bed. The nurse tried to wake Melek up, without success. She pressed a button, and in a few seconds a doctor and another nurse appeared. They asked the two men to step outside.

The last thing Christian saw before leaving was the doctor trying to reanimate her with a defibrillator. The sight of Melek's naked chest frightened him. He felt relief when the nurse firmly shut the door in his face.

From the moment I opened my eyes in the morning, I felt like a schoolboy whose teacher had just announced they would be going on a school trip. I had woken up early to pack my equipment and everything else I would need for a weekend away. After two difficult days, what I had been impatiently waiting for was finally here. My acquaintance with Persie had intensified my wish for this trip to happen.

Even though I had been taken aback by what had unfolded in the theatre the previous evening, I kept glancing at the phone, willing it to ring and call me downstairs where they would all be waiting for me in the mini-bus that was to carry us to the seaside town of Galaxidi. Luckily, reestablishing the shoot had gone without a glitch, as the magazine was very keen for it to go ahead. Persie rarely gave interviews and now, given the success of the show, everyone wanted to secure one. I was the lucky man chosen to photograph her. I had decided not to mention anything about the previous incident unless she did, even though I was dying to find out more. Not only about why her boyfriend had been so aggressive, but also about what had made her change her mind and go ahead with the shoot. Other than photographing Persie, I was planning to take some landscape shots to add to my portfolio if our schedule allowed it.

Lost in my thoughts, I jumped when the phone rang. My heart sank when I looked at the screen—it was my father, and I had no wish to speak to him. I declined the call, hoping that would make my intentions clear to him.

I had spoken to my mother earlier, and she had seemed unaware of our altercation. I kept it to myself, not wishing to upset her. She was glad to hear the trip was going ahead, and we arranged to have lunch the following week in a quiet little taverna and catch up. I really wanted my father to know that I now knew their secret; the secret my mother had revealed a few days ago. I was dying to spit the words in his face, so he would realize that I no longer lived in ignorance. However, I could not do it without my mother's consent. I knew that he would take his fury out on her, and it was the only thing that had held me back thus far. Of course, one last outburst might be the final straw, the excuse she needed to finally leave him and escape his clutches after so many years. I shook my head to shake these thoughts away—I was determined not to let anything spoil my mood this weekend.

The phone rang again and snapped me back to reality. This time I grinned widely when I saw who was calling, and immediately answered. Persie informed me they would be here in a couple of minutes, her voice calm and sweet. I realized that she, too, needed a distraction after what she had just been through. I picked up my bags and went downstairs, grabbed my keys, then hurried out the door, slamming it behind me. Too impatient to wait for the elevator, I slung my bags over my shoulders and trotted down the stairs, nearly tumbling down in my haste.

I left the apartment building and stood in the shade of a nearby tree. It was still early, and the road was deserted. I had gathered there would be quite a few of us on the bus. It was a big production; the concept had secured the magazine plenty of advertising that more than covered the cost. I would be getting paid well for this job. Now that I had met Persie, though, I would have done it for free, just for the chance to capture something of that woman's essence on film. I intended to ask her to pose for my portfolio too, once the shoot was over. I was dying to photograph her eyes ... that deep green contrasting with her hair made her look like a fairy, an elven queen. Seeing her up close yesterday, I thought two emeralds were reflected around her pupils. Intense memories from the performance still ran through my head like a film reel, over and over. If someone had asked me to describe the show in two words, I would have said: nightmarishly erotic. The story had been based on the myth of Persephone but had spun an entirely different interpretation, shone a different light on the familiar legends.

A rickety old mini-bus that looked like it belonged in a '60s film arrived, and the driver cheerfully honked. Persie was waiting inside, accompanied by Theo, an assistant named Mary, and two other girls who I guessed were hair and makeup. I shoved my bags in the compartment at the back and ran to the side of the bus. Everyone was wearing hats, sunglasses, and bright smiles. The doors swooshed open and I stepped inside.

My good cheer faded a little when I saw that I would be sitting next to Theo. Persie was sitting in front of us, next to

Mary. I could have kicked myself for indulging in a fantasy where I spent the next couple of hours seated beside her, our knees touching as we squeezed in the narrow seats. Well, near was better than nothing, I told myself.

Just then, Persie stood up and greeted me with a kiss on the cheek, and once again I became a clumsy teenager, gawping at her, speechless. Without a trace of makeup, she looked as stunning as she had the night before, even with the dark glasses hiding her luminous eyes. Theo seemed to pick up on my nervousness and gave me a mischievous look. He nodded at me to come sit so the driver could close the door and we could finally be on our way. I fumbled my way to my spot and threw myself in it.

The traffic had picked up, and it took a while to get out of Athens and onto the highway. We decided to stop along the way to load up on coffees and water bottles for the journey, but I was so impatient to get to Galaxidi I would not have minded driving straight down. A half hour later, we pulled up in the parking lot of a large roadside coffee shop. Persie stayed on the bus and chatted with Theo, gesturing that she would be coming along shortly.

I walked inside with the others, and we began placing our orders. I glanced at the menu mounted above the serving counter, but nothing looked tempting. Besides, they told me that we would be stopping at Delphi to have lunch with one of Persie's friends.

I felt the coolness of Persie's fingers brushing against the back of my hand as I stood staring at the coffee machines on the opposite wall. I must have given her a strange look, because she pulled her hand away awkwardly. "Will you get me an iced tea while I run to the bathroom?" she asked.

"Yes, of course," I replied, trying to hide my surprise at the unexpected touch.

She drifted off in the opposite direction, and I discreetly turned around to watch her. She walked as if her toes made no contact with the ground, as if her feet were skipping in the air. Her hair was pulled back, and she wore a long white dress. The memory of her standing naked in her dressing room danced before my eyes. I had fallen asleep with the image of her body seared behind my eyelids.

The voice of the girl behind the counter harshly interrupted my wild daydreams as I watched Persie go. I turned and gave my order.

Our arms loaded with goodies, we lined up to enter the van and resume our journey. I don't know if it was by accident, but this time the only seat that remained empty as I stepped on the bus was the one next to Persie. She gave me a smile and motioned that I should sit. I tried to disguise my enthusiasm, without success, as I nearly spilled the tea all over her in my haste to hand it to her. Everyone laughed at my gaffe, and I laughed along, trying to release my nervousness.

Soon enough, we were back on the highway. The breeze, gushing in through the open windows, kept the rising temperature at tolerable levels. The sound of music with a strong drumbeat—African, I think—filled the bus. Persie turned towards me and our eyes met. She drank a sip of tea and touched my hand as it lay on the seat rest between us. She mouthed a soundless *thank you* and gazed at me fixedly from behind her dark shades. I don't know why, but I still felt unbearably gauche, unsure of how to act.

She turned to look ahead, silently singing along to the tune blaring from the speakers. It was as if the fight after the show had never taken place. I so longed to find out more about it, but I did not dare ask—not now, when everything seemed to find a sense of balance, some harmony. The *thank you* she had whispered was not about the tea I had bought her—at least, that's what I wished to believe.

We arrived at the exit that led up the mountain to Delphi and then descended to the coastal town of Galaxidi, our destination. Persie's phone had rung several times, but she had rejected the calls after giving the name on the screen a quick glance. I could guess who it was, but I still avoided the subject, confining my conversational gambits to the show and how much I had enjoyed it.

After a while, we pulled up all the windows to make the calls we needed in preparation for the shoot, which would begin that afternoon. Some final details still had to be settled. I had asked for everything to be ready one hour before sunset, so we could enjoy the soft, warm light of the departing sun. Today we would be going to a tiny island in the bay. The pictures I had seen of the place had impressed me, and I thought it would be ideally suited to the concept of the shoot, the atmosphere of the photos.

Persie asked the driver to make a brief stop as we wound our way up the mountain. She stepped off the bus on her own and walked to the side of the road, where one of the tiny chapels dedicated to people who had lost their lives in a car accident along this stretch of road stood. I thought it must have been a friend or a loved one, but I kept my questions to myself. She would tell me if she wanted to. She returned to her seat without comment.

I was startled to see the village of Arachova up the road; time had flown by quickly. Here, spring was still hanging on, and the mountain slopes were a vibrant, vivid green as far as the eye could see. I always envied the sedate pace of the Greek countryside. People appeared relaxed, slouching on rickety chairs outside cafés, seemingly not caring about what went on in the rest of the world. We slowly made our way through the village's narrow streets. I remembered that in winter, especially on weekends, crossing the village could take hours as skiers swamped the village heading to the snowy peaks of Mt Parnassos. Now, things were much calmer.

We left picturesque Arachova and began our descent to Delphi. The smell of thyme and rosemary filled the bus, wafting in through the open windows. Persie gave an interview over the phone and then fell silent again, gazing out the window at the splendor around her, the nature rolling by as we coursed down the winding road. I guessed she was thinking about the events of the previous day, or whatever else was preoccupying her.

I mustered up my courage and touched her hand, pointing to a string of horses trotting up a small slope. As if she had been waiting for it, she gave my hand a tight squeeze and leaned across my seat to get a better look, imperceptibly brushing her body against mine. I could not tell whether she realized how much I liked her, whether it was all random or just the way she usually behaved. Whatever her intention may have been, I felt flustered, and it took all my meagre acting skills to hide it.

Delphi slowly appeared on the horizon with the archaeological site on our right, brimming with visitors and large buses ferrying hundreds of tourists.

"It's a beautiful place. I wish I could photograph you here," I said, turning towards the ancient theatre.

"We can, if you want to, but just the two of us," she said, looking in the same direction.

"Okay, we'll do it on the way back," I said, and then instantly remembered that we would not be traveling back together. She would be spending an extra couple of days with her friend at her family home, while the rest of us would be returning on Monday morning, if not the following evening. Nonetheless, she said nothing and seemed to like the idea.

We entered the village and pulled over. Persie was keen to see her friend Paul, and we would be grabbing a bite at his restaurant. The fresh countryside air had left me famished ...

Christian, a suitcase in hand, appeared at the exit of the airport of Ioannina. He looked around, and spotted the man walking towards him. He greeted him, and the man led him to a car parked a little farther away. He handed over the keys and helped him load his luggage. They spoke for a few seconds, and the man left. Christian looked at the sky and got behind the wheel. The overcast skies did not match the time of year, and darkened his mood.

From the moment he had left the hospital in Paris, he had devoted himself to finding the starting point of the story Melek had told him. He carefully studied all the details of the case and laid the necessary groundwork before catching a flight to Greece. He had access to a good network in the country, and the fact that he spoke the language had proved invaluable. The envelope she had handed over contained information from that time, her recollections, and everything she had managed to dig up during her early research years ago. Unfortunately, she had fallen into a coma and had not awoken since. The doctors doubted whether she would come out of the intensive care unit alive.

Christian typed his destination into the navigator. His information had led him to begin his search in Ioannina, a city he was visiting for the first time in his life. He had rented a car and would be staying at one of the large hotels in the city center. All his moves so far had been veiled in secrecy, and no one knew the reason for his trip to Greece.

The lawyer handling Melek's affairs had demanded absolute secrecy. If his search proved fruitless, her fortune would go to charity.

But Christian was determined to leave no stone unturned. Melek had touched his life in the past in a way that had marked him. Now, he was determined to find her child. He was not motivated by the vast fee he would receive should he prove successful. He wanted to shed light on the murky past, solve the crime, and bring those guilty to justice, even after all these years. He had handed all his cases over to his associates and, when he had uncovered something that tied the past to the present, he got on the first plane to Athens and a connecting flight to Ioannina. He knew that Melek was still alive, and he still hoped against all odds that he might find the child and bring him or her to Melek, so she could go to her final resting place having found some peace.

The splatter of raindrops that hit the windshield mystified him. He had not expected this kind of weather in Greece, had not packed for it. As he neared Ioannina, he saw he had the choice of two routes leading to the hotel: one through the city, and the other alongside the lake. He opted for the latter; Melek had mentioned the "enchanted lake" numerous times in the notes she had left him. She had secretly spent some of the happiest times of her life on its shores, in the arms of her beloved.

Its waters had become his final resting place after those two monsters had left him there to drown, monsters Christian had now come to find. However, none of his searches had turned up a record of a drowned man washing ashore at that time. Many men had lost their lives in the lake, intentionally or accidentally, but none of them tied in with the time or other evidence he had. His frustration grew as the rain began to come down in sheets. He had been hoping that he would at least be able to enjoy Greek sunshine outside of work, and had instead arrived in the heart of winter.

He reached the road beside the lake. The downpour crashed against the lake's surface, creating a foggy cloud that spread like a veil. Despite being melancholy, it was a captivating sight. Christian's frustration eased, and he pulled over to enjoy the sight.

He tried to recall all the details Melek had recorded in the directions she had left him. It had not been easy to know where to start with the meagre hard facts he had at his disposal. The previous morning, after a report from one of his collaborators, he felt he had a chance to uncover one of the main culprits. He had been surprised to find out that the man was now a respected citizen in Ioannina. So, he'd hastily travelled here so he could verify whether the man in question was one of the two men who had committed those crimes against Melek and the other women back then.

Christian had been informed that the man would be one of the main speakers at a book launch this evening, and had secured an invite. His plan was to approach the man in the crowd, thus throwing him off balance. He did not have enough time on his hands—he had to act with swift precision. This mode of action suited him perfectly. He was not risk-averse, was unafraid to follow unorthodox methods at work, always careful and always passionate in everything he did.

The downpour continued, more violent as time went on, limiting visibility to the area just around the parked car. Christian leaned his head against the headrest and closed his eyes. He thought back to the endless nights filled with passion that he had spent with Melek. He had spent the rest of his life searching for the same kind of magic he had shared with her, which had been the most real thing he had experienced until then, though purchased. Even when he had abandoned all efforts to find her, he kept hoping at the back of his mind that one day their paths would cross. He had never expected they would reconnect under these circumstances, that he would be meeting a woman whose eyes were the only thing left to remind him of the person he had fallen in love with.

The encounter had shaken him, made him fully grasp the meaning of "life is too short." He had never had a family, always afraid to commit. Now, he found himself yearning for a child. Seeing Melek fervently searching for hers even as her life drew to a close had made him reexamine many of his own decisions. That would be the one thing he would change once this case was over. He realized that he would never meet the perfect woman, that he would have to make small compromises if he wanted a family. The years were passing fast, and he would have to act if he did not want to end up completely alone.

The rain began to abate, and he decided to head to the hotel. He was tired, having spent the past few days working around the clock on the case, studying it, searching for any clue. He intended to find out as much as possible about the man in question before attending the book launch that evening. Who was he? What kind of connections did he have? His position made Christian's task even harder—it would be easy to tie this man to the past. He realized people would not be forthcoming, but he trusted his own abilities to loosen reticent tongues.

He started the engine and drove slowly and carefully to the hotel. The weather seemed to be turning, and a bright rainbow had sprung up in the middle of the lake, spanning the city and resting on the foothills of the snow-capped mountain, a vestige of the heavy winter that had left its traces behind ...

After the wonderful lunch at Paul's restaurant in Delphi, we resumed our journey towards Galaxidi. The views from this high vantage point were spectacular. Olive groves stretched for miles before us all the way down to the coast. The sun had passed the midpoint of the clear blue canvas of the cloudless sky. The days were long and clear, and we all decided not to waste any time and head straight to the shoot on the small island.

Initially, I thought there was only a small church on the islet, the chapel of St. George. I had just been informed that there was an even smaller second chapel, St. Andrew's. I had not seen anything resembling such a building in the photos I had come across when I investigated the location. I could never understand people's obsession with erecting chapels in the middle of nowhere as a votive offering. Why not build a home for a poor family instead? How could someone choose to use the money to build a church that opened its doors a couple of times a year, if at that?

We were due to arrive shortly. Persie was twisted around in her seat, chatting with Theo. I stared out the bus window and let myself get lost in my own thoughts, gazing at the faraway horizon and the sea.

At the restaurant, Persie had spent most of her time getting her hair ready for the shoot, then sat beside her friend, catching up. I must confess to feeling jealous in the beginning, but then I realized that this was a childhood friendship that had not faded with the passage of time. I saw her become tearful at some point as she spoke to Paul, but she quickly tried to hide it. We all carry our own secrets and burdens, things we never share.

I, for one, had not spoken to any of my friends about what had happened recently. I was reserved by nature, afraid to share my feelings. My father had played a part in my reticence, raising me to never trust anyone. Whoever approached my family was an enemy in his eyes, someone who just wanted to take advantage of me. It took me a long time to react to such paranoid behavior.

The only time I heard a word of approval escape his lips was when I was accepted to medical school. Only then did I hear "Well done!" accompanied by a pat on my back. He had forbidden my mother from praising me, saying it would make me weak, a pushover.

I made an effort to chase these thoughts away and return to the happy present. I turned towards Persie and looked at her. She felt my gaze and returned it. Then she seemed puzzled, as if she had been waiting for me to say something. When she realized I was looking at her for no reason, she smiled and returned to her conversation. I was sure that everyone had picked up on my crush but, despite my embarrassment, I made no effort to hide it.

I shifted in my seat and leaned my head against the window. The truth was, I was still under the spell of her performance. I could not believe this heavenly creature, who could shift so easily between demon and goddess, was sitting here beside me. The way she danced was breathtaking. I had never seen anyone move their body with such harmony, such passion. I closed my eyes and replayed the show in my head, scene by scene ....

In a daze, I felt a hand gently stroke my cheek. I realized then that I must have fallen asleep, and the hand tenderly caressing me belonged to Persie, who was trying to wake me up. I sat up and smiled. We had stopped near the sea and everyone else was already getting off the bus.

"Are we here? I'm sorry, I didn't get much sleep last night," I said, trying to excuse myself.

"It's okay, Constantine, you obviously needed a nap. Take your time; the boat will have to make two trips to ferry us to the islet. The others have set up umbrellas to give us some shade and everything else we might need," she replied, and slipped soundlessly out of the bus.

The way she moved seemed to defy the laws of gravity. Even off stage, every movement seemed like a dance, without any pretentiousness. I felt embarrassed she saw me like this, but the truth was that I had slept very little these past two nights with everything that had happened.

I jumped out of the bus and felt sweet sunshine warm my body. I heard the voice of Sophie, my assistant, shouting hello from the boat that was already setting off for the chapel of St. George. She looked like a tomboy with her closely cropped hair. There was no one better at what she did, and I felt lucky she worked for me.

I waved back, quickly took down my equipment, and moved to join the others in the shade of a large pine tree. More than ten people had gathered for the shoot. The plan was to take a few shots against the backdrop of the two chapels and then wait for the sun to begin its descent, to make full use of the sunset colors. Across the bay, on the islet, a small tent had been set up, housing the clothes Persie was to wear. Clothing companies usually sponsored such projects.

I opened my bag and pulled out a hat, sunglasses, and lighter clothes, as we would be spending a lot of time in the sun, and moved behind the bus to change. From the corner of my eye, I looked through the windows and realized that Persie was turned towards me. Perhaps this was tit for tat for the previous evening, when I had spied on her through the door of her dressing room. I hastily pulled on a pair of shorts and a shirt.

When I reappeared, she dashed towards me so fast I was taken aback. She reached out, removed my sunglasses, and, before I could react, began to smear my face with sunscreen.

"We would not want you to burn," she said as she smothered every inch of my face.

We were standing very close and I looked deeply into her eyes, surrendering to her every gesture. Her hair was pulled back and her face, now melancholy, shone in the daylight, perfectly suited to the photoshoot concept. We would be keeping her make up as minimal as possible, going for a very natural look, not that that would cause any difficulties. She had one of those faces that were uniquely beautiful even when left completely bare.

Our eyes met for a moment, and her movements slowed down. I could feel the energy emanating from her fingertips course through my body, making me numb. Once again, I could not withstand her piercing gaze and I looked away towards the others, who were calling out something. I wanted to keep looking at her, to enjoy the feel of her touch, yet I awkwardly avoided it. I stood there like I had a split personality, wanting to do one thing and doing the exact opposite.

When she was done, she handed over the sunscreen tube and told me to cover anything else I needed, as the sun was treacherously hot. I wondered what she made of my gawkiness.

I gathered all my equipment and sailed towards the tiny island with those that had waited for the second boat ride. From this distance, the islet looked no bigger than a football field. Seeing it from afar, I thought that if I ever got married, I would like to have my wedding at just such a location. As if she'd read my thoughts, Persie said loudly for everyone to hear, "Nice place to get married!" and laughed, casting me a sideways look. I was too embarrassed to confess that the same thought had crossed my mind, too fearful that I might sound ridiculous—so I just nodded in agreement.

A little while later, we were all on the small island, looking more like a gang of castaways than professionals visiting for work. We set up quickly and began shooting against the backdrop of the chapel. Persie had assumed her part with ease and, as I clicked away, I enjoyed her beautiful eyes, their emerald color, the melancholy they exuded as she looked at the lens. I snatched moments and, ignoring the clothes, focused on her glance. In fact, I shot one frame for the magazine and one for me. Sophie, holding a large umbrella made of transparent tulle, softened the light of the sun. She patiently listened to my directions as we changed poses and clothes.

I meticulously avoided turning towards the makeshift dressing room. I was determined Persie would not see me steal a glance again, so I busied myself with the angles and lenses I intended to use. At one point, when she posed with her back turned to me, her tattoo of a small pomegranate became visible above the low cut of the dress she was modeling. It now appeared clearer and brighter than it had the previous evening. I wanted to ask her what it meant. I focused on it and took a few shots, clicking rapidly, afraid of missing the slightest detail.

Just before we finished taking the shots that centered around the white outfits, I heard the familiar text alert coming from my phone. I pulled it out as we changed positions, and cast a hasty look. I clenched my teeth, seeing that my father was the sender. I nervously pulled up the message and froze to the spot.

*You may have found out the truth—but now you have lost all fatherly protection ...*

A moment ago, I was happy, but again my father was doing his best to spoil things for me. Luckily, I had managed to capture some good frames before reading the message—

from that point onwards my hands shook so badly that I could not continue.

Persie walked up to me, having witnessed everything from afar. "How about a break? I think we are done with these clothes and the shots we need."

I was impressed that she had sensed the change in my mood, as if she could read my thoughts. At least, that is what I wanted to believe, not that my agitation was so evident that anyone could spot it. In any case, it was time for a break to change backdrop, as the sun was setting fast. The idea was that she would wade into the sea, with the sun slowly dipping behind the mountains on the shore we had just left.

Realizing that it would take a while for her to prepare, I decided to go for a swim. I wanted to let the water wash away the thoughts that had returned to torment me. I walked to the other side of the islet, just behind the chapel, and laid my things on a rock. Shielded from everyone's view as I was, I stripped naked and waded into the water.

I felt the cold hit my body hard. I had thought it would be warmer, but I was mistaken. I wavered for a moment, but then I took a deep breath and dove in. The icy cold stunned me to the point where I thought I'd never be able to catch my breath again. I swam away from the shore with furious strokes, trying to warm up. I kept the frantic pace up for a while, trying to conquer the cold, but I already felt my spirits begin to rise. Without realizing, I had covered a great distance. From where I was, I saw everyone dotted all over the island as if they were taking part in some religious festivity.

For a moment I forgot about everything and floated on the surface, looking up at the sky. The silence surrounding me filled me with energy and strength. I knew that I would have to confront my past as soon as I returned to Athens. No matter how hard I tried to escape it, it always waited for me at every twist and turn. Perhaps now I was being given a chance to finally rid myself of everything, especially my father.

I must have been so lost in my thoughts that I floated for quite some time and started to feel the cold again. I began to swim back to the shore. When I was close to land, I lifted my head out of the water to see how I could safely get out, surrounded by rocks as I was. I was startled to see Persie sitting by the sea. She was waving a towel, showing that she was expecting me. How could I walk out completely naked and dry myself?

I stood up, the water reaching my chest. Persie was in a bathing suit, a sarong wrapped around her waist. I was not sure she understood that I was naked, but she was patiently waiting for me to come out. Hoping that someone would eventually call her away, I began to tell her how cold the sea was, how beautiful the place was, how pleased I was with the photos we had taken.

She gestured once again. "Come out, you'll catch a cold! I can see your teeth chatter!"

She was smiling strangely. No way was I appearing before her, even if it meant freezing to death. She stood up, dropped the towel on a rock, and turned to walk away. "Fine, I'll leave you to it ... even though you owe me one for last night."

I tried to understand what she meant as she walked away. I was now certain that she knew I was naked and that she had probably seen me peering at her the previous evening. Perhaps this was her revenge. Or was she referring to the near naked scenes of the performance? I did not know what to believe and, as soon as she was some distance away, I got out as fast as I could and wrapped myself in the towel. In a few moments I rejoined everyone, and we waited for the sun to reach a lower point so we could continue shooting. Persie was already swimming along the tiny coastline.

Anna sat on the balcony of her home and looked at the sun with teary eyes as it set behind a tall mountain, spreading its last rays across the horizon. She was nearly sixty but looked older, as if she was carrying the heavy burden of her difficult life on her shoulders. Silently, she waited for the door to open and Nick, her husband, to arrive.

A terrible argument had erupted between them over the phone concerning their son, Constantine. Without meaning to, she had blurted out that she had revealed the secret they had kept hidden from him all those years. She'd regretted the words the moment they'd left her lips and had tried to backtrack, but it was too late. Her anger had finally gotten the best of her, and she had been careless. She could no longer stand to hear Nick speak so ill of their child, as if he was someone despicable, a social pariah. As a mother, she knew her child better than anyone else. She had been the one to raise him, after all, almost single-handedly. Her husband's input had been confined to bringing home a paycheck and making life difficult for both of them. He had never loved Constantine, had treated him badly from the start.

She wiped the tears streaming down her wrinkled cheeks with the back of her hand. An old burn mark run down her arm, scarring it all the way down to her fingers and adding a nightmarish look to her gentle exterior. It was all that was left to remind her of the past, of everything she had gone through with that man. She regretted not only things she had not done, but things she had done as well. She wished fervently she had taken Constantine away and raised him on her own, far away from the shadow of his fearsome father. But, even now, she had never stopped being terrified of Nick, knowing what he was capable of. The fact that he was a policeman meant absolutely nothing. She wished she had found the strength to speak up, to let everyone know that behind the mask of the good cop hid a monster, a man so ruthless he would stop at nothing to achieve his aims. She was puzzled at how he had managed to get away with it for so many years; none of his despicable acts had ever seen the light of day. On the contrary, he had risen up the ranks.

Rage boiled inside her. If not for their son, she would have killed him. Sometimes, when she watched Nick sleep beside her, she was overcome with the desire to plunge a knife in his heart. She often dreamt of his death, to the point where she would sometimes wake up expecting to find the sheets drenched in his blood from the multiple wounds she had inflicted in the land of dreams. As disgusted as she had felt, however, she had not summoned enough courage to call Constantine and tell him that his father now knew about her revelation. The truth was that she had not told her son everything, only what concerned his life—what had happened before his birth remained secret.

The familiar sound of his keys unlocking the door echoed inside Anna, and a cold fear gripped her heart. She knew what was coming. Without looking away from the sun, whose crown still peeked over the mountain top, she listened as he walked into the living room.

Then she frowned, puzzled. She thought she could hear singing. She could not believe the tune that was coming from his mouth. It was the tuneless melody more than the lyrics—she remembered the lyrics, but could not understand what he meant by it now.

She stood up and walked to the kitchen, to find Nick standing before the fridge, munching on something. He was in uniform but looked a mess. His shirt was hanging out, creased. His tie was undone and about to drop to the floor. Once again, he was drunk. When he sensed her presence, he turned and smiled as if nothing had happened. As if he was in a joyous mood, he kept monotonously repeating the chorus of the song, looking at her with eyes blurry with wine.

*Even if he cheated on you,*

*Even if he hurt you,*

*This love makes your eyes glow*

*Like a golden palace ...*

Anna knew the song well—it reminded her of one of the worst moments of her life. She had not heard it for years, but it always triggered a flood of unbearable memories. She kept watching him, waiting for his outburst. He kept stuffing his face with whatever he could lay his hands on, still singing and spitting crumbs everywhere. Finally, satiated, he slammed the fridge door shut and indifferently pushed past her, stumbling off into the bedroom without saying a word.

Anna was stunned, having expected a painful fight after everything that had happened. She thought it must be the drink. On an almost daily basis he would drink himself into a stupor. His colleagues often brought him home in a terrible state. She snuck over to the open bedroom door and saw him lying on the bed fully clothed. She turned and walked back to the balcony, taking the phone with her to call Constantine. Her husband would be snoring until the following morning. Taking a deep breath, she dialed the number with shaky fingers ...

The shoot was almost finished. Dusk was fast approaching, but I kept at it, taking as many shots as I could in the dim light that lingered as Persie posed in the water. I confess that, as soon as she stripped down to her waist, the same feelings I had experienced the previous night when I had watched behind the door of her dressing room returned. I felt like flinging my camera aside and wading through the water towards her, touching her ... But of course I would not do it, so I tried to stifle my raging imagination.

None of those photos would make the magazine, shot as they were from certain angles. That did not mean I could not see her ... It was not the first time I was photographing the naked back of a beautiful woman, but the one standing before me exuded such a sensuous aura that I was filled with tension and awkwardness.

I was impressed she had managed to stay in the water without feeling the cold for so long. She had explained she swam through the winter, but her stamina was nonetheless remarkable. She never complained and followed my directions without objection, taking the poses I indicated. We only paused a few times, so she could take a few calls.

Her sangfroid following the events of the previous evening had impressed me. She was either one of those people who could skillfully hide their feelings, or was a very resilient person. In the brief time I had known her, I concluded she was probably a mixture of both. I would lose all track of space and time as I worked with her, often succumbing to the illusion that it was just the two of us. I enjoyed a special connection to her through the lens. I could feel her piercing glance and just clicked away, hoping to capture her singular beauty which shone so bright. Like on stage, she could metamorphosize from one moment to the next, from a diva to girl next door. That chameleon-like quality was obviously one of the great secrets of her success.

The others began to pack up and ferry everything across the bay, hoping to beat nightfall. I felt my phone vibrate and cast a hasty look. It was my mother, but I did not reply. I did not want to keep Persie any longer; she must have been getting tired. I dropped the phone back inside my pocket.

Even though I really wanted to find out what had happened with my father, I decided to call my mother back later when I would be able to talk more freely. I could imagine how hard all this must have been for her—to carry the burden of regrets and a guilty conscience all on her own. I intended to ask her to move in with me as soon as I returned to Athens, to finally escape her misery. I don't know why, but I felt that my father's period of grace was about to come to an end, that he would soon pay for everything he had done to my mother and me.

Realizing it would be excessive to continue in the twilight, I decided we should stop. "I think we are done for today. You can come out now," I called out to her. Everyone broke into cheers and applause.

Her friend Violet and some other friends would be waiting for us in Galaxidi for dinner in an hour. I tried to concentrate so that no photos would be lost due to a careless error. I gave Sophie instructions to take the camera and save everything. She gave me a puzzled look at such thoroughness but said nothing and took the equipment from me carefully.

Soon enough, we had packed up. Persie had pulled a white dress on and was on the phone, walking towards the other side of the island where the boat awaited us.

Theo approached me with a smile and whispered conspiratorially, "Ready to depart. Do you want the last spot, and I can wait here with Persie for the boat to come back?"

I don't know why, but I felt that he was purposely giving us a chance to be alone, trying to bring us closer together. Initially at a loss, I spoke with difficulty, trying to think of a good excuse that would explain my desire to stay. "No, it's okay, I'll stay. You go and load up the cars so we're not late for dinner, and we'll come join you."

As if Theo had been hoping for such a reply, he turned and skipped towards the boat before I could even finish my sentence.

The last rays of the sun still tinted the sky, as if daylight was refusing to let nighttime arrive. I felt the freshness of a light breeze and turned towards Persie. I could make out her shadow and the faint sound of her voice. She was still talking to someone on the phone. The loud engine of the departing boat sucked up every sound until it was some distance away and everything returned to its previous calm. It was a little strange to find ourselves alone on a deserted island; unfortunately, the boat would be returning soon to pick us up. Now, only the sound of the waves lapping the rocky shore could be heard.

I don't know why, but it felt good to be here, so far away from the world. It was as if the islet had suddenly transformed into a castle that kept everyone outside.

When I was sure Persie had hung up, I slowly approached her. She was standing still, looking towards Galaxidi, where the lights of the town lit up the surface of the sea. *Another photo I would like to have*, I thought, watching her attentively.

As soon as she sensed my presence, she turned around and our eyes met. Her white dress lit up her smiling face. I sensed that her mood had once again changed, no matter how hard she was trying to hide her true feelings.

Suddenly, she looked serious and motioned for me to keep quiet. Her eyes were fixed on a spot behind me and, for a moment I felt fear. She tiptoed towards me and pulled me by the hand, crouching and forcing me to bend down low. We kept walking in this position towards the spot she had been staring at. Perplexed, I scanned the area ahead but could not see anything. I turned to ask her what was going on, but she shushed me and pointed at something. "Look!" she whispered. "Wild rabbits."

Just then, I saw something move. To my great surprise, I saw that she was right. Our cheeks were almost touching as we glanced right and left, trying to make out the bunnies hopping everywhere. A few moments later they vanished, and we slowly turned to face each other.

"How did they end up here?" I asked, perplexed.

"I don't know ... I remember them hopping around since I was a kid. I thought there weren't any left, but I was wrong," she replied with a smile.

I felt a smile form on my lips, and we burst out laughing, still very near one another, as if we had heard the funniest joke. The powerful woman I had seen on stage had now given way to a small child. I was fascinated by the changes in her behavior. I had never met anyone whose mood could change so swiftly, not just on stage but in real life.

As soon as our laughter subsided, she took my hand. "You gave me great courage last night. That is why I am here today, and I thank you," she said. Once again, I was taken aback by her forthrightness.

I had not realized I had been of any help. She stood facing me, looking into my eyes, and all I could think about was how to find the courage to move closer and kiss her. I was rooted to the spot, however, fearing her reaction. Having learned that she was already in a relationship with the man she had argued with the previous evening, I would not be the one making the first move. Besides, I was not sure she had any feelings for me, having noticed that she was very warm and tactile with everyone.

"I think they are coming for us," she continued, as it was now clear I would not be responding. She straightened up and looked at the approaching boat. I felt my heart sink, realizing I had let an opportunity to connect with her pass me by.

She had opened a path for honest communication, so I summoned all my courage and said, "I'm glad I could help you, even unwittingly, but I would like to know more. What did I ...?"

"Maybe I won't tell you, so you can do it again ..." she replied with meaning, and began to walk towards the spot where the boat would pick us up.

My limbs felt heavy as I followed her. In less than twenty-four hours, she had succeeded where every other woman before her had failed—she had managed to impress me in the truest way a person can: with her simplicity.

# Ioannina

In the city of Ioannina, Christian sat at one of the back seats of a packed library hall between two ladies he had just met. Just before his arrival, he had received a call from Melek's lawyer in Paris, informing him that she had woken up for a few moments and was asking for him, before losing consciousness once again. This small revival had given them hope that she might reawaken.

He was at the launch event of a history book covering the Ottoman period of the city. He was generally familiar with the topics covered by the speakers, but at this moment Mark Ganas, the man at the podium, had fully captured his interest. He could be one of the two men who had snatched Melek's child and sold it. His skull was shaved, a method chosen by many men to cover severe hair loss, while his whole appearance and manner were at odds with the evening—he was like a fish out of water. Only the way he held the microphone showed some ease with public speaking.

Christian observed Ganas carefully, and the more he watched the more he became convinced this was the man he had been looking for. It was not just the man's aura, but also his gut feeling that whispered he was on the right track. The man was the main shareholder of a local football team and the owner of a large slaughterhouse, as well as one of the sponsors of the book being presented.

Christian's information left some room for doubt about whether this man was one of the two guilty parties, and he had struggled to find proof to link him to the events of that time. The other man, the policeman Melek had mentioned, remained elusive. It was as if such a man had never existed. This was not surprising—many members of the criminal world disappeared overnight and were never heard from again.

Ganas, pausing often, reached the end of his speech, talking with great emphasis. "The Turks and Ali Pasha may have called her a whore ..." Silence fell at the sound of that word. For a moment he froze, as if the word had slipped out of its own volition. He tried to overcome the *faux pas* with a small cough and ploughed on. "That was the excuse they used to drown her and the other women in our lake. To us, however, Kyra Frosini[6] will always be the symbol of a Greek woman who refused to bow to the conqueror's sword. Thank you ..."

Lukewarm applause greeted his final words. There was tension in the air. Christian instantly sensed it, and it confirmed his research about that man.

The woman coordinating the presentation stepped up to the podium. "Thank you all for coming to tonight's presentation of *Ioannina, from Ottoman Times to the Present*. The author will sign books now and a small

---

[6] TN: Euphrosyne Vasileiou (1773 – 11 January 1800), better known as Kyra Frosini, was a Greek socialite who was executed for adultery in Ioannina by the Ottoman governor Ali Pasha of Ioannina along with 16 other women.

cocktail party will follow in the foyer, offered by Mark Ganas Ltd. Thank you for your presence."

Everyone clapped politely and began to rise from their seats. Some moved to the foyer, others to the stage where the author was signing her book. Christian realized it would be pointless to approach Ganas now, and decided to wait and meet him at the cocktail party. He patiently waited for everyone to step into the foyer. Ganas was already there, posing for photos with the other speakers.

Soon everyone had moved to the bar, where a band was playing live music and the party was livening up. Christian was chatting with the two women who'd been sitting beside him earlier; they seemed delighted to have made his acquaintance. He had introduced himself as a historian, specializing in war crimes. They followed him with interest as he spoke. His Greek was rather good, and they were happy to complete his sentences whenever he fumbled for a word. He was elegantly dressed in a cream suit and a white, tight-fitting shirt that accentuated his toned torso. Barely ten minutes of polite conversation had passed, and they had already invited him to lunch the following day.

Soon enough, Ganas made his appearance at the hotel bar. As soon as Christian saw him, he said with feigned indifference, "It is good to see businessmen sponsor efforts such as this one. I wish there were more men like Monsieur Ganas ..."

One of the women sighed and was about to speak, but her friend, who was holding a rose, interrupted her. "You are right. The contributions of private enterprise are a great aid to art."

Ganas, as if sensing they were talking about him, walked towards them and greeted the two women. He cast a questioning look at Christian, who had fixed his eyes on him. The woman holding the rose made the necessary introductions. "Mr. Ganas, meet Mr. Ledu, a French historian of Greek descent."

Their eyes met as they shook hands. "Pleased to meet you ... I have a feeling we've met before. Have you been here before?"

"First time," Christian said. "My mother's parents were born on the island of Kea. I spent many summers there as a child. I have traveled around Greece of course, as a tourist, but this is my first visit to your city. So, unless you have lived in Paris ..."

"I have been to France only once, but not in Paris ... What brings you to our city, if I may ask?"

The same woman interrupted them. "Mr. Ledu is here because he is writing a book about crimes committed during the wars ... Isn't that so?" she said, and looked at Christian.

"That's exactly right. The book talks of those crimes. More recent crimes will be in another book I'm planning to write," he said with a smile that left doubts as to whether he was joking. He was preparing the ground for his upcoming attack.

Ganas's smile vanished when he heard that last sentence. He turned towards the women, evidently ill at ease, and encouraged them to have another glass of wine. Then he spoke, looking at Christian, "Let us not talk of crime any more, but have another glass of wine. It is local, you know; we have vineyards around here. I hope you will find it up to your standards."

"Anything made with dev—" Christian paused, struggling to find the right word.

"Devotion!" jumped in the same woman, with undiminished eagerness.

"That's right … Anything made with devotion is bound to be good," Christian said, smiling at the woman who had taken on the role of assistant.

"You should also try the food," Ganas said. "Locally-made delicacies—and delicious! It was a pleasure to meet you."

Ganas turned to leave. Before he could move away, a young woman flung herself into his arms.

"Daddy, I only just arrived from Athens and I missed your speech!" she complained loudly.

He gave her a tight hug. Joy beamed out from his every pore. He kissed her and put an arm around her shoulders as they walked away. Christian was startled by this happy encounter and looked after them, speechless, as they made their way to the buffet tables. The love emanating from the girl was palpable. She looked not a day older than twenty-five.

His thoughts were interrupted by the chatty woman, who waved her rose around as she spoke. "It's his daughter, Caroline. A wonderful girl; she is studying in Athens now. She has a scholarship to study abroad next year. She moved to Athens after her parents' divorce, but visits often. Her mother, you see, has married again and lives in Australia now ..."

The other woman nudged her unstoppable friend in the ribs. Christian was stunned at how much one could learn in so brief a time. You could just drop a hint, and rumors would be spreading through the city like wildfire. People knew much about the lives of others in small communities. Details that were personal, family preoccupations, would become common knowledge. This was proving most useful in the circumstances.

He wanted to find out more, but the two women had turned their attention to some friends who had approached them. Christian smiled a temporary goodbye and drifted off in the direction of Ganas and his daughter. He lined up to get a drink, and the smell of food woke hunger pangs, reminding him he had not eaten properly all day. A glass of wine in one hand, he sampled the delicious spread. He tried hard to appear relaxed, but he knew that every minute that ticked by was precious time lost ...

People had begun to leave the cocktail party. The rumors about the visitor from France and the history book he was writing had spread, and Christian had not been bored. People kept walking up to him to meet him and find out more details. He kept waiting for the right moment to approach Ganas without attracting attention.

In the meantime, he had managed to find out a few things about the past. He had understood that people would not be forthcoming on certain matters, but in his charming way he was beginning to loosen some tongues. An elderly teacher he had met a short while ago had spoken of the time period he was interested in. He had asked him discreetly about brothels and bawdy houses in the seventies. The elderly man, no longer fearing his wife—who had long departed this earth—had confessed to visiting some of them. Christian quickly did the math in his head and realized it did not match the time when Melek worked there. But the man knew, like everyone else, about the fire that had consumed the brothel and some of its residents. The fire no one realized had been lit by the hand of Melek as revenge against her tormentors and the abductors of her child. The elderly man informed him that the tragic event had forced the police to take a stand and crack down on the many illegal activities they had been turning a blind eye to. The man had then grown tired and wanted to leave, but they agreed to have a coffee the following morning near the spot where the brothel had once stood. He promised to bring newspaper clippings he had kept from that time, having amassed a large archive throughout his life. Christian had not expected to discover such a source so early on. Used to the pace of big cities, he was not familiar with how fast wheels could spin in the countryside.

A few minutes later, Ganas's daughter passed in front of him, giving him a warm smile. Unable to resist his weakness for women, he returned the smile. Finally, he was left face to face with the man who had been the cause for his presence that evening.

Christian eyed him up like a beast might eye its prey before attacking, and moved towards him. He decided to be forceful, fearing he might not have another opportunity to approach him. Ganas would be vulnerable now, especially given the presence of his daughter.

Christian moved closer. Ganas saw him approach, smiled, and raised his glass. "To your good health, Mr. ..."

"Ledu," Christian replied, seeing him struggle to remember his name.

They clinked glasses, and each took a long sip.

"Will you be staying long?" Ganas asked.

"I hope not too long. Just as long as it takes to track down the information I need."

"If I can be of any assistance, I would be glad to ..."

"The truth is, you can. Possibly more than anyone else," Christian replied, having decided to go for broke.

Ganas seemed taken aback, but rallied quickly. "I beg your pardon? I don't understand ..."

His daughter returned just then with a drink, interrupting their conversation. Sensing the tension, she realized it was an inopportune moment and apologized. Christian said hello and introduced himself, then raised his glass, urging them to follow suit. He wondered how she would react if she ever learned of her father's hideous past actions. Melek must have been younger than his daughter back then. Their glasses touched in the middle of the impromptu circle they had formed. Christian made his toast before they could take a sip. "To the memory of all the innocent lost in the lake ..."

Ganas appeared irritated before he even heard the end of the sentence.

"And to all those who burned later ..." Christian added in a clear voice.

Even though he had brought his glass to his lips, Ganas did not drink, and gave him a hard look. His daughter realized something was going on between the two men, and left them under the pretext of saying hello to a friend she had just spotted. The two men remained silent, sizing each other up. Ganas cracked first, and spoke in a harsh voice, which in no way resembled the polite tones of the man who had taken to the podium. "Who are you? What do you want from me?"

"I already told you who I am. I bring greetings from a mutual friend. Perhaps it would be better if we spoke somewhere else, not here … Certainly not in front of your child …"

Christian knew how to hit where it hurt. Ganas's reaction confirmed that the right man was standing before him. His response came swiftly, but his voice now was filled with the anger of an injured animal, under attack and fighting back. "We have nothing to discuss unless you tell me what you want from me and who the mutual 'friend' is."

"No need to get so wound up, my friend. Here is my card. I will wait for your call tomorrow morning, so we can have a quiet little chat," Christian replied. He handed over a card and placed his wine glass on a table. He saluted Ganas and made to turn away. Just then, he fired his parting shot, a sentence he had thoroughly practiced in his head. "The woman who says 'Hi' told me you were there when times were hard. It seems you both made it in the end."

Ganas lost his temper and grabbed Christian by the arm, grunting through gritted teeth, "You don't know who you are messing with, Frenchman. You have no idea what you are getting into …"

It was the reaction Christian had been expecting. He had saved the best for last. "Fine then. You want to know right now? So be it." Christian leaned forward and hissed, "An old friend from the past sends her greetings. Melek says, 'Burn in hell.'"

Ganas froze at the sound of that name. His breathing became labored. Slowly his face turned ashen, as if he had just seen a ghost …

We had just arrived at the taverna for dinner: everyone who had been at the shoot, and also some friends of Persie. We had barely had enough time to dash to our rooms to quickly shower and change. All I had managed to do was check with Sophie that all the photos had been saved.

It was a small town, meaning distances were insignificant, and the little taverna by the port was beautiful. The sailing boats completed the perfect picture, firing up my secret dream of learning how to sail someday. Persie already had a Yachtmaster qualification, and she told me that she disappeared on some vessel in the Greek seas most summers. I now associated her with sailing—along with everything else. Since last night, I felt like all my life revolved around her. Even now, all that I cared about was seeing her arrive.

We sat at a long table that could barely seat so many people. Persie was the only one missing, due to arrive any moment now with her friend.

I had managed to call my mother earlier. She had kept apologizing for telling my father that I now knew the whole truth. I tried to convince her that I did not mind, and that there was no reason for her to be upset. She sounded willing to leave him, and we agreed to discuss it when I returned. Although it would be hard for me to financially support the both of us, I was prepared to make every sacrifice for the woman who had raised me with so much love, sacrificed so much to make me happy.

I suggested that she move to my house for now, and promised to join her as soon as possible. She made me swear not to return before my work was done, even if I felt she needed me by her side. After everything she had revealed, I could not even imagine how my life would have turned out if it had not been for her, if I would still be here today.

No one other than us three knew the truth about our family, and I feared my father's reaction. He seemed out of control, and I was sure his downfall was near. No matter how well-connected he was, his friends in higher places would not be able to salvage his reputation. Every time I went to their home, I could tell he had leverage. He had gathered information people would rather be kept secret, and in exchange they protected him and his dirty deeds. If I could get my hands on concrete proof I would have turned him in, but he was an expert at hiding his tracks.

Everyone turned at once, and I realized Persie must be arriving. I turned around in my seat and, seeing her arrive accompanied by her friend Violet, I stood up. Simply dressed in a plain blue dress, she glowed once again. Despite feeling both dazzled and dazed by her glance and her mischievous smile, I turned towards her and greeted her. She introduced her friend, and we all sat down. The other diners were looking at Persie, who was greeting everyone she knew in the room. It was evident that people here loved and admired her.

Violet took the seat across from me. Persie had told me much about their friendship, which had begun in childhood. Persie sat further down the table next to some of her other friends. I just hoped she would not spend the entire evening there.

Her friends looked at me, and a young woman whispered something in Persie's ear. Persie whispered something back. What I wouldn't have given to be privy to those words!

Although she'd initially shown me no particular interest, Violet was now fixing me with her gaze every time I looked away. I spoke to her, but my mind was at the other end of the table. She showed great interest in my work and asked me many questions. She owned a small bookshop, and the following day we would be shooting outside her store. We laughed a lot when I mentioned the wild bunnies, and Violet told me of a rare flower with a distinctive smell that only grew on the island in spring, a type of daffodil locally known as *meriza*.

"It's Persie's favorite flower," Violet said. "Whenever she's here and they happen to be in season, she goes to the island just to smell them. The funny thing is, though, she never gathers any ... She just kneels down and smells them."

I felt as if she was pointing out everything I ought to know. Even though it was rather funny and bizarre, I liked the way she spoke about her best friend. The more that time passed, the more I wished Persie would stay at the other end of the table, so I could find out more about her life. As Violet explained, Persie had lost both parents in a car accident many years ago and still missed them sorely. I remembered the moment when we had stopped at the side of the road for her to visit the roadside votive chapel. After the tragic accident, she had gone to live with an aunt in Athens and professionally pursued her great love: dance. After she graduated from highschool, she moved abroad to continue her studies.

I kept stealing glances in Persie's direction. She now looked serious; troubled. I was sure it had something to do with the events of the previous evening. I still had not brought it up, trying to be discreet. On the other hand, I didn't want her to think I did not care. I would try later to raise the topic in an effort to help her. She sensed my eyes on her, smiled, and stood up to join us. She sat next to her friend, facing me. She raised her glass as if trying to chase her dark thoughts away, and we followed suit.

"A toast to the most talented photographer in Greece," she said loudly. Almost everyone clapped and cheered. Giggling at my blush, she fixed her eyes on me. I fell under her spell every time she looked at me this way. As far as I could recall, I had taken some unique photos of her eyes with the sea spreading out behind them.

Violet took out her phone and took a photo, probably to post it on social media. Generally, I did not like to share my personal moments, but I did not object this time.

The waiters placed large platters of seafood on our table, and we all tucked in, famished, savoring "the fruit of the sea" as Violet called them.

Michael's home on Patmos was one of the fishermen's sheds lining the shore on the west coast of the island. These small buildings mostly served as boathouses for the tiny fishing boats, but he had converted his grandfather's shed into his refuge. He could not spend winter here; the humidity would seep through and temperatures dropped as the northerly wind battered the shore. But as soon as spring made its early, timid appearance, he would pack up and move to his hermitage, where the only sound that could be heard was the waves splashing against the rocks. In the winter he would rent a small house further inland, although he spent many nights at one of the monastery's cells.

His life was austere, in no way dissimilar to the life and vows taken by the monks. He followed their routine for the most part, not just the religious but also the dietary aspects; however, he liked having the choice of secluding himself from their community whenever he felt the need. The small structure also housed his studio, and he would paint, looking out to the sea, whenever he found a spare moment.

A small bed and a wooden bench holding the essentials were all his belongings. A gas lamp and a few candles lit up the room, particularly the sketch that Renée had found in the library, which now stood on an easel. The face of the woman with the long auburn hair and the emerald green eyes could now be seen more clearly, as the aquarelle stood in the brightest spot in the room. At its corner, a few words had been painted in cursive, like a title.

Michael was sitting on a low wooden stool, holding a brush and nervously correcting the lake backdrop of the painting. His long hair was pushed back loosely, away from his face. The door was open, and the soft breeze filled the room with the salty scent of the sea. To his right, on a smaller easel, stood a sketch of a fishing boat at the port of Patmos at midday. On it, the figure of a man was faintly visible, lying on a small plank and shielded from the hot sun. His hand was hanging down by his side and resting against the floor of the boat, a sign that he was fast asleep. To the right, small text was inscribed in cursive:

*I peeked through the door and caught a glimpse of the sea inside you ...*

Such poetic words, so fitting the image of the fisherman in repose. It was a reproduction of an old photo of his grandfather, who had been sleeping inside the boat when a photographer had stolen that moment of serenity. It was the only picture Michael had of him, having seen him only a few times in his life when he was a young child. The text had been written on the back of the photo. He did not know whether his grandfather or someone else had written it, but he loved it, and had used it as a kind of signature.

Michael dabbed tersely away at the canvas, at the point where the lake faintly filled the backdrop. The woman's eyes were so imposing, it was hard to take in the rest of the painting. Even though her face was expressionless, it exuded a strange power that drew you in. The melancholic mood of the setting, the sadness and pain in her eyes, dominated the picture.

Despite the tranquil atmosphere, Michael was not in a good mood. He had just found out that the book Renée had donated to the monastery would be arriving in Athens the day after tomorrow, and he had been charged with taking delivery and transporting it to Patmos. He had not been to the capital in years, and he did not relish the prospect, but he was the only one who could perform this duty. Besides, it had been one of the conditions Renée had imposed—that he should be the one to go to Athens and meet the man who would be flying with the manuscript from Paris. Patmos was his castle—he felt safe here, as if the energy of the island cast a shield of protection around him. He would have to stay in Athens overnight due to the ferry routes and departure times.

Upon hearing of his upcoming journey, Peter, the elderly monk, had asked him to take some holy water and an icon to his sister who was in the hospital in Athens. It would not be a pleasant visit, but Michael could not refuse his brother, as he called him, and so he accepted. He feared spending an entire day in the city. This inexplicable dread had filled him with tension, which he tried to dispel by painting. Athens was nothing but a jungle, he'd often said.

In a few minutes he abandoned his paintbrushes, fearing he was doing more harm than good, and stepped outside. A narrow path to the side of his home wound down to the beach. He loved walking there in the afternoon, while the island was still quiet. At this time, it was unlikely that he would meet anyone.

Walking along the coastline, he reached the sparkling pebbles that still glimmered in the setting sun. He found a dry spot and sat down. He looked to the island of Samos on the left. It had been a clear day and visibility was perfect. A little further back, the lights on the coast of Turkey twinkled faintly, piercing the approaching darkness.

He untied his pony tail and felt the breeze run its fingers through his hair. With a contented sigh, he let nature fill him with peace. This was the moment when he cleansed his soul. He sought tranquility, the balance that could be found in nature. He felt that this was his way to be nearer to God. It was how he understood religion. He did not believe churches and temples were the only place where an encounter with the divine was possible.

He had revisited the grotto that afternoon with Peter, wanting to ask the old monk who sat vigil there why he'd chosen that particular excerpt from the Book of Revelation to speak to Renée. Michael did not know the monk beyond a friendly greeting. He was a reserved man, and Michael had respected that, not pushing for further communication than the monk was happy to engage in. Peter, however, knew him well and, using something he needed to attend to as an excuse, had offered to accompany Michael and talk to him.

Michael and Peter found the old monk finishing his evening prayers, and they all sat together outside the grotto. Guessing the purpose of their visit, the monk addressed the matter before they could ask. He told them of a trip to Paris before he'd moved to Patmos permanently. Renée's movie had just come out, and had been condemned by the church as blasphemous. He had joined the protests outside movie theatres. In one of those protests he had met her, although he was sure she did not remember him. He had verbally attacked her, and her bodyguards had hit him, then handed him over to the police, who later released him. The monk had never forgotten the incident, or the humiliation they had inflicted on him for protesting the offensive spectacle. The phrase had been written outside every cinema back then: *And I gave her space to repent of her fornication; and she repented not.*

When the monk had seen the actress again at the grotto, he'd felt he needed to remind her of the sin which, according to him, she had committed. Michael and Peter did not comment, just let him explain the reason behind his conduct. Even though he did not apologize for his actions, he seemed to soften a little when he learned of her donation, and dropped the subject.

Michael was happy to let the matter go. For him, it was enough that the verses were not directed at him and his past life ...

The book launch event at Ioannina had drawn to a close, and Ganas was driving away. His daughter sat in the passenger seat. As soon as they had put some distance between them and the hotel hosting the event, she reached out and touched his hand. "What's the matter, Dad? What did that man say?"

Ganas tried hard to hide his turmoil. He turned on the radio and cast her a sideways glance. "Nothing, sweetheart. I just have a lot on my mind right now; work stuff. Nothing serious. Are you planning to stay for a few days?"

She did not seem satisfied with his answer, but did not push the matter. "I'm staying for a week to work on an assignment. I will head to Metsovo tomorrow and spend the day there working. Come have lunch with me and catch up."

As if he had not heard a word of what she had just said, Ganas stared at the road ahead. The headlights of oncoming cars intermittently lit up his face and the fearful expression that still haunted his eyes, ever since the moment Christian had spoken that woman's name.

"I'll drop you off at home," he said without looking at her. "There is something I need to do."

He could feel her gaze studying him. Had rumors about him reached her ears? He knew that people loved to gossip, not just about his work, but also about Caroline's mother. She had moved to Australia permanently with her new family. Her new husband owned a large construction company and might be able to offer Caroline a nice job. With things in Greece going from bad to worse, Ganas made sure Caroline lacked for nothing. The last thing he wanted was for his ex-wife to lure his only daughter away. Thankfully, Caroline had not met her mother in over two years, so that seemed like a distant prospect.

Ganas pushed the thought away as he pulled up outside the garden gate of their home. They had not spoken another word during the drive. Their house was in the suburbs, up on the hill, with a view of the lake. He got out and kissed her goodnight, waited for her to get inside, and then hurriedly drove off.

He parked on a small, deserted street and pulled out his phone. His forehead shone with tiny beads of sweat. He clumsily wiped them away with the back of his hand as he scrolled through the list of names. The blue light of the screen cast its hazy glow on his face, highlighting the anxiety that twisted his features.

Ganas pressed a number and brought the phone to his ear. He did not like what he heard, and swore. He dialed again— still no answer. He let a few seconds go by and tried one last time, hoping it would get picked up. All his attempts proved in vain. It was late, and the person he was trying to reach was probably asleep.

He pulled out a small bottle of whisky from the glove compartment and took a long sip. He instantly drained it, and flung it on the passenger seat in disgust. He turned back to the phone and tried again. The robotic voice at the other end of the line asked him to leave a message. Deciding he had no other choice, Ganas said in a shaky voice, "It's me, Mark. Call me as soon as you get this. It's urgent. I had a visit today ..." He paused, and thought it would be safer not to disclose any more details. "Anyway, it's urgent ... Something to do with the past ... Call me now!"

He hung up, irritated. Darkness filled the car once again. He looked out the window, towards where the lake could be faintly seen in the moonlight. Christian's words still echoed in his mind.

*To the memory of all the innocent lost in the lake ... An old friend from the past ... Melek ...*

Only Persie, Violet, and I were still sitting at the long table scattered with empty wine glasses and plates, the remnants of a sumptuous dinner. We had all had a fair amount to drink, and I was enveloped in a sweet haze. We were all very tired, but lingered, enjoying the music and the relaxed atmosphere, an old *rebetiko* song blaring through the speakers. I was impressed that Persie was singing along every now and then—I had not expected a woman like her to enjoy this kind of music. Although her voice could barely be heard, I liked it.

Softly and sweetly, she broke off in mid-conversation to sing the chorus. I had recently heard one of the songs and, coming from her lips, it sounded more melodious than I remembered.

I was beginning to believe that I would like anything she did. I watched her all the time, as discreetly as I could. At one point I felt her leg touch mine under the table, but unsure whether it was intentional, I pulled away. I was enchanted by her, but inexplicably something would come over me and I would pull back from being demonstrative. I constantly felt out of sorts, and kept trying to hide it.

When I realized we were about to leave, I signaled to the waiter for the bill, but Persie stopped me. "We have already paid, Constantine ..." she said, and slowly stood up to follow Violet.

Her expression was so firm it left no room for protest, so I thanked her as I walked towards them. There was no way I would be going to sleep, so I said goodnight when we reached the boats, saying I was going for a walk and then back to the hotel. Persie looked at me, puzzled. "Violet is going out for a drink, but I'm not up to it. Do you want to walk me home? It's on your way anyway."

I could not utter a word, so I just nodded. That was all I wanted, to spend a little time with her. We said goodnight to her friend and began to stroll alongside the small harbor. It was evident from Persie's pleasant mood that she was also a little tipsy. She seemed to savor every moment, as if this was her fist visit here. Every couple of paces, she would pause and examine the sailing boats with curiosity, observing some of their technical characteristics. She spoke of those attributes in detail, not that I could understand much. I just enjoyed the sight of her happily walking along in her blue dress, ignoring the few people we met on the street.

Without realizing it, we found ourselves across from the restaurant. The place resembled a lake, the way it circled and protected the harbor from the open sea. Along the pier, fishing boats were lined up, large and small, along with other pleasure boats. There were not many houses at this end and, walking through an alley, I thought one of those must be hers. I said nothing and carried on walking beside her.

Persie spoke of her childhood, vividly describing how she had spent the happiest time of her life in this area. All mention of her parents, however, was absent from the memories she recounted. It was lucky that Violet had told about Persie losing her parents; otherwise, a couple of questions concerning them might have escaped my lips, and would have probably woken up painful memories. She looked so happy; I did not want to do or say anything that might spoil that.

The smell of pine followed our every step, waking childhood memories in me from long ago. Mostly the voice of my mother complaining about my resin-smeared clothes, but then telling me not to mind her and giving me a hug ...

Persie halted for a moment. "Do you want to walk in the woods? It's dark, but we can see our way in this moonlight. We also have our phones to light the way, if need be," she said, and looked up at the half-moon above us.

"Yes, of course. I love walking, so long as you know the way ..." I said. She smiled, and reached out to take my hand to guide me.

Like two puzzle pieces that perfectly matched, our hands gripped tightly. We crossed the street and, taking a small foot path, began to wind our way through the small woods. *Pera Panta*, they called it, the faraway side. *What a funny name for a wood*, I thought.

It got darker as we walked farther inside the woods, and from a certain point onwards we could see just enough to avoid the large pine tree trunks. Along the way we came across a few couples kissing in quiet seclusion. After a brief trek, still holding hands, we arrived at the highest point and turned to walk down to the shore.

"I want to show you my favorite place in the world," Persie said happily, as we approached the tiny beach just visible ahead.

A few steps before we reached the water, however, she changed course and pulled me in the opposite direction, taking an even narrower path. Straight ahead, as far as I could discern, stood a small indentation among the rocks. When we reached it, Persie motioned for me to sit on a large stone that looked like a tiny armchair, sculpted as it was by the wind and the brine. Faint moon rays interrupted the shadows of the pine trees. I slowly lowered myself to the spot indicated and she sat beside me, as if we were on two narrow seats in the middle of nowhere.

She leaned back against the smooth rock, and I followed her lead. A large opening in the trees before us created a natural screen framing the sea. The reflection of the moon tinted the watery surface silver, and faded out against the shore. A soft breeze blew, as if conversing with the trees, forcing them to whisper a unique sound. Even with my eyes closed I would have known it was the swaying pine needles.

*Every tree sings its own tune, so long as you know how to hear it*, my mother had once said, and I always remembered it whenever I heard the rustle of leaves. We fell silent for a moment, enjoying the sound of the waves mingling with the wind in the woods. We were like two children, patiently sitting beside each other, waiting for a performance to begin. It was strange to be here, all alone with her, but I chose not to ask her anything and unwittingly spoil this beautiful moment.

Persie's voice rang out sweetly in the silence. "My parents used to bring me here to wish upon a falling star … Sometimes, I made many wishes. Other times, the stars did not get 'hugged by the sea,' as my father used to say, when I would ask where the stars went after they had fallen from the sky …"

A sigh escaped my lips. I both envied her memories, and was glad to hear them at the same time. I had never experienced anything similar with my family. My fingers were running through her hair, and I could sense how much she enjoyed it. For a moment, I could not hear her breathe, and I was perplexed. I leaned gently towards her and saw why. Tears were streaming down her cheeks, shimmering in the faint moonlight like melting crystals.

I was surprised at this sudden change of mood, and took her hand. I felt like I should not immediately ask her what the matter was. I wanted her to know that I sympathized, that I was there for her. The quieter I kept, the more she cried—silently at first, then with soft, quiet sobs. I stroked her hair and tried to soothe her. I struggled to find the right words, but failed. All I could utter, with great difficulty, was a gentle "talk to me."

My voice sounded tender, filled with genuine concern, for at that moment I truly wanted to ease her suffering, unless the tears were a source of relief for her. Slowly, without looking at me, she leaned towards me and rested her head on my knees, looking out to the sea …

"I miss them so much ..." was all she could say, before bursting into heartbreaking sobs.

I did not know what to do ... what to say ... She somehow understood that I knew about the loss of her parents. I tried to show her that I sympathized, that she could count on me, gently stroking her cheeks and hair. All her previous joy had crashed against the memory of her family. As if she had been trying to contain intense feelings all day, her barriers now collapsed, and she allowed herself to get swept away in the torrent of memories that had welled up inside her and now sought release.

She tried to speak again but was choked by sobs. Her crying became louder, and I struggled to find a way to help her. Events had taken a turn I had not expected, if I was to be honest with myself. When she asked me to walk through the woods, I had begun to imagine our tryst in my mind. And now this. Still, while she sobbed against my knees, I felt she was gifting me something precious, the way she had surrendered to me.

Most men think you conquer a woman when you make love to her body. I had been guilty of that misconception, too. I had sought carnal pleasure even when I knew it would end in nothing of substance. But I had never felt anything like what I now felt, as I held this magical creature curled up in my arms. Weak and fragile, she had leaned on me. I felt as if she had chosen me, chosen to make herself vulnerable and bare her soul, and I wanted to show her that I was there for her. Her tears had soaked my hands, but I did not mind. I spoke to her gently, pleading with her to calm down and forget what was paining her. She had curled inside my arms like a child, reminding me of one of the dance recital scenes, when the dancer with the fearsome mask had brought her back from the bowels of the earth, making her appear as small and fragile as she now did. And then, she had immediately transformed into a woman that had swept up everything in her frenzied dance like a dragon.

The sweet smell of wine drifted from Persie's lips, and I wondered whether the drink had brought on this outburst. For a second my hand moved lower and I touched her naked leg, as her dress had been pushed up. I pulled it away immediately, as if I were doing something wrong. In any case, she was lost in her thoughts and probably did not realize. But that moment was enough to feel the velvety texture of her skin.

Her sobs began to subside. I kept quiet, knowing that the outburst was a way for her to unburden the heavy load she carried inside her. I knew tears provided a release for many people. She raised her head and sat up beside me, taking my hand in hers. "I'm sorry ..." she said, and looked at me with moist eyes.

I smiled so she could see I did not mind at all, trying to cheer her up. I realized that after her tears, the moment had come for me to ask everything I had avoided asking until that moment. I let a few seconds pass, and tried to lighten the mood. "You sing well, don't you ... *rebetiko* too!"

Persie smiled, still tearful. "My father used to sing them. He had a beautiful voice," she replied, and I bit my lip for having reawakened what had already brought her down moments ago.

I was about to change the subject, but she spoke first. "I will not cry again. The song I sang at the taverna was his favorite. It reminds me of him so much. I like to think about them; it's just that so much has happened during these last few days, I could no longer keep it bottled up. I wonder what you must think of me ..."

"If I tell you, you'll want to have nothing to do with me," I spontaneously said, but it worked. She smiled.

"You don't look like the big bad wolf, so I'm not afraid of you," she said with a laugh.

We both turned towards the sea at the same time and looked far away again. The island of St. George, where we had held the photo shoot, was now a dark mass in the middle of the silvery surface, and the shadows of the two chapels stood out. I did not want her mood to turn somber again.

"Well, as we barely know one another, how about we improve our acquaintance?"

I must have sounded funny, because she burst out laughing, making me laugh too.

"Fine ... Even though it sounds bizarre, I'll play along. I'll go first," she said, trying to stifle her giggles.

She shifted on her seat, pulling down her dress, which had gathered up, and covering her naked legs.

"I grew up here. I have danced since I was a little girl. I started out at a small, local ballet school. My father was a singer, and he travelled around Greece with his band, playing mostly folk music. He never managed to find what we would call 'renown,' because he loved my mother too much and he believed that if they left for Athens it would spoil their relationship. He was asked to go to Athens and make a record many times, but he always refused."

Persie paused, as if she needed to summon more strength, and then continued. "When I was twelve years old, my parents died in a car accident, where we stopped outside Arachova ... I just wanted to leave a flower at the place where I lost them forever. I immediately moved to Athens to be looked after by my aunt, our only close relative. We used to spend summers in Galaxidi at my family home, where Violet now lives. I was a child, and the only thing that gave me joy, that helped me forget, was dancing. So, I dedicated myself to what I loved with all my heart, as it washed away my sorrow and the bad memories. When I finished high school, I studied dance. I won a scholarship to study in London for three years, and I went there after the death of my aunt. I have not stopped dancing since my return."

"And you do it so beautifully," I said, wanting to express my admiration about her recital once again.

She smiled, then returned to her story. "A few years ago, Steve, who you met yesterday, and I formed our own dance company."

She looked at me, expecting me to say something, but I opted to say nothing at all. I knew they were a couple and I did not want to show anything. Realizing I would not speak, she sighed and spoke once again.

"We've been together for many years ... Actually, we *were* together for many years, because I don't think we have a future together, not after last night. We are still bound together by other things that will not be resolved as easily. I do apologize again for last night, but believe me, it will not happen again. Serious things have happened in my life, and I honestly do not know what the future holds. I have not told anyone anything. You are the first to hear all the details."

I was surprised she had confided in me so easily. I could not see her face well in the dark, and I tried to tune into her mood, which was never constant. "I understand this is hard," I said, "but it is good for things to change when their end has come. Thank God you have your work, which is going well. I'm surprised you did not extend the run, given the success of the show."

"Constantine, if you knew what has happened in my life these past few months, you would understand," she said, and looked away.

"We might not know each other well, Persie, but I felt like I knew you from the moment I first met you. Your performance moved me, but it's not just that ..." I lost my train of thought just then, because I did not want to confess that I liked her, that I had been obsessed with her ever since that first moment I saw her dance. I quickly changed tone. "If it makes you feel better, I'm happy to hear about what's troubling you. You never know; I might be able to help in some way."

"I wish it were so easy," she replied, and took a deep breath.

"Sometimes things get rebuilt as easily as they get destroyed," I offered.

"Sometimes, but not always ... I can't understand why I'm here with you, telling you these things ..."

"There is nothing to understand. We are here because we want to be here and, for my part, there is nowhere else in the world I would rather be. Please, tell me whatever you desire."

Persie looked down. "A few months ago, Steve convinced me that an investment he would be making abroad would quickly triple our money. He had done it before, he said, and he persuaded me to hand over my savings. I so wanted to own my own theatre, and he made it sound like that dream would materialize very quickly, so long as I trusted him, which I did."

She looked up, meeting my gaze. "Unfortunately, nothing turned out as he'd promised. The details do not matter; the point is that now I am nearly bankrupt. My home here is mortgaged, and I will have to sell everything to cover the debts."

"But the show, surely ..."

"The profits from the show wasn't even enough to cover the expenses. Yesterday, Steve came to lay his hands on those profits, but Theo and I had already used them to pay everyone's salaries. That was why he was so furious. The reason we did not extend the run is because the theatre rent has not been paid. Steve never made those payments, along with many other expenses, so they asked us to shut the show down. It's as if I'm starting not from rock bottom, but even lower ..."

"I understand," I said gently. "You feel everything is ruined. But you can't let that defeat you. Whatever you do from this point onwards, it will be a huge hit. People love you; I saw that. You are not starting from scratch. You have already built so much you can rely on; it might take some time, but you will get back on your feet. What's important is that we learn from our mistakes; that is the point of them. To teach us how to not repeat them."

I genuinely believed every word I'd said. With a little help, she could overcome this. I was sure of it.

"You are right," she said. "I know you're right. But the burden I have to carry feels too heavy, and I don't know if I can bear it. It's serious. I spoke with a lawyer, and things are not that simple. Your presence at the theatre yesterday ... I don't know why, but it gave me hope. I can't explain it, but you gave me strength." Her voice trailed off. Before I could speak, she turned to me, a determined look on her face. "I think I've said enough. Your turn to talk about your life, and I'm sure it will be a much more pleasant story."

I was glad to hear her say that. However, I was at a loss where to begin. My childhood, or what I had recently discovered that had shaken me to my core?

"I'll start my story at the beginning then, too. My childhood memories are scattered all over Greece. My father is a policeman and, back then, he used to get transferred a lot, as if he could not lay roots down anywhere. My mother and I were swept up along for the ride. When people used to ask me about my home town, I would not know what to say. Now, after everything I have recently discovered, not only do I not know where my home town is, I'm not even sure where I was born."

Persie seemed perplexed, justifiably so, so I reassured her. "I'll get to it, and you will understand everything. After spending years moving from place to place, we ended up in Athens when I was sixteen. I graduated there and got into medical school. I was following my father's wishes.

"We were never close, my father and I. We had a tumultuous relationship. I envied you when you said you came here with your family to wish upon a falling star. I have no such memories, except a few moments snatched with my mother, when he was away.

"I always loved photography, so I took lessons secretly while I studied medicine. Eventually, I could no longer keep up the pretense; I felt like I was suffocating. So, I decided to follow my own dreams, rather than my father's. When I announced that I was dropping out of med school to pursue photography, it was the end of our so-called relationship. I felt like that man hated me."

I had never shared any of this with anyone. I looked at Persie, and realized she was anxiously waiting to hear the rest of the story.

"There is no point in telling you too much about my relationship with him, as I recently discovered he is not even my father ..."

She sat rock-still, clearly trying to understand.

"Recently, I had a huge fight with him," I explained. "Afterward, my mother told me that I was not their biological son."

She gaped at me open-mouthed, filled with suspense.

"My parents met in Ioannina, where my father was first posted as a policeman. They got married a few months later. My mother knew she could not have children because of health reasons, so she asked him to adopt one. Even though he would not hear of it at first, she managed to convince him and, using whatever network he had, he turned up at home with a baby one day. She tried to ask him for details, but he never said anything. He just told her that my birth mother had abandoned me at the hospital, and he had managed to swing a quick adoption. When we returned to Athens for the first time a couple of years later, they presented me as their own child. That's what I believed until now, that my mother was the woman who had given birth to me. I can stop if you are tired ..."

"You will stop when you want to stop. Now it is my turn to listen, to be here for you. Isn't that what you said ...?"

I realized she truly meant it, and I continued.

"I had always wondered how a father could be so cold-hearted towards his child. Now I know why ...

"It was a shock to learn about my adoption, but you know what? I'm not upset. Who knows where I would be now if they hadn't adopted me. It's just that I feel they haven't told me the whole truth, that there are more secrets, maybe even things my mother doesn't know. What upsets me is the way my father always treated my mother, taking it out on her every time something went wrong in his life. I've lost count of the times I saw her trying to cover up her bruises from me. All the times he ..." I paused, my throat suddenly dry. I shook my head. "Anyway, my father is dead to me. When I return to Athens, my mother will leave him and move in with me. Then we'll figure things out ..."

Persie was dumbstruck. "I imagine it must be very hard to discover something like this. It must have shattered so many things inside you," she said, with some difficulty.

"If I had a normal relationship with my father, perhaps I would not have minded at all."

"What became of your real parents? Have you looked for them?"

"No. After everything my mother told me about the way the transaction went, I would not even know where to start looking. Knowing my father, it may have even happened against their will."

"Unbelievable. Do you think they snatched you, and that your birth parents might be out there right now, not knowing what actually happened to you?"

"It's very likely. To find out anything I would have to talk to him and beg him to tell me. But, even if I decided to do that, I don't think he would give me the slightest hint. My first thought when I found out was to look for my birth parents. But then I realized there was no point running around looking for *ghosts*. I wanted to leave all this misery behind me and move on with my life without anything tying me to the past."

"I think it was a wise decision," Persie said. "I would have done the same. When I was young, my mother used to say that no one knows the hidden aspects of a person's life. When I would ask if there were secrets that I should know, she used to tell me I would know when the time came, that no secret stayed buried forever, no one can escape the secrets of those around them ..."

How right her mother had been! I had not been able to escape the secrets of my parents, and now I had to live with them and with whatever else they might bring into my life.

A cold wind blew, and Persie's dress fluttered, revealing her tattoo. Timidly, I touched it. "It's very pretty. I took many photos of it, and I think you will like them."

She paused and looked at me. I pulled my hand away because I thought she might be annoyed with me. It was hard to read her reactions in the dark.

"What does it mean for you?" I asked, trying to hide my discomfort.

She sighed before replying. "I had it done three years ago, when I decided that someday I would stage the dance recital you watched. You want to hear what the myth says?"

"I do. I like to hear you talk ..." I said, and leaned back against the rock.

"Persephone was the daughter of the goddess Demeter and the god Zeus, who turned himself into a bull and seduced the goddess. A girl was born named Persephone, and she grew up to be so beautiful that she caught the eye of Hades, the god of the Underworld. He fell madly in love with her and abducted her, taking her down to his kingdom of the dead.

"Demeter searched everywhere for her daughter, to no avail. Her grief killed all the crops, and the land withered. The sun, who could see everything, told her where her daughter had been taken. She demanded that Persephone be returned to her, otherwise she would not allow anything to grow again. Zeus, swayed by humanity's hungry cries, ordered Hades to release her.

"Hades obeyed, but first he gave Persephone a pomegranate. You see, when you eat food in the Underworld, you are forever bound to Hades and his domain. Persephone ate six seeds, and thus sealed her fate. She was to remain with Hades for all eternity.

"Demeter was furious, and Zeus suggested a compromise. For every seed eaten, Persephone would spend a month in the land of the dead. So, she would spend half the year with Hades, and half the year with her mother. When Persephone is in the underworld, Demeter is sad. Leaves turn yellow, and autumn and then winter comes. When Persephone returns, Demeter's joy breathes new life to nature and everything blossoms."

She paused, then said, "Shall I continue?"

I nodded eagerly.

"A pomegranate symbolizes fertility and good luck when cracked open. Of course, it brought me nothing of the kind. I got the tattoo because, when I was young, my father would carefully take out the seeds and offer them to me, like a small gift. Our garden here is filled with pomegranate trees."

"You said 'cracked open,' but yours is closed. Does that mean something?"

"It's made in such a way that it can be adjusted when I want to change it."

I wanted to ask when and why that would happen, but I was afraid she would think I was being too intrusive. I did not have to, because she gave the explanation herself after a brief pause.

"If I ever have a child, it will crack open ..." she said, and turned to look at the sea, melancholy once gain.

Although I did not understand full well what she meant, I dropped the questions. But how could the pomegranate crack open when she had a baby ...? I decided not to pry, and reached out to stroke her hair. I froze mid-gesture when I heard a noise, and Persie sprang up and turned towards the direction the noise had come from.

We breathed a sigh of relief when we realized a young couple was walking in our direction. Seeing us there, they changed course and moved towards the small beach. They obviously knew this spot, but we had gotten here first. I could tell from the sound of their voices that they were young. Their laughter rang out in the stillness of the night, and only their dark shadows stood out as they descended the path that led to the water. Then they hugged, and their voices faded into a passionate kiss. We held our breaths, as if afraid to disturb them. Their youth, their vigor, was palpable, and I must confess to feeling a tinge of jealousy.

Our mood had changed completely. Persie rose carefully and gave me her hand so I could follow her. I obeyed, and she pulled me up, close to her. Even in the semi-darkness I could make out the color of her eyes. We made no move; just looked at each other. I thought that I had to take the first step, but knowing she was in a relationship with someone else, I did not want to. I was rooted to the spot, unable to find courage either to kiss her or to walk away. My temples throbbed as I tried to make up my mind, as she seemed to be expecting me to make a move.

"Thank you for being here tonight, for listening," she suddenly said.

I tried to think of something to say, but could not. Evidently discomfited by my silence, she added, "I suggest we turn back now. We have an early start tomorrow for the photo shoot."

It was as if the cat had got my tongue. I wanted to say so much to her, but I could not. She took my hand again and turned to the path, taking the first step. I was dying to pull her back into my arms and kiss her, but I could not summon the courage, so I meekly followed her back through the woods. I berated myself for letting another chance go by like that. I wondered what she must be thinking of me.

We barely spoke as we walked back. Moments ago, we had been baring our souls, and now we were suddenly frozen. We quickly returned to the road and could see the narrow alleys leading to the houses. We chatted awkwardly about where we would be shooting tomorrow, and I began to tell her once again how much I had enjoyed the dance recital. She was not exactly cold, but I could tell we had lost our previous sense of connection.

The town was nearly deserted at this hour, except for the noise coming from a couple of bars by the port. We approached an old, single-storied house, its garden brimming with trees and flowers. Persie stopped at the gate of this beautiful home, and I realized the time had come to say goodnight.

The smell of jasmine tickled my nostrils and forced me to take a deep breath. We stood face to face once again. Even at this last moment, I could still do it. But just as I had drummed up enough courage to kiss her, she moved swiftly towards me and gave me a peck on the cheek, quickly saying goodnight. Caught off guard, I just froze. Even as she sauntered up the stairs, I stood there, immobile, as if my feet were nailed to the asphalt. She opened the door and turned around to look at me. She waved goodnight tenderly, and vanished inside the house.

I had not felt so disappointed in a long, long time. I was never particularly brave, but my cowardice now exceeded any shyness I may have ever felt. For some inexplicable reason, I felt like she exerted a strange power over me, one that rendered me a complete imbecile. Exhausted, I managed to drag my feet to my hotel ...

Ten minutes later, I was in my room. I picked up my phone and found Persie's name. I wanted to text her, but every word I wrote I then deleted. I felt as if I had let the evening end incompletely. We had left so hurriedly, so abruptly after the couple had arrived ... I could not make any sense of it. Only moments ago, we had been so vulnerable with each other, so connected. I finally ended up texting: *Thank you for being there tonight ...*

I pressed Send, switched off my phone, and dropped it on the bedside table. The ceiling of my bedroom was hand-painted, the mural depicting a flowering garden guarded by cherubs. I looked at their cheerful faces for a moment, then, turning the light off, I lost myself in the memories of this eventful day.

Persie and Violet were sitting on a large couch in the living room of their home. Soft music filled the room from a speaker in the corner. A low table lamp barely lit their faces. Persie had brought her friend up to date on what had happened with Steve, and the two friends were ready to go to sleep.

Naturally, Violet had also asked many questions about Constantine and their moonlight walk. Yesterday, she had thought the photo shoot had been cancelled, and she had been surprised to learn that it was going ahead. It had been easy to guess that the young photographer's visit had played a key part in changing Persie's mind.

Although Violet had never expected her friend to engage in a flirtation with another man while she was still involved with Steve, she soon understood the reason why her friend had sought the company of another man, if nothing more. She could not believe that Steve had struck Theo and almost got into a fight with Constantine. Persie explained everything in detail, from the moment Steve had started using her money to make investments. Violet had been in the dark, and tried hard to understand what had happened and how it had led to such a dire outcome. She did her best to maintain her composure, but was mortified at what she had found out. Not just because her own savings had just been wiped out but also because of her friendship with Persie as well.

Violet had been living at Persie's house for a few years now. Although she did not pay rent, she covered all the house's maintenance costs and other expenses. The ground floor was reserved for Persie's use whenever she would visit. Persie had dismissed her friend's offers of money. Violet, despite being older, was her best friend. The pretty bookshop she owned in the center of town just about covered her living expenses.

She was a solitary person who liked to read and travel. Not that she did not wish for someone to share her life with, but she had been burned in the past and now was cautious. She had married some years before, mostly succumbing to social pressure, but her marriage had not lasted long. She was an old-school kind of woman, who wanted her man to be romantic, a gentleman.

Violet had stood by her friend, supported her following the loss of her parents, and Persie was filled with gratitude. Now, Violet understood that once again Persie was going through hard times, and she was trying to think of ways to help. She had never liked Steve but had kept her views to herself. Now, after hearing what had happened, she regretted not speaking up. Strangely enough, her main concern was how she could help Persie; not how she could recover her own savings. Her friend was facing a very serious situation that could prove catastrophic.

Trying to order her thoughts, she shifted closer to Persie and tried to comfort her. "What could they do to you? It's not that easy to lose everything. How can that happen when you are so successful?" she asked, and held her hand.

"Look, Violet, I spoke to my lawyer already. Some things I can contest in the courts, but the essence is that I was the one signing all the documents for the company we had set up, and everything appears to have gone through me. We have a meeting next week to decide how to proceed, but he made it clear that the best-case scenario if I don't find the money to pay our creditors is that I avoid a prison sentence. Everything else will be lost, including the house we are in right now, as it is mortgaged. Foreclosure is only a matter of time."

Violet froze. Yes, she would be forced to leave a house she loved so much, and that pained her, but what chilled her to the bone was the realization that things were truly dire. Persie had no savings, putting everything she earned back into her work.

"Don't worry about how you'll make ends meet. I've managed to put some money aside, and it should see you through for a few months. I owe you ..."

Persie raised her hand to silence her. "You owe me nothing. I haven't forgotten the sum you lent me. Thank you for your offer, and if I really need the money, I will tell you. What worries me most is that it would be hard to do anything else, like put on another show or start teaching, while I owe money. Especially to the banks. I was thinking of taking the show on the road this summer, but how can I if I am bankrupt? No one will agree to put on the show and then wait to be paid until after the ticket receipts come in—and that's assuming it's a success. There is always the possibility that we will not be allowed to perform, especially in the countryside. There were days in Athens we needed police protection for the performance to go ahead. I wish I could disappear like Persephone, and return to find everything back to how it was."

"Yes, but you don't want to visit the Underworld!" Violet teased. "Everything happens for a reason, and you know it. It's not like you've had it easy. You have been through much worse and managed to not only land on your feet, but achieve so much. You can do it again. You were but a girl then, and you surmounted all those difficulties. Even Constantine ... I don't think it's a coincidence he has come into your life right now. I have not seen you look at a man like this in a long time, and he seems fascinated by you too. He kept asking me about you ..."

Persie sighed as if she did not wish to reply, and Violet changed track, speaking in a lighthearted, chirpy voice now. "Let's go get some sleep and, when the shoot is over tomorrow, we'll find a solution. Worst comes to worst, we'll go door-to-door and sell my books to raise the money you need," she said, and smiled, trying to cheer Persie up. She succeeded for a second, as a faint smile crossed Persie's lips.

"Don't laugh it off, I'm ready to hit the sailboats tomorrow with a cartload of books ..." she added.

They rose slowly from the couch and hugged, trying to give each other courage. "It will all work out, you'll see," Violet said, and accompanied her to the staircase that led to the ground floor.

Persie kissed Violet on the forehead and said goodnight. She walked downstairs and headed straight for bed. She was sleep-deprived and was dying to curl up under the covers.

She picked up her phone to set an alarm for the following morning, and was surprised to find a message from Constantine. She read it, and a bright smile lit up her face, her mood immediately lifting.

Persie would not be here tonight were it not for him. His mild, straightforward manner had caught her attention from the start. She liked his shyness, enjoyed playfully putting him on the spot. She saw his pure, unadulterated hunger for her in his eyes, and liked it.

She chose not to reply, and went to bed. The thought of spending the following day with him filled her with joy. Just before turning the light off, she looked at the photo that stood on her bedside table. Her younger self was standing between her parents, their arms around her, on a beach in Galaxidi, that last summer they had spent together ...

As soon as she heard the sound of movement coming from the bedroom, Anna sprung up from the couch where she had spent the night. Her husband was up. He appeared moments later, his phone glued to his ear. He ignored her and headed towards the bathroom. Whatever was being said at the other end of the line made him stop in his tracks. His back still turned to her, he reached out a hand to steady himself on a kitchen counter, as if he needed the support to keep upright. Anna could tell something was seriously wrong, but said nothing. She just sat in an armchair and kept a discreet eye on him.

Nick slowly turned towards her. His eyes seemed lost, two beads staring into the distance, as if he had just heard something terrifying. He rubbed his cheeks nervously, as if trying to wake himself up. Anna felt worried for a second, thinking it might be something to do with Constantine. As if suddenly slapped, he rallied and walked to the bathroom, slamming the door behind him.

His face was dripping with water when he stepped back out. He returned to the bedroom and, she could tell from the noise he was making, tried to get dressed. Something serious had happened, but what? She could hear muffled cursing as he thumped closet doors and rattled drawers. Anna did nothing, just sat impassively in her chair. She enjoyed hearing him struggle. It was a small moment of schadenfreude.

Even though she worried about her son, she concluded the trouble must be something to do with work; otherwise he would have told her, if only to hurt her. He reappeared in the living room and irritably began to collect his things. He cast her a look filled with hatred and left, slamming the door so hard the windows rattled.

Anna was used to his strange behavior, but had rarely seen him lose control. She wished deep inside her that whatever had befallen him would cause him great torment, that it would be the worst thing that could happen to him. She also found it odd that he was heading to work so early.

She desperately wanted to speak to her son. She had been on edge ever since she had revealed the truth, and did not know how to handle this new situation. Even though she felt somewhat relieved, she knew she had not disclosed the whole truth. At present, she could not find the courage to tell him everything. She would, however, once Constantine came back and took her with him.

The burn marks were not the only scars the terrible fire had left on her body—her lungs often failed her, with violent coughing fits. One such fit had seized her when she had told her husband that Constantine now knew the truth about his adoption.

Nick exited the garage with reckless speed. He pulled up at a square near his house and took out his phone. He quickly dialed a number.

"Have you lost your mind? Why did you call a hundred times? Have I not told you not to call me here? What ... Speak up! What did he say? Hang up. I'll call again."

Evidently upset, he opened the glove compartment and took out another phone. While he waited for the cell phone to come to life, he violently swore at it, as if that could frighten the phone into working any faster. When the screen light came on, he quickly punched in Ganas's number and brought it up to his ear. "It's me," he hissed. "Never, ever use the other number! Now, talk. Who was that man? What do you mean, French? ... Not a chance ... He is bluffing ... She burned ..."

While he listened to Ganas, he nervously loosened his tie and rolled down his window to let some fresh air in. He felt like he was choking. In the distance, the blue waters of the sea shone in the brilliant sunshine among the towering apartment buildings, but the world had turned dark for Nick. His voice was angry, and he slammed his palm on the wheel. "Shut up and listen. I don't know what that jerk told you, or how he ended up here, but you must make him understand he is in over his head. He must have got information from somewhere, and now he is trying to blackmail us. Did he mention me? Don't let my name slip, you hear? He'll want money, but be careful what you say ... Go on ..."

His expression softened as he listened to Ganas, processing the news. Then he looked around carefully, as if someone might be watching, and spoke more determinedly. "I'm still here … I'm thinking … Yes, you are right. Let's hear him out calmly; listen to what he says first. Find out what he knows, and then we'll see how we deal with him. Just remember no one, nothing, ties us to what happened. Talk to him and then text me. I'll call you. Be careful. You act clueless, and let him show his hand. Do not give him any information until we speak. Remember, you had nothing to do with it. So, I'll be waiting for you to make contact, and not a word to anyone."

As soon as Nick hung up, the world around him sank in darkness once again. That was the last thing he had expected. He'd thought that chapter of his life was closed.

He shut his eyes and leaned back against the headrest. Long-forgotten memories from that time returned as if not a day had passed. *High flames ravaging a house and people standing outside, helplessly watching the wooden building be consumed. Beside him, the clothes of a woman smoked as he lifted her in his arms to carry her away.*

He opened his eyes abruptly to chase the pictures away and straightened his tie, looking into the rearview mirror. Then, almost in a trance, he drove off. There was nothing to do but wait for news from Ganas.

The bright sun lit up the lake of Ioannina, which reflected its golden rays like a mirror towards the spot where Christian sat sipping his morning coffee. He was leafing through a local paper, trying to remember his Greek. He was not as fluent in the written form of the language, so he was struggling to understand what he was reading. Photos from the previous evening's book launch graced the front page—he could even spot himself in the background of some of them.

He wore sunglasses, and was casually dressed in jeans and a t-shirt. A sweatshirt was loosely draped over his shoulders, its sleeves tied in a knot across his chest. It was a glorious morning, in sharp contrast to the stormy weather of the previous day. Only the scent of evaporating water belied that it had rained before. Visibility was good, and he could make out not only the mountains, but also the snow that still capped their peaks. He wondered why the area across the town had been undeveloped. If he ever lived here, that is where he would have opted to build a home.

Earlier, he had called the hospital in Paris and been informed that Melek's condition remained critical but stable. He was waiting for the elderly teacher he had met at the event to arrive, so they could talk about that time. He had not slept much, because he had spent quite a few hours trying to find out as much as he could about Ganas and how he might fit in with the events Melek had described.

Despite having promised her not to share what she had said with anyone, he had sent a long message to his closest associate, explaining what he was doing in Greece. He wanted to ensure that they would know where to look for him should anything happen to him. He understood the kind of man he was dealing with.

Charges had been brought against Ganas in the past, but he had never been sentenced. Money laundering and bribery seemed like a walk in the park compared to his other crimes that lay below the surface. He always managed to get away with it, and had been an active philanthropist in recent years, a strategy followed by many when they wanted to erase the sins of their past. His company was doing very well, so he now had the funds to invest in football by acquiring a team. He employed many people, and had bought the loyalty of many in this way, especially now that the country was in the grip of high unemployment.

Christian wanted to find some clues about the other man, too, the one who had fathered Melek's child. *Memory is short and selective,* he always said when dealing with difficult cases. He was always impressed by how personal interest could trump reality and blind people, pushing them to forget terrible things.

Moreover, he was convinced that Ganas would be calling him at any moment. Ganas's behavior had been proof that he was one of the two men he was after. The way Christian had approached him had not left him room to react. It was one of his go-to techniques. He had also had the good fortune of the daughter's presence, which had made Ganas vulnerable—what a gift that had been!

The elderly man he had arranged to meet was walking up behind him. His hands struggled to grip a bulging envelope filled with newspaper clippings. Christian jumped up and greeted him, relieving him of his load and placing it on the table. George, now a pensioner, must have been around seventy. Trim and smartly dressed, he looked like a man who took great pride in his appearance. He sat in a chair and ordered Greek coffee with just a touch of sugar, *just a touch* he stressed when he addressed the waiter, who ran up to him as soon as he saw him.

"It's a nice day today," George said, and looked at the lake where the early boats began to make the crossing to the small island and the Ali Pasha museum.

"Yes, so different to yesterday," Christian replied.

George smiled and pointed to the lake. "Pretty, isn't it?"

"I must confess I did not expect the town to be so picturesque. I walked through its narrow alleys last night and I was impressed. And the lake is magnificent, especially the view across. I wonder why that part has not been developed ..."

"You speak Greek very well, I must say. With a nice French accent, but perfectly. What were we saying? Oh yes ... We don't have the right politicians, son, otherwise this town would now be one of the best resorts in Europe, but no one cares ... Such a beautiful area, history, scenery ... So much unemployment, but all they care about is their own families, nothing else. Let's see if the new mayor is any better."

Christian was impressed by the passion behind George's words. What little he had seen had convinced him of the beauty of the region. "You are right," he agreed, and looked at the envelope, trying to lead the conversation to the subject he was most curious about.

However, it appeared that the teacher inside the old man had reawakened, and he began to talk of the history of the town, the lake, and the tiny island. Enthusiastically, he encouraged Christian to visit the Ali Pasha museum, the former ruler's sitting room. Christian learned that the bullets that had assassinated the Ottoman ruler had left holes on the floor, still visible to this day. Every time George mentioned the Turkish occupier hatred colored his words, particularly when he spoke of the death of Kyra Frosini, whom Ali Pasha had drowned in the lake along with sixteen other women. *Efrosini Vasiliou*, he called her, her alleged real name, and added that she was rumored to have been the Pasha's mistress, and that the love affair had been the cause of her death.

Gesturing wildly, the old man recounted the story with great emphasis—how she was a beautiful, educated woman, how the Pasha had coveted her despite her being wedded to another man, how she had fallen in love with the Pasha's son, and how Ali Pasha had drowned her in a fit of jealousy. Of course, he stressed, that was one variant of the story, one of many versions and legends out there. He had taught at the school on the island, he added, his favorite time in his teaching career. On the island, he could maintain the illusion of being cut off from the humdrum grind of everyday life.

Christian heard his phone ring—not without considerable relief. He prayed that would put an end to the teacher's ramblings. He apologized, and stood up to take the call a few paces away. He suspected who it could be, as he did not expect a call from many people. It was Ganas, who informed him that if he wanted them to meet, he could come see him at his office.

Christian's face glowed like that of a fisherman feeling the tug of a fish at the end of his hook. Even though Ganas asked him to come over now, he declined, saying he could make the meeting in a couple of hours. He wanted to appear relaxed and in control. Of course, he was burning to have the meeting and get the ball rolling, but he hid it well. His strategy had worked so far, and he intended to stick with it. Ganas reluctantly agreed to wait for two hours.

He returned to the table, expecting to hear more stories from the teacher, but was pleasantly surprised to find George emptying out the large envelope. Under other circumstances, Christian would have enjoyed hearing about the city. But he could feel the clock ticking and the pressing need to find out as much as possible about the case right now.

George handed him an old newspaper clipping showing the faded picture of a burnt house. A caption above the picture read: *Brothel tragedy. Three prostitutes and owner dead. Police investigate causes.*

"This is what I have from that time," George said. "Much was written, but I don't think you will find it. You can, if you want, search newspaper archives more thoroughly. Unless someone has made sure a part of the archive disappears ... I've photocopied what I could find for you. Like I told you yesterday, I was a client a few years before the house burned down. Many of the women were kicked out and replaced by others to keep everyone happy. Some would stay longer, either because they would find a boyfriend or because they were good and kept clients coming back. I was still single back then; I did not have to account for what I did to anyone. I had a good time in there ... I respected the women ... I know you only have my word for it, but I did. But, you know, not all people are the same. Many were cruel to them and used their bodies without caring that they belonged to human beings ..." A sigh escaped George's lips.

"Can you tell me if you remember or found out anything about the women who worked there at the time of the fire? Who was the owner, and what happened after the fire?"

"Look, son, I had just got married. I had decided it was time to have a family; I wasn't getting any younger. But I stopped going for another reason. I found out that some of the girls were kept there against their will. There were rumors the police were in on it too, but who could do anything against them back then? Nobody dared stand up to them. They say that the drunkard who was the owner died in the fire too, but I had stopped going for some time. I was teaching at a village outside the town and did not come to Ioannina often; my wife had followed me to the village, you see. We did not even hear about the fire immediately, and I don't think many people cared about what had happened. Most were happy to see it gone, even if lives were lost."

The waiter arrived, setting down a fragrant cup of Greek coffee in front of George. The old man reached into his pocket to pay, but Christian was faster. George thanked him and took a loud, careful sip, his lips barely touching the surface of the hot liquid, and then shook his head with disappointment.

"Already turning cold," he grumped. "When I see that silly boy ... Anyway, what was I saying? Oh yes, there was a rumor that someone had fallen in love with one of the girls and set the fire to burn them all, but no one really knows what happened. The police, as you will read in the article, declared that the fire was an accident caused by some old stove. No further investigation. They were just happy they had one less brothel to deal with. We are strange creatures, us men; we only care about what happens in our own backyard and nothing else."

Christian was listening carefully, but he needed something more specific. "Were the women working there Greek?"

"Not exclusively. They came from Greece, but also all over the world ... Exotic, some of them were." George spontaneously let out another sign of relief and continued. "I told you, they came and went. Sometimes they would all change in the space of a month. To tell you the truth, when I heard that the house burned down with some of the girls, I felt guilty. In a way, we had all played a part in what happened. There was a lot of talk about a Turkish girl that worked there, and they said she died in the fire too."

Christian felt the hair at the back of his neck stand, but showed no particular interest on his face. "Such as?"

"Everyone wanted to sleep with her ... She was one of the prettiest women to pass through here. They were always talking about her long red hair and her blue-green eyes ... I know what you are going to ask. No, I never saw her up close. Like I said, I was married. But I heard what they said, and she must have been striking ... She died, too, burnt to a crisp. They only found a few bones. I think that they let the fire rage all day on purpose, even though they could have contained it, making sure the house burned to the ground ... Maybe they wanted to purify the sins that lingered in there like a curse."

George kept up his end of the conversation for a while longer, but added no new information. It was clear he had said all he knew. The time for Christian's meeting with Ganas was approaching, and he had to return to the hotel first and then go see him. He thanked George and gathered up all the clippings to go.

While he was shaking the old man's hand, George gripped his hand and said, "You won't find out anything else here, my son. You are on the right path, though, you should know that. Like I said, the police covered everything up. Those who were involved back then could be in high places now ..."

George handed over the clipping with the picture of the burnt house as he said those last words. Christian tried to understand what the old man was actually trying to tell him. He smiled and picked up the envelope to place everything inside. Just then, he noticed another clipping that had remained inside the envelope all this time—the color photo of a policeman headlined a brief article.

It was no accident, he realized. The cunning old man was trying to make a point. He nodded with understanding, and George returned the nod emphatically. Slowly, Christian sealed the envelope and turned away. He understood that the teacher knew more than he'd let show, but had opted to pass the crucial piece of information in code.

Christian began to walk in the direction of the town. Behind him, the elderly man sighed and stared out at the lake. Softly, he began to whistle the first bars of an old *rebetiko* song. As Christian moved further away, he could faintly hear his sweet voice ...

*Even if he cheated on you,*

*Even if he hurt you,*

*This love makes your eyes glow*

*Like a golden palace ...*

Kostas Krommydas

# Ioannina, Spring, 1978

The street on which the brothel stood was veiled in darkness. Even the red light hanging above the door was now dark. It was the time of night when even the strangest human shadows pause to rest. No one was outside. The breeze carried the sweet smell of roses with it from the surrounding gardens. Like a well-oiled clock, the monotonous hoot of the scops owl announced that spring was here to stay.

In the narrow alley beside the wooden house, the figure of a man crept noiselessly. When he arrived beneath a window sill, he bent down and picked up a small pebble. He aimed at the closed shutters and threw it. Without a sound, the shutters opened, and a woman appeared at the window. Cautiously, she looked behind her and up and down the street.

Once certain that no one was lurking around, she stepped over the sill slowly, legs first, and then her whole body. She tiptoed on the tin roof of a small porch, creeping to the edge, where he was waiting for her to come down. She sat at the edge of the roof, legs dangling. He grabbed her legs and supported her as she slid down his body until her feet touched the dirt path. Their bodies did not part, and their lips met in a passionate embrace.

Still wrapped up in his arms, she pulled him to a darker spot, under a tree in the abandoned garden of a nearby house.

"Michael," she whispered as she surrendered to his caresses and kisses.

He peeked into the street and, after making certain no one was out and about, he pulled her down the narrow path that led to the lake. Like children, they stifled their giggles as they playfully ambled down the path. They stopped often, hungrily kissing and touching, trying to quench an insatiable thirst. The lake appeared, and Michael pulled her towards the bushes, where a hidden path led to a secluded spot by the water. Hand in hand, they stopped and looked at the calm, dark surface of the water. In the distance, the snow that still covered the mountain peaks was barely discernible. At their feet, a small boat was roughly tied to a large stone that jutted out like a knife.

Michael helped her onto the boat and gave it a light push, then jumped in and grabbed two small oars. The soft, monotonous splash of the wood as the oars sliced the water was the only sound in the stillness of the night. He looked up at the clear sky and pointed out the sparkling stars. "Melek ... Look," he said gently.

She tilted her head back and followed his gaze towards the countless stars that shone above their heads. Captivated, they both contemplated the infinite bright sparks that dotted the heavens above them. She reached out her hand and touched his shoulder to stand up and come sit beside him. He began rowing again slowly, steadily carrying them away from the shore towards the small island. She nestled in his arms, wrapping her overcoat around them both.

In the dim light of the stars, they reached the small island. Melek had learned some Greek by then, although her accent still betrayed she was a foreigner, a fact she could not hide no matter how hard she tried. Michael loved hearing her talk in her unique way. It was like a game between them, him teaching her new words, and hearing her repeat them back to him.

It was a balmy evening, and he led the boat to a safe cove. Stepping into the water, he pulled the boat to the sand so his beloved could step ashore. He picked her up in his arms and carefully set her down. Then, he stowed the boat among the roots of a large tree that snaked into the dark waters of the lake. They walked away from the shore to a tiny grove that gave them just enough cover.

He took off his coat and spread it in a tiny clearing amidst the large stones, asking her to sit down. Melek obeyed and, pulling him gently, brought him down beside her. Softly, she wrapped herself around him as if seeking shelter. Across the bay, the lake reflected the few lights of Ioannina.

Michael tenderly lifted her chin up and hungrily sought her lips. His hand slipped under her blouse and touched her breast. Gently, Melek took his hand and brought it to her lips. Surprised, he said nothing and let her lead him. She shifted on the ground, turned on her back, and leaned her head back against his knees, looking up at the sky. The light of the stars twinkled in her eyes as Michael gently stroked her hair.

"What's wrong, Melek? Don't you like it here? We can go back whenever you want," he whispered.

"I like it very much, Michael, and I wish we could stay on this island forever. If only no one could find us and harm us ..."

"I promise you, soon no one will be able to harm us. Be patient, and we will leave this place forever. I swear we will be safe on the island we will go to ..."

Michael caressed her cheek, and was surprised to feel it damp with tears. He instantly sat up and bent closer. "What is the matter, my love? Talk to me. Did they hurt you? What happened?"

Melek dried her eyes and sat up to face him. "No more than what has been happening since I arrived here. That is not the reason for my tears ..."

"Then please, tell me, what's wrong?" he asked anxiously, trying to convince her to unburden herself.

"I'm afraid we will not be able to leave as planned ... Not for a while ..."

"Why?" he asked in surprise.

"Because I'm pregnant, Michael ..." she replied after a brief pause, trying to choke her sobs.

He did not know what to say. The news struck him like a thunderbolt. He did not want her to think that he was losing his courage or hesitating, so he pulled her into a tight hug.

"How do you know? Could you be wrong?" he asked tensely.

"I know. I'm not wrong, I know!"

"You are still coming with me, no matter what. I love you and I will not leave you. This child is one more reason to take you away from this hell even sooner than we planned," he said, summoning up all his courage.

"You know it will not be easy. They will not just let us walk away."

As if suddenly stung, he still tried to persuade her. "Listen, I have a little money set aside. Give me a few more days to see what else I can do, and I will take you away. We will go to my grandfather's island; no one will look for us there. We can then start a new life. We will have to hide at first, but it will all work out in the end, you'll see. Nothing can be worse than what you are going through right now. Hear me out. I will work all day, take any job I can get. Once we have what we need, we will run away. We will hide somewhere at first, and then we will leave. Everything will work out in the end."

"Michael, you know it will not be easy to hide. These people have connections, associates … and … and I'll be pregnant, and then there will be a baby …"

Determined to go for broke, he put his fingers on her lips and shushed her. "If you truly love me, if you mean everything you said before, you will follow me, and you will see that we can do this. Maybe what this baby is telling us is that now is the time to run away. We will make it, I promise."

She said nothing, just looked at him, trying to believe what he was saying. She wanted to escape the nightmare that was her life, but she knew it would not be easy.

"I wish I could leave with you. I have been pretending to be ill for a while now, so I have not been working. They brought in a woman yesterday who deals with ... with this kind of thing. She told them it was too late to take the child now. I don't know what they plan to do. What I do know is that if they catch us, you will pay for it first, and they are not joking around. I don't want you to suffer for me any more ..."

"I would die for you," he declared solemnly.

Melek stared at him, stunned, unable to utter a word. From the moment she had met him, when she had tried to run away and they had taken her to the police station, she had learned that good people existed in the world. It was the first time in her life she had met someone who was kind. For months, Michael visited the brothel and paid just to see her, until the owners realized something was going on and banned him. He did not give up, though. He found a way to secretly communicate with her. He was the only person who seemed to truly love her. Now, she could clearly see how passionate, how determined he was.

"You are crazy, you know! Not that I'm any better. Yes, Michael, I will do as you say ..." she replied after a brief pause. They fell into each other's arms and kissed clumsily, thirstily. He held her at shoulder's length and looked into her eyes. "The baby ... Do you know if it's ..." he asked shyly, struggling to pick the right words.

"I don't know, Michael. I don't know ..." she sadly replied, understanding what he meant.

"It will be our child, no matter what. I don't care who ... You understand ..."

"Yes, I understand," she said, wrapping her arms around his waist and pulling him closer, as if she wanted them to become one. She looked at him and stroked his face. "I can't remember the word you taught me the last time I saw you ..."

"Destiny," he immediately replied.

Melek cupped his face in her palms and smiled. "My destiny ..." she whispered, and kissed him tenderly.

In the rustling leaves of the small grove that sheltered them, the song of the nightingale rose out of the darkness.

We had been shooting in the narrow alleys of Galaxidi for a while now. I had slept well and felt rested, my spirits restored. Although I had expected an answer to my text message, I had received no reply from Persie.

The first thing I'd done in the morning had been to speak to my mother. I sensed she was holding something back, but could safely guess things at home must be very tense. I pleaded with her to leave my father immediately and go to my house, but she insisted she would wait for my return. *What's a few days more, when it's already been a lifetime?* she said, and reassured me that everything was under control.

After speaking with my mother, I had breakfasted at the hotel, and then set off for the location where we were due to take our first photos.

Based around Violet's bookshop, I had taken many photos in the surrounding streets, playing with the daylight and the sun's rays as they filtered through the houses and lit the faded walls of some old buildings in a strange way. I wanted today's backdrops to emphasize the old, timeworn part of the city. Especially where the color of the houses had faded, I found ideal angles to photograph her. The decay in contrast with Persie's vibrant face captured a very special mood, making her seem like an otherworldly creature. Simply dressed, naturally made up, she effortlessly shone once again.

I had asked her to also take some photos for my portfolio. The material I already had and what I was shooting today was enough to curate an exhibition entirely devoted to her.

We would be entering the bookshop shortly to take some shots among the old books and its stone walls. Luckily, most of the clothes Persie had been given tied in with the general concept of the shoot, so we could proceed quickly.

We had not said much to each other since meeting that morning. It was as if the previous evening's confessions had pushed us apart. We had both revealed landmark moments of our lives. For my part, I had never revealed so much about myself to anyone so easily. I could tell that Persie, too, had trusted me and confided in me about everything that was troubling her.

Although I could feel the intensity of her gaze through the lens, we only spoke about the shoot whenever I walked up to her, without any reference to the previous evening. At this pace the shoot would end early, and then we would have the remaining day to ourselves. I desperately wanted to suggest we go somewhere just the two of us, but had mentioned nothing. I could never have imagined that such a tragic story was hiding behind this remarkable woman. Now, I admired her even more.

Persie stood under an old balcony, where a bougainvillea bursting with dark red flowers spilled down over the railing. Through the lens, it seemed as though the branches sprang from her hair, as they had the same color. Everyone else hovered around us, holding up shades or touching up her hair and makeup.

I moved closer to her and brought her hair forward, so it flowed down her neck. My hand brushed her skin, and she gave me an intense look. Imperceptibly, I felt her respond to this otherwise accidental touch. Her pupils widened and I lifted the camera between us for a close-up.

I could feel her breath against my face. I wanted to fling my camera aside and kiss her in front of everyone. I was drowning in passion and desire, but at the same time I could not express myself freely. Her strength frightened me, the strange mix of intensity and aloofness that was vacillating between us from the moment we had met. Under the gaze of a photographer's lens, most people will tense up or pretend, but she did not seem fazed. Her every move overflowed with alluring, instinctive eroticism.

The beguiling sound of jazz music distracted me. It came from the bookshop, where Violet, Theo, and the others were sitting in the shade of the entrance. The pretty wooden sign with the bookshop's name swayed in the light breeze. It was time to take a small break before moving inside for the remaining shots.

"I think we are done here; we can move inside," I suggested, slinging my camera over my shoulder.

"Good morning," Persie said, despite us having exchanged that greeting hours earlier. It was as if she wanted the day to start anew between us.

"Good morning," I replied with a smile and, bolstered by this small shift in the mood between us, I ploughed on. "When we are finished, I would like to take some photos of you at some other locations I scouted and then take you out to lunch, just the two of us. My turn to treat you."

"I would love to, Constantine, but I have some things to attend to this afternoon."

I felt crushed, but tried to hide it. If we did not manage to speak today, we would never get another chance. I was leaving the following morning, and she would be staying here for another couple of days.

"That's fine, never mind," I said as impassively as I could, and turned to join the others.

She grabbed my arm lightly, drawing me back to her. "Thank you for last night," she said. "It really helped. I'm caught up in a maelstrom and I have no idea how this will end. If I find some time this evening, maybe we could meet up then ...? I do want to see you, you know."

Once again, I was at a loss for words and looked at her, dumbfounded. She took my hand and gently pulled me towards the bookshop. Both our lives were being marked by change and upheaval at the moment. I could not believe we had met by chance, that destiny was not at play ...

Kostas Krommydas

# Ioannina

Ganas's young secretary led Christian down a corridor that ended outside a large, wooden door. A small plaque on the door read *Never bite the hand that feeds you.* Christian smiled ruefully at the man's arrogance.

The secretary knocked on the door and Ganas's hoarse voice barked at her to enter. She opened the door and stood aside to let Christian pass through, shutting the door behind him. Across the room, behind a massive, expensive desk, sat Ganas. The man who probably knew what had become of Melek's child after it had been snatched from her nearly thirty years ago.

Without rising to greet him, Ganas pointed to a chair across his desk. Christian sat down and glanced at the gaudy décor around him: brightly colored walls, and a haphazard selection of famous prints hanging indiscriminately. A large screen transmitted real-time feed from the building and the exit. An aquarium behind him brimmed with all kinds of fish, like a tiny ark. The strong smell of stale cigar filled the room, and an ashtray overflowed with cigarette butts on the desk. The only pretty thing about the room was the large glass windows that overlooked the lake. Boats filled with students and tourists crisscrossed the waters to and from the island.

"I'm all ears," Ganas said.

Christian had anticipated this approach, and decided to play his game. "I think it makes more sense for me to hear you out. I have nothing further to add …"

Ganas looked him up and down, as if sizing him up. There was no way he was divulging anything, Christian guessed. Not before he could gauge what his intentions were.

As Christian expected, when Ganas spoke it was to throw the ball in his court. "Yesterday, in all that hubbub, you mentioned some names and various other things that made no sense. I was wondering what I've got to do with any of that. I apologize for any rudeness, but I do not like to be pressed."

"I know that," Christian said, and smiled sardonically.

Ganas pursed his lips and gave him an angry look. "I have neither the time nor the patience for games. Tell me what you want, or …" He pointed at the door.

Christian could sense the anxiety that hovered behind Ganas's uneasy eyes. Ganas was staring at him with a frown, trying to faze him, without success. Christian decided to attack with all the weapons in his arsenal.

"I have no time to lose, dear Monsieur Ganas, so I will get straight to the point, since you pretend to not understand. It would be easy for me to go to the police, but I have my reasons for not doing so. It will depend on the outcome of this conversation.

"Thirty-five years ago, in a nearby brothel with which you were associated, one of the women held captive there gave birth to a child. A child, which you and some others snatched and made disappear."

Ganas, leaned back in his armchair, his face so hard he might have been a marble statue.

"I want to know what happened to that child," Christian continued. "The mother is looking for it. If you help me find it, you have my word that I will not bother digging up any dirt about all the crimes you committed back then. Not only against Melek, whom I represent, but all the other women too. I do not know how you managed to cover them up so well, but I can promise you that unless you tell me the truth, now, the whole of Greece will find out about your activities back then. I wonder how your daughter will feel when she finds out how you spent your youth? Just in case you think I'm taking shots in the dark here, I must inform you I know all about your associates, too."

It was evident this was not the first time that Ganas had found himself in a tight spot. The course of his life, the fact that he occupied this desk before him, belied a man who could handle being cornered. However, Christian was hoping that Ganas had never expected that something he had long thought buried in the past would rise to haunt him.

"You must be confusing me with someone else," Ganas said smoothly. "I have nothing to do with any of this. I don't know why you persist ... But even if, for the sake of argument, we assume things are as you say, why did this woman only think of her child now, after all these years? What was she doing before?"

"That's another story. Listen carefully, Ganas. You don't want to find out what I am capable of doing, so let us not waste any more time. It will prove costly to both of us. All I want is to know where the child is. Imagine the field day the press will have when they get the story. Your phone will be ringing off the hook ..."

"I told you from the start—I don't know what you are talking about. Maybe I can help you if you give me more details. Ask around, find something out ..."

Christian, sensing it would be all or nothing, stood up and took the folded copy of the press clipping George had given him earlier that day by the lake. He placed it on the table and turned to leave. "Maybe I should talk to the police then. I think I'll start with your friend in the photo. I have a feeling he might be more interested than you are ..."

As Christian slowly walked to the door, Ganas picked up the piece of paper and unfolded it. The photo of Nick Papadogiannis in uniform covered most of the page, accompanied by a small article about his actions against drugs and prostitution. He threw the photo on his desk like it had burned his fingers.

Before Christian could leave the room, he called out, "Wait. Close the door and come back."

Ganas stood up and walked around his desk. Sweat trickled down his forehead. His shirt was already drenched in some places. Christian closed the door firmly and turned to face him.

"I don't know who is paying you to go looking for ghosts," Ganas hissed. "But I can tell you they are lying. Tell me what you really want, because if you think I believe a dead hooker is suddenly looking for her child you've got another thing coming. Is it money? How much do you want? Careful what you ask for; there are more ways than one to settle a bill."

Christian, full of confidence, sat back in the chair and smiled sarcastically. "How do you know the woman is dead? Were you there when she died?"

"I don't know who told you we had anything to do with this. The house burned down back then, and so did the owner and all the women who were inside. I was just a client. As far as I know, they found a few bones, all that remained of the three corpses. So, drop the charade and tell me what you want. I'm beginning to lose patience ..."

"I can see that," Christian said pointedly. "I told you from the start: all I want is to find the child. I have evidence that ties you and your friend the cop with the brothel and all the crimes you committed against innocent women."

Ganas looked like he was about to explode. It was obvious he did not know how to handle these developments. "I need some time. Let's talk again in the afternoon; I can't tell you anything right now."

Christian guessed he needed to talk to his accomplish. He was very close to his goal, he could feel it. "You have half an hour. Then I'm calling the police and handing over the evidence. I will also be giving them Melek's witness statement about what happened back then. I'll go for a walk to the lake and, when I return, I hope you'll have come to your senses. I know you have a tendency to drown people in these parts, so you should know there are others here with me. If anything happens to me, things will still take their course."

Ganas turned white with the sudden realization that the man sitting in his office knew much more than he had suspected, things that went beyond their involvement in the brothel.

As soon as he watched Christian walk away through one of the surveillance cameras, Ganas picked up the phone and called Nick. Quickly, he recounted their conversation. Nick informed him that he was trying to find out more about the Frenchman's identity and would call him as soon as he had something.

Nick sounded genuinely shaken when he realized that his past had become known. He insisted that Melek could not possibly be alive, that something else was going on. They decided to stall the Frenchman for as long as possible and offer him some money to start with, to check his reaction. If he refused the payment, they agreed to give him a clue, so he could start digging around and they could buy themselves some time to find out who he was and what he wanted.

In the meantime, they would try to locate the missing child—its existence was the most solid proof of everything Christian was alleging. Nick's last words had shocked Ganas: the suggestion that if the matter did not go away, they would have to make the child disappear.

When he protested, Nick reassured him that he would handle it, that he could track Melek's child down. The fact was that Ganas had not preoccupied himself with what had become of that baby in all these years. He knew some details about the identity of those who took it, but not much. After the fire, he'd tried to clear his name and suppress everything that linked him to the brothel. He had done well until now. Christian's sudden arrival was turning his life upside down.

They hung up after a few minutes, then the phone on his desk rang again. Ganas was startled, not expecting Christian back so soon, but his pulse slowed down again when his secretary announced that his daughter had come to see him. He was surprised, but not unpleasantly so, because she was supposed to be going to their country house in Metsovo for the day. Caroline entered his office, gave him a quick kiss on the cheek, and sat in the chair Christian had vacated earlier.

"What happened? You changed your mind?" Ganas asked, thinking about the visitor who would be returning any minute now. He did not want the two to meet.

"I decided not to go, Dad. I wanted to talk to you, but I can tell you are busy, so let's do it another time ..."

"It's true, I'm swamped right now. If it could wait for this afternoon it would be great."

He stood up and kissed her forehead. Her faced clouded over, and she reluctantly got up. "I understand ... I'll go now, and we can talk some other time."

Her father felt bad. He had seen so little of her recently. He sensed that she wanted to say something important. He looked at his watch and decided he still had a few minutes to spare, so he decided to hear her out.

"Wait here ..." he said, and called his secretary. He asked for no interruptions until his daughter left. He believed that Christian would wait for a few minutes if need be.

"Sit down, sweetheart." Ganas pulled up a chair and sat beside Caroline. She was pleased, and gave him a small, nervous smile. Then she became serious.

"Dad, I have an announcement to make. I have made an important decision, and I want you to hear me out. This might not be the best moment, but you need to know ..."

Ganas had no idea what to expect, and his heart began to pound louder and louder in his general panic. "Tell me, please. You are scaring me."

"Well ... I'm going to Australia, to Mum."

Was she leaving him? Ganas quickly chased the thought from his head. She hadn't seen her mother in two years and was missing her, that was all. "I can't say I'm happy to see you go, but of course you have every right to visit your mother. But how will you manage with your classes?"

"Dad, I'm not going for a visit. I want to try living there permanently. For a few months, at first, and then I'll see. I can't stand living here any longer."

Ganas felt like someone had punched him in the gut. The room's walls were closing in on him. First Christian's threats, and now his daughter's announcement that she was abandoning him. "Tell me you're joking," he begged.

She slowly shook her head. The look in her eyes told him she was being serious.

He walked to the large window, his legs suddenly leaden. He could see Christian strolling up and down the shore of the lake, his phone glued to his ear. Ganas felt trapped, caught between a past that ominously loomed over him, and a dire future filled with the absence of the person he loved most.

Caroline stood up and came to the window. She gave him a hug. "I want you to understand that this has nothing to do with you. I need to make a fresh start. In this country, my whole life is funded by you. I feel completely useless. I might return in a couple of years to work for you. Even if everyone here is always whispering behind my back ..."

Blood rushed to his face. "What do you mean, whispering behind your back? Who? Why?"

"That's not the reason ..." she said, clearly trying to change the subject.

He would not be so easily distracted. Wanting to find out exactly what she meant, he insisted, "Please tell me what they told you. Whatever it is, I'd like to know."

"Dad, no one said anything *to* me ... I mean, who would dare? Please believe me, that's not the reason I'm leaving. There are many reasons. Things are not working out for me, not personally, not professionally ..."

"Why have you not said anything before? Do I have no say?"

"Dad, I tried to talk to you about it, but you have so much on your plate I did not want to burden you with this. You never even asked what happened with Tom, why I don't even see him anymore. I should inform you we broke up three months ago. Remember how many times I asked you to come see me in Athens, and you kept postponing it? Do you know you've never been to my house, not even once? I'm not blaming you. You have your own life; I understand. Now, I need to have mine, to be in control of it. I need to at least try and, if I fail, then I'll see ..."

Ganas was frozen to the spot. His temples throbbed. The room swayed. Even a hardened man like him could not endure so many repeated blows. He knew that much of what had happened in the past was still gossiped about in Ioannina, but he had tried to shield his daughter from it. This was more difficult now that she was grown up. He decided to make one last effort to at least persuade her to postpone her departure.

"Listen, sweetheart. I would like you to give me some time to see if we can work something out ... I know I have been neglecting you, but I will make up for it, I promise. You know that I can help you do whatever you want ..."

"But that's exactly what I am trying to leave behind me, don't you understand? I need to stand on my own two feet, do something of my own ... without having everyone say that I'm doing it with my dad's money ..."

He could tell someone had been putting ideas in her head. "I just hope all this is not your mother's doing."

"No, Dad. Don't blame Mum. All she did was hear me out when I needed to talk. I asked her if I could go stay with her. Please keep her out of this."

Ganas felt he would crumble under the mounting pressure. Once again, he played for time. "When are you thinking of leaving?"

"When I hand in my final paper ... in a month, at most."

It was nearly time for Christian to return, and Ganas's breathing became shallower as his anxiety grew at the prospect of that meeting. He did not want Caroline to see him here, not after what had happened the previous evening.

"Here is what we will do," Ganas said. "We'll go have dinner together this evening and talk this through, calmly. I just want you to hear me out. If I don't manage to convince you, I will accept your decision. Not only will I not stand in your way, I will be here for anything you need. I will always support you." He pulled her into a protective hug. "You are the only family I have, and I want you to be happy. Just give me a chance before you make your final decision. Please."

After a long pause, Caroline said reluctantly, "Sure. We can talk. I just want you to know I have given this a lot of thought already."

The phone on Ganas's desk rang, and he realized Christian must be waiting outside. Even though he had not wanted the two to meet again, there was nothing he could do about it. He walked Caroline to the door, kissed her goodbye, and stepped into the corridor to walk her to the lift. Christian was sitting in an armchair and smiled at her politely as she walked in front of him. She returned the smile.

Soon enough, the two men found themselves back inside the office. Ganas, drenched in sweat, wasted no time. "I have a proposal to make; a solution that suits us both. I have all the goodwill to help you, but you must tell me first why you are looking for this child. It will not be easy to find, but I will do everything in my power so long as I understand what it is that you truly want. The woman claiming to be the mother cannot possibly be alive. I'm telling you this because I think they are lying to you, too."

Christian said nothing, watching Ganas carefully.

Ganas took a cigar out from a box on his desk and fingered it nervously, then put it in his mouth without lighting it. Seeing that the other man was not willing to speak, he continued. "If the issue is money, name the sum and we will see if we can put this long-forgotten story to rest. I just want you to know that if you do not keep your end of the bargain, you will never rest again. We will find you."

Christian grinned widely at his threatening tone. "You look like a smart man. Only a cunning man could keep such horrors secret for so long. I am not a judge, nor am I God. It is clear what I am asking in return for letting your secrets stay buried; not only those that concern Melek, but the other guy too. Believe me, everything I say is supported by evidence. I don't want money. If you help me find the child quickly, you will never hear from me again. I don't intend to become a crusader, chasing you and your friend Nick in Athens. It's very simple.

"I know you are trying to find out who I am, so let me save you the trouble. I am a professional, and I have a mission. Give me what I want. I can find out in other ways, but they will prove costlier to all of us ..."

For a while only Ganas's heavy breathing could be heard in the room. The sound of an incoming text message broke the silence. It was Nick, informing Ganas that the man in his office was a private investigator based in Paris, of Greek descent. The fact that he had not already gone to the police verified his claims. Nick was still not convinced about Melek.

"Where is she, then, if she is alive as you say?" asked Ganas. "Why did she not come look for her child herself, and sent you instead?"

"Her memory is still good; she remembers what she went through last time she found herself in your company. She will appear when the time is right."

"Suppose the child is found. How do I know you won't try to drag us into this mess then?"

"You don't. You will have to take my word for it. I'm afraid you do not fully grasp the choice before you, so let me explain once again. Either I leave this office with the information I need, or I make a phone call and every TV station in the country will be camped outside your doorstep by the end of the afternoon while you are answering questions down at the police station. Is that clear? Don't try my patience any longer. I will not explain this again. I bring you your last chance to atone for your sins. Soon, it will be too late. I have no time to play games ..."

Ganas's breathing became more labored. He brought his hand up to his chest and tried to undo more buttons, his face twisting in a spasm of pain. Ragged, choked breathing escaped his lips.

Christian ran around the desk and tried to hold him.

Ganas's eyed bulged and he fell to the floor with a thud. Christian felt for his pulse, and then ran to the door, shouting at the secretary to call an ambulance. He dashed back to Ganas's side, rolled him over, felt for his pulse again. Without wasting any time, he crouched beside him and began pumping his chest.

The cries of the secretary brought some more men into the office, anxiously asking what had happened. Christian hurriedly explained Ganas had collapsed. He kept feeling for a pulse, but Ganas was unresponsive.

The last thing Ganas remembered before darkness swallowed him was Christian tilting his head back and breathing into his mouth, then pressing his palms rhythmically on his heart, still trying to save him ...

A few hours later, Christian was in a taxi driving towards Ioannina airport. He had left his rental car at the hotel and had been lucky to find a seat on the small plane that serviced the city. The flight to Athens would be departing soon.

He had just left the hospital, where Ganas was in intensive care. The doctors spoke of a heavy stroke, and would soon be operating on him. They'd also told Christian that had he not given Ganas first aid, he might not have made it to the hospital alive. Under different circumstances Christian might have left Ganas to die, but right now he needed him alive.

When the ambulance had arrived, he had taken Ganas's phone and copied Nick's number. He had called him a short while ago and, after informing him of his accomplice's condition, they agreed to meet in Athens. Nick was perturbed by this twist of events and asked for some time, claiming he needed to verify that what Christian was telling him was true. When he'd checked that Ganas was indeed in the hospital, Nick reassured Christian that tomorrow he would get the information he was after.

Christian could tell Nick was buying time, but he had no other choice. If there was a small chance that the child was still alive, he had to move swiftly so mother and child could meet while she was still alive. Christian had to make all the necessary compromises. He also had to decide how to handle things in case time did run out. In the meantime, he was in constant contact with Paris, where Melek was still in a stable condition.

He had also asked his associates to track down any information they could get about Nick Papadogiannis. They collaborated with a private investigator in Athens and gained instant access to a wealth of information, although Christian wanted no one to know the reasons behind his interest in the man. Their appointment had been set for the following morning, and he wanted to arrive prepared.

The taxi pulled up at the airport and he jumped out, pulling his luggage behind him. He dashed to the ticket desk to settle his purchase. As the plane took off an hour later, he looked down at the city. He had really liked the place and wanted to return under different circumstances. The view of the lake captivated him, and he stared at it, entranced, until it disappeared from his window ...

# Piraeus

The ship had just dropped anchor and the crowd spilled out from its bowels onto the dock, spreading among the cars that slowed down as the throng snaked its way to the exit. In vain did a port official try to manage the flow of cars and passengers to allow those waiting to board, and the ferry to depart once again without delay.

Among those disembarking, Michael walked along the concrete pier towards the exit, a small bag slung over his shoulder. He only carried the bare essentials, along with a small box with an icon of Saint John and some holy water, which he would be taking to Peter's sister at the hospital the following morning. She was very ill and had asked for the icon and the holy water in the hope of a miracle. Michael was happy to oblige his good friend and spiritual father in Patmos.

The odor of the city settled on him unpleasantly as he slowly walked through the ferry terminal. The smog spewed by the ferries' chimneys made the air grimy and stifling. Michael looked around in surprise, as if this was the first time he was here. He had not been to the port of Piraeus in years. He watched people jostling rudely to make it through the gates first. He disliked crowds, and patiently waited for his turn to leave.

As soon as he found himself on the pavement, he turned towards a waiting car, a police light flashing on the roof.

The monastery had asked for police assistance, as Michael would be taking delivery of a priceless manuscript. Indeed, the following morning, a special car would be transporting it to the monastery. A small handover ceremony would take place at his hotel in a few hours. Several politicians would be waiting for him there, wanting to benefit from the publicity surrounding both manuscript and donor.

On the boat, Michael had been informed that Renée herself would be attending the ceremony. He had been glad to hear it. He had liked her, and was looking forward to receiving such an important book for the history of Patmos from her.

He greeted the man waiting for him, then climbed into the passenger seat of the police cruiser. They drove towards the hotel, Michael sitting silently and watching what he called "the jungle" through the window. He could not understand why so many people had decided to live in such stifling proximity. He could not wait for the two days to pass so he could board the ship once again and return to his beloved island. He suddenly felt like an animal trapped in a cage. He felt the cement monster that rose all around him swallow him up.

The driver informed him that the ceremony would take place in one of the hotel's large reception halls. They chatted about politics and the upcoming elections for a few minutes. Then Michael, not particularly interested in the topic, turned back to the images unfolding outside his window.

His thoughts returned to the past, when he had set sail from this same port as a fugitive. He brought his amputated hand close to his face and closed his eyes, surrendering to the memories. Like a nightmare, he saw himself under the water, struggling to rise to the surface, the blood flowing freely from his missing digit, and then a hand suddenly pulling him up by the hair and lifting him onto a boat.

A few minutes later, they pulled up outside the luxury downtown hotel beside the parliament. As Michael walked up the stairs, he looked towards the Tomb of the Unknown Soldier and the gathered crowd waiting for the changing of the guard. The sun was about to set, its last rays softly lighting the large building. He stopped and took in the sight for a few moments, then followed the driver inside the hotel.

Michael unpacked his few belongings and prepared to go down to the hall where he would be receiving the valuable manuscript from Renée. He carefully combed his hair and pulled it back into a ponytail, then took the elevator to the ground floor. Many people were already gathered there, and the driver introduced him to a man representing the ministry, who led him to the hall. Clerics and politicians filled the room. He did not know any of them, but politely met and greeted as many as he could—he was there as the monastery's representative.

Camera flashes lit up the room, announcing Renée's arrival. She stood still, allowing them to take as many photos as they wanted so they would not chase her around the room disrupting everything. When the photographers left, she approached Michael to say hello. She was glowing in her red dress. Michael greeted her with a smile.

"It's a pleasure to see you again," he said. "I found out you would be coming on my way to the port, and I was very glad to hear it."

Holding his injured hand, she replied, "The truth is I do not like such formal ceremonies, but I had to do it. Knowing you would be here to receive my small gift made the prospect more pleasant. I know you went to a lot of trouble to be here, but I did not want to entrust it to anyone else. I am sorry for the inconvenience it caused you."

"It was no inconvenience. It is a pleasure and an honor to be here, and I promise to take care of your gift for as long as I live," he replied, as her words washed away his fatigue.

Renée smiled. "Yes, I would not want it to be eaten by that bug you mentioned. What was it?"

"Woodworm," Michael replied. "No, I promise we will look after it as we should; keep the bugs away."

Some others approached them to greet Renée, and Michael walked to his seat. When she finished talking to them, she came and sat beside him in the front row, despite the seat bearing her name card being elsewhere. The minister of culture took the podium and made a speech in English about the importance of Renée's donation to the monastery of Patmos. Then, he tried to draw parallels between this gift and the Parthenon marbles, highlighting the necessity of their return.

In a special glass case beside the podium lay the manuscript Michael would be receiving. The minister of culture called for Renée, and everyone stood up to applaud her. She moved close to the microphone and, when everyone sat down again, she looked at Michael and spoke in English tinted with her slight and sweet French accent.

"I am very happy to be back in Greece. I was holidaying in the Aegean recently, and I had the opportunity to visit the monastery of Patmos. There, I was given a tour of the library and the Cave of the Apocalypse by the people of the monastery. During my brief visit, I understood the important work that they were carrying out to rescue and conserve works of such great cultural value. This great manuscript came into the possession of my family some years ago. It is said to have been written on Patmos and was stolen during the Ottoman period, along with many other important artifacts. After my visit, I thought it would be best if it returned home."

She looked at Michael again and paused briefly. "On Patmos, I met the man in charge of the library, the guardian of this intellectual treasure. I am certain the manuscript could not go to safer hands. On behalf of my family, I now call him to receive this significant heirloom."

Michael shyly rose, surrounded by applause. He had not expected such formality and was unsure how to react. No one had prepared him for such a glamorous ceremony. He thanked Renée with a warm handshake. She stepped aside to allow him on the podium. He had never addressed so many people before. He looked over the expectant audience.

"On behalf of all the monks of the monastery of St. John, I thank you for your gift. We were honored to welcome you at the monastery, and would be happy to see you again. With the support of the monastery, our library is currently one of the most important sources on the history of Christianity and the region. For many years, Patmos has been the destination of a lifetime for many people, and the monastic community has played a great part in this. I would like to take this opportunity to encourage anyone who may have Christian manuscripts or books in their possession to contact us. Many of these heirlooms are destroyed with every passing day, kept in conditions that are not suited to such old artifacts. I hope today's event will spur on the return of other treasures to their proper homes. We thank you."

His imposing presence and speech entranced the audience, which burst into loud applause as he received the case containing the manuscript from Renée. Camera flashes lit up the room as the case changed hands. When all was quiet again, she approached him and handed him a book covered in wrapping paper. "This is a small present for you, to thank you. I hope you will read it at some point."

Michael took the book and thanked her warmly. She lowered her voice and spoke again. "I want to ask you something personal, and please feel free to answer only if you want to."

"Yes, of course," he replied willingly.

"The painting I accidentally saw in the library bore a little blue flower and an inscription, like a signature, or a title ..."

Michael opened his mouth to explain what it said, but was interrupted by a group of dignitaries approaching Renée. He discreetly stepped aside and lost himself in the crowd, still holding her gaze as he moved away.

At the end of the shoot, as we were packing up inside the bookshop, Steve, Persie's boyfriend, suddenly appeared. We all froze for a second. I had already decided that if he became aggressive, I would not just stand there and watch. Even Persie seemed stunned to see him before her. Luckily, he now seemed much calmer and was patiently waiting for her to gather her things. Violet kept glancing anxiously in my direction, as if she was very scared.

Persie approached me before leaving and whispered that everything was under control and she just needed to have a word with him. She asked me if I was planning to return to Athens that evening. When I said I would be leaving the following morning, she gave my hand a tight little squeeze as if she was glad to hear it. Most of the others would be returning that evening. I had just enough time to tell her that she could call me whenever she needed me, no matter what time it was. We exchanged a fleeting glance under the watchful eye of Steve, who was impatiently waiting for her, and then they departed.

I spent the rest of the afternoon walking all over town, trying to wear myself out and vanquish the tension I felt. Where had Persie and Steve gone? What were they talking about?

Just before midnight, as I made my way down a dark alley, Violet called. She told me she had spoken to Persie, who had reassured her that everything was under control. I had not asked her to keep me posted, but she must have sensed my worry.

I was beginning to believe that I would not manage to see Persie before my departure the following day. I played out various scenarios in my head. I imagined that maybe they had sorted things out between them, were back together, and I would now have to erase the special moments we had shared. A long wait often makes people dwell on the worst outcome, and a bad feeling now gripped me. Partially because Persie was out there right now with that bastard, and partially because of the conversation I'd just had with my mother.

I had just spoken to her on the phone, and she could barely utter more than a couple of words. She was suffering another bad asthma attack. I'd struggled to convince her to go to a hospital, and she'd finally agreed to go see a doctor friend of mine the following morning before I returned.

She had not had an attack in a while. It was due to the fire that had scarred not only her skin, but her lungs too. The details of the fire were another family secret. I only knew their home had caught fire at some point. She rarely mentioned the incident, and changed the subject whenever I asked for more details.

A dog ambled up to me in the alley I was standing in and caught my attention. He was wagging his tail as if he knew me. I stroked him and, encouraged, he playfully rubbed against me. The truth was that I was not in the mood, so I left him and began walking towards the sea. The dog, however, followed me, keeping a short distance behind me. Whenever I stopped, he would do the same, and raise himself on his hind legs.

We passed a taverna and he stared hungrily at the kitchen. The aroma of grilled meat spilled out onto the street. Without thinking about it, I motioned at the dog to stay, and walked inside to buy some food for myself and my new companion from the streets. He wagged his tail ecstatically when he saw me come out holding a plastic bag. I asked the waiters if they had seen him before, and they told me that he had been roaming the streets for a few days. Maybe someone had abandoned him.

I walked to the harbor and sat on a bench. I pulled out a paper plate and put some of the meat on it. I had never seen a dog wolf everything down so hungrily. I had bought something for myself too, but, seeing how famished he was, I handed over my portion as well. I would not have sought out food if I had not met him in any case.

Once the meat was gone, he sat at my feet licking the plate and the pavement slabs. His appearance had worked as a welcome distraction, but my thoughts returned one by one as I sat looking at the sea.

It was getting late, and I still had not heard from Persie. I knew I would not be able to sleep without knowing what had happened, so I decided to call Violet, despite the late hour. She answered immediately, as if she had been waiting for my call. My heart sank when I heard the news. Persie had called her and asked her not to wait up—she would not be coming home that evening. I was surprised she was so willing to share this information with me, but then I thought that maybe she did it so as not to give me false hope. Violet had sensed how much I liked her friend.

Disappointed, I decided to return to the hotel. The dog rose as soon as I did, and waited to see which way I would be heading. He was a cute dog and I patted his head, wanting to thank him for the company. He followed me all the way back. I had never had a pet, but I suddenly felt the desire to adopt him.

When we reached the hotel, I thought about taking him to Athens with me. But as I stood at the entrance, he barked, wagged his tail, and disappeared up the dark alley. I waited for him to return, but he never reappeared. *Unlucky and abandoned, yet again*, I thought, and felt sorry for myself.

I walked inside, closing the heavy glass door behind me. No one was behind the reception desk, but I did not mind, as I had my hotel card with me. If I had my own car, I would have left right there and then. Sleep seemed unlikely, so it would have been better to get a head start on the long drive back to Athens.

I opened the door to my room and fumbled in the dark to find the card slot for the lights to come on. I flung myself on my bed without bothering to remove my clothes. I felt empty, drained. I could not believe our acquaintance was ending in this manner, so ingloriously. Just when I thought we were becoming closer, I was proven wrong, and I kicked myself for not being more assertive, more forthcoming.

A sound came from outside the room, and I assumed another guest was walking in the corridor. Suddenly, I realized it was coming from the window shutters. I walked towards the window and pulled the shutter open without asking who it was. Before I could react, the shadowy figure of a woman threw herself into my arms. In the dim light of the bedroom, I realized it was Persie.

Without speaking a word, our lips met thirstily, like parched soil soaking up the first raindrops of autumn. I was so surprised I could not believe the woman kissing me so hungrily, so desperately, was Persie. Without any resistance, I shyly responded to her passionate attack. I wondered if I was dreaming as I surrendered to her caresses and took her face in my hands, wanting to make sure it really was her. I could not imagine how she had managed to climb onto the balcony, not that I really cared at that point.

I pushed the shutter shut to shield us from curious eyes and, without parting for a moment, ran my hands all over her body, trying to remove her clothes. From the moment I had met her, I had felt like a torrent swelling with desire. Now I was ready to burst my banks and sweep everything in my path.

She wrapped her legs around my waist and, climbing on me, slowly removed her top. I held her up in the air, hugging her as tightly as I could. The sound of our breaths filled the room. Slowly, she unbuttoned my shirt and threw it on the floor. I felt the warmth of her body fill my belly as she gripped me.

She tried to lower my trousers with her toes, like a small, wild animal refusing to touch the ground. So strong was her grip that the only button in her way became loose, succumbing to the strength of her leg muscles. She slid down my torso until our bodies became one.

The sensation of our first, slow union filled every pore of my skin. She leaned back suddenly, arching her body until it nearly touched the floor. If I did not have my hands around her waist already, I would not have been able to support her. Waves of pleasure washed over me as she swayed softly against me. Her hands were touching the floor and pushing the rest of her body towards me. It was as if she was dancing, suspended from me, with slow, sensuous movements.

I could not get enough of her, and thirstily brushed my lips against her skin, trying to make this magical moment last forever. She pushed herself up until we came face to face and began to untie her legs from around my waist. Our parting lasted but a moment. As soon as her feet touched the floor, I turned her back towards me and pulled her into my arms. My hands touched her breasts and I pulled her closer, biting her neck. She turned her head, her lips searching for mine. As she moved, I felt every muscle in her body.

I entered her as we stood there. Our bodies were covered with sweat, and my hands slipped on her velvety skin, pulling her closer, closer, still behind her, making her mine. We did not say a word, just tried to assuage the thirst, the hunger, the fire that had sprung up inside us from the moment we met.

She gently pulled me towards the large bed, still in charge, and lay back on the mattress. I lay down between her legs and moved to the rhythm of our bodies that sought ever greater pleasure. The ecstasy, the pleasure, filled me, and still I could not believe this was not a dream. Nothing I had ever imagined could measure up to this.

I realized she was nearing the moment of climax when she began to pull me even closer, more violently. She began to tremble, and I felt her fingers dig deep into my flesh as her moans filled the room. I tried to pull back, but I felt her nails tear my back, trying to keep me inside her so we could finish what we had started together, as one. For a moment, it was almost an out of body experience, as I abandoned myself to the ecstasy of the climax she was offering. With a loud cry she shuddered and fell quiet, our passion spent, lying against each other, our bodies still one.

We said nothing, only looked at each other in the semi-darkness. Her moist eyes watched me hungrily. I was about to say something, but she covered my mouth with her palm. She slowly turned to her side and curled up, pulling me softly against her. Blindly obeying her every command, I came near her and enveloped her with my body. Our bodies fit perfectly, like pieces of the same puzzle.

The early morning sun crept in through the curtains and woke me up. For a few seconds, I tried to order my thoughts, trying to understand whether I had just woken from a vivid dream. The feel of Persie's skin still lingered on my fingertips so strongly, it could not have been a figment of my imagination.

The white gauze that covered the four-poster bed canopy had been untied and shielded most of the room from my view. I wondered how that could have happened, as I remembered them tied to the posts. Persie must have untied them while I slept.

I raised myself on one elbow and heard the click of a camera shutter. Across from me, naked, Persie had turned the lens towards me and was snapping away. She was resting her arm on the sofa's armrest as she reclined on it. Satisfied, she stood up and came near me. "Good morning," she said, and lay down beside me to show me the photos she had taken.

"Good morning," I replied, and began to scroll through the pictures.

The white fabric hid me in the first few shots. Then all the photos, taken from different angles, focused on my body. I was genuinely impressed—some of them were exceptional. I was surprised she could handle such a complicated camera with ease, to frame photos in a way that exuded atmosphere, that captured the mood of the moment.

Feeling the warmth of her skin as she lay next to me, I placed the camera on my pillow and shifted near her. Persie tugged on the sheet, as if she wanted to cover her nudity. There was so much I wanted to ask, but I didn't, afraid of spoiling this moment. I hugged her and turned her towards me. I could not understand where we now stood. I was dying to find out how her meeting with Steve had gone, but I bit my tongue again.

All my worries washed away when she began to kiss me sweetly. I instantly responded, and our bodies moved closer. My hands began to explore her body, touching her and pulling her on top of me. I could now see her blue-green eyes clearly, and the redness of her hair seemed starker against the white sheets. I began to explore her body with all my senses once again ...

Christian had arrived in Athens the previous evening. He had gone for a short walk downtown, grabbed a bite, and then returned to the hotel to talk to his associates about cases in Paris. His sudden trip had left many cases pending, but he did not care at all. Indeed, he had delegated most of them to his associates, wanting to dedicate himself to Melek's quest. Only one trusted associate knew some of the details of the mission he was on.

He knew many people in Athens, but he chose not to meet anyone. Despite spending most of his time on the phone, he enjoyed the view of the Acropolis from his balcony. This was one of the rare occasions he spent his evenings alone while on a business trip. He usually sought out an escort. He feared commitment and preferred fleeting, paid encounters, secure in the knowledge that he was free to leave at any moment.

The unexpected encounter with Melek had shaken him. Suddenly, he realized how many years had passed, and that if he wanted to have a family he would have to change, quickly. The carefreeness of a life without commitment was beginning to tire him. Moreover, he had been stunned by the fervor with which she sought her lost child after nearly thirty years. All this now acted as a strong incentive to focus on this task exclusively.

He read up on anything he could find. He was trying to understand how Ganas and Nick had managed to get away with it all these years, how the latter had even managed to rise through the ranks of the Greek police. The latest news from Ioannina informed him that Mark Ganas was still in intensive care and unlikely to recover. Christian had wanted to see him pay for his crimes, but it seemed that a higher power had already decided what his sentence would be. This was one of the rare occasions where he believed that an invisible judge was delivering divine retribution, only doing so selectively, allowing many to go unpunished.

There were many reasons behind Christian's desire to successfully complete his mission, the main one being how moved he had been to meet the woman who had taught him the secrets of love making again. He would have been willing to help her for free; but his reward, if he discovered the child, was substantial enough to change his quality of life. He had always dreamt of a house by the sea on his beloved island of Kea. That would be his first purchase if all went well. There was a plot of land on the island that had belonged to his grandparents, land he had not sought out yet. He knew it was somewhere near the sea. He was already beginning to imagine spending his remaining years there, accompanied by his future wife.

He slept late, but rose at dawn to prepare for his meeting with Nick. He grabbed a quick coffee on the pedestrian street close to his hotel, then hailed a taxi that would take him to his destination.

Christian stood outside the entrance of the Athenian central police headquarters. They checked his passport and then let him through to be escorted by a policeman to Nick's office. He had been surprised Ganas's accomplice had wanted to meet him here. Evidently it was a power move, to show Christian that he had nothing to fear.

The news from Paris that morning had been distressing. Melek had taken a turn for the worse during the night, and there was nothing more the doctors could do. Her lawyer had told him that they might have to jointly decide her fate soon. He was upset, feeling that he was so close to the truth now, that all he needed was a little more time, so that mother and child could be reunited while she was still alive.

The policeman opened the door to an office and ushered Christian inside, leaving him alone with Nick, who rose from behind his desk to greet him.

"Welcome! Do come in." He pointed to a small seating area beside the desk.

Nick was unkempt, overweight, and looked in bad health. Deep, dark circles under his eyes emphasized the sickly pallor of his skin and the redness of a drinker's nose. After a formal handshake, Christian sat down, puzzled at the man's politeness. Nick returned to sit behind his desk.

A large map of Greece hung behind the desk, various locations marked with tiny red flags. Nick followed his gaze.

"Greek cities where I served," Nick explained. "Almost every one of them ... Well, I'm all ears. I hear the news is not good for Ganas, but that's life." He shrugged. "Everything can change in a single moment ..."

"Mr. Papadogiannis, the truth is I have no time to lose. We already spoke on the phone yesterday. You know the reason for my visit, so let's cut to the chase."

Nick leaned back in his chair. "I am at your disposal; you can ask me anything. I must say your Greek is excellent for someone who grew up abroad. I imagine the time you spent in Kea as a child explains it ..."

Christian realized that they had completed their background research on him and that Nick was now posturing. He had nothing to fear, nothing to hide in his past or present. He did not reply, just gave the policeman a sharp look to make him understand that he had better start talking soon.

For a moment, Christian thought he would be reliving the scene in Ganas's office. He hoped the man behind the desk did not collapse before revealing his secrets. One look at Nick's pasty face, and he decided to take a milder, more careful approach.

Nick, under the scrutiny of his gaze, spoke first. "I don't know what you expect me to say. You'd better ask me something, so we have somewhere to begin."

"I know you are already fully informed about what I am looking for, so I will be very precise. I want to know where the child you snatched from Melek thirty-five years ago is. If you help me find it, you have my word this will remain between us, as I already told your accomplice. No one will ever hear about the crimes you committed against those women."

"Well, my dear Christian, I don't know what you have been told but you have been misinformed. To start with, I'm glad to hear Melek is alive, because we all thought she had died in the fire back then. Maybe she has been reincarnated, but that remains to be seen.

"You mentioned crimes, and I really don't understand why. All we did was visit that brothel, like so many other men, and pay for the services provided. On the contrary, we protected those women. Do you think anyone will care if so many years ago I visited a brothel and protected the women from some of the animals that would frequent it? If that is the crime, then half the male population of the country should go to prison," Nick said with a loud, forced laugh.

"I told you, I don't care about the criminal aspect of your activities," Christian said. "I just want to know where the child you abducted from a helpless woman is."

"We did not abduct anyone! She asked us to take the child. She did not want it. What we did was give it to a family that could raise it in a loving home, not in the corridors of a brothel or a dark alley. I am still not convinced that woman is alive, but if she is, I don't understand what has come over her. Why is she looking for a baby she did not want to keep in the first place? Now she suddenly *cares*?"

Without wasting any time, Christian went on the counterattack. "It's easy to spin a story how it suits you, but that is your version of the truth, not *the* truth. You and the monster dying in Ioannina as we speak kept her there against her will. When she tried to run away, you kept her prisoner and drowned the man who was trying to help her in the lake. Did you do that out of love, too?"

Nick flinched when he heard about the drowning. He stood up somewhat nervously. "I don't know what you are talking about. I told you what happened. If you truly want to find the child, you will have to tell me the real reason you are looking for it. I don't believe this nonsense about its mother looking for it. She is not alive. So, spit out why you are really doing this and be done with it, or go to the floor below and make a statement ..."

Christian's mind was now working at lightning speed. He realized he was dealing with a formidable opponent.

"I don't know why you believe I would not do that," Christian said. "If you don't help me, you leave me no other choice. Maybe the ensuing outcry will loosen your tongue. I have evidence, witnesses that place you there. The best outcome for you is that you get fired, although I think you will end up in jail if you do not manage to run away. Okay, let's move faster. Have a look at this and tell me if it reminds you of anyone ..."

He put his hand in his jacket and slowly removed a photo of Melek. It had been taken during her Paris years, and she was standing before the Eiffel Tower. Nick slowly took it and when he saw who it was, his hands began to shake.

"I see your memory does not fail you ... This was taken some years after her 'stay' at your brothel, when she managed to stand on her own two feet again. She has not changed much, has she?"

Nick threw the photo on his desk and walked to a filing cabinet in the corner. He removed a bottle and splashed something into a cup of coffee. He took a long sip and sat down once again. The smell of alcohol spread through the room.

"A photo does not mean anything," he said, emptying his cup. "Suppose I help you find this child. What's to prevent you from spreading these lies afterwards?"

"Absolutely nothing. All I can promise is I will keep this to myself—*if* we move fast. So, don't waste any more of my time. You know very well that if they start digging around in your past, much more will come out, and you don't want that. Everything you have done ... and I'm sure there are many who would enjoy your downfall. I promise you that if you don't help me, I will make it my purpose in life to destroy you."

Nick leaned his elbows against the desk and sank his head into his palms. He stayed like this for a few seconds. It felt like a lifetime to Christian. The windows were open, and the sound of traffic filled the silence between them.

Taking a deep breath, Nick lifted his head and looked Christian straight in the eye. "Your threats do not frighten me ..."

Christian swallowed the sarcastic laughter that rose to his lips, and let him continue.

"I am not convinced that anything you say is true, but I have nothing to fear. I will tell you where the child is. It does not know anything about its birth mother, and imagine suddenly finding out your mother was a whore. Is it worth digging up the past for this? Do you realize how much this person's life will change? Think of the family, that obviously chose not to reveal the truth to their adopted child. What will become of them after such a shocking revelation?"

"The child has a right to know. That is enough. Tell me where the child is," Christian replied, sensing the moment of truth was near.

"I could lie, you know. I could tell you the child is dead, or that I don't know what became of it."

"But you *do* know," Christian interrupted, leaning forwards.

"Yes, I know. I know all too well. Maybe we weren't the nicest people, but we are not criminals," Nick replied, and poured himself another drink.

He emptied the cup in a single gulp. "I know that boy better than anyone. I know him because I raised him like a son. I took him from the whore, to give him a chance in life. I married one of the women who worked at the brothel, and we raised him as if he were our own flesh and blood. That's the kind of monster I am. A monster who married a woman to save her from destitution, and adopted a child to give him a better life than he would have had with his whore of a mother. And instead of being thanked for doing a good deed, I get threats ..."

Christian stared at him, open-mouthed. It was the last thing he had expected to hear. Melek had told a different story, and although he had his reservations about what he had just heard, he did wonder whether she had not revealed the whole truth either ...

As much as I wanted to stay with Persie, it was time to leave. Sophie was waiting for me in the small hotel's lounge. She looked surprised to see us come downstairs together, and tried to hide it without success.

After we'd breakfasted, I loaded my bags in Sophie's car trunk and then walked up to Persie. I knew she had a difficult day ahead. She had told me that Steve had turned up last night like he was a different person, apologizing and asking her to give him another chance. But her mind was made up that it was over. Today, she would be meeting with her lawyer to try and find a solution to her financial situation. The truth is we did not talk much about her ex. She laughed a lot when I told her the story of the dog, and told me she had seen him wandering the streets as well.

Now, I was finding it hard to part from her, and I fumbled for the right words to say. "I could stay with you if you want, and leave later."

"No, Constantine. You have your own stuff to deal with. Go to your mother; she needs you. I'll be back tomorrow at the latest. I have a heap of stuff to deal with in Athens, too," she said, and took a step closer. "If things were different, I would be asking you to say. I don't know what this is, but I've never felt this way before ..."

"Me neither, Persie. I don't want you to worry about a thing. We'll work through this. I'll do everything I can to help you ..."

Forgetting that we were standing in the middle of the street, I bent down to kiss her. She gently put her hand up between us. "The whole of Galaxidi will be gossiping about us ..." she said, and looked at me intently. She changed her mind immediately and pulled her hand away. "Then again, who cares? They'll gossip whether you kiss me or not, so ... kiss me!"

I felt the warmth of her lips against mine, and closed my eyes. "Drive safely," she said, and swiftly walked away, leaving me rooted to the spot.

Just before I got inside the car, I turned and looked in her direction. She did the same and, for a moment, our eyes locked under the brilliant sunlight. Persie raised her hand and waved, then disappeared around the bend.

If it were not for my own pressing concerns, I would have been unable to part from her. I had only known her for a few days, but I felt as if she had been a part of my life for years. I had forgotten everything that had happened with my father, and the only thing urging me to leave was the need to be near my mother. She would be arriving at the hospital shortly, and I prayed all would be well. We had arranged for her to pack her things in the afternoon and leave my father. I still thought of him as my father out of habit, but I was glad the reality was different.

Lost in my thoughts, I was startled to realize we had left Galaxidi behind and were winding up the mountain towards Delphi. As we drove, Sophie and I chatted about the photo shoot and how to deliver the material to the magazine the following day. I opened my laptop and tried to make a first selection of photos I liked best. I was very excited by what I saw.

When we neared the spot where the small monument to Persie's parents stood, I asked Sophie to pull over. I left the car and walked to the tiny stone chapel. The weather-worn inscription on a small marble plaque was barely legible. *To the memory of my parents, Nick and Lucy Stefanou.*

The black and white photo of her parents, the way they held each other, showed a couple filled with love.

The dates beneath the inscription had become invisible, as if time had wished to keep them a secret. In the middle, the flower Persie had left was wilted and ready to scatter its petals with the first strong gust of wind.

My phone rang, and I pulled it out of my pocket as I walked back to the car. It was my mother, and I immediately answered. She told me her appointment was in an hour but she felt much better, so she was thinking of canceling. I managed to convince her to go. My friend, the doctor, had arranged for her to undergo some general tests in any case. I mentioned my father, and she informed me that he had left for work early that day, and she had not told him anything about leaving him. I was surprised when she asked me precisely what I was doing at that moment. Without giving her any details, I said I would be back in

Athens in a couple of hours. We'd talk when I arrived, and decide accordingly.

We hit the road again, and I could not get Persie's face out of my mind. I shivered, fearing that I would suddenly discover that it had all been a dream. I could not recall another time when I had felt so many intense emotions in such a short time. I was always cautious, reserved, needed time and space to feel at ease. Persie, sensing this weakness, had taken the situation in hand and led me in a magical way.

I did not understand what it was that I had said or done that evening at the theatre that had made her change her mind about coming to Galaxidi. It must have been some detail that escaped me but had meant something to her. I intended to ask her the next time I saw her. If there was a next time, of course. I had loved the words she said when we were parting. I felt like a teenager in love, not that my teenage years had included anything like this. I closed my eyes and thought back to the passionate moments we had shared the previous night.

Christian was trying to put all the information he had just received in some kind of order. "How can you have taken the child? The boy, as you say, was given to a couple. What happened to them? How did he end up with you and the woman you say you married? You married Anna, didn't you?"

Nick flinched. It was obvious he had not expected Christian to know so many details.

In the written information Melek had given Christian, she had mentioned Anna as a woman who had tried to help her, but she thought the woman had also perished in the fire. Christian had decided to take a gamble by mentioning Anna's name, and smiled inwardly when he saw it had paid off.

Nick stared at him blankly. Christian could tell he was trying to think, but the alcohol was making him hazy. He stood up with difficulty and stumbled to the window, opening it wide to let the fresh air in. The back of his shirt was soaked with sweat. He slowly returned to his desk and leaned against the edge.

"When the boy was born," Nick said, "we gave him to a family that wanted a child. When the brothel burned down, we left the city and looked for the child. Anna and I felt guilty about Melek's death, and wanted her son to have a better fate. We took the boy back, saying Anna was the birth mother and now we were married and could care for him ourselves. When they saw her burn wounds, the tears in her eyes as she pleaded with them to return the child … they changed their mind. So, yes, we lied to get the child back. If I should be punished for these actions, please, go ahead." He pointed to the door.

"How old is your son?" Christian asked abruptly.

Nick, who had not expected the question, paused before answering. "Thirty-four … I mean, thirty-five …"

It was Christian's turn to pause and think. He could see the effects of the heavy drinking, and wanted to verify what Nick was saying. "Let me get this straight. You claim that, after the birth, you gave the child to a family because Melek did not want it …"

"That's right," Nick replied.

"And that, after the fire, your guilty conscience made you look for it and take it back from that family."

"Yes, and we raised him as our own, without telling him anything. He thought we were his birth parents for years. Recently he found out he was adopted, but he knows nothing about his real mother."

"Why now? What happened?" Christian asked tersely.

"You don't have any children, so it is hard for you to understand the difficulties that come with raising a child, especially one that is not your own. Well, I've told you everything. Now you must tell me what you are *really* after, and why."

Christian ignored the question, trying to order his thoughts. "You'd better not be lying to me; otherwise, prepare to spend the rest of your life in jail."

"Your threats mean nothing to me, Frenchie. Don't try my patience; I will not hesitate to have you thrown out of this office."

Christian realized there was no point in arguing with a drunk. The man before him was near breaking point anyway. All Christian cared about was successfully completing his mission.

"How can I contact your son?"

"I would like to be present when he hears the truth. I think he is away, but will return to Athens today. I'll set up a meeting between the three of us ..."

"What about your wife?"

"Best to take things step by step. I will tell her. So, I will make arrangements for this evening. I'll talk to him and let you know ..."

Things had proceeded quickly, and Christian was finally getting somewhere. But something about Nick's story did not sit well with him. Maybe it had been his reactions, or the fact that he took time to think before replying, or his condition in general. On the other hand, why would he lie now, when a DNA test would soon prove whether his son was Melek's child? Nick must have known there would be a test, so he had to believe what the man was telling him.

Christian would have preferred to have seen the son straight away, as time was of the essence. But wait for the evening he must. He wrote the hotel number on the back of his card and handed it over. Nick glanced at it indifferently. "So, Melek is really alive?"

"She is, and you'd better pray she stays alive for a long time to come." With that, Christian turned and left the office.

Alone in the room, Nick picked up the phone and nervously dialed a number. "Anything new? I'm running out of time. I need to know as much as possible by lunchtime. Especially who he meets, who he talks with ... Find out. Call me as soon as you have something ... Anything! I'm running out of time, don't you understand?" he hissed, and slammed the phone down with a curse.

Melek's photo was still on his desk, face down. He picked it up and looked at it with blurry eyes. "So, you got away with it, did you?" he spat out with hatred. "Fooled us all into thinking those were your ashes ... Looking for your bastard now, eh? Why now? Why?"

He threw the photo back on the desk and leaned back in his chair, deeply troubled.

Michael, carefully holding the package Peter had prepared for his sister, walked down the hospital corridors searching for the room number the nurse at the front desk had directed him to. Walking past a small waiting area, he paused and looked at the large posters depicting different locations from around Greece. One of them caught his eye, and he froze to the spot: a lake, a boat in the middle, and Ali Pasha's island in the distance.

It was enough to wake a flurry of memories that were both a nightmare and the best moments of his life. In the waters of the lake, he had once told his friend Peter, he had both died and been born again. It was not the first time he'd encountered something related to Ioannina, and the trigger always unleashed an avalanche of mixed emotions.

Michael gathered himself and walked on, finally finding the room number he sought. He lightly knocked on the door. No reply came, and he hesitated, unsure of what to do next. He did not have much time. The next ferry would be leaving in a few hours, and he couldn't wait to be back at his beloved sanctuary.

He asked a passing nurse if he could go in, and she opened the door for him and showed him the bed of Peter's sister. He thanked her, and walked inside. Three beds were in the room, but two of them were empty, although the bedside tables belied that they were occupied. An elderly woman was lying on the third bed, her eyes closed.

Michael hesitated, trying to decide what to do next. He removed the small package from his bag and looked at the woman, who was fast asleep. The door opened, and another elderly woman walked in, leaning heavily on a walking stick. She realized he was there to visit her roommate, and explained that she had had a very difficult night and the doctors had just sedated her so she could get some sleep. Michael asked if he could leave the package with her, explaining what was inside so she would be careful with it. He waited a little longer, but Peter's sister did not wake up. He alerted a nurse about the package he had brought, and turned to go.

A police car would be taking the manuscript straight to the port. Michael could not understand such a waste of resources, as he could have transported it himself, but arrangements had been made and that was that. Indeed, another ceremony awaited him on Patmos late at night, upon the ferry's arrival.

He patiently waited outside the elevator for the doors to open and carry him to the ground floor. He squeezed into the crowded elevator. The smell of chlorine was pungent, making the atmosphere stifling. He glanced around, as if sensing something imperceptible, and raised his head to look at a woman who seemed vaguely familiar. Old burn scars crisscrossed the largest part of her arm. He was sure he had seen her before.

Sensing his eyes on her, she turned to give him an annoyed look. Michael saw her discomfort and immediately looked away. As hard as he tried to recall who the woman was, his memory failed him. But the niggling feeling of familiarity persisted. The woman was drawing him like a magnet, despite his efforts to resist.

They reached the ground floor and slowly exited the elevator. Michael looked at her again, and saw her move towards a counter holding a bundle of papers. His brain was about to burst with the effort, and he paced back and forth in front of the elevator doors, trying to remember.

As if his memory had suddenly cracked open, he froze in his tracks and stared at her. Scattered memories tore through his mind like lightning. Rooted to the spot, he watched her intently.

Sensing his eyes on her again, she turned her head and dread flashed on her face for a split second. She quickly glanced around, as if the presence of so many other people reassured her.

Michael was still staring at her, no longer caring about the effect he had on her.

Finishing up at the counter, she gathered her papers and carefully moved away, occasionally glancing over her shoulder. In a trance, he followed her a few steps behind, all the way to the stairs outside the exit.

Suddenly, she stopped, obviously aware that she was being followed.

She could not understand what the strange man wanted from her, Michael realized. She must have decided to confront him here, among the crowd milling outside the hospital doors. He stood beside her.

"Why are you following me?" she snapped. "Do you want me to call the police?"

The sound of her voice was another detail, another puzzle piece that dropped to complete the picture slowly forming in Michael's mind, convincing him he knew her.

He had to concentrate hard to utter something in response. "I apologize, but … I think I know you."

Hearing his quiet voice, her features softened, and she looked at him curiously. "I think you are mistaken, sir."

"You're Anna, aren't you?"

Surprised, she gaped at him and nodded. He could tell she was unable to recognize the man beside her.

Michael moved nearer. "It's been many years, Anna; it's no wonder you don't remember me. If it weren't for your burn marks, I would have mistaken you for a ghost. I thought you were dead … I didn't know anyone had survived the fire in Ioannina …"

She blanched. "Wh-Who are you?" she stammered.

"I'm Michael, Anna …"

A small cry escaped her lips at the sound of his name. Startled, she brought her hand to her mouth, as if trying to stifle her words. "Michael who?"

He did not reply, letting her own memories return to her.

"It can't be …" she said slowly. "It's not possible. Who are you? Is this some kind of sick joke?"

"Anna, we have thought each other dead for so many years, and now we both realize it is not so …"

"No. No, it can't be … Something else is going on! Who are you? Please, tell me!" she whispered, taking a step back.

"I understand this is difficult for you, but I need to ask you something. Please hear my question, answer it, and then I promise I will disappear if you do not want to talk to me. But there is something I need to know …"

He could see that she was reeling from the shock. So many memories must have been locked away, but now the lock was broken and they were all coming back. All she could do was nod.

"Melek …" Michael said. "What happened to her? Is she still alive?"

As soon as he spoke her name, Anna broke down in loud sobs. A hacking cough seized her, and she fought to draw breath. Seeing her struggle, Michael took her by the shoulders and led her to a nearby bench. He waited for the coughing to stop, for her to tell him whether the woman who had marked his entire existence was still alive …

She calmed down a few minutes later and looked at him as if he was a ghost who might disappear at any moment. Michael knew she had seen him arrive at the brothel so many times, always going to see Melek, and was certain that everyone knew that they'd loved one another.

Silently, she listened to him tell her about his life. All she said was that she was certain Melek had perished in the fire. Michael then told her that they had beaten him up, badly, when they'd found out about his relationship with Melek, trying to scare him off. When he'd tried to run away, however, they'd thrown him into the lake and left him to drown. In the dark, he'd managed to swim away from the shore and was rescued by a fisherman, letting everyone think he was dead. He had hidden for some time, and had tried to follow the couple who had taken Melek's baby the night of the snatching, but had fainted at some point. When he'd came around, they had disappeared.

His voice quavered with emotion. "After all these years, it still feels like yesterday. I was hiding in an abandoned house and, when I heard the noise of the fire, I ran to the house. So many people were there, and nobody did anything to help, as if they wanted the place to burn down. By the time the firemen arrived, nothing was left standing. Everything had turned to coal and ash. I approached carefully, so as not to be seen, and realized no one could have survived. When I heard they were looking for an arsonist, I realized that I would become their scapegoat if I appeared. Not that I cared much. Everything precious to me had been consumed by the flames.

"I left and, after many adventures, arrived in Paris to study. I was lucky enough to meet people who helped me build some kind of life. I ended up on Patmos, where I still live. I can't believe you are still alive! How did you manage to get out of the house?"

Anna shook her head. Her silence was interrupted by the sound of her ringtone. She took the phone out of her bag. It was Constantine, asking where she was. She looked at Michael, as at a loss as to what to do.

The sound of an ambulance seemed to snap her back to her senses, and she told Constantine she was already at the hospital. "Okay, I'll see you in ten minutes," she said after a brief pause, her voice cracking with emotion. She hung up and turned to Michael. He could see her trying to breathe calmly. "My son is coming, and I don't want him to see us together. I hope you understand ..."

Michael gently touched her scarred arm with his injured hand. "You have nothing to fear from me, Anna. I have left the past behind. Your secrets are safe. All these years, I thought no one had survived. I always felt that I had played a part in the events that led to that tragedy. If you want to say nothing, I understand. We both share a bond to that time, as you can see." He showed her his missing thumb. "My missing flesh is a daily reminder of that nightmare, but every day I move past it and try to lead a useful life."

Anna touched the old injury and looked deep into his eyes. "So much has happened since then, so much you do not know. But tell me: what are you doing on Patmos? Are you a monk?"

"No, but I work at the monastery. I have been in charge of the library for many years."

# Lake of Memories

"Michael, listen ... Like I said, I don't want my son to see us together. So much has happened in my life recently that I don't think this is a coincidence. I want to see you again, to talk."

She hastily pulled a piece of paper from her bag and scribbled down her phone number. Michael took it with shaking hands. "I will be returning to the island in a few hours," he said, "but if I am ever back in Athens, I would like to see you again too. I'm glad you managed to escape such an inhumane life and have a family."

Anna looked surprised at the peace he had found. She was gazing into his tranquil eyes, still holding his hand, when a car honked, startling them.

Michael knew she had to go. He sensed her turmoil. "No one knows who I am, Anna. No one will find out. I hope we can meet again someday. If you ever find yourself on Patmos, come see me at the monastery library. I plan to spend the rest of my days there ... God be with you." He guessed that the car was her son's and he let go of her hand.

Anna waved at car that she was coming and stood up. "You didn't ask me about those responsible for what happened to you, to all of us, and I wonder why. Don't you want to know what became of them?"

"I have forgiven everyone who hurt me, Anna. The only one who has not received forgiveness since then is me. That is the forgiveness I have sought since the day Melek died."

The car honked again but Anna stood there, speechless. Michael sensed that she was torn between her son's impatience, but still had so much she wanted to say. He smiled soothingly. "Go. Your son is waiting for you. If we are to meet again, it will happen like today, when we least expect it. The universe will take care of it. Thank you, Anna, and forgive me if I upset you. I hope your troubles are temporary ..."

"I was happy to see you too, Michael. God bless you, and I hope we meet again someday. Goodbye." Anna stood up to go, but halted, as if suddenly remembering something. "She loved you too, you know. She loved you so much ..."

Michael had managed to keep his cool this whole time, but at the sound of those words his eyes brimmed with tears. He swallowed hard. Anna patted his shoulder and ran to the waiting car.

I was struck by the appearance of the man talking to my mother outside the hospital. I asked Sophie to wait a moment, and stepped out of the car to greet her. The moment my mother arrived at my side, I kissed her and asked, "Who was that man? Are you crying?"

She took a deep breath, but her cough returned before she could say anything. I tried to comfort her. I had spoken with the doctor, who had told me that although her situation was not serious, her health could deteriorate fast. A minute later the coughing subsided, and she could breathe more easily.

"He was an old friend of mine, son. I had not seen him in years. His wife passed away at the hospital today."

I squeezed her hand in sympathy and helped her inside the car. I looked back towards the bench, but no one was there. I looked around, but the man seemed to have suddenly vanished from the face of the earth. I kept looking as Sophie drove us out of the hospital grounds, but he was nowhere to be seen.

Still surprised, I turned towards my mother in the back seat and held her hand, trying to comfort her. I asked her if she had said something to my father, who had not stopped calling me and leaving me urgent messages to contact me all morning. He had just texted me asking to meet me near our house that afternoon. She replied that she had barely seen him since the previous day. I had not called him back, wanting to avoid a scene in front of Sophie.

Trying to change the subject, my mother told me about her visit to the doctor and kept asking me questions about the photo shoot and the trip to Galaxidi. I could not say much in front of Sophie, so I motioned at my mother to be patient, and that we would talk once we got home. Besides, so much had happened that I did not know where to start.

I wondered how my father would take it, when he came home to find his wife had left him. Or when he discovered she had moved in with me. I would not be surprised if he showed complete indifference; on the other hand, he was so selfish that I doubted he would take such a rejection lightly.

We would shortly be arriving at my house, where I would pick up my own car. Then we would go collect my mother's things. I fell silent, giving her some time to unwind. Today would be a landmark day for the both of us.

We picked up the medication my mother needed, and Sophie dropped us off at my house after I gave her instructions about the photos she had to send to the magazine. I had managed to get a lot of work done during the drive, and all that remained now were some details. Most of Persie's takes were exceptional, and I could not get enough of them. I could fill an exhibition space just devoted to her. As if I did not have enough to contend with, Ella kept calling me all the time. I felt uncomfortable after the incident with my father and avoided her calls, realizing she was not calling about my work but to hear my news. Even though I liked her as a friend, I did not feel like talking to her at this moment in time.

My mother and I thanked Sophie for the ride, then quickly walked upstairs, dropped my things off, and then got inside my car to go to my parents' house. It was midday, and the sun was sizzling hot. We heard the weather forecast on the radio announcing rising temperatures during the following days, the beginning of a scorching summer.

I pulled up outside my parents' house just as my father called for what felt like the hundredth time. I felt like hurling my phone out the window. I motioned to my mother to keep quiet, and answered the call.

Enraged, he screamed at me for not calling him back. As soon as I told him we were at the house, he announced he was coming to pick me up for some kind of meeting, then hung up. I was mostly afraid of how he would behave towards my mother. There was no way I was following him anywhere, and I could not understand his persistence. If he dared lay a hand on me again, I would respond in kind. This situation had to end; our lives had to follow their course on a new foundation.

We walked up to their apartment and, without wasting any time, my mother began to pack up her belongings. There was much I wanted to ask about my adoption, but I thought it best that we get out of here as soon as possible and talk about it later, when we would have all the time in the world. There would be many opportunities to talk and connect from this day forth.

I picked up a small bag and filled it with some photos and personal belongings of my own; that way, I would never have to set foot in this house again. All the while, I tried to psychologically prepare myself for the upcoming confrontation with the man I had thought was my father for so many years.

My mother kept tearing up. When I asked her if she regretted her decision, she reassured me that her mind was made up and that she was crying for another reason. Maybe the strange man at the hospital was the cause of those tears after all ...

# Ferry boat to Patmos

Michael had boarded the ferry a couple of hours ago. With the assistance of the ferry captain, Michael and his police escort had sealed the manuscript in the ship's safe to keep it safe during the voyage. Then he'd stepped out on the deck and watched the port of Piraeus fade into the distance as the ship set sail for his island.

He had learned to control his feelings over the years, but the unexpected encounter with Anna had awoken a host of well-guarded memories. Two men struggled inside him now. Michael, the young man from the past, every cell in his body pulsating with love for Melek, who would be reborn at the slightest knowledge of what had become of her; and Michael, the recluse, who had left his old self behind after many years of meditation and recollection, forgiving even the men who had tried to kill him. His memories now overwhelmed him—everywhere he turned, he saw the beautiful face of the woman he had loved.

He had been sorely tempted to get off the ship and go find Anna, to ask her all the questions that burned inside him. Had it not been for the manuscript and his sense of duty, he might have done so. As the ship sailed away, however, he felt some of his previous tranquility return.

Michael took the piece of paper with Anna's number on it and held it up. The wind tried to rip it from his hand and swirl it into the sea. He felt hostage to the paper, and did not like the sensation. He had acted on impulse when he had seen Anna, spoken to her, but now he wanted nothing more than to return to his own world, a world that shielded him from everybody else.

He did not loosen his grip on the paper, as tempting as it was. Instead, he folded it and pushed it back inside his pocket. The return trip suddenly seemed endless.

Although Michael had a cabin at his disposal, he spent most of his time on deck, looking at the sea. The ship was not full, but nonetheless carried many visitors to Patmos or the other ports of call along the way. As summer progressed, the number of visitors to the island would rise. He preferred autumn and spring, when the island was quiet but still lively.

He could not get the picture of Anna out of his mind. It is a shock to see someone you thought dead standing before you, no matter what the circumstances might be. What was most important to Michael, however, were the memories the encounter had awakened, memories he had thought long-buried but which nonetheless resurfaced to remind him not only of the pleasure, but also the pain of that time.

He still had Renée's gift with him, which he had not found the time to unwrap. He decided that now was the right time. The sun was beginning to sink into the sea. He took out the present and carefully peeled off the wrapping paper. It was a French book, and the title stood out in red letters on the cover: *Destin*, meaning destiny. He smiled, because he remembered teaching his beloved the meaning of the word in Greek.

Michael scanned the back cover, and decided to start reading it now, as he still had many hours ahead. He held it in both hands as the wind rushed to turn the pages for him. The sea was not calm, but the massive ferry moved smoothly as it crossed the rising waves.

He read a few pages and realized it was a sort of biography, a retrospective of Renée's career in film and theatre. The first chapter devoted quite a few pages to that movie which had caused such a stir, characterized as blasphemous by the Orthodox church. He then remembered the monk at the grotto and his words when he had seen her.

Michael read Renée's biography until the wind became too strong to stay on deck any longer. Tucking the volume under his arm, he went inside, bought a bottle of water from the ship's bar, and retreated to his cabin to rest.

Christian was shortly due at the meeting with Nick and Constantine. His research had not brought up any information that could shed more light, and he hoped the corrupt policeman was telling the truth.

He had looked up Constantine, and realized that he was nothing like his father. Constantine was by all accounts a talented up-and-coming photographer, and had most recently posted a photo of himself and a woman at a restaurant in Galaxidi. Social media made Christian's job so much easier; sometimes all that was needed to uncover what you were looking for was a few clicks, and the information appeared before you in real time. The men he investigated often gave themselves away all on their own by posting their exact locations on social media.

Constantine was a good-looking young man with a piercing gaze who appeared very modest. He reminded Christian of his younger self. Christian didn't see much of Melek in him, but that was no reason to think they weren't related.

He had booked two seats on a flight to Paris the following evening, just in case Constantine really turned out to be Melek's son. If they hurried, and Melek clung to life a little longer, there was a chance mother and son might be able to reunite. Of course, Christian would have to fill him in on some significant details beforehand. How would Constantine react when he learned the truth about his past? Whatever his initial reaction may be, Christian was certain that when he learned of his inheritance, he would reconsider his attitude and then accept it, as would most in his situation.

Christian got ready and walked down to the lobby, asking the receptionist to call him a taxi. He was in high spirits, convinced he had Nick cornered and that he was on the verge of solving the mystery. His phone rang as he was about to step outside. It was Melek's lawyer.

He answered confidently, bolstered by the good turn events had taken, but suddenly stopped in his tracks. Expressionless, he listened to what was being said at the other end of the line, and struggled to utter a few words. "But how? She was better yesterday. What happened? What? ... The doctors said what? ... No! No, don't do it! I need two days at most, and then ... Yes, very close ... Fine, then."

Christian felt the ground give way under his feet. He did not want to believe what he had just heard. He answered a few more questions mechanically and hung up, staring vacantly ahead.

Melek's voice rang out in his ears melodically, *my darling Chris*, the way she called him whenever they were together back then. Blinded by tears, he stepped out onto the street. Now that everything was so close to the end, the news from Paris made him despair. Brain activity had ceased, and she was on life support. She had seemed to be doing better, and then suddenly relapsed. And, according to the lawyer, just before she'd fallen into the coma, she'd opened her eyes and faintly whispered a single word: *Michael ...*

Even though Christian knew the end could come at any moment, he'd still harbored some hope that she might improve. He had been convinced that mother and child would finally reunite after their violent parting so many years ago. Fate, however, seemed to have other plans, and he felt enraged by the injustice. It wasn't just his desire to successfully complete a mission, but the personal relationship and the beautiful moments he had shared with Melek. He had not known what had become of her for so many years, had even thought she might be dead. Now, he was faced with reality, and the unfairness of it all rankled him.

But she was still alive, if clinging to life. Perhaps even now he might still make it in time …

Christian jumped into the taxi and shouted out his destination. The windows were rolled up, and he felt suffocated. He politely asked the driver to turn the air conditioning off, and roll his window down. He brought his face close to the open window and tried to fill his lungs with fresh air.

He had to push the news aside for now, gather his strength, and complete the mission and return to Paris, with or without her son. Despite his disappointment, he yearned to complete what he had begun, fulfilling her dying wish. He wanted to be there for her when they turned off the life support more than anything in the world. When he had brought the lawyer up to date earlier that day, he had been stunned at the speed with which he had moved, untangling this complex web. He had never dedicated himself to a case to this extent before. Every waking hour had been spent searching for that child. Now, he was near the end, even though doubts still lingered inside him.

He was not unaware of the possibility that Nick was presenting Constantine as his son for some obscure reason of his own, or to buy time. Was this the end of this incredible story, or was there more he did not know, another twist further down the path? He hoped Melek had not kept anything from him, that today he would find out the whole truth.

It was early afternoon, and the driver informed him they might be late. One of the roads up ahead had been closed without warning and they would have to take an alternative route. Christian was annoyed, impatient to arrive there as soon as possible. He realized he had no other choice but to show a little more patience ...

Only a few people were out and about in the narrow alleys of Galaxidi so early in the morning. Persie, Violet, and another man were among them. The man was a lawyer, an old friend of Persie's father, who was now advising her on all matters concerning her debts. She wanted the opinion of someone she trusted, but, as the documents she had signed were binding, he did not tell her anything she did not already know. To pay off her debts she would have to liquidate all her assets, and even then, the sums raised would not be enough to clear her debts. It would buy her some time; although, with the economy being in the state it was, it would be hard to dig herself out of this hole.

Steve had informed Persie earlier in the day that he was going abroad, disappointed with the end of their relationship. She knew that he was really running away from his responsibilities and leaving her to shoulder the burden of his recklessness. She understood full well that she could expect nothing from him.

They arrived outside her house. In the garden, the cicadas had begun their summer concert on the pomegranate trees. She thanked the lawyer and he drove off, leaving two troubled women behind him.

"Would you like me to make us something to eat?" Violet asked as she walked up the steps leading to the front door.

"I think I'll go for a small walk," Persie said. "You go ahead without me."

The sorrow in her face saddened Violet, who walked back towards her. "It will all work out in the end; you'll see. We'll just have to be patient and decide what to do next. Try to focus on the good things in your life right now and everything else will sort itself out ... I did not ask you where you spent the night, but this morning, you were glowing. I haven't seen you so happy off stage in a long time. I was so happy for you, you know. I saw how he looked at you all evening. I've never seen a man so besotted."

It had all happened so fast. Every time Persie thought of Constantine, she could feel her spirits soar. Persie smiled at her friend as she remembered the beautiful moments she had shared with him. She squeezed Violet's hand without a word, then took off down the street that led to the sea.

Pulling out her phone, Persie texted Constantine as she walked. She had to sign some papers the following day, and then she would return to Athens. She had no idea how things would turn out between them, but she could not wait to see him again. She liked his humility, how he did not try to hide his timidity.

She arrived at the harbor and walked up to a sailboat that had just dropped anchor. She dreamt of one day owning her own. In fact, that had been the reason behind her decision to hand over her money to Steve, and now she had lost it all. She looked at the yacht longingly, then turned to leave.

The sound of an incoming message made her look at her phone again. It was Constantine. Her face lit up, and the dark thoughts that had just plagued her scattered. The sun was burning her face and she had forgotten to take a hat or sunglasses with her.

A few steps away, she noticed a dog walking towards her. He had no collar around its neck and matched the description of the dog Constantine had shared his dinner with. His fur was the color of cinnamon, except for his black snout. He walked up to her and rubbed one of her legs with his nose. She bent down and petted him tenderly.

When she stood up, she did not need to ask him to follow her—he was already doing so. Soon, they were outside the house, and she opened the garden gate to let him in. Obediently, he walked inside the garden and went to the small fountain, where he thirstily lapped up the trickling water. Persie picked up a flower pot saucer and filled it with water.

Violet had heard them arrive, and stepped into the garden. She was thrilled to see their new visitor, and crouched down to pet him. The two friends exchanged a look, and Violet said, "I hope he likes roast chicken and fries." They both savored this unexpected moment of kindness and tenderness, trying to make it last.

We did not talk much while my mother gathered her belongings from the home she shared with my father. It must have been strange for her, to be starting a new life at this stage, to be making such a radical change. An only child herself, she did not have many friends or relatives. Her few relations had emigrated to Germany with her parents, abandoning her with her grandmother. For some reason I never learned, she'd lost all contact with them. A few years ago she found out they were both dead.

My mother's past was veiled in mystery. She did not like to talk about her life, and I was left with countless unanswered questions. Maybe now we would have a chance. Maybe, away from my father, she would find the courage to open up.

I heard the sound of a text message and began to look for my phone. My mother brought it to me with a cheeky grin. I realized why when I looked at the screen and saw that the message was visible in its entirety. It was a text from Persie. *I wish you had "abducted" me this morning.*

The reference to the show I had watched and loved so dearly was evident. When we had woken that morning in Galaxidi, I had told Persie that when I had seen her dance, I had felt like going up on stage and taking her away with me.

I immediately texted back: *I regret not doing so ... I'm waiting for you.*

Seeing my expression, my mother stopped what she was doing and looked at me. I was sure she could clearly read my feelings.

"You haven't said much about this dancer, but I think you really like her."

It was important to me that my mother forget her own worries even for a moment, but we had to hurry—I did not know how my father would react if he found us here.

"I'll tell you everything, Mum, but later. Please just pack enough for a few days, and we'll come back for the rest."

The sound of the key in the lock startled both of us. Neither one of us had expected him back so soon. My father staggered into the living room, drunk once again. I wondered how they put up with him in this state at the police headquarters.

He walked up to us without a word, looked at the luggage around us, and burst into loud laughter. "I see you are heading out! Why did you not ask me to help you move?" He turned to look at my mother. "Do you think I will stop you from leaving?" he hissed. "So long, farewell, adieu! Send me a postcard some time! Know only this: once you leave, there is no coming back. Think about it while I'm out with your son and make up your mind. But be ready to face the consequences, little woman."

Her eyes brimmed with tears at his disparaging words. I was at a loss as to where he wanted us to go.

"We have a meeting with a man who wants to talk to you about something important. It concerns you."

He stepped closer to me, and now I could really smell the alcohol on his breath.

"I'm not going anywhere with you," I said. "Not unless you tell me who the man is and what he wants from me."

"You'll find out in a moment. Come on! Follow me!"

I felt my blood boil. "I'm not following you anywhere. I'm not one of your lackeys or your dog!"

Suddenly, catching me off guard, he grabbed me by the collar. "You do as I say, boy! Stop wasting my time. Come on!"

I pushed his hand away. "I'm not going anywhere. Don't you dare touch me!"

As if he had not heard a word, he clumsily grabbed me again. I did not have time to react. My mother pushed him back suddenly, trying to keep him away from me. Without even looking at her, he raised his hand and slapped her across the face.

Seeing her stagger and hold her cheek, I put my hands on his chest and pushed him back roughly. He stumbled and, drunk as he was, lost his balance, crashing into a small coffee table which shattered under his weight. My mother screamed.

I stepped over him, ready to hit him again if he tried to get up, but he did not move. I bent over him and desperately tried to revive him. He did not respond. My mother's sobs sent shivers down my spine.

The paramedics struggled to carry my father's heavy, unconscious body to the waiting ambulance. Despite the hatred I felt for him, I was terrified at the thought he might be seriously injured. It was not just the fear of possible consequences, but the fact that, regardless of the pain he had caused me, he was still the man who had raised me. I regretted pushing him, but I had lost all self-control when I saw him slap her. Now he was unconscious and had to be transferred to the hospital.

Terrified, tears streaming down her cheeks, my mother stood beside me trying to comfort me. When we reached the ambulance, they swiftly placed him inside and asked us who would be accompanying him. I stepped forward, but she pulled me back. "I'll go. You follow us in the car ..." She cupped my face and spoke emphatically. "Constantine, this is not our fault. Don't say a word. We'll say he fell over. He was blind drunk. If he comes around, then we'll see what we'll do. Okay?"

I did not want to lie, but I nodded so the ambulance could be on its way. I ran upstairs to grab my keys and, by the time I returned, a small crowd had gathered in the street. A man arrived beside the ambulance and inquisitively looked inside. I was struck by his curiosity, the way he was slowly watching us, but I paid no more attention to him—the ambulance was pulling away, and I needed to follow them.

I got into my car and, as I pulled away, I saw the strange man across the street outside the café where, according to my father, we were due to meet someone who needed to talk to me. He saw me and stuck out his arm, motioning for me to stop, but I ignored him. I stepped on the gas and sped off to get to the hospital as fast as I could. I did not care about anything other than being near my mother.

In the rearview mirror I saw him run after the car and then stop, looking disappointed. The image of my father lying unconscious on the floor flashed again before my eyes, making my pulse race. I prayed, despite the hatred, that he would be okay.

Christian, at a loss as to what had just happened, looked for a taxi to follow the car that had just sped off. He had arrived at their meeting place and the first thing he'd seen had been the ambulance, then Nick being carried on a stretcher, unconscious. He recognized Constantine from the photos he had seen and tried to get his attention, but the young man had dashed off. He assumed the woman standing beside him must have been his adoptive mother.

Seeing Nick in this state had shaken him. The more the case progressed, the more he felt that some invisible hand was pulling the strings, that they were nothing but the puppets in some divine master plan. First Ganas, then Melek, and now Nick being carried to the hospital, unconscious. *Not only good things come in threes*, he wryly thought. It was as if divine retribution had decided to no longer wait for men to deliver justice.

But why did Melek have to be punished? The two monsters responsible for what had happened to her, yes, it seemed only fair, but why her? Had she not disclosed the whole truth to him after all? Did the need to atone and receive forgiveness in her final moments lie behind her desire to meet her child? Or did she just want to spend her last days with the child she had been deprived of? Christian always used to say that fate is not guided by reason and that people are the prisoners of chance. Chance had brought Melek into his life all those years ago, and now led the lives of everyone involved whichever way it wanted.

No taxi was to be found, so he broke into a run towards a more central road. He had missed the chance to follow Constantine, but he was not deterred. He could easily find out the name of the hospital. Having the address, he could locate the ambulance, which he did after a quick phone call to the ambulance coordination services. He flagged down a taxi and gave the name of the hospital. He wanted to complete the mission more than anything else, and, once everything was settled, he would return to Paris having fulfilled Melek's dying wish, for her child to see her alive ...

I anxiously paced the floor outside the emergency room, waiting for some news of my father. A doctor soon appeared and asked if we were his relatives. He hastily told us that my father had suffered a brain hemorrhage, and they would know soon if and when they would operate on him. For the moment, they were waiting for test results, as his blood alcohol content was too high, and then they would decide how to proceed.

When they asked us what had happened, my mother took over and said that he had slipped and fallen against the coffee table. The doctor took down some more information and asked her to follow him into his office, to inform him about his medical history and any medication he might be on. I said I would wait for her, and began walking towards the waiting area.

I took out my phone. Persie had just sent me a photo: she was smiling, her arms around the neck of the dog that had followed me the previous evening. I smiled too. Despite her own problems, she was honestly trying to stay positive. Looking at the photo, I wondered whether I should tell her what had happened, or whether it would be best not to worry her. *He suits you ... but I'm jealous,* I texted back.

I put the phone back in my pocket and kept walking. My smile froze when I saw the man who had been waiting outside my house standing in the corridor. I was truly perplexed. Why was he following us? He must have some serious reason, and the time had come for me to find out.

I walked up to him. "I saw you outside our house. Who are you?"

He glanced around, as if making sure no one could overhear us, and then introduced himself. "Christian Ledu. I'm a lawyer. I don't know if your father spoke to you about me. We were supposed to meet today outside your house, but I saw something happened and you moved him here. Is it serious?"

I tried to remember if I knew him, but drew a blank. Even though his Greek was good, his accent betrayed that he either lived abroad or was a foreigner.

"We don't know yet. We are waiting for the doctors to tell us. All my father said was that it was an important meeting. Why did I have to be there?"

"Please accept my wishes for a speedy recovery, for a start. Would you like to move somewhere quieter? I will answer all of your questions since your father did not have time to explain the matter to you."

I looked behind me to see if my mother had left the doctor's office. "We can go to the waiting room around the corner; I would like to stay near my mother."

I pointed to a sofa near an open window, and we walked there together. The area was nearly empty, just a couple of people in the armchairs some distance away.

"Please get straight to the point. I would like to return quickly," I said impatiently.

He nodded thoughtfully for a moment. "To be honest, I don't know where to begin. It might have been better if your father was here. This morning your father revealed some information about your past, events about which you might have no idea."

I immediately thought of my adoption. What else could my father be revealing about my past?

"Well, as you said, he can't be here, and we don't know when or if he will ever be. So, either you tell me now, or wait for his recovery. It's not up to me and I am in no mood for riddles. Please get to the point."

The window overlooked the roof of another wing of the hospital, cracking and peeling with humidity. The droning hum of the air conditioning units flitted into the room and set my nerves on edge.

The man shifted nearer and spoke in a low voice. "I will get to it straight away. Things have been moving at lightning speed these days anyway. I know that you recently found out that the people who raised you are not your real parents."

I had guessed the reason for his visit correctly. I suspected what would follow would not be good—nothing good ever came out of my father's strange dealings.

I immediately replied, trying to keep this conversation as brief as possible. "Yes, I found out recently. And to save you any trouble, I might as well tell you I have absolutely no interest in finding out who my parents are. There is nothing there, no ties with them. At this point, their existence is the least of my concerns. If that is the reason you are here, well, see you later."

I tried to get up, but he placed a hand on my arm and pulled me back down, gently yet firmly. "Constantine, please hear me out. I will be forthright and brief. I am not a lawyer, but a private investigator. You will hear things that may sound extraordinary, but please do not rush to any conclusions.

"A few days ago, in Paris, your birth mother instructed me to find her child, a baby that had been violently snatched from her. Your father confirmed that you are that child. There is a process to verify this, and, if you really are that woman's child, you will find out the rest. If you really want to find out what truly happened and why you ended up with the people who raised you, the people you naturally thought of as your parents, you will have to come back to Paris with me. There, you will take a DNA test and, if the results are positive, we will proceed to the next stage. We could do the test here, but it would take longer, and time is pressing. The story you will hear is a very unhappy one."

When my mother had disclosed my adoption, she had refrained from giving me any details. The truth was that I wanted to be done with the past, with everything that connected me to my father. Like a ball and chain, I had dragged it along for years and it had hindered my movements every step of the way. Following Persie's sudden appearance in my life, I wanted to make a new start, to live unhindered.

All that being said, his words had piqued my curiosity, especially the part about being violently snatched. Suddenly, a dozen questions sprung up in my mind. "What do you mean, they snatched me? Where is that woman now? What's the point of proving whether I am her child or not, after so many years?"

"I wonder whether this is the right place to have this conversation?"

"Let's get it over and done with," I snapped, burning up with curiosity.

"Fine. You must promise to hear me out 'till the end."

I nodded and gestured that he should go on.

"I will not go into the details; it would take too long. You will find out later. You were born in a brothel in Ioannina, thirty-five years ago. Your mother was forced into prostitution and kept there against her will."

I stared at him, open-mouthed. He gave me a look of compassion and continued. "When she fell pregnant with you, they made her give birth at the brothel and took you as soon as you were born. They gave you to a childless family—sold you, actually. Some time later, your birth mother set fire to the brothel in revenge. The two men responsible survived, as did the woman who raised you. The burn marks on her body are the result of that fire.

Everyone, however, thought your mother had perished along with the other women. It was a devastating fire.

"No one knew who had managed to survive in the general upheaval. Your birth mother managed to run away, and her survival never became known. Eventually she ended up in Paris, where she lived tormented by the harm she had caused, as the only ones who had died in the fire were blameless prostitutes. Her thirst for revenge had blinded her to the fact that there might be innocent victims. In the meantime, the couple you know as your parents tracked down the family that had taken you in, took you back, and raised you as their own. They convinced your first adoptive family that you were their biological child."

"I … I don't believe it! What did my father have to do with the brothel? How did he end up involved?"

"This is another unpleasant part of the story, Constantine. The man who raised you was one of the men who kept the women captive and exploited them in the worst possible way."

My head was spinning. I did not know what to think. "My mother … not my biological mother, the woman who raised me … what was she doing in the brothel?"

"I think it's better if she answers that question. The story I just told you is a mix of everything I have been told by your biological mother and your supposed father. I met him this morning, and he told me some of this."

I needed time to process this. I felt completely overwhelmed and horrified at the same time. "This is crazy, but I still have to ask—why now? Why is my birth mother looking for me only now, and did nothing all these years?"

"As I told you, it's long and complicated. I've just told you the basics. We need time for everything else. I am bound to tell you that, if you prove to be her son, you will then receive a letter she wrote to you. I am following very specific instructions. I am also obligated to tell you that you will inherit a large fortune, which would have gone to charities if I had not found you."

I did not want to believe a word of what I'd just heard. I could not understand whether the woman was still alive or not. I had just found out another shadowy aspect of my father's character: he was a despicable pimp, and the woman I had known as my mother had been a prostitute. I sank my head in my hands, trying to order my thoughts.

"I'm in shock," I mumbled. "This is really difficult. It all sounds so outlandish. Whatever the truth may be, my real mother is here, in the doctor's office as we speak. No inheritance will ever change that. Maybe it's best to let it all go to charity ..."

"Constantine, you don't have to decide anything right now. Besides, you have no idea about the size of the fortune we are talking about. It is a vast inheritance ..."

"I told you, I don't care. Maybe this conversation is pointless."

If everything I had heard was true, my father did not deserve to live. I was sorry he had not died on the spot back at the house. Christian watched me, waiting for me to speak.

"I can't tell if the woman you say is my birth mother is alive or dead."

"She is in bad health, Constantine, and has been for some time. She fell into a coma earlier this morning and is not expected to regain consciousness. She is on life support, in the hope that at least her child can see her before she dies. There is that letter I spoke to you about, in case she ... It's very important to her that you receive it and read it. I will hand it over to you once we are certain you are the child we are looking for. She fought hard for many years, but now the end is near. That is what had stopped her from looking for you. All she wanted was to see her child before she passed away. She did not even know the sex of the baby she had lost. Once you know the whole story, you will understand why she did not look for you earlier."

I felt thunderstruck. Even though I felt nothing for her, a tightness gripped my chest when I heard what had happened, and I realized that I needed to know more. So many secrets had risen to the surface all at once, escaping the souls and memories of those who had kept them buried, to see the light of day.

Christian suddenly stared ahead. I turned, and saw my mother and a nurse approaching.

"There you are!" my mother said. "I've been looking for you. Come quickly, your father is worse. They are taking him to the operating theatre."

"Stay here!" I shouted at Christian as I hastily followed them.

I was praying for my father to recover for one, and only one, reason. If everything the French detective had told me was true, I wanted to scream in his face how much I hated him, and then make him pay for his crimes.

We had just signed the consent forms, and the doctors had taken him to the operating theatre. His rapidly deteriorating condition meant they did not have much choice. They had to act fast to save his life.

My mother and I left the doctor's office and paced the hospital corridors, where panic had seized the people who dashed around us. I did not know how to start talking about the latest revelations that Christian had brought with him. He had told me that he would fill in the details at a later point, but I did not know whether it was for my mother to find out what was happening from him or myself.

She looked unwell, coughing all the time. Seeing her in this condition, the doctors had given her an inhaler to ease her breathing. No matter what she may have done in the past, I had only fond memories of her, full of love and care. I really wanted to hear her side of the story. Perhaps it was best to do so in the detective's presence.

I took her shoulders and turned her to face me. Her eyes were red with crying, and for a moment I hesitated. I didn't want to upset her more, but at this point it would be best to close that chapter of the past. There was no point in keeping these secrets buried any longer, eating away at the souls of their keepers, tormenting them like the furies. I wanted to clear up everything, so I could enjoy the good fortune that had brought Persie into my life. I had not stopped thinking about her. The previous night we had spent together had been magical, an unprecedented experience for me. She had stormed into my life, swept me off my feet.

I stroked my mother's burned arm and wondered how painful it would be for her to now relive that part of her life. She was looking at me with a puzzled expression, trying to understand why I was acting like this. Behind a glass partition, I saw Christian watching us intently. The time had come.

"Mum, this might not be the best place to tell you this, but we need to talk …" Surprise and suspicion mingled in her eyes. "Whatever happens, I want you to know that you are the person I love most in the world. I do want us to finally put the past behind us, and that means no more secrets. Some things have come to light, and all I want you to tell me is if they are true, or slanderous lies. I will believe you; only you. Whatever you tell me, I will accept as the whole truth, and then we can all move on. We can have a future free of secrets and the shadows they cast."

"Constantine, what's the matter? I don't understand? What's happened?" She sounded scared.

I did not want to prolong her agony, so I came straight to the point. "You have told me some things about my adoption, but not everything. I know we were supposed to talk about it after you left him. However, just now, the man who we were supposed to meet followed us here. He told me a story about my birth, about the woman who gave me life ..."

My mother gawped at me, and I pointed at Christian behind the glass wall. "That man knows a lot about the time you lived in Ioannina. I want you to hear him out and tell me whether he is telling the truth. You are the only mother I have ever known, and you will always be my mother. I need you to believe me when I say that. I just want us to be free, to no longer be haunted by the ghosts of the past."

She turned and looked at him. "Constantine, that day may now be here. I've wanted to tell you for years, but your father kept threatening me. I hope God sends him the punishment he deserves. I don't know who that man is, but I agree—it's time to finish this. This is not a coincidence, everything that has been happening since this morning. Let's go talk to him, and I promise to tell you the truth, no matter how ugly. I have carried a great burden all these years. I have spent my whole life trying to protect you, and now is the time to keep you safe, but no longer in the dark."

I was impressed by her readiness, and realized that she wanted everything to become clear, too. We walked towards Christian, who had been patiently waiting for us. Arm in arm, we arrived at the small waiting area, and I introduced them. We agreed to go somewhere more secluded to talk. My mother gave one of the nurses her phone number, so they could reach us if need be.

We took the stairs and walked down to a quiet little garden behind the hospital. It was late afternoon, and the sun was hiding behind the towering apartment blocks that surrounded the garden. Two small benches stood in the shade of a welcoming oak tree. A flock of pigeons rose in the air as we crossed their path.

We sat down and Christian, without wasting any time, briefly told my mother the same story he had told me. My mother sobbed quietly as she listened to him, and I could see the memories waking up inside her, becoming flesh and blood. Regret, nostalgia, and terror alternately twisted her features. The most difficult moment was when she heard that my biological mother had survived and managed to run away. She needed a moment to recover from the hacking cough that seized her, and then Christian could continue.

He spoke about another missing part of the puzzle: the man who had been my father's best friend and accomplice. He said that the man was lying in intensive care after an unfortunate incident. Concluding his story, he told her that Melek was in a coma in Paris since that morning.

My mother lowered her head and cried silently. She looked haggard and worn. She took out her inhaler and took two sharp breaths. I had no doubt she had not known some of what she'd just heard. I asked her if she wanted us to stop, but she shook her head. I was surprised that Christian mentioned nothing about the fortune he had tried to tempt me with. I was sure he would, just to see her reaction, although I could have already told her myself.

Now we both waited for her response. She took a couple of sips from the small water bottle she had been holding. It was evident that her soul was in torment. Not just because of the detective's story, but also as a result of all the years she had spent harboring the secrets that were eating her up inside.

Before telling her side of the story, she asked how my biological mother had survived and how her subsequent life had been. Once Christian answered those questions, she took a deep breath and struggled to speak in a hoarse voice.

"Everything my husband told you is a lie ... That's not how it happened. He is twisting everything to suit his purpose, but the truth is different. I am ashamed of many things I have done in my life, but I never harmed anyone ..."

The sound of her phone interrupted her. She took it out of the bag and answered faintly. She visibly paled at what she heard.

"What's happening?" I anxiously asked her.

"Your father ..."

"Is he dead?" I asked, not knowing whether to be sad or glad if it were the case.

For a few seconds she said nothing, prolonging my agony as well as Christian's, who was hanging on to her every word.

"No, he is not. They did not operate in the end. He woke up, and now he is asking for me."

I could not believe my ears. How could he recover so swiftly, to the point where he was asking to see her? He had been unconscious only minutes ago and the doctors were telling us how serious his condition was.

I wanted to ask her to stay, but that would have been inhumane, so I did not stop her from getting up and dashing back inside. My father's hold on her was still strong. Fear had nestled inside her and was preventing her from leaving him behind, from freeing herself. He had ruined her life and still she ran to him whenever he called.

Stunned, Christian looked at my mother, then me as I watched her go. I motioned for him to follow me. I was curious to find out what my father wanted from her. Like a bad penny, he kept turning up ...


We stood in the corridor waiting for her to come out of his room. I could barely stop myself from bursting in. In the meantime, a doctor had informed us that they had not operated because my father unexpectedly regained consciousness, and now it seemed like he would pull through. He was being closely monitored, and they would not allow another visitor, although he had asked for me too.

After a few minutes of tense silence, Christian spoke up and revealed his personal relationship to my birth mother. On the one hand, I felt uncomfortable hearing so many details about her; on the other hand, I wanted to understand why she had waited so long before looking for me.

Eventually the door opened, and my mother stepped outside. Her face was harsh, expressionless. "We can leave if you want. I'm done here. I want us to go home and talk about everything, taking our time. I'm fed up," she declared in a steady voice.

"What did he want?" I asked.

She scoffed. "What else would he want? He wanted me to shut up, to lie. He threatened me with everything under the sun, but I no longer care." She looked at us and took my hand. "Let's go home. It's time to talk about it and move on."

I was surprised at how everything was suddenly coming to the forefront in such a strange way to untangle this complex web.

We walked ahead, Christian following closely behind. By leaving my father alone, I felt as if I was slowly parting from a large chapter of my old life.

The sun was setting over Galaxidi and Persie was packing her bags. Violet sat on the bed and anxiously watched her.

Constantine had just called to give Persie the news about his father's injury. He also told her that it had been a day full of revelations about his past. She had been worried, but did not press him for details, sensing that he was pressed for time and that the long day was nowhere near the end for him. He had been speaking in a low voice, as if he did not want to be overheard, and she'd grasped the gravity of the situation. She had asked him whether he needed her, but he had asked her not to drive in the dark and come the following morning if she could.

Persie had initially agreed, but changed her mind a few minutes after they'd hung up, convinced that he needed her. Violet agreed with Constantine, and was trying to dissuade her from going. "Persie, please, you promised Constantine, remember? You can't drive up and down the mountain alone. You haven't slept in two days! Why don't you wait until tomorrow morning?"

"I want to see him anyway. I'm just doing it a few hours earlier than expected. It's not the first time I'm doing this trip during the night. It's better that I arrive in Athens tonight. I must meet my lawyer tomorrow at lunch anyway, to decide how to proceed. This way, I'll have some time to see Constantine in the morning. You know, I don't think meeting him now is a coincidence; you know I believe in karmic meetings. It's as if destiny has brought us together, and I don't intend to ignore any of the signs," Persie replied without breaking her stride.

"And you are planning to take that beat up old car? It won't even make it to Delphi. Come on, this is crazy!"

"It will do fine. I toured the whole of Greece in that car."

"Ten years ago!" Violet said, and stood up. She grabbed Persie by the shoulders and looked her straight in the eye. "Persie, come to your senses, please. I don't know what kind of spell the guy has cast on you, but if you want to be near him, it'd be good if you made it in one piece."

Persie simply stared at her with such determination that Violet sighed in defeat. "Fine. We'll go together, and we'll take my car. You'll drop me off at your house, and then you can do whatever you like. It's a chance to take care of some business I have in Athens. It's also the only way I'm letting you go. Don't forget I have all the keys."

"What about the bookshop?" Persie asked.

"I'll ask a friend to cover for me. It won't be the first time."

Persie opened her mouth to say something, but Violet did not let her. "I'm going to pack ... unless you don't enjoy my company?"

"Don't be silly. I just don't like the thought of you going to so much trouble. There is no reason ..."

"Yes, there is, and it's a serious reason. We'll set off in half an hour. I'm going to find someone to feed the dog while we are away," Violet said, and walked to the staircase that led to the first floor.

Persie looked out of the window at their four-legged friend in the garden, smiled, and returned to her suitcase. Although her own troubles were never far from her mind, she could not wait to be near the man who had so suddenly given her life new meaning and woken so many feelings inside her.

I drove all of us back to my parents' house. With my father in the hospital, we now had all the time in the world to talk and pack up my mother's belongings before leaving. The drive had felt endless to me. I wanted to know the truth so badly, but kept running into unexpected obstacles. But now, the time was finally here. Christian appeared cooler, and was waiting patiently for the moment of truth. My mother had not spoken a word since we had left the hospital, lost in her own thoughts. We did not talk much, either. We all gathered our strength for what was to follow.

As I waited for my mother to change in the bathroom, I called Persie. I couldn't stop myself from telling her everything that had happened. I was pleasantly surprised by her reaction. In a heartbeat, she had said she was on her way, but I persuaded her to wait until the morning, when she would be rested for the long drive back to Athens.

For some reason, I thought back to the small chapel by the roadside where her parents had died as I said those words. I did not want her to risk such a dangerous drive at night when she was so tired. I did not share my fears so as not to scare her, but I tried to dissuade her. Besides, we would not be able to meet this evening anyway.

Nonetheless, I had been pleased with her willingness to come. It showed she really cared for me, that we were not just two ships passing in the night. Maybe it was the first flush of love, but I had surrendered to her charm and quirky personality.

While I spoke to Persie, Christian flipped through an old photo album and cast glances in my direction, as if wanting to make sure I was the same person as the child in the photos. Even though he had appeared out of nowhere, I felt that he had been honest with me. I was still guarded as to what his real intentions might be, given how peculiar the story had sounded, but he had presented the necessary proof. Who else could know about the past in such detail? The impending death of my birth mother had affected me, and I wanted the light of truth to scatter the shadows of the past.

Now that I'd had some time to think, I considered my options and thought that maybe I could help Persie with this fortune I would supposedly be inheriting. I felt immediately ashamed of myself for having such thoughts while the woman was still alive. At the same time, a voice inside me told me that I might not be her child. I don't know whether it was subconscious denial because of my mother's past, but the voice in my head kept whispering that this was not the end of the story. Maybe it was just my natural suspicion towards the man we had left behind at the hospital, the man I had once thought my father, who was a consummate, unscrupulous liar.

When I saw my mother come out of the bathroom and into the living room, I went and sat on the sofa. She came and sat beside me, facing Christian. She seemed calmer and more determined than ever. She had a long, terry cloth bathrobe on and was drying her hair with one of its ends. Her movements were robotic, absent-minded. I asked her if she wanted something to drink, but she declined the offer. She looked at Christian for a few moments before speaking.

"My parents abandoned me with my grandmother. I thought I had done something wrong, that this was my punishment. In the beginning everything was okay, but as I grew up things became difficult. My grandmother forced me to drop out of high school and take a job. I was barely sixteen when I decided to follow my own path. I dropped out of school and fell in love with the first man to pay attention to me.

"I was unlucky; he just wanted to take advantage of me. We moved from place to place and eventually I ended up in Ioannina, in that brothel. I was an adult by then. I met your father as soon as I arrived, and he decided to keep me for himself. Compared to giving my body to just anyone, I was happy to do it just for him, in exchange for the protection he offered. He was a young, good-looking policeman back then, and I hoped that one day he would take me away. The truth is he did, but sometimes I think it would have been better if I had died in the fire."

She turned towards me and her eyes welled up. "If you had not come into my life, I would have died years ago. You kept me ..."

I gulped hard and squeezed her hand. I did not say anything, waiting for her to continue. Christian also waited silently.

"The details of my past don't matter at present. We can talk about it later, Constantine … When they brought Melek to the brothel, she was just a frightened young girl. Pretty as an angel, she was. That's what her name means, you know … She had been sold to a local man, and he brought her to the brothel some time later. They put her to work straight away. I remember she ran away once and went to the police. Little did she know she would find my husband there, that beast … He brought her back, of course, never having to account for his actions to anyone.

"All the city's high society visited the brothel, and they protected him and Ganas. We never learned who the true owner of the brothel was; he never made an appearance. It was rumored that it was someone high up, rich and powerful. A decrepit old man was in charge of collecting profits from the brothel and bringing them to the owner; he burned in the fire.

"Everyone came to the brothel to satiate their needs and perversions, and all the poor women earned were a meal and a bed to sleep in. Those who managed to get away had no chance of making a living and would come back, begging to work in the brothel again. I tried to help them as best I could, but it was not easy.

"Your father saved me from such deprivation. But if I could turn back time, I don't know what path I would have chosen. Those were hard, impoverished times. People did not care what was happening right under their nose. The kept their heads down and their mouths shut, even after the fire. That's how those bastards got away with it. I'm glad to hear Ganas is suffering, and I hope he dies. He was far worse than your father. I can't even begin to describe what he did to those girls, the humiliation when he brought his friends over … Like a pack of wolves, they were, ready to tear their bodies to shreds."

The cursed cough seized her once again, and I immediately brought her a glass of water and her inhalator. For a few seconds she struggled to breathe, but then it seemed to subside. I could tell she still had much to say, that more revelations were coming.

"That's when Melek ran away and went to the police station. There, she met Michael and they fell in love. Those two animals tried to kill him, but he survived. They cut one of his fingers off …"

Christian started. "What do you mean, he survived?" he asked. "Did they not drown him in the lake?"

"That's what we all thought, that he had drowned back then. But he managed to survive, even though we thought he was dead all these years."

"How do you know he is alive?"

My mother paused, her eyes filling with tears. We were hanging on her every word.

"I know he is alive because I met him at the hospital this morning. It was purely by chance; he was the man sitting beside me on the bench …"

Christian stared at her, open-mouthed, and I struggled to put my thoughts in order.

"Are you sure you are talking about the same man who fell in love with Melek all those years ago?" Christian asked, stunned.

My mother nodded. "When he came up to me and told me who he was, I thought someone was toying with me. But then I realized it really was him. Many things change with the passage of time, but the eyes stay the same ... Everything that had stayed murky for thirty-five years is suddenly clearing up in a single day," she said, wiping away her tears.

Christian, still reeling, asked more questions. "How can he be alive? Where has he been all these years? Why did he not look for her if he loved her?"

"He told me that after his near-drowning he hid for a few days, injured and scared. When the brothel burned down, he believed that no one had survived. Thinking Melek was dead, he left the country. He travelled for years, then moved to Paris, and now he lives on Patmos."

"Do you know when he was in Paris?" Christian asked.

"He did not say exactly, but I understood it was some years later."

"Do you have a way to contact him?"

"He told me he works at the library of the Patmos monastery, but I don't have a number, if that's what you mean ... I imagine he will be shocked to hear Melek is still alive. I don't know if he should even be told the truth of what happened; I'm sure it would pain him greatly. Maybe they met in a brothel, but it was true love. He spent all his earnings, poor man, just to be with her. I remember hearing them in her room, him trying to teach her Greek. We were all envious, knowing we would never have something like that," she said with a wistful sigh.

"This is an important development, and maybe we should let him know ... But please, carry on, I'm sure you have a lot more to tell us," Christian said, waiting for my mother to resume her story.

Although I was fascinated by what I was hearing, I could not wait for the part that touched me most: the story of my birth.

"When we found out Melek was pregnant it was too late for an abortion, and they decided to let her have the baby and then sell it to a family. They did that whenever a girl fell pregnant. Melek tried to run away with Michael, but they did not make it, and they banned him from the brothel and threatened to kill him. The two would meet in secret, taking a boat to the island. Nothing could stand in the way of their love. I am ashamed to say it, but I saw them one night. I never told anyone, though, because if they found out they would have drowned them both."

Christian, so far patient with the slow pace of her narration, now asked her impatiently, "Could you tell me how Constantine ended up living with you? After they snatched him from Melek that evening. I am confused by what Nick said and what you told us before, at the hospital."

My mother took my hands in hers. "Your father lied. He must have wanted to gain time for some reason." She looked to Christian. "At the hospital, he tried to convince me that you were a crook. He suspected you were just trying to blackmail him. He also wanted to convince Constantine that he was the son of a whore, by way of revenge. He thought it would fill him with shame."

She looked back to me, gaze intense. "The alcohol has taken away any brain he had left, not that he ever used it for anything other than evil. He threatened to kill me if I told you the truth, but I no longer care. What else can he do to me?" She turned again to Christian. "Michael this morning, now you with all the revelations about Melek ... it is as if God has suddenly decided to give an end to the story that began in Ioannina decades ago. I'm afraid you will be disappointed to hear this, but Constantine is not the child you are looking for ..."

Once again, we were speechless. Christian looked worried. "What do you mean? I don't understand. Please, if there is the tiniest chance that we might solve this while Melek still alive, tell me ..."

My mother raised her head determinedly. "I was present when they snatched Melek's baby, and I know for certain that that child is not Constantine."

The French detective looked at her with suspicion. Even I thought that something else was going on, that my mother was trying to throw him off his tracks by spinning another version of the story.

"I am starting to get muddled with all these different versions," Christian said. "Please, in the name of the love you claim you had for Melek, tell me the truth. If Constantine is not her child, then who is?"

A strange smile spread on her lips; a smile of despair. She leaned over and placed a hand on his knee. "The baby that was born that night cannot be Constantine because Melek did not have a boy; she had a girl. And I could never forget this, because I was the first person to hold her before they made her disappear. I still remember her eyes, the way they fluttered open. She looked so frightened then, as if she could sense what was happening. They threatened to beat us if we told Melek anything about the baby's sex. Poor Melek ... We took Constantine a year later, when the doctors told me I could never have children. I had contracted something at the brothel ... I knew he could do it, so I pressed him to find a child for us ..."

She beat her breast with her fists, as if she wanted to punish herself. "He never told me the details, just made arrangements so we could present you as our own son, as if I had given birth to you. I was so happy to have a child of my own that for many years I did not care what he did or how he treated me. It was enough that I could raise you."

Christian looked frustrated. "I find it hard to believe your story, unless you have some proof that this is the truth and not another fabrication. Do you have any proof about what happened to Melek's child?"

The seconds of silence that followed were the most tortuous of my life.

"I may have no proof, because I truly do not know or remember, but ... there is someone who does. And I think you know who I'm talking about," she replied, and then burst into tears.

When my mother's sobs subsided, we let her rest for a few minutes. I cannot say with any certainty whether I was glad or sad that I was not the child. Perhaps the only reason I had hoped it would be me was so that I could help Persie financially. I still had my reservations about what my mother had said, knowing the influence my father exerted on her.

It was getting late, and the lights of the ships crossing the sea could be seen through the balcony doors. Christian, rooted to his seat, was waiting anxiously for my mother to reply.

Finally, in a whisper, she spoke again. "The only person who knows what happened to the girl is Nick. He made all the arrangements and took the money. I asked him about it only once, and he swore at me, saying he did not remember. I heard him talking to Ganas, however, and I could tell he knew. Even when he was drunk and let other things slip, he never mentioned this matter."

Christian rose and walked to the window. He must have been so confused with all these stories. There were still aspects I could not fathom. The detective walked back to my mother and knelt beside her, taking her hand.

"I understand this has been difficult," he said, "and I don't mean to tire you more than necessary, but I need you to understand my position. I'm here looking for the child not simply as a professional, but as a ... That woman was important to me—*is* important to me—and I accepted the case in a heartbeat. I wanted to reunite her with her child while she still lives, and that possibility is fading away. I swore to do my best, and if there is still a way to find her true child in time I will do it, no matter what."

She looked down at him sweetly, as if approving his intentions, but said nothing.

"I beg you," he said, "be honest with me. Are you telling me the truth? If not, all you will manage is to delay me, because I *will* find that child. I am close to cracking the case now, and there is no turning back ..."

"I have told you the truth. There is another detail I have just remembered. I did not think of it before but now, I think it might be related somehow ... Just after the fire, I heard Ganas talk of a man ... 'the singer,' he'd called him. I think he was referring to the man who had taken the baby. Perhaps I should go to my husband and ask him to tell me the whole truth ..."

After all that I had learned today, I would never allow her to be in the same room as my father again. Christian voiced my thoughts before I could. "There is no way he would say anything to you. I just wanted to make certain that he does know. Leave the rest to me. I will visit him tomorrow, and you can be sure he will tell me everything. He will have to ..." Christian jumped up. "I think I should contact Michael. Did you tell your husband you'd seen him? Do you have his last name, or any other information?"

"No."

"Did he at least tell you where he could be found?"

"All I know is what I've already told you. That he works at the library of the monastery on Patmos."

Christian nodded. "That should be enough to track him down. I think he should know. Maybe he would like to see her before ..." Christian paused for a second, but then ploughed on. "I will do it as soon as I return to the hotel. If I don't find him this evening, I will try again in the morning. I think I should go now and let you get some rest. I hope everything goes well, and that we don't have to discuss such matters again, although I make no promises."

We stood up and shook his hand, and he headed to the door. My mother stopped him just before he stepped outside. "I don't know if Michael will believe you. If he doesn't, let me know so I can talk to him. There is one other thing I would like to ask of you."

The Frenchman nodded.

"Please tell me when you find the girl. And, if she agrees, I would like to meet her."

"If all goes well, I promise to do all I can to bring you in touch. You understand I am in no position to know what her reaction will be when she hears about her past. I hope your husband will help me, and I promise to do my best ..."

Christian closed the door behind him, and I took my mother in my arms.

"I'm sorry, son ..." she said, and hugged me tightly.

I pulled back and looked at her. "Don't apologize. I should thank you for managing to give me so much love after everything you went through. I don't care about the past. We will make a fresh start. We have all the time in the world to talk about this, to examine it. But it does not change how much I love you. Now, go get some rest. I think we should spend the night here, pack up in the morning, and then leave. What do you say?"

"I agree. We've spent so many years here, what's one more night?"

"Do you still want me for your son now that I'm not an heir?" I asked with a laugh, trying to lighten the mood. It worked, and a faint smile spread on her lips.

I turned to go to my room, but she stopped me.

"I'm proud of you, son ..."

"I'm proud of you, too," I said, and kissed her forehead.

As soon as my mother fell asleep, I took a shower and poured myself a large glass of wine. There was always plenty of alcohol in this house. It was a balmy evening, and I needed to wind down before going to bed.

As I stepped on the balcony, I saw my phone light up with a text from Persie. I smiled. She must have sensed me thinking about her, as I had just been about to call her.

*Violet and I have just arrived in Athens. Tell me if you need anything, otherwise I'll see you tomorrow morning.*

I may not have wanted her to drive so late in the day, but I was nonetheless glad she did. I leaned back in my armchair, looking at the sea, and typed back.

*All I need right now is to talk to you ...*

*At your service! I'll call you in five minutes,* she texted back, and I felt my heart flutter.

I drank a sip of wine and realized I had so much to tell her I did not know where to begin.

Night had spread its black cloak over the island of Patmos. Michael had just handed Renée's manuscript to the monastery hegumen. A small ceremony had taken place at the entrance of the castle, but now all was calm and monastic life resumed its tranquil pace once all the guests had left. Peter instantly noticed a difference in Michael's behavior, and suspected that something must have happened in Athens. Michael should have been happy, but he looked dazed and lost, as if something serious preoccupied him.

He and Peter were both seated on the ramparts, enjoying the view of the sunset over the port of Patmos. There was no wind, so silence reigned. Only the faint sounds from the port occasionally reached the high walls. Michael told Peter everything that had happened at the ceremony and then, as if in a trance, recounted his encounter with Anna at the hospital the following day.

On the walls, beneath the evening star that glimmered in the sky, Michael began to tell his life story in detail to someone for the first time. It was as if he was opening the gates to his memories that had remained sealed for years. His speech sounded more like a confession than a narration. It was as if he were asking the monk to pardon him for his actions in the past.

Peter listened carefully, a stunned look on his face.

Michael could understand his friend's surprise. He hadn't shared any of this with anyone all these years. Every time he mentioned Melek, his eyes filled with tears he could barely hold back. He believed his meeting with Anna had been no coincidence, that there was some reason the two had met again after all these years. He did not stop talking until he had said it all.

Michael knew that this was the first time Peter—or anyone—had seen him in this state. In all these years, Michael had always hid his pain and secrets. He stared vacantly into the distance. Tears streamed down his cheeks as more and more memories rapidly surfaced.

Peter gently touched his friend's shoulder. The monk's voice made Michael turn towards his friend.

"You did well, Michael, to open your heart to someone, and I am glad I was here for it. We all carry not only our sins, but the sins passed on to us by others too. I know you are a virtuous man, and I also know that we are but puppets and someone else pulls the strings of our existence. There is no greater judge than our own selves, for we all carry God and the devil within us. It is clear who wins the battle between good and evil in your soul. I will not judge what you said, or the time you chose to say it. Maybe that woman crossed your path today for a reason: for your salvation."

Relieved to hear those words, Michael took Peter's hand and gripped it with gratitude. Peter was more than a friend to him. Their spiritual relationship had been a great support during the years he had spent on the island. Peter almost never followed the traditional route of religion when he approached another person, an attitude that had won over Michael. Imperceptibly, Peter had helped him move on, drawing out the hatred that had filled his every pore. Peter taught him that only through forgiveness could someone cleanse their own soul and find lasting peace.

"All these feelings were still buried inside me, and I thought I had left them behind ... They rose again to torment me the moment I met that woman again. I thought I could forget everything, but as soon as I stepped on the island, the energy of this blessed land woke every single one of my memories, even things I had long forgotten," Michael said, visibly moved.

"You had not forgotten them, Michael. They were buried deep inside your heart, waiting for the right time to reveal themselves. Tell me, though, what is this woman doing now in her life? It would be good to see her again and talk it over. She too, as I understand, must be wishing to find peace, if she has not already done so."

"No, Peter, she hasn't. We did not talk for long, but I understood she has been hiding her past all these years. At least she managed to have a family and leave that way of life. That is something ..."

Peter fell silent for a moment, as if something was troubling him. "There is only one thing I would like to ask you, and you don't have to answer."

"Peter, you can ask me anything," Michael said eagerly.

"What happened to the child? I wonder why you never looked for it. Did you not wish to, or could you not?"

"I could not. I was unconscious when the child was taken, and after the fire, I was convinced anyone who knew its whereabouts had died. I would have asked around Ioannina, but I knew they would blame me for the fire, so I chose to leave. When I returned to Greece, I did think about looking for it, but I realized it would be fruitless without so much as a name—or even a sex—to go on.

"My arrival on the island showed me that I had to leave the past behind me and move on. Which I did, until this morning. I do not know if I acted out of fear all these years. How could I reveal, if I found the child, that it was the child of a prostitute, and not the family that had raised it? Everything had ended for me with Melek's death. Every time I thought about taking some other course of action, I looked at my missing finger and remembered."

"She gave you her number, though."

"Anna? Yes, hurriedly, because her son was waiting for her."

Peter said no more, leaving Michael to complete his train of thought. Slowly, Michael brought out the piece of paper with Anna's name and number, and looked at it.

Michael stayed on the ramparts for some time, enjoying the stillness of the evening. He then went to check on the library before returning to his house to get some rest. As he unlocked the door, he heard the phone ring, and wondered who it could be at this hour. He hesitated for a moment, then picked up the receiver.

At first, he could not hear properly through the static, so he hung up. The phone instantly rang again, and this time he waited until a voice came on at the other end of the line. He was thunderstruck. It took some time for him to become convinced that what he was hearing was true. He collapsed into an armchair, his legs unable to hold him any longer.

"I want to be there," he said in an unsteady voice. "I will come, I don't care. Just tell me how it can be done."

Michael's hands shook so badly he could barely hold the pen and scribble something down. He ended the call and then leaned back against the armchair, a shell of a man. His serene expression was gone. His eyes stared at the opposite wall and the icon of John the Revelator ...

Christian arrived at the hospital early the following morning and headed straight to the room where they kept Nick. He had barely slept during the night, searching for anything relating to the case, so he could extract the truth from the policeman. Unfortunately, he had discovered no information that could independently lead him to the woman who was Melek's child.

If he did not manage to crack the case today, he would be forced to talk to the press and take the case to the police. Too many conflicting versions had surfaced, with not enough evidence to support any of them. This was not the kind of decision he could make lightly. Melek's lawyer had asked him not to make her identity public while she was still alive. Christian was fully aware of the publicity such a case would generate. Perhaps he should just wait for Melek to pass; last night, the lawyer had spoken of her arrangements for her funeral. But then she would miss her only chance of discovering the truth about her daughter's identity.

As Christian walked through the hospital, his head filled with troubled thoughts, he observed the patients along the way. He wanted the case to be over and to never set foot in a hospital again. He had been marked by the last image of Melek as she lost consciousness, when they were ushering him out of her room. That weak, skeletal body had nothing to do with the sensuous creature he remembered sharing pleasure with years ago. It was as if the cursed disease had sucked the life out of her. From the moment he had met her at the hospital, he'd begun to seriously ponder his own future. All he had done was work endless hours for many years, without enjoying the simple pleasures of life. He had enough set aside to enjoy a good life. His fee, if everything went well, might ensure he never had to work again.

When he arrived outside Nick's room, he was surprised to find two uniformed policemen already talking to him. Christian stepped aside, pretending to talk on his phone, and watched the scene discreetly through the half-open door. A male nurse sitting behind a nearby counter smiled at him, and Christian walked over, putting the phone back in his pocket.

"Good morning," the nurse said. "How are you? You were here yesterday too, weren't you?"

Christian didn't remember the man at all, and was astonished he was apparently so memorable to him. The nurse kept looking at him intently, and finally Christian got the message. It was not just the man's observational prowess that was at play here; he was interested in Christian.

He was used to men flirting with him, and although Christian did not return the nurse's interest, he was still flattered. It was also an excellent chance to discover what was going on with Nick and the police officers.

"Yes, I was here yesterday," Christian said, smiling back. "Mr. Papadogiannis and I have an appointment for this morning, but I can see he is busy ... Do you know what's going on?" he asked, summoning all his charm and pointing to the room.

The nurse glanced around, then gave Christian a conspiratorial nod and ushered him into the nurses' room. After closing the door behind them, the man whispered, "It's been happening all morning. Other policemen have been here too. Something is going on with your friend. I think he'll have police trouble once he leaves the hospital."

"How do you know that?" Christian asked.

The nurse hesitated, and Christian pulled out his wallet. When the nurse realized what his intention was, he stopped him. "You don't have to do that. I'll tell you for free, so long as you never say it came from me."

Christian just nodded reassuringly.

"Earlier this morning, a doctor overheard a policeman tell him that it was all over, and that his dirty laundry would now be aired. That's it, nothing else."

The nurse opened the door and they stepped back outside. Christian saw the two uniformed policemen leave the room, and decided to move towards them. He touched the nurse's hand. "Thank you, I really appreciate it ..."

"I'm George ... My shift ends in a bit. I'll buy you a coffee in the canteen ..." he said in a tone full of meaning.

Christian smiled without giving him a definite response, not wanting to crush his hopes. He would need this unexpected ally for as long as Nick stayed in the hospital.

He walked swiftly to Nick's room and entered without knocking. Nick gave him a look filled with resentment. "Just who I needed ..." he grumbled.

"I can see you have a whole lot of other trouble ..." Christian replied sarcastically.

"Yes, I do ... Do you want to solve it?" Nick snapped, and raised himself up on the bed.

"I can't solve your troubles, but I can make sure they don't multiply. The trouble I am about to heap won't be as easy to handle," Christian said, and sat in a small, faded armchair across from the bed.

The policeman looked rough. He was dressed in a white robe, his hair was a matted mess, and he looked more like an inmate in a psychiatric facility than a patient in a hospital.

"I'm listening," Nick said. "I imagine you had time to catch up with my family. Tell me what you want."

Christian quietly observed him for a moment. A wreck of a man sat before him. Gone was the arrogant look. His eyes now exuded fear, like a trapped animal.

"All I need you to tell me right now is where Melek's daughter is."

Nick laughed sardonically. "So, she told you everything! I save the woman from a brothel, give her the chance to live a respectable life, and this is the thanks I get! Where would she be now without me, without my protection? She obviously didn't tell you about when she got sick from all the filthy scum that lay with her, that I was the one who saved her. She couldn't even have children, and I gave her one. This is the thanks I get … I many not have been the best of men, but at least I tried …"

Christian, in no mood to hear his ramblings, interrupted him. "I do not care about anything other than finding the girl, Nick. You can tell your wife everything else when you see her. Give me what I want, and you will never have to see me again. Believe me, you don't want to add me to your list of enemies. You've already wasted my time once. You don't want to do that again."

Christian did not intend to let things drag on any longer. He was seething inside. If Nick had told him the truth from the start, the girl might have managed to meet her mother in time. He wanted to extract the information first. Then he would extract his revenge. He decided to play his last card, although he sensed the man would crack any moment now.

"All you need to tell me is where the *singer* who took the baby is …"

Seeing Nick's shock, Christian feared a repeat of the Ganas incident. He needed Nick to stay alive, to reveal the names of those who had taken the baby. But if he backed down now, he might never gain the answers he sought.

"As you can tell," Christian said, "I am very near. If you say nothing, you will just gain another enemy and a couple more days at most. But I have not shared the good news with you! Michael says hello …"

"Michael who?" Nick frowned.

"Michael whose finger you cut off and then tried to drown in a lake. Guess what? He is doing fine and would be glad to come testify. So, make up your mind ..."

A high-pitched, nervous laugh escaped Nick's lips. He shook his head, as if this could help him ignore the truth a little longer. The laughter became louder, raucous, and then began to subside. He fell silent and stared at the floor, muttering oaths and cursing his wife and son. He sat at the side of his bed and touched the floor with his naked toes.

"The dead have come back to life ..." Nick whispered. "I don't even remember their faces. All these years, I never thought such a moment would come ... yet here it is. I'll tell you what you want to know, but I need a favor, too."

Christian said nothing. Had Nick finally realized he had no other choice but to tell the truth? If so, the last thing he wanted to do was interrupt him.

"All these years I thought her body was among the ashes left behind by the fire," Nick mumbled in a voice so low, a whisper could drown it out. Then, louder: "I want to meet her. That is all I want."

Christian's eyebrows shot up at this but he managed to keep his voice void of emotion. "I hope you meet soon. You will have plenty to talk about. Until then, speak!"

Nick gave him a cold look and turned to face the window. In a shaky voice, he finally began to tell Christian everything he knew about the people who had stolen the baby with his assistance.

We had arrived at my house some time ago. I had to return to my parents' house and collect a few more things, but for the time being my mother and I unpacked and tidied up what we had already brought.

I emptied a room I used as a workshop for her. The plan was for her to spend a few days here with me, and then we would look for a small apartment for her nearby. It would not be an easy transition for either one of us, particularly for her—the change was too great in any case, and the added upheaval of all these revelations was making it even more difficult. The French detective had turned our lives upside down and now we needed time to process everything and move forward, leaving all these unpleasant memories behind. I did not intend to keep digging up the past. Maybe it would be better if I never learned the whole truth. Sometimes ignorance is better than all the truth in the world.

If my mother had not insisted on meeting Melek, I would have asked Christian to never contact us again. I had nothing against him as a person, just the turmoil he had brought into our lives. Everything I had learned had saddened me, and I tried to push it aside and focus on Persie.

We had talked for over an hour the previous evening, and I had told her everything. She had been stunned, just like me, and was struggling to believe her ears. I did not hide anything about my mother's past or the terrible deeds of my father. I wanted her to know who I really was, and I confessed everything without fear. We were both discovering my past almost simultaneously, as everything had happened so suddenly, so abruptly. She agreed that there was no point in me looking for my birth parents, and that now I had to focus on supporting my mother as best as I could. Even though she did not comment on my father, I could sense she was disgusted by his actions.

She wanted to pass by my house and see me, even for a few minutes. In the end we decided to rest for a bit and meet for lunch later. I could not wait to see her again. The memory of her body against mine was so strong it was as if we had parted moments ago. The way we had made love was as if our bodies had known one another for years.

I had managed to capture some unique moments on the small island and in the alleys of Galaxidi. Before sending the final copies to the magazine, I wanted to show Persie the ones I had chosen. Sophie had finished touching them up and they were ready to be sent off. The magazine was anxious to receive them and had heard we had done a good job. I was sure it would be an excellent spread.

My mother had sensed something was going on, and asked me about Galaxidi. Without going into too much detail, I let her understand that these past few days had been an emotional rollercoaster for me. As soon as I was paid for the job, I intended to rent a house on an island where we could go for a while and recover. I understood that, at this point particularly, she needed to rest and recuperate. All these revelations had taken a physical and mental toll on her, worried as she was about how I would react and neglecting her own wellbeing in an effort to make things easier for me.

Only time could heal those wounds. I just prayed we did not have more trouble with my father, especially after the detective's visit. Christian was still searching for the girl that had been snatched from the brothel. What would happen if everything became known? Media and the police would probably hound us, trying to find out the details. Christian had said that if my father revealed everything he knew and led him to Melek's child, he would leave him alone. Besides, after all these years, the statute of limitations had "erased" most of those crimes.

Whatever the outcome of this case, I hoped we would be rid of my father's presence for good. Before I'd learned of his past, I hated him just for the way he treated my mother. Now, I loathed him, realizing how ruthless he was.

I was startled to hear music in the living room. It was not just the fact that the radio was on, but the tune it played, a song I had recently heard Persie sing—her favorite song. I walked over to my mother. She was holding a picture frame. It was a photo of the two of us from when I was a baby. I put an arm around her shoulders.

"That's our very first photo, Constantine. It was taken the day your father brought you home," she said, stroking the baby's face in the photo tenderly. The final verse of the *rebetiko* song filled the living room, and she sang along ...

*Even if he cheated on you,*

*Even if he hurt you,*

*This love makes your eyes glow*

*Like a golden palace ...*

Nick had disclosed enough information for Christian to be able to track the child down. He had left him at the hospital in a bad state. The ruthless beast of a man was beginning to break down. In the end, realizing the gravity of his situation, Nick had begged Christian not to say anything and swore that he had just told him everything he knew. Although he blamed most of their actions on Ganas, saying that he was the one making all the decisions, Nick begged Christian to let him meet Melek and ask for her forgiveness.

Christian had not revealed anything about Melek's condition to Nick, wanting to find the child first. He had been puzzled by Nick's request, and had vaguely replied that he would try.

He returned to his hotel room and spoke to an associate on the phone while he searched the internet for information on the child, cross-referencing clues. After a brief, agonizing wait, the associate gave Christian a name.

Christian typed the name into the search engine and hit Enter. His eyes bulged as images began to appear on the screen. Stunned, he stared at the photos of the woman who, based on the evidence they had gathered so far, appeared to be Melek's child. He asked his associate to call him as soon as anything new turned up, then hung up.

He could not believe the similarity of the two women. The eyes, the color of their hair ... This young woman reminded him of the Melek he had met in Paris when she was young. He hungrily read everything he could find out about her, burning with curiosity. Everything he discovered matched Nick's story, and this time he was almost certain that his search was finally at an end.

His associate called him again, providing Christian with some more information, as well as a phone number. He picked up the piece of paper where he'd scribbled everything down, and tried to imagine what the young woman's reaction would be when she found out her real identity. How much did she know about the past? Christian thought it unlikely that her parents would have disclosed that her real mother had been a prostitute. Although the similarity was striking, only a DNA test could confirm their kinship. Until then, he wanted to be cautious, especially considering all the twists and turns of the previous day.

Not wanting to waste any time, Christian dialed the number. He knew it would be difficult to convince this woman to meet with a complete stranger, so he decided not to tell her the true reason he wanted to see her. She sounded suspicious of his intentions at first, but eventually agreed to meet him; although only for a few minutes, and she would be bringing someone else along.

They agreed to meet downtown around lunchtime. Christian knew how to be patient, but now he had been swept up by the fast pace of events and was trying to end his mission as quickly as possible. He spent a few more minutes searching the woman's past, and then decided to get ready to meet her.

My mother and I had just arrived at a nice taverna in Plaka. We would be meeting Persie, Theo, and Violet there, to have lunch and get to know each other. The weather was great, and the Parthenon hovered imposingly above us. Smiling tourists strolled in the narrow alleys and bought souvenirs in dozens of little shops, having travelled from all four corners of the world to enjoy the sights of our city. A little further away, a band played a tango, sweeping us to faraway lands with its Argentinian rhythm. The mood was festive.

According to the latest update from the hospital, my father was doing better and would be allowed to leave the following day. Just before we'd left the house, his colleagues had called, asking questions about the circumstances surrounding his injury. They found it odd that neither my mother nor I were at the hospital with him, and my mother excused herself by saying she was ill and housebound. It seemed my father had not revealed that I had pushed him; maybe he did not remember it? In any case, we decided to no longer preoccupy ourselves with the matter. I wanted to talk with a lawyer as soon as possible to begin the process of their divorce and everything that would entail.

My mother seemed to be enjoying herself greatly, looking around with a smile on her face. I had not seen her smile like this in a long time, but I empathized—she was free at last. I think that the greatest release was not her separation from my father, but the revelation of the truth she had kept hidden for so long.

Now, she was fretting about what Persie would be like. Persie had insisted on meeting my mother after everything she had heard the previous evening. She claimed it was not good for my mother to be left alone, and that I should bring her to our lunch.

I sensed Persie's presence before I could even pick her out among the crowd at the end of the alley. Her white dress made her sparkle in the sunshine. Accompanied by Violet and Theo, she was walking in our direction. I looked at her, entranced, unable to get enough of her exotic beauty. She must have sensed my admiration, because she smiled widely as she came nearer. My mother turned to watch her too, and then fell strangely silent.

My mother and I both stood up, and I walked around the table to greet them. I felt rather awkward, unsure of how to behave. As if sensing it, Persie gave me a peck on the cheek and turned to my mother, who kept staring at her.

I introduced everyone to my mother, and we sat around the table. I had asked Persie, for the time being, not to show that she knew anything about my mother's past, because that might make her feel uncomfortable. She sat down next to my mother and held her hand, indifferent to the burn marks. What surprised me was the intent way my mother watched Persie.

"It's so good to meet you, Anna," Persie told my mother. "It's very pretty here today ..."

"Isn't it just? I haven't been here in such a long time," I said, and looked at Violet. "Not as pretty as Galaxidi, though. Right, Violet?" I teased.

Violet smiled. "Every place has its beautiful spots, Constantine. This place is great! I haven't been here in years, and it hasn't changed one bit ..."

I felt a leg brush against mine, and looked at Persie. She gave me a sneaky smile and kept talking to my mother, who seemed a little more relaxed now but was still acting strange, observing Persie closely as if studying her. Persie's leg gently rubbed mine, and I immediately responded, careful to make sure no one noticed.

We all chatted carefreely for a while, until the waiter arrived to take our order. Our feet never parted for a second. Even though we all had our fair share of trouble, we forgot about it for as long as we were there, enjoying each other's company and Violet's jokes as she kept teasing Theo. I now better understood those two were Persie's family; the only family she had left.

I shifted my weight on my seat, trying to hide how much I wanted to be alone with Persie. We had arranged to go somewhere after this, just the two of us, and, as lovely as lunch was, I could not wait for the moment when nobody else would be around us. I also kept trying to understand my mother's bizarre behavior, without success. Even though she joined in the conversation and answered Persie's questions, she seemed very preoccupied. Maybe it was normal, after everything she had gone through these past two days, although she had given me the impression that she was much better this morning. She probably needed some time to put her memories behind her, if such a thing were even possible. Perhaps it is better to learn to live with our past, rather than try to bury it so deep its tentacles cannot reach us.

We ate and mostly chatted about *Abduction*, and my mother showed great interest in all the allusions to the myth of Persephone. Persie showed her a short video of the performance on her phone, and my mother seemed impressed. She knew about the protests, of course, but she had never seen a clip of the actual show.

When we were done, I asked for the bill, wanting to repay everyone for the dinner at Galaxidi. I ignored their protests and paid.

The plan was for me to take my mother home, and then pass by Persie's house to pick her up. As Persie walked around the table, her phone rang. She replied instantly. From the few words that reached my ears, she was trying to explain where we were to someone. As soon as she hung up, she walked up to me and spoke in a low voice. "Constantine, is it okay if we meet a little later? I have a meeting in a bit, and it might take a while …"

I was surprised she had not mentioned that meeting, but of course I was fine with it. "Yes, no problem. Call me when you are done so I can set off. I hope everything is okay …"

"Yes, all good. Violet, Theo, and I are meeting this weird, foreign guy. He says he is interested in taking the show abroad and, given my financial situation, I should at least hear him out. That was him, just now. I'll wait here for him with Theo and Violet. I'll call you as soon as we're done ... I can't wait for us to be alone." She took my hand tenderly, and I smiled.

I was glad to hear someone was interested in her show. Other than the fact that I would get to watch her enchanting performance again, it would help her pay off some of her debts. But I did not get a chance to tell her that; my mother was anxiously calling out my name.

I turned towards her, trying to see what the matter was. She gestured at me to look towards Theo and Violet. I turned, and gasped.

Christian stood at the taverna's entrance, looking equally taken aback. I could not believe that once again he was standing before us. Persie walked up to him with an outstretched hand. "You must be Mr. Ledu ..."

He nodded awkwardly, keeping his eyes on me. I felt my blood boil. "What are you doing here? Are you following us?" I snapped.

"I'm sorry, do you two know each other?" Persie asked.

Christian looked equally surprised to see my mother and me here. Still looking at me, he replied, "I have a meeting with Miss Stefanou ... What are *you* doing here?"

I tried to understand what was going on, but could make neither head nor tails of it. Both Christian and I started talking all at once, muddling things even further. Persie, trying to resolve the misunderstanding, motioned at us to be quiet. "This is the man who was interested in my show. How do you two know each other?"

If I told her who he was in front of my mother, she would know that I had told Persie our family secrets. Besides, what did Persie mean, he was the man who was interested in her show? It made no sense.

Christian spoke before I could reply to Persie. "I guess you did not tell me the whole truth," he said to me. "I was honest with you, explained the gravity of the situation. You knew everything and kept it from me, fobbing me off with crocodile tears. Why?"

My mother, who had been silent all this time, suddenly flared up. "We did not lie to you," she said angrily. "What does anything we said have to do with your presence here now?"

Christian seemed at a loss, not knowing how to reply. He glanced first at Persie, then at Theo and Violet, who were as confused as everyone else, including me.

"Can you tell me why you are here?" I asked.

"I will, but let me explain first. Miss Stefanou, I am the man who called you, but I am not interested in your show. I told you a little white lie so you would agree to meet me ..."

"What do you want, then?" Persie demanded.

"I think we should all sit down, because this seems to concern all of us. This is not some accidental meeting ..."

"You didn't answer. Why are you here?" I asked him, fed up with his games.

"I am here because this is where your father's information has led me. But now I see you are all playing some kind of game, and I wonder—"

"Are you trying to tell me that he gave you Persie's name when you asked him about what you were looking for?" I interrupted.

"No, he did not give me her name, but rather information that led me to her."

I tried to put my thoughts in order. My father, who evidently knew about my acquaintance with Persie, had told him that she was the child Christian was looking for. Why would he do that? What could he possibly gain from it?

We were beginning to attract stares from the other tables, standing up and arguing in the middle of a restaurant as we were.

"I think it's better we all sit down and clear this up. We have not lied to you, and this is obviously my father's doing..." I said, and pointed to the table we had just vacated.

Violet was looking at Christian, and shifted to vacate the seat beside her. She and Theo had said nothing all this time. After shooting me a puzzled look, Persie sat down, and the rest of us followed her lead.

Christian spoke first. "Isn't it better to have this conversation with just the three of us?" He indicated himself, my mother, and me.

"At this point, I don't think it would make any difference," I said. "Besides, Persie already knows quite a bit about this case." My mother gasped. "Please tell us what my father said, because this doesn't make any sense."

"I don't know what to believe anymore," he replied with a frustrated huff. "I saw Nick at the hospital this morning. His colleagues are already investigating him about other cases he is involved in. When I pressed him, he told me that Melek's child was purchased and taken away by a couple passing through Ioannina. He claims that the man was an acquaintance of Ganas's, a singer, and had made all the arrangements with him. His name was—the man is dead now—Nikos Stefanou. He told me that the couple died in a car accident many years ago, somewhere near Delphi, and he lost all trace of the child after that."

Persie and my mother looked aghast. I, however, was certain my father's twisted mind had dreamt it all up. "I don't believe a word of it," I said. "He knew I was in Galaxidi, and he made sure to find out some details about Persie's past life. Now he is muddying the waters once again, trying to hide the truth. He will not give up, and wants to make our lives as hard as possible."

I turned to my mother, waiting for her to agree with what I was saying. She just looked at me with eyes wide with fear. "Constantine, maybe he didn't lie. Remember what I told you yesterday about *the singer* ... It might be him. There was a *rebetiko* singer in Ioannina at that time. I didn't make the connection until now ...". She turned and looked Persie up and down. "The moment I saw you, I thought it was *her* ... You look so much like her ..."

Persie looked pale, lost, her eyes flitting between me, Christian, and my mother. She tried to speak, but her voice refused to obey her. "P-Please ..." she stammered. "Tell me what's going on. Is this some kind of sick joke?" She looked ready to burst into tears, and my heart ached for her.

"Persie, I swear this is not a joke," I said. "Please be patient until we can figure out what's going on." Turning to Christian, I added, "This is the first time I'm hearing any of this. Let me see if I got this right: are you telling us that, based on what my father said, Melek's child is *Persie*?"

"I am not that child!" she shouted. "I know very well who my parents were, so stop this at once!"

Violet stroked her hand, trying to calm her down. "Darling, you know I would never lie to you. Everything I have heard just now, although I didn't follow most of it ... Well, I think I need to tell you something that might be related to what they are saying." She turned towards us. "If I understand correctly, this child was taken from a prostitute in Ioannina. Is this so?"

"Yes," I said.

"Years ago, when my grandmother was at death's door, she told me something that surprised me. I paid no heed to it then, thinking it was the ramblings of an old woman. She told me not to be friends with you, Persie, because you were not the daughter of the people who were raising you, but had been born in a brothel in Ioannina. That they had snatched you. That's why they called you Persephone ... And that God punished your parents for what they did, killing them in the car accident. I had never planned on telling you any of this, but after everything I just heard ... Maybe she knew something after all."

I couldn't believe what I was hearing. If this were a movie, I would have laughed it off as preposterous. I was sure it was one of my father's satanic schemes to confound everyone, and that he was laughing with glee at the hospital this very moment. But what about Violet's story; how did that fit in with such a scenario?

Persie was staring at her friend, dumbstruck. A strange laugh escaped her lips, and she turned to look at the Acropolis. Christian, who had been watching everyone carefully all this time, evidently decided we were not lying to him, and spoke next. "We still need to clear up some things, as you can tell. What we must do first is check whether you are truly Melek's child. The resemblance is striking, but the only way to know for sure is for you to take a DNA test. I wish we could do it here, but it would be faster if you came to Paris ..."

"So, you are telling me that my real mother is a prostitute?" Persie said. "And that, based on what Constantine told me last night, she is in a coma as we speak?"

"That's right," Christian replied. "And if you agree to come to Paris with me, you will have a chance to meet the woman who gave birth to you before she passes away."

"And you initially thought Constantine, who I met a few days ago by chance, was the child you were looking for, but now it turns out that it's *me*?"

"I know it sounds entirely improbable, but the evidence and your striking resemblance seem to indicate this. If you come with me to Paris, we will all know for certain within the day. In case you don't know it already, you are to inherit a considerable fortune. There is also a personal letter she has left for you."

Persie shook her head, as if she did not believe a word. "I don't care about inheriting something that does not belong to me, and I'm not going anywhere. I just want you all to leave me alone!"

She pushed her chair back and ran off, disappearing into the narrow alleys of Plaka.

Violet stood up to follow her, but I held her back. I then rose and ran after Persie and, once I caught up with her, followed her, walking a few feet behind. I could see her pomegranate tattoo through the opening of her dress, and I remembered the story she had told me that evening in Galaxidi. I picked up my pace and fell into step beside her.

Persie looked at me with moist eyes, and I felt my heart break. The tears, ready to roll down her cheeks, were like tiny drops of sea. She looked ahead without a word and began to walk up the steps leading to the Acropolis. The cluster of small, low houses that lined the street belonged to an island, not the center of a busy city like Athens. Flowers bloomed everywhere, and the white washed yards looked like a postcard. It would all have been picturesque and beautiful, but Persie's sadness cast a shadow over everything.

Although I had my doubts about this latest version of events, I decided to stand by her. It would be a difficult time for her, watching everything she had known about her life come crashing down, especially given the warm, loving relationship she had enjoyed with the people who had raised her. She needed time to calm down and see how she would deal with it, as did I.

A group of Asian tourists walking in our direction forced us to step aside, as most held open parasols to shield them from the scorching sun. I took Persie's hand and held it as we watched them walk behind their tour guide. When the last tourist had passed us by, I looked at her and pointed to the shade of a small olive tree that had sprung inside the cleft of a large rock. "Come, let's stop here for a while," I said.

We sat down on the dark stone mass that protruded from the narrow pavement. We fell silent for a few moments. The passing tourists smiled at seeing us under the shade of the olive tree.

Persie broke the silence first. "Constantine, I felt as if my life changed when I met you, as if everything had suddenly become brighter. If you feel the same way, I need to you to tell me the truth. Did you know any of this before you met me?"

"I told you everything as I was finding it out. I'm as shocked as you are, and I still doubt you are the child. But I think everything happens for a reason. I really believe that."

"That night, when we sat by the shore in the woods, I mentioned something my mother told me shortly before the accident. Do you remember?"

"Of course I do. Not the exact words, but what she meant. That everyone has their own secrets, and that you would find out the secrets concerning your life when the time would be right."

"Precisely. Maybe this is the secret she meant."

"That's possible ... Look at all the secrets my parents had kept. It seems that neither one of us was raised by our biological parents."

"When I think of all these coincidences, I can't accept any of it is true. How can it be?"

I turned to face her. "Look, Persie. As I told you, I believe everything happens for a reason. Maybe that woman, if she really is your biological mother, did not reappear by chance just when you needed financial assistance the most. Maybe it was meant to be. If you are her daughter, you will inherit a large fortune and it will make your life easier. Maybe that's why it's all happening now, and not earlier. Maybe the common points in our past are what will now determine our future.

"Also, remember the man on Patmos who was there at the time? I don't know if Christian has had a chance to bring him up to date. Incredible as it may seem, everything is conspiring for the truth to be revealed in the lives of all three of us, at long last. The doctors in Paris are doing everything they can to keep Melek alive, and this may be your only chance to see the woman who gave birth to you while there is still some life left in her. There is something stronger than us out there, that we can't even begin to conceive of, but it seems to be showing us the way forward."

Persie looked at me, perplexed. "What do you suggest I do?"

"Agree to take the DNA test. You have nothing to lose. If you do not meet her now while she still lives, and it turns out that she *is* your biological mother, I can only imagine the guilt and regret you might feel later over the missed opportunity."

"But I don't feel anything for her!" Persie shouted. She took a deep breath, regained her composure, and continued. "I don't know what I want to do. But, if I decide to go, I want you to come with me. Otherwise, I won't do it."

Things were moving so fast that I was starting to think I was dreaming. It was as if the pace of my life had spiraled out of all control. I stood up and gently pulled her towards me. "I hear Paris is beautiful this time of year ... I always wanted to visit ..."

I bent my head towards her and kissed her tenderly. Our lips did not part until we heard the wolf whistles of a group of tourists taking our photo against the backdrop of the Acropolis.

Inexplicably, I thought of the *rebetiko* song that not only my mother had been humming this morning, but that Persie had also sung in Galaxidi ...

Kostas Krommydas

# Paris

---

I did not have to try hard to convince Persie to make the trip to Paris. Besides, the way fate had intertwined our lives, all we could do was wait for the outcome of this unpredictable series of events that had turned our lives upside down. Both of us, for entirely different reasons, wanted this story to be over and done with, so we could carry on with our lives once the mystery was solved. The revelations we had been subjected to surpassed anything we could have ever imagined. At present, all I could believe was that destiny had set the pawns on a chessboard as it wished, so that not only the snatched child would be found, but also so that Persie and I would meet. As far as I was concerned, our paths crossing was what mattered the most. Things now magically seemed to slot into place, rectifying the injustices of the past.

My father left the hospital and was immediately taken to the police station to answer a host of other accusations. Things looked bleak for him, although I still feared he would dream up some new scheme that would allow him to get away with it all. Ganas, my father's accomplice, was still in the hospital in Ioannina in a critical condition.

Christian had asked my mother and I if we wanted him to take what he knew about our case to the police. We thought it best not to bring anything to light yet, and wait and see how the other investigations into my father progressed. I wanted my father to rot in jail, but I did not truly wish to be the cause.

My mother stayed in Athens at my house while Persie and I travelled to Paris, and I had asked Sophie to keep an eye on her. I think she needed to enjoy quiet solitude for a while, having been deprived of it for so many years beside my father.

The only missing piece of the puzzle was Michael, Melek's long-lost love; but even he, too, had now been found. We met up with him in Athens and, together with Christian and Violet, had all boarded the plane for Paris.

Michael had barely uttered a few sentences since meeting us. The tragic irony was that he had thought Melek dead all these years. He stared out of the plane's window absent-mindedly, and only spoke when someone spoke to him. Persie sat beside him; the two had spoken a little at the airport. He had been startled by her resemblance to Melek when he had seen her. We could see him struggle to contain how overwhelmed he must be feeling right now.

Persie occasionally would take Michael's hand in hers, trying to comfort him. Christian had filled him in on all the recent developments. The thing that seemed to impact Michael the most was the fact that his old love was still alive, and that Persie was probably the child that had been violently snatched from her.

We traveled business class, and a limo was waiting for us at the airport. I was impressed by how much money was being spent on us, but we had agreed not to jump ahead of ourselves until we got the results. We would be driving straight to the hospital, where Persie and Michael would say goodbye to the person who had indelibly marked their lives.

Melek's immobile body lay on a bed in the middle of the hospital room. Cables linked her body to countless machines, and the robotic sounds filled the room while screens flickered around her. An oxygen mask covered her face.

A nurse entered the room, followed by Persie and Michael accompanied by a doctor. They were wearing scrubs and masks, and they carefully approached the bed. Persie appeared the most shocked at the sight of the woman's weak, skeletal body. She had refused to heed the advice of the doctor to cancel her visit, and had decided to go with Michael and see the woman who appeared to be her mother by all accounts. Christian had chosen not to join them, and stayed behind with Constantine and Violet.

Persie had just given a DNA sample, and even now remained convinced that results would show she was not the child they were looking for. Seeing Melek on her deathbed, all she could feel were waves of shock washing over her.

Michael walked to the other side of the bed and looked at Melek somewhat impassively. The only signs of life were the monotonous beeps of the life support machines. The doctor motioned for Persie to come closer, explaining Melek's condition and what would follow, now that her legal representative had given his consent to take her off life support.

When he was done his explanation, Michael asked the doctor in fluent French if he could stay alone with Melek for a moment. The doctor did no object, and opened the door, waiting for Persie to follow him outside.

She hesitated for a moment and stood there looking at Melek, as if trying to imagine growing inside the woman, to forge a connection before leaving her. Head bowed, she avoided looking at her face. Then, she cast a glance at Michael, who was rooted beside the bed, and followed the doctor, who closed the door behind them.

The machine sounds pierced Michael's body, as if suddenly louder. He leaned over Melek's pillow and pulled his mask aside, just enough to reveal his mouth. He stroked her hand, then gently grasped it. A few seconds later, he began to speak to her in a low voice, as if she could hear him.

"Not a day has passed that I did not think of you. If I had known you were alive, I would have come for you, but ..." His voice choked with emotion, and he could barely hold back his tears.

He took a deep breath. "I will never forget the nights we spent on our little island. I can still see the stars lighting our way, countless stars lighting the heavens just for you and me. I hope you kept my flower, that forget-me-not ... Remember? You swore to never forget me ... Forget-me-not, for we will meet again ..."

Michael started, and stared at her in shock; he could have sworn he'd felt her give his hand a faint squeeze. He desperately looked for a sign that what he had felt had been real, and not a figment of his imagination born of his desperate desire to communicate with her.

A faint tremble of her lips made him bow his head over hers, trying to hear something, anything. He put his ear close to her mouth, his senses sharp, desperate. With great difficulty, as if reaching out to him from some other dimension, he heard the faintest of whispers:

"Forget me not."

Before he could even tell if what he had heard had really been said, the sharp beep of the machines startled him, and he gently placed her lifeless hand on the bed. The doctor ran inside and went to the machines. Another two doctors arrived behind him, looking at Michael, who stood by her bedside, his arms hanging limply at his sides.

A tear trickled down his cheek and wet the corner of his mouth. Devastated, no longer caring, Michael knelt by the bed and brushed his tear-soaked lips against her hand.

I never left Persie's side for a minute, barring the few moments she had returned to the room to see the lifeless body of Melek. She needed some time to recover from what she had seen. She did not say much, clearly trying to banish the image from her mind.

Christian informed us that if Persie proved to be Melek's daughter, there would be a series of legal steps that would need to be taken so she could come into her inheritance. The lawyer had let us understand that Melek's fortune was sizeable. The following day Melek would be cremated, and we were invited to attend the small ceremony.

Persie and I went straight from the hospital to a restaurant that Christian had recommended, needing to be alone with each other. The lawyer had given us a folder containing old photos of Melek, and we looked at them as we sat at the bar. From the little Persie had said, I realized that the relentless disease must have sucked every last drop of vitality from Melek, who looked so vivacious in the photos.

Violet had stayed behind at the clinic to keep Christian company, and I suspected there was more to her interest than friendly concern. Michael had decided to go for a melancholy walk through the streets of Paris and revisit his own haunts. I think he needed time to grieve for the lost years in his own way. I had been deeply moved by the fact that Melek had drawn her last breath when just the two of

them were in the room. As if she had been waiting for him
...

All the large windows in the breezy restaurant were
thrown wide open. Everyone was enjoying the balmy
evening, with drinks in hand and a lively jazz band in the
corner. The name of the restaurant was yet another
coincidence: *Déjà vu*. Not that I felt as if I had lived through
anything similar in another lifetime, of course. It was just
that all the striking coincidences recently had led me to
believe that only some unfulfilled karmic force could be
shaping the flow of these events.

A pleasant scent of baked cinnamon filled the air, though I
was unable to detect the source. Christian's insistence that
we come here was more than justified. The friendly
atmosphere was exactly what we needed after such a taxing
day. Persie, visibly moved, was looking at one of the photos.
Her resemblance to Melek was striking, particularly the
shape and color of her eyes.

The barman approached and held out a platter of finger
food, as if trying to find somewhere to set it down. He held
two shot glasses in the other hand, which he placed
between us. He only spoke French, and we had struggled to
order food. The big platter looked delicious, and we
thanked him. He took away our empty wine glasses and
asked if we wanted another round of the white wine he had
recommended. We nodded.

As he walked away, Persie and I picked up our shot glasses,
exchanged a longing look, and emptied them. I instantly felt
the sweet flavor of cinnamon pleasantly tickle my palate. So

this was what had filled the room with the aroma of cinnamon. As if we wanted to share flavors, we pulled closer and kissed.

We were anxiously waiting for Christian to call us back with the test results. It was a phone call that could change our lives forever, yet we drank on, refusing to let our future hang on our phones. In the meantime, Violet was supposed to call us if anything else came up, but we no longer cared— we had each other.

I slowly twirled my bar stool in Persie's direction and touched her face, gently stroking her neck. I could not get enough of her beautiful eyes.

"I want to ask you something," I said, as she leaned in and gave me another sweet kiss. Without waiting for her reply, I continued. "I want you to tell me what you are thinking of doing if you prove to be Melek's daughter ... How do you see your life after this?"

Persie smiled, detecting the real fear behind my words. "All I can tell you right now is that I want you in my life no matter what ... If it were not for my debts, I might not be here today. I am fascinated by Michael and Melek's love, however, that it lasted for so many years. Even when they thought each other dead, they carried on living in the shadow of their passionate relationship. It's no coincidence she chose to pass away the moment Michael said goodbye to her."

Yet again, she had left me speechless. "I am awestruck by it too. A relationship that includes you, don't forget that!" I said, and felt that a similar love was being born between us.

Casting another glance at the photo, Persie said, "Honestly, even though we look so alike, I still think I'm not the one they are looking for."

"We'll know that shortly ..."

We paused as the barman brought two glasses of white wine. I felt the tiny droplets of humidity outside the glass wet my fingertips as I picked it up. We clinked glasses, and I took a gulp. I did not know much about the wine, but this one had a refreshing taste.

"How do you imagine your life after ...?" she said, returning my question.

I laughed at her cheekiness. "I think our vision of the future is very similar," I said, and grinned as I pulled her closer.

The sound of her phone interrupted us. Christian's name flashed on her screen, announcing the changes his call would bring. She picked it up and fell silent, agreeing with whatever he was saying. She hung up and looked at me. I felt my heart racing.

"He told me that they have finished with the tests and he is expecting us at the clinic to give us the results ..."

"So, is it you?" I asked.

"He said he would tell us when we arrived."

Although I was dying to find out now, I decided not to rush. "I suggest we enjoy our last carefree moments before our lives take a different path ..."

"Whatever the path, the destination for me remains the same," she said, bringing her glass against mine and gazing at me with her stunning eyes ...

*Standing on a boat in the middle of the sea, a woman with bright auburn hair gazes at the horizon, where the sun is slowly dipping into the water. She wears a white wedding dress that billows in the strong gusts of wind, fluttering behind her like creamy wings of lace. The strands of hair escaping her veil also sway in the sea breeze. Their color is unnaturally red, the color of ripe roses.*

*Michael is slowly swimming towards her, but she seems unaware of his presence. He is trying to reach the boat, but she is drifting along on the sea current. He is using all his strength, struggling against the rising waves to reach her. He opens his mouth to call her name, but the water gushes in, choking him every time he tries to make a sound.*

*The boat keeps drifting farther and farther away, no matter how fast his strokes. He seems stuck on the spot, as if bound by an invisible hand. A loud, animalistic sound escapes his lips in a last effort to catch her attention.*

*Her boat, as if halted by his cry, stands still and the wind suddenly drops. The veil drops from her hair like a stone. All he can hear is the sound of his breathing, nothing else. Slowly, the wooden boat begins to turn towards him, and her face is revealed. Melek, her eyes dark. He is unable to tell if they are open or shut. She is holding a baby, its face scrunched up as if it is crying, though no sound comes. Between her legs, the wedding dress is bright red with blood, which drips down into the boat.*

*Summoning his remaining strength, he makes one last effort to swim towards her, and a loud, piercing scream tears from his lungs. The blood soaks the boat and drips into the sea.*

*He can hear someone calling him, over and over, and a hand grabs his shoulder and pulls him down beneath the surface, steals his breath as he begins to sink in the crimson veils that have enfolded the sea ...*

Michael opened his eyes, breathing heavily and drenched in sweat. He rose from his bed unsteadily, still trying to get his bearings. The dim light pouring in from the half-drawn drapes pulled him to the window like a magnet. He tugged them open and remembered that he was in Paris.

The nightmare still haunted him. He pushed the window open to let the fresh air in. The glittering lights spreading beneath his balcony fully justified Paris's reputation as the city of light.

Michael had not looked up any of the old friends who had once helped him. He was thinking how he would not be here if it were not for his random meeting with Anna, how he would never have had the opportunity to say goodbye to the woman he had loved so much.

This was the second time he was mourning her loss; yet his feelings, the true love they had shared, had remained unaltered by the passage of time. After so many years, however, he felt that a huge chapter of his life was now closing.

Gazing at the city, Michael pondered the tragic irony that both he and Melek had been in this city at the same time, but had been unaware of each other's existence. Fate had not been generous with them, had not arranged some random meeting back then. His only consolation was that her child still lived, and that she had grown up to be such a wonderful person. He did not intend to ask Persie to investigate his paternity. Not because he did not want to know, but because he was terrified that she might not be his daughter.

The soft breeze ruffled his long hair, and he moved closer to the edge of the balcony. A wide avenue separated his hotel from the large river that crossed the city center. He climbed onto the marble ledge and slowly sat down, his feet dangling over the void. His turmoil mingling with the strong sensations of the dream made him close his eyes and turn his face to the sky.

Just below, some passersby noticed him and stopped in their tracks, trying to fathom his intentions. Ignoring the rising noise, Michael opened his eyes and watched the blurry dots that were the stars bereft of their glimmer, snatched by the city lights. A feeling of completeness rose up inside him and pushed him to open his arms wide, as if expecting the force that reigned from the heavens above to sweep him into its arms and carry him away.

All was dark and quiet at Constantine's family home. Only Nick's loud snores echoed from the bedroom down the hall. The following day would be a difficult one. He had to return to the station and make a statement about all the illegal activities he had committed for years. His breakdown, the news that he had been taken to the hospital injured and drunk, had been the final straw for his superiors. In a domino effect, his misdeeds began to come to light one by one.

Despite all this, Nick slept soundly. He still held onto the belief that his friends would once again spread a veil of protection around him. He was wrong—everyone was trying to distance themselves from a man who seemed to be collapsing, afraid that he would take them down with him.

His snoring was broken up by the faint sound of a key turning in the lock. A small sidelamp timidly lit the living room. Slowly and carefully, Anna stepped inside the house and soundlessly closed the door behind her. She paused, listening to the snoring. Once she was certain Nick was fast asleep, she began to creep towards the bedroom.

The air was stale with cigarette smoke and the faint whiff of alcohol. In the twilight, she saw him lying on his stomach in bed, head turned to one side, relentlessly, rhythmically emitting the annoying sound that made his lips shake. His clothes and gun belt were carelessly flung on an armchair in the corner.

Anna slowly pulled out his gun and held it. She turned the ceiling light on and sat on the edge of the bed, hiding the gun behind her back and waiting for him to wake up. Nothing seemed to disturb his deep slumber, so she punched his leg.

Nick jumped up in fright. Shielding his eyes with one hand, he stared at her as if she were a ghost. "What ... What are you doing here?" he gasped.

Anna stared at him intently without saying a word. He tried to push himself off the bed, cursing her loudly. She swiveled her burnt arm around and pointed the gun at him. He froze to the spot, then slowly leaned back against his pillow, wiping the saliva from his chin.

"Remember how you taught me how to shoot, and I said I'd never need to so what's the point?" Without waiting for his answer, she ploughed on determinedly. "Guess you now get to find out what a good teacher you were."

She raised the gun and aimed straight between his eyes. Nick tried to appear calm, and failed. He lifted a shaky arm in front of his eyes, desperately trying to shield himself from the gun. "It's not funny ... Stop it! Why are you doing this?"

Anna burst out laughing. "I have a million reasons to pull the trigger, so don't act like you don't understand. You'd better try to find *one* reason why I shouldn't."

Stunned, he seemed unable to think of an answer, still trying to shield his face like a frightened, trapped animal. Seeing him like this, Anna spoke with even more confidence. "As you seem unable to think of something, I will give you a reason why I should not blow your filthy face away. I will be clear, and I hope we will understand one another. Agreed?"

Nick nodded without a word.

"If you ever bother me or Constantine again—if you even *think* about bothering us again—I will sneak back in here, and you won't even have time to hear the gunshot. I know what you are thinking right now, so let me tell you that if anything strange happens to me, all your crimes will be made public and you will rot in jail. You are the one who told me what a good time corrupt cops have in jail, remember? Let me remind you of the photos and documents you asked me to burn in Thessaloniki all those years ago. Let me inform you they are still in good condition, waiting to reach the right hands if anything happens to me or Constantine."

Nick seemed to have lost the power of speech. He made to move towards her, but she motioned for him to stay still. She moved closer to him and pressed the barrel of the gun inside his mouth. He trembled violently as the metal scraped against his teeth. His eyes bulged with terror.

His torment did not last long—Anna suddenly pulled back the gun and backed away, flinging the gun onto the bed.

"The choice is yours," she said. "Just stay out of our lives."

He lunged for the gun and held it for a moment, trying to decide what to do. She had already walked out of the bedroom; should he follow? But he simply stayed on the bed, unable to react. He now knew she had kept information that could tie him to a serious crime in Thessaloniki many years ago: a woman's rape and disappearance.

The sound of the front door closing brought him back to reality. She had left. Still stunned, he tried to reconcile the fearless woman who had just threatened him with the terrified creature he had dominated for so many years. He threw the gun back on the bed and held his head in despair. His now ex-wife's message had been well and truly received.

On the shores of Lake Ioannina, Violet, Theo, and Christian stood in a huddle. Persie, Michael, my mother, and I sat in a boat sailing towards the island of Ali Pasha. Michael had deferred his return to Patmos to be present at this final farewell to his beloved.

We had returned from Paris two days previously and, following the final instructions Melek had left in her will, had all decided to come here and scatter her ashes. Although I had been here before, many years ago, I had never crossed the lake. According to Michael, this was the route the two would take back then, when they lived their love in secret.

When Christian had initially contacted him, Michael had thought it was all a distasteful joke. I could not imagine how he must have felt when he found out that the woman he had loved more than any other had actually survived the fire she herself had set. It must have been harder for him, because, thinking Melek dead all these years, he had not looked for her. When he learned that they had both been in Paris at the same time in the years that had followed the fire, he had nearly collapsed. It was heartbreaking to think of them both in the same city, at the same time, both mourning the other's death. Now, it must be painful for him to be here and relive the nightmare of his attempted drowning and escape.

Michael had told us his side of the story the previous night and, despite knowing some of it already, we had been engrossed. He showed no hatred towards the two people responsible for that tragedy. I was impressed by how serene his face looked despite the turmoil that must have been ravaging his soul. Aside from a few moments when his voice cracked, it was hard to discern what he was feeling. His stay at the monastery of Patmos for so many years had helped him find that inner peace we were all looking for.

Michael and Persie had been inseparable since our arrival in Greece, and I was trying to let them enjoy this otherwise tragic meeting. Persie, upon finding out that she was indeed Melek's child, had broken down, trying to understand why her parents had told her nothing about her adoption. I tried to ease her distress by telling her that they surely would have done it when she was old enough to understand. Besides, that must have been what her mother had meant when she had spoken of secrets to be revealed at the right time.

We had spent two days in Paris, and would soon have to return to finalize the paperwork that would give Persie access to the large fortune Melek had bequeathed her. During our short stay there, Christian had taken us to the house just outside the city center where Melek had spent her final years. We attended the formal reading of the will, and Persie had received the letter Melek had written for her child. Melek had stressed that she wished for the letter to be read here, at the place of her child's birth, but Persie had not opened it yet. She intended to do it immediately after we scattered Melek's ashes.

From the moment we had left for Paris I had let anything else drop by the wayside, and all I now wanted was for this whirlwind of revelations to be over. Provided nothing else was waiting in the dark for us …

The local helmsman brought us to the middle of the lake and we all fell into an uncomfortable silence, unsure of what to say or do. The weather was good, and the sun lit up the clear atmosphere. The fresh, green color of the trees on the island reflected on the surface of the lake, blending in with the cloudless sky in a cornucopia of blue-green shades. Under other circumstances I would have brought my camera along and captured these incredible images, but the occasion did not allow this.

As soon as the helmsman silenced the engine, we knew the time had come. Persie left her seat beside me and moved to where Michael was sitting. He opened a box and removed the porcelain urn holding Melek's ashes. He tenderly held it in his arms as Persie carefully removed the lid. They exchanged a look, and we all stood up. In a few seconds this woman's life journey would formally come to an end, a journey that had begun in the depths of Turkey, and ending here today. Everything happened without a word, as if we had all secretly vowed to stay silent.

The two of them leaned over the edge of the boat towards the water and slowly upturned the urn. Its contents flowed to the surface of the water and the soft breeze scattered the ashes, creating a small cloud that quickly began to settle over the tranquil lake.

When all the ashes had been scattered, Michael ceremoniously dunked the urn into the water and rinsed it out with calm, assured movements. He hugged Persie, and she returned to my side. My mother moved closer to Michael and they held hands, exchanging an emotional glance. With this modest and silent ritual, we bid Melek goodbye as she reached her final resting place.

"Now something of her will always live on in the lake she loved so much," said Persie, looking up at me with moist eyes.

I hugged her shoulders without a word. I felt no words were enough to express what I was feeling, so I chose to stay silent. Our helmsman, realizing our purpose was done, set sail for the small island. We would take a walk there and give Persie some time to read her mother's letter alone. I pulled her closer, and she buried her head in my shoulder. She was so vulnerable at this moment and I tried to give her strength.

We arrived shortly, and moved through the reeds towards a tiny pier. We all stepped off the boat and left the helmsman there to wait for our return. Persie and I moved ahead. I intended to leave her alone to read the letter she was already holding in her hands, ready to open.

"I'll go back to join the others and we'll wait for you ... Are you sure you don't want me to stay with you?"

"We'd better follow her exact wishes," Persie replied, and gently touched my lips as she turned to walk towards a small stone dock looking onto the city of Ioannina across the lake.

In the distance, small boats had begun ferrying the tourists away from the pretty island. I watched Persie as she walked away, and had a strange feeling that something was still incomplete, some detail that remained elusive. Although everything seemed to be falling into place, something inside me could not find closure. I paid no more heed to my feelings and turned to leave. Just before losing sight of her, I saw her sit on a large rock and slowly unfold the letter ...

As soon as we returned from the lake, we all made our way to the hotel. When we arrived, Persie insisted we go somewhere just the two of us, and I immediately accepted. Although Violet and Christian wanted to follow us, they realized we wanted to be alone, so they arranged to go somewhere for a drink. My mother would grab a bite at the hotel with Michael, and then they had arranged to go for a walk in the town, which may have changed but surely still held many memories for them. The following morning we would all return to Athens, and then Persie would be preoccupied with all the legal matters that awaited her attention.

Persie came out of the lift, and we made our goodbyes to the others before stepping onto the main street that led to the town square. She seemed to be going through some kind of internal conflict, but I could not tell the reason.

It was getting dark, but people still milled around the shops, making us start and stop along the way. We passed in front of the large town clock just as it struck the hour. A little farther down the street, we took a turn down a narrow alley towards the lake. I asked Persie if everything was okay, and she replied that she was fine. Her eyes were still moist, and I realized she was still preoccupied with the contents of the letter.

Once again, we reached the shores of the lake that now seemed to dominate our existence, too. The streetlights were coming on, and many people were taking an afternoon stroll or having a late coffee at one of the many shops lining the lake. Persie still looked troubled, but I did not want to press her. It was a delicate matter, and I thought she should be the one deciding how to handle it.

We reached the calm waterfront and stopped beside the statue of a woman overlooking the lake. Her name was carved on the stone pedestal: *Kyra Frosini*. Behind us stood a café, its wooden sign bearing the same name. Persie observed the marble face of the woman for a while, then turned to look in the same direction.

"Do you know her story?" she asked me, glancing at the statue once again.

"I know the Turks drowned her here, but I don't know why ..."

"There are many versions, but the most prevalent one is that Ali Pasha did it because he was jealous that she was his son's lover. It must be a terrible death, drowning ..." A frightened shadow flitted across her eyes. "They say that the Turks drowned many other women that day with her, because they were allegedly immoral ..."

She gave me a loaded glance as she spoke the last word, obviously trying to link Kyra Frosini's story to ours. I walked behind her and hugged her, our faces turned towards the lake. She backed into me, and we stood gazing at the lights twinkling on the dark surface and the boats skidding across the lake. The dark waters were both frightening and beguiling, the mystery they exuded in no way resembling the calm allure of the sea. I felt her strong arms pull me even closer. We stood like this, silently, looking at the liquid darkness. Eventually, she spoke in a soft voice, without turning to look at me.

"Do you think the water can record everything? The feelings, the pain so many people experience beside it, on its surface, in its depths? Does a part of them still survive in the lake, something we just can't perceive? I wonder if its composition changes when such strong emotions are at play ..."

Although I sensed those were just rhetorical questions, I decided to share my own views. "Water is a source of life, so it can't remain unaffected by everything that happens ... especially when the emotional charge is great ... like death, or hatred, or love—"

"I wonder if it will feel what I am about to tell you ..." she interrupted. "Will you marry me?"

I thought I had misheard, and said nothing, taken aback. If she had said what I had just heard, then she must be joking. Persie, however, continued. "Shall I take your silence as a refusal?"

I was speechless. Her posture, the tone of her voice, showed that she was serious. "What do you mean? Are you actually proposing to me?" I asked her, confused.

"I know it's rather unusual, but yes, I am asking you to marry me. Soon ..." She paused, and then giggled. "Don't forget I now have a large dowry ..."

Persie laughed, and I laughed along with her. When our laughter subsided, and we caught our breath, she startled me once again by suddenly turning serious. She turned around and looked deeply into my eyes. "Constantine, I'm not joking. I'll understand if you decline, but I mean it when I say I want to marry you ..."

I could now clearly see that this was no joke. I replied without wasting a moment. "If you really mean it, as you say, then it will have to be done properly, otherwise I will refuse ..."

It was Persie's turn to give me a puzzled frown. I looked around quickly. "Can you wait here a moment?"

"I can, but if you are planning to run away, you'd better tell me now. It'd be a shame for me to spend the rest of my life waiting by a lake," she said with a smile.

"No, I will be right back, and things will happen as they should," I replied, and gave her a quick kiss.

I ran towards the shops that lined the street behind us, trying to find a shop that had caught my eye on the way here. I slalomed among the small tables lining the square until I spotted the jewelry store. It was closed.

Then I spotted a souvenir shop, its counters loaded with lake memorabilia. I ran towards it in the hope of finding something that would suit my purpose. The shop assistant let out a startled cry as I dashed inside. She smiled when she realized I was a customer and not there to rob her.

"Hello," I said, examining the merchandise around me.

Paintings and posters hung from the walls and countless knick-knacks filled the shelves, but nothing resembling what I was looking for. The faces of Ali Pasha and Kyra Frosini dominated most of the paintings.

"Do you have any rings?" I asked, and she looked even more surprised.

"Not much, and certainly not men's jewelry," she replied.

"It's for a woman."

She pulled out a small drawer from a display case and placed it on the counter before me. I looked at the rings and felt my heart sink. Some looked childish, and none were remotely suitable.

"What exactly are you looking for?" she asked, seeing my disappointment.

What could I say, and would she even believe me? At this point I had no choice, so I summoned my courage and said, "I want a ring for a marriage proposal ..."

A tortuous silence ensued. Overcoming her surprise and realizing that I was not joking, she awkwardly said, "No, I'm sorry, I have nothing like that ... You can visit the jewelry store next door tomorrow when it opens."

"I need it right now ... I don't have any time," I said. Disappointed, I turned to leave.

Her voice stopped me just before I stepped out. "Hold on a moment ... I have something else, although I'm not sure it's entirely suitable."

I turned to see her climb on a wobbly stool and pull down a large box from the top of a tall display case. She carefully placed it on the counter and dusted off a layer of dust with an apologetic look. She took a small pouch from inside the box, opened it, and pulled out something wrapped in tissue paper.

"I don't know if this will do. I had stored it away because no one was interested. It's silver, so it's more expensive than the other merchandise."

I did not have a lot of money on me, but I was sure we could work something out if I liked it. She unwrapped the ring and placed it on the glass countertop. I could not tell what the ring represented, but when I picked it up, I saw the body of a dancer, wrapping her arms and legs like tree branches around a small flower in the center of the ring. It was not what I had imagined, but the more I looked at it the more I succumbed to its unique appeal. Having no more time to lose, I looked at the price tag. I pulled out my wallet and counted my cash. The shop did not take credit cards.

"You want it?" the shop assistant asked.

"Yes, it's just I'm a bit short on cash and it says you don't take credit cards."

She looked at the paper bills I'd left on the counter. "This is fine, I'll give you a discount. Besides, it's a pre-crisis tag. Give me a moment to wrap it up properly. I gather it's going to its destination immediately," she added with a smile.

She must have been impressed I was proposing so spontaneously, and was trying to help as best she could. In a few minutes, I ran out of the shop and back towards the shore, tightly gripping the box in my hand.

I found Persie exactly where I had left her, dreamily gazing at the lake. As soon as I was near enough, I asked her to turn towards me. Out of breath as I was, the words came haltingly out of my mouth. Persie covered her mouth in surprise. I got down on one knee and proffered the box.

"Persie, I have thought long and hard ..." I began.

We stared at each other for a moment, then both burst out laughing, attracting the stares of passersby.

Trying to overcome my awkwardness, I started over. "Persie, I love you. Will you marry me?"

She pulled me upright and snuggled against me. Flipping open the box, she took the ring out and held it up to catch the light of a nearby street lamp. "It's very pretty ... Where did you find it?"

"I've been looking for months," I joked.

We laughed as carefree as children unwrapping their Christmas gifts. She slowly pulled the ring on her finger. Then she brought it up between our lips that were only a breath apart, inhaled slowly, and looked at it for a few seconds. "Yes, yes I will ... On one condition," she whispered.

I was surprised, and waited anxiously for her to continue.

"Whatever may happen to us, never forget me ..."

The boat had just arrived at the port of Kea and was unloading cars and passengers who had arrived to spend their August vacation on the island. Violet disembarked on foot and scanned the passing cars, waiting for someone. A small car pulled up in front of her amidst a cacophony of crowds and honks. She opened the passenger door and stepped inside.

Christian smiled at her as he drove them along the dock, passing fishing boats and sailing boats that had dropped anchor there. It was the peak of the summer season and the island was packed. Even as they sat stuck in traffic, both looked happy, and exchanged longing glances.

A mutual attraction had sprung up between them from the moment they had met. When the case was closed and Persie was proven to be Melek's child, Christian had returned to Greece mainly to see Violet again. It did not take long for the two to become close, and they had been together now for about a month.

They'd decided to travel to Kea, Christian's favorite island, for a few days, leaving the others behind. Besides, he really wanted to build a house here, and would be combining their holiday with a visit to the plot of land that belonged to him. Moreover, he would research permits and everything else that was required. His view of life had changed, and he was determined to make all his dreams come true. He decided to work less and spend more time doing things that pleased him. What he wanted most was to have a family.

Even though they had not known each other long, he could tell how well-suited they were. Violet had left her bookshop in the capable hands of a friend and had come running when he'd called. Seeing the speed at which Constantine and Persie's relationship had progressed, they felt emboldened, ready to seize the day. They both had enough life experience under their belts, and now sought the same things.

"It will take ages to get out of here," Christian said, looking at the traffic up ahead. "How about I park the car and we go for a walk by the port, grab a bite, and then go to the hotel?"

"Good idea," Violet replied, and tenderly touched his hand.

They left the car and strolled along the port arm-in-arm. The music from the tavernas and bars reached their ears in a strange jumble. The crowds, the children running around happily, all created a festive atmosphere. Christian looked around curiously, trying to remember details from his last visit.

"What do you think of it after all these years? It must be very different now," Violet said, guessing his thoughts.

"If I did not know where we are, I'd think we were on a different island," he said, still looking around, impressed.

She was leaning against him, and he kept his arm protectively around her shoulders as they ambled along. This was what they had both been searching for: the carefree and tranquil life of people who don't constantly need to be on the go to stave off boredom.

Violet noticed a group of people hovering around a shop. They moved in that direction and, as soon as she saw it was a bookshop, she smiled and looked at him. "Do you mind if we go there for a bit?" she asked, despite knowing he would not refuse her.

Christian nodded agreeably, and they walked toward it. The sign above the door was decorated with a painted cat.

"I'd buy a book, but I don't think I'll have much time for reading," she said, giving Christian a look full of meaning.

He tried and failed to keep a poker face. "Yes ... no time for reading," he replied, and tenderly kissed her neck.

They watched the people waiting in line to get their books signed. "It's some kind of book signing," Violet said, curiously examining the large poster in the window.

"I think you need a vacation ..."

Christian pulled her away towards the small beach across from the bookshop. She smiled and did not object, casting a last look towards the people and the books in their hands. They sat on an old wooden boat and looked at the sea.

"We used to come here often when I was a child," Christian said. "Back then, there were barely ten boats at the port. My grandmother liked to be close to people. She was afraid of secluded beaches, because my mother had almost drowned on a secluded beach once when the weather suddenly turned bad. Before I was born, of course ..."

Violet leaned against him and he stroked her hair. They sat still, eyes fixed on the ferry exiting the port, people crowding its deck. The summer was over for most of them.

"Do you know what my fondest memory from the island is; one I will never forget?"

She turned and looked at him, all ears.

"I had one of the most breathtaking experiences of my life the day of my grandmother's funeral. Our house was up on that hill." He pointed at the hill rising behind them. "It is some distance to the church and the graveyard, but they carried the dead by hand back then, not by car."

The sudden round of applause and the noise coming from the bookshop forced them to turn their attention elsewhere for the moment.

"Please, don't stop," she urged him.

"As the funeral procession moved along the hill, people who lived there would step up and take the coffin. When they reached another neighborhood, the people who lived there would come out and take over, to honor the dead and allow the others to rest. This kept happening until the final destination, the coffin changing hands along the way, everyone sharing its weight. I can still hear the women's laments. In this way, it was as if the whole hill was accompanying one of their own on her last journey. I don't know if they still do that, but I will never forget it."

Violet, moved by the story she had just heard, said nothing as she turned his words into images in her mind's eye.

"So, do you know what I want right now?" Christian asked after a prolonged silence. Before Violet could reply, his enthusiasm got the better of him and he said, "I want us to go to a small taverna I've heard great things about. It's by the sea, and I think you'll like it. I don't remember its name, but I have directions. Let's go find it. What do you say?"

"Sure! I'm starving," Violet said, and jumped down onto the sand.

He followed suit and they found themselves face to face, the waves lapping their feet. They moved closer and their lips met for a few seconds, then reluctantly parted as they turned to walk back to the car. They passed by the bookshop before vanishing into the dark alleys. The voice of the writer could be faintly heard behind them, bringing his presentation to a close:

*No love can lift you as high as a love led by instinct ...*

Kostas Krommydas

# Two months later

Boats were everywhere I looked, either just arriving or having dropped anchor around the island of St. George in Galaxidi as guests approached from every accessible point. Everyone was smartly dressed and walked towards us as we waited for Persie to arrive at the church accompanied by her own friends. My mother smiled and greeted everyone, mostly friends and acquaintances.

The afternoon sun was slowly making its descent behind the tall mountains. A few scattered clouds did not threaten to spoil what we had spent three days setting up. When we had first arrived here in early summer, everything had been lushly green. The hot days that had followed had changed nature's palette, giving the island a different kind of beauty.

Ever since we had received permission to hold the wedding ceremony here, we had done all we could to further beautify the already charming island. The two small chapels now looked entirely renovated after our intervention.

Barely four months had passed since the fateful evening when I had first set eyes on Persie as she danced on stage; and, now, we were getting married. The day we had scattered Melek's ashes on the lake, Persie had read the letter her birth mother had left her. The envelope Christian had given her contained the French hand-written letter and the translation necessary for Persie to be able to read it. I never learned what the letter had said. I never asked, and she had never volunteered any information.

When we walked by the shores of the lake that same day and she asked me to marry her, I realized that the unexpected proposal must have been due to the contents of that letter. I must have been one of the few men to receive a marriage proposal from a woman, especially after so brief a relationship. My instinct told me there was more, things Persie had never spoken about. Whatever may have pushed her to pose the question, however, here we now were, about to get married.

Peter and another priest behind me were making the final preparations for the ceremony, which would take place at the entrance of the small church. Michael had suggested that the monk—who had been his spiritual guide and friend all these years—officiate the ceremony, and we had gladly accepted the offer. So, Peter had accompanied Michael from Patmos. Besides, as Michael told us, Peter's wish for Michael to visit his sick sister that fated morning at the hospital had been the cause of his meeting with my mother. Persie had asked Michael to walk her to the altar that day, wanting to show him that she now considered him her family. I wondered whether there had been something in Melek's letter that had encouraged her to give him the role of father.

After the story of Persie's true parentage leaked to the press, we had spent the whole summer avoiding journalists. The magazine containing our photo shoot in Galaxidi sold out three times over. Luckily, we escaped most of the uproar by spending more than a month in Paris as we settled all the legal matters surrounding Persie's inheritance. Red tape kept us in Athens for the rest of the summer. We had found a pretty house in Plaka about a month ago, and lived there now. My mother kept my old apartment, which was nearby.

My mother seemed stronger than ever. I was impressed my father had not bothered us. Perhaps he was busy with his own legal troubles. We agreed with Christian not to give anyone the details of his actions with Ganas. The latter would be spending the rest of his life in a nursing home, unlikely to ever recover fully from his stroke. He could not even feed himself anymore, and was by all accounts in a pitiful state. His daughter had moved to Australia to be with her mother. I couldn't think of a worse punishment than what had befallen Ganas. It seemed that fate had decided the punishment that would befit those two.

Persie did not seem to object to our decision to keep a distance from both of them, and I think Michael and their frequent conversations had gently pushed her in that direction. When he had arrived three days ago, he had asked for permission to bring a special guest to the wedding. We accepted, of course, though he had not yet revealed the surprise guest's identity.

Our family had grown even larger with the addition of the stray dog we had met in Galaxidi. Persie called him Pluto. I had just spotted him sniffing among the rocks, evidently looking for the wild rabbits that must be hiding in their burrows, alarmed by the noise. Today, Pluto would be the mascot of our wedding.

The more I got to know Persie, the more I realized that our decision to marry had been right. We could not get enough of each other and wanted to spend as much time alone together as possible.

The fortune Melek had left her daughter was sizeable, and I was still struggling to grasp its true scale. Persie settled all her debts and kept the house in France where her mother had spent her final years. Her ex, Steve, had reappeared asking for a loan to pay off his debts, but she did not give in, convinced that he was lying to her once again. I had never liked the man and all I asked of her was to be careful, especially now that she had refused him money. She told me after the meeting that she would rather the money go to a good cause than be wasted on Steve.

In a few days, the construction of a large building by the lake would begin in Ioannina, funded by Persie. It would house a hostel for abandoned or neglected children. It was the least she could do to honor the memory of the woman who had given birth to her. People in the city were glad, and were waiting for us to arrive for the inauguration of the construction.

Persie had also rented one of the largest theatres in Athens on a twenty-year lease, intending to renovate it and stage her own productions, as well as large productions from abroad. She wanted to start rehearsing a show based on *rebetiko* music, and was already in talks to acquire the rights to some of the songs. She had included her father's favorite song, the one she had sung that evening by the sea.

I had come to realize what a generous person she was during the few months we had been living together. Without ever appearing in a rush, she moved at amazing speed. "I want to make the most of every moment," she used to say, and I fully understood what she meant. What we had just been through had made both of us realize that life and the things we love should not be postponed for the future. *Better do something imperfectly than never do it at all,* was our motto.

Following that motto, we would become man and wife shortly. Christian and Violet would serve as best man and bridesmaid, and were due to arrive with Persie shortly. I knew there was something going on between them and I was glad, because I liked them both. They were well-suited. Now that I had gotten to know them better, I realized that their meeting was not accidental either ...

As prepared as I was for the wait before the ceremony began, I felt increasingly anxious as I watched for them across the water. We had not formally invited anyone to the wedding, announcing that anyone who wished to attend was welcome. As a result, half the town had arrived on the island, which I imagined was sinking under the weight of so many people. Countless friends had also arrived from Athens, booking out most of the hotels.

Sophie, a sardonic smile on her face, brought me my phone. *Ready?* read the text message Persie had just sent

I smiled and replied: *From the moment I laid eyes on you at the theatre ...*

The sound of boat engines made us all look up. A small flotilla of joy was coming in our direction, blasting its horns. I stepped closer to the shore to get a clearer view, and I spotted Persie standing at the prow of the first boat, like the commander of a fleet about to lead a raid on the tiny island. The closer she came, the more I realized how much I wanted her.

Her auburn hair streamed behind her, and she looked like an elf in her white wedding dress, floating in her small blue boat over the calm waters. I so wanted to take the camera from Sophie and take as many photos as I could, but I had given her and the other photographers precise instructions to take photos from many different angles. Countless phones rose in the air as the guests captured the moment with their own cameras, so that nothing would go unrecorded.

More than ten small and larger boats were sailing behind my beloved, loaded with guests. Her boat berthed at the makeshift pier and Michael jumped out first, carefully helping Persie onto dry land. I only had eyes for her. She looked at me, and suddenly it was as if we were the only two people in the world. Only when they were near me did I notice Michael by her side. The two of them were the prettiest sight I had seen in a long time. Theo stood beside them, wearing a quirky white suit, tailor-made just for our wedding.

When they reached the little church, I took Persie's hand and brought her closer. Before I could kiss her, she asked me once again with her offbeat sense of humor, "Have you seen any wild rabbits, or did they all swim away?"

I tried to stifle my laughter, and failed. I whispered, "I think Pluto has scared them so much they will never resurface ..."

Christian and Violet came and stood beside us, both looking very handsome. Persie was overjoyed to see her friend so happy after such a long time. We kissed to the sound of applause and cheers.

As the cheering died down, Persie and I turned to greet Michael. His eyes glistened in his calm and collected face. He stepped aside and gently ushered a woman forward, who seemed strangely familiar. "Allow me to introduce Renée ..." he said.

She looked like an actress whose movies I had watched some time ago, but how could it be? I then remembered a story Michael had told us about a famous actress who had donated an important manuscript to the monastery. It had to be her, but I could not understand how she had ended up here.

Persie noticed my surprise, and said, "That's how I felt, too, when I first met her. We'll tell you the full story later."

Impressed, I shook Renée's hand warmly, and turned back to Persie. Together, we walked towards the monk and the priest waiting under a white canopy for the ceremony to begin ... Beside them, as if he had been trained for this,

Pluto was standing on his hind legs, patiently waiting for our married life to begin ...

Lost in a blissful trance, I only came back down to earth when I heard the priest wish us congratulations and everyone cheer.

I was holding Persie's hand tightly and trying to convince myself I was not about to wake up from a beautiful dream. If someone asked me to define happiness, I would have said this moment, under the clear blue skies, surrounded by people who loved us and shared our joy. I did not even have time to kiss her once the ceremony was over, too lost in hugs and kisses as everyone rushed to congratulate us.

The sound of live music joined the happy chatter. It was one of Persie's surprises, and it lifted my mood to even greater heights. The sun was beginning to hide behind the mountain, and I knew we needed to hurry. Persie and I had agreed to take one of the small boats, so I could photograph her on my own against the backdrop of the small island and the sunset, just like I had the first time we had come here.

We smiled, posed for photos with our guests, and then decided to make a run for it. We asked everyone to make their way back to Galaxidi and the wedding reception waiting for them in the harbor. It was important to make it back before it got dark, for everyone's safety.

I took Sophie's camera and slung it over my shoulder. Then I lifted Persie in my arms and walked towards the boat as everyone cheered. I struggled to scoop up all the material of her dress, but managed in the end. My mother, ecstatic, never took her eyes off us. I winked at her and walked on. Violet, Christian, and Theo kept showering us with handfuls of rice as if they had brought endless supplies with them. I tried to shield Persie's face with my hand, and finally made it to the small boat.

I set her down inside and straightened her dress. Pluto ran up to us and barked, worried. "We are not leaving you behind, don't worry ..." I said, and patted his head before stepping into the boat.

Persie looked at his frantic state in surprise, then gunned the engine and we moved away from the wooden pier. Our guests called for us to look back so they could take more photos. We obeyed, striking a series of silly poses. Once we were some distance away, I asked Persie to keep going so she could be aligned with the setting sun. The other boats had begun to make the crossing back to the mainland, passing by us, the laughter and shouts of our guests distracting us.

Persie sat at the prow, looking at the sun. I zoomed in with my camera, asking her to look at me, to look at the sunset, to turn up to face the sky that was bleeding in crimson. *Just at the right time*, I thought to myself as she balanced precariously on the edge of the small boat. The wind blew her voluminous wedding dress towards the sea, and I kept snapping away without looking through the lens. Reality was so much more seductive, so I stole a few glances for my own pleasure, forgetting about the photos.

One of the boats came closer—someone wanted to take a photo of the two of us on the boat. I returned to my lens and did not stop taking pictures until I felt the boat shudder, hit by the bow wave of a passing boat.

Persie, unprepared, lost her balance and tried to hold on, grabbing the rope that tied the prow to the small mast. It was not taut enough, and she leaned over. To avoid smashing against the boat's edge, she jumped into the water.

I confess I could not hold back my laughter. She had fallen so comically, letting out a yelp of despair at the impending ruination of her dress. I was surprised not to hear her call out, and I leaned over the side to pull her up. I could not see her, and I assumed she must be on the other side of the boat. I called out her name.

When I could not spot her over the other side either, I began to worry. Dropping my camera, I dashed to the prow. The light was rapidly diminishing, and I could no longer see clearly. I felt my heart race. The passing boat had stopped, and I could hear everyone's anxious cries. I held onto the edge and leaned over the spot she had jumped from. I prayed she was playing a joke, that she would burst to the surface at any moment.

In the dim light, I saw something that turned my blood cold. Her white wedding dress was blurrily sinking a few meters beneath the surface, and I could see nothing other than the floating fabric and the shadow of her flailing arms as she struggled to rise to the surface.

I fell in the water, clumsily, and swam down to find her. I opened my eyes and saw Persie below me, fighting against the weight of the soaked wedding dress that was pulling her down to the depths. With hardly any oxygen in my lungs, I swam downward with all my strength, trying to reach her. The more I moved, the deeper she seemed to sink.

My lungs began to ache, but I kept pushing on, refusing to resurface to catch my breath. I would not lose sight of her, no matter what, even if our fate was to drown here, together.

When I finally reached Persie, I grabbed a handful of fabric and began to rise to the surface, using the last of my oxygen reserves. The dark water hindered my eyesight. Gripping the dress tightly, I summoned all my strength, trying to rise with her. Despite my efforts, we moved with painful slowness. Bubbles of air escaped my lips, and I watched Persie, who seemed to be losing her strength, her movements becoming slower as she abandoned all effort.

I took her face in my hands, desperate. Frightened, her eyes sought mine, and she grabbed me. I felt someone pull my hair, tugging me upward, and I managed to grab Persie's arm with the last of my strength, pulling her with me. Every ounce of my being was focused on holding her arm.

I felt the water rushing into my mouth, scorching my lungs. I closed my eyes and, as I lost consciousness, I felt her arm slowly slipping from my grasp ...

# Patmos

As much as you may want to believe that you will one day find your life's destination, there comes a moment when everything either scatters like dust before you, or a new, magical world suddenly forms. Such a new world, filled with intense feelings, was born inside me when I first saw Persie on stage, interpreting the myth of Persephone. The way fate had woven our lives together was not only rare, but inconceivable for anyone who was not present during the events that shaped our paths. Everything happened with lightning speed, as if the portal that destiny had opened in the fabric of time would not last for long. The thirst of the past to see justice rendered in the present was assuaged, leaving salvation behind for some, and punishment for others.

I don't think I will ever forget the fact that we managed to escape our watery tomb. Our saviors later told us that they'd managed to pull us out literally at the last minute. A fisherman had dived down and pulled me to the surface with the help of a rope. My grip on Persie's arm had saved her; otherwise, the water that had turned her wedding dress to lead would have dragged my beloved to the bottom of the sea.

Despite being practically unconscious, I did not let go of Persie until we were both at the surface. I recovered my senses back on the boat almost immediately, and anxiously watched Renée trying to resuscitate Persie. Thankfully, she recovered quickly enough, putting an end to my agony. They took us both to the hospital, where we received first aid and they kept Persie overnight.

I still remember our guests, suddenly finding themselves outside a hospital instead of a wedding party, waiting for the test results as if Persie was their own child. Renée turned out to have been a competitive swimmer before she got into acting, where she had learned about resuscitation from drowning. After the doctor cleared me, I took her into the hall and thanked her profusely for saving the love of my life.

Renée had been on the boat that had rocked us, and had watched the whole scene unfold. She had quickly understood what had happened, and dived in with Michael and everyone else. Then they had all climbed onto the boat, and she had given Persie the kiss of life.

The following morning, Persie got a clean bill of health and left the hospital. The doctors had said that she would quickly be able to resume her normal life because of her excellent physical condition. Our wedding feast may not have taken place, but at least it had not been followed by the most detestable ceremony of them all ...


Gazing at the sea, I felt how vast and how small at the same time our world was. I watched Persie swim away and, admittedly, after everything that had happened, I felt anxious seeing her in the water. As if I were afraid that some force would pull her down to the depths. The image on the cover of the *Abduction* program, of Persephone struggling to surface, had almost proven morbidly prophetic for Persie.

The Stone of *Kalikatsou* rose beside me on the beach, like an ancient stone altar. The hotel owner had told me that it was named after a bird locally known as *Kalikatsou*, which used to nest on the top of the rock and lay its egg. He also told me that some claimed the strangely shaped rock had been placed there by aliens.

I always loved to hear the stories behind a name or a legend. Such stories abounded in Greece, always fascinating and never ceasing to impress me.

As Persie swam in my direction, her body left a wavy line on the calm surface of the sea. Michael had given us a wonderful wedding gift, handing us an envelope the day after the wedding when everything had calmed down. We were now enjoying his present on Patmos, where we were staying at one of the nicest hotels I had ever seen. It was not just the luxurious accommodation, but the friendliness of our hosts. Most had heard our story and understood our need for seclusion.

Although it was early October, the weather was very good and the tranquility of the island just what we needed after our adventure. It also provided a welcome escape from the journalists clamoring to learn everything about us. Renée's presence at our wedding had drawn more attention to our already well-known history. She had become the heroine who had saved Persie's life.

We had arranged to meet with her during our next trip to Paris, as we now felt that her presence at our wedding had not been a coincidence. Persie, half-jokingly, would say that she had been reborn thanks to Renée. Reborn: that is what Renée's name meant in French.

We had done our best to keep the trip to Patmos a secret, and the hotel personnel had played a decisive part in that. We stayed at one of the nicest rooms in the hotel, and I had already scouted numerous locations I wanted to photograph. I had been impressed by the attention to detail they had paid when they renovated one of the old state-owned hotels. I hoped others would follow their example throughout Greece.

We wished we could stay longer, and agreed to return the following summer or during Easter. Everyone told us that Easter on the island was mesmerizing, mostly thanks to its monastic community. Besides, we had a lot of work waiting for us back in Athens. Persie intended to put on her show just before Christmas, and was already scheduling appointments and auditions. She was very happy because, during our stay here, she had learned that she had been licensed to use the *rebetiko* songs she'd wanted, and one of the best-known bands in Greece had agreed to perform them live for her show every evening.

There were hardly any tourists on Grikos beach in front of our hotel. The season was drawing to a close and the island was quiet. As soon as I sensed Persie near me, I stood up with a towel, ready to shield her from the cool autumnal wind. Water dripping from her hair, she walked up to me and took the towel to dry her skin and hair.

Michael would be arriving shortly to take us somewhere, a surprise. He had been very specific about the departure time, for some reason only he knew. He had also told me to take my camera with me. Persie, on the other hand, wanted to give him a small gift, without disclosing any more details.

We had arrived the previous evening, and had only now stepped out of our room. It was such a lovely room, we could have happily spent our entire honeymoon holed up in there. However, we did not want to miss out on the beauties of the island, and were planning to visit the library and the grotto at the monastery the following morning.

Now, we had to hurry to be on time for our meeting with Michael, who treated Persie as his own flesh and blood ... When we had arrived, he had gifted her a portrait of her mother he had painted. Its title had stayed with me: *Forget Me Not*, written in cursive, and only Persie seemed to understand what it truly meant ...

I hugged her and, in a playful mood, lifted her high and twirled her. She cupped my face and kissed me. I put her down on the sand and she turned to go, motioning for me to follow her. What I saw just above her bikini bottom startled me: the pomegranate that marked her back now seemed to have cracked open, a tiny seed lying beside the original design.

I wondered when she had gotten it done, and how I had not noticed it the previous evening. Then I remembered that she had turned the lights off the moment we had stepped inside the room, and pulled me down onto the bed. I could not believe I had not noticed it. I chose not to ask her anything yet, and tried to remember the explanation she had given about the fruit cracking open with ripeness back then, that evening in Galaxidi ...

Michael drove the small car up a narrow street. Persie made herself comfortable in the passenger seat, and I sat in the back, holding her hand over the backrest. Like a tour guide, Michael spoke of the history of the island and the time of his arrival here. I imagined how difficult the revelations about the past must have been for him. His love for Melek had been so strong that after her supposed death he had been crushed. It had changed his life forever.

It was always hard to tell what Michael was feeling. Today was a rare exception—he seemed cheerful, happy to see us. Although Persie had wanted to make a donation to the monastery, he had insisted that she use the money for her children's charity in Ioannina. He told her that was where the money was needed the most, and stopped her sweetly yet firmly whenever she raised the matter.

Rather quickly, the two of them had built a warm relationship. From the open car window, she excitedly pointed to a rock standing in the middle of the sea, as if it had been dropped there by a human hand. Michael instantly pulled over.

"That is the famous *petrokaravo*, the stone ship in the sea," he said, looking at the rock, which was so intricately sculpted that it looked like an upturned boat. Although we did not ask, our curiosity was evident, so he continued. "Legend has it that many years ago, when pirates raided the island, they did not only loot homes but the monastery too, taking the votive offerings with them. The Saint cursed them as their ship sailed away, and ship and pirates all turned to stone on the spot."

Persie fixed her gaze on the stone. "It's my first visit to Patmos, and everything I had heard about the island pales in comparison to the energy of the place. Ever since we set foot here ... I don't know how else to explain it, but I feel like I've been here before ..."

I had briefly visited the island some years ago for professional reasons. Now, however, I felt just like Persie. I'd initially attributed it to the strong emotions of what we had just been through, but in the end, it was something else.

Michael, seeming in a hurry, started the engine and glanced at the sun, which was preparing to make its descent. His eyes were glued to the road. "I watched excerpts of your show ... *Abduction*. Although many in the monastic community do not like it because of the references to the Book of Revelation, I must admit your performance was breathtaking ... Not that I know much about dancing ..."

"You are an excellent judge," I jumped in, and they both laughed.

Persie, always modest, touched his shoulder in thanks. "It's a shame you did not watch it live. There is a video of the entire performance, but it's not the same ..."

"I'll watch your next show, which will be just as good if not better," he said, giving her a glance filled with pride.

We reached the end of the road. Just above us, on the mountain's peak, stood a small chapel. According to Michael, we were near the highest point of the island. We left the car behind and began to climb the whitewashed steps that led to the Church of Prophet Elias. I slung my camera over my shoulder and took Persie's hand. We looked towards the sunset and followed him, understanding then why he wanted us to be here at this precise hour.

As soon as we reached the chapel, Michael motioned for us to sit on the stone wall encircling the tiny church, which was locked. We obeyed, and turned our eyes to the west. The absolute stillness and the view filled me with a sense of completion. Persie sat between my legs and leaned against me. The shades of nature reflected in her eyes and tinted her face. I refrained from bringing out my camera. It was a moment to capture in our minds forever, and nowhere else.

None of us spoke. We enjoyed this magical moment as if we were the sole inhabitants of the island. The sun's glow dimmed as the crimson disk sank into the waters of the Icarian Sea, yet the sky surrounding it became ecstatically vibrant. We sat there, at peace, until the last bright fragment was lost over the horizon.

As if a gate had suddenly opened, a cool breeze brushed our faces, alerting us to the approaching nightfall. Michael had stood leaning against the chapel wall all this time, his dark clothes sharply contrasting with its pristine whiteness. My eyes drifted towards his hand. His missing digit would always be there to remind him of those nightmarish moments. I fought against the urge to photograph everything around us, not wanting to break the spell of this moment.

Persie turned towards Michael. "Thank you, Michael, not just for the wonderful gift of our hotel stay, but for this moment. I feel my soul has become lighter up here ..."

He smiled and came closer to us. "This is what I do when I want to lighten my burden, Persie. The realization that, as I watch the sun set someone on the other side of the world is watching it rise, attunes me to the circle of life and gives me the strength and energy to go on ..."

"Michael, there is something I want to ask you, but feel free not to answer," I said, unable to keep the question inside me any longer. He smiled and waited for me to pose the question. "Those two men—Ganas, and my alleged father—harmed you grievously, and you did not even ask whether they would ever face the consequences of their actions. Are you not angry that they stole your future?"

A faint smile spread on his lips as if he had been expecting the question. "Anger and a thirst for revenge keep us prisoners, Constantine. I overcame them years ago. As Kazantzakis said, there is no greater punishment for evil than kindness ..."

He glanced at the horizon, and his mood changed. "I'll leave you the car and return on foot. We'll meet at the taverna for dinner."

I felt bad he would be returning alone, and I tried to change his mind. "Come with us, we can leave now too ..."

He interrupted me with his calm voice and pointed to the sunset. "This is the best time to enjoy the view ... I like to walk in these parts, and I haven't done it in a while."

Persie then jumped out of my arms and took Michael's hand. "I was planning to do this at the taverna, but I don't think there is a better place than this ... Please wait for a moment."

She ran down the steps. We exchanged a puzzled look, as I too had no idea what she was talking about. She grabbed something from the car and returned. She caught her breath and stretched her palm towards Michael. A small wooden box tied in a red ribbon lay in her hand. "My mother left this box in the envelope with the letter, and I think you should be the one to have it," she said.

Perplexed, Michael gingerly picked up the box and untied the ribbon. He slowly opened it and removed a faded piece of paper wrapped in a plastic membrane. He carefully unfolded the piece of paper, his movements cautious, ceremonial, largely due to his work at the library. Something was inside the folded paper, and he peeked inside before unfolding it completely. He gave us a look of incomprehension, and delicately opened it up.

A dried flower lay there, a very old blossom. Persie waited for the flower to be entirely revealed, and only spoke then. "My mother left the flower in the letter, saying it was the flower you had given her on your first visit. Her only instruction was that I do not forget her, and she left it to me in the belief that you were dead. I think it belongs to you ..."

Michael looked at the flower in disbelief. We kept still, anxiously waiting for his reaction. The wind blew his long hair against his face. He spoke softly. "A legend tells of a beautiful blue flower that grew on the banks of a river. A young couple, very much in love, happened to pass by. The girl spotted the pretty bloom on the steep banks and admired it. Her young lover, ignoring her cries of alarm, ran to fetch it for her. He cut the blossom and, as he was about to give it to her, he slipped and fell in the water. He struggled against the current, but it was too strong for him. She watched him get swept away and her tears echoed in the valley. The young man, before succumbing to the river bed, managed to throw the flower to his beloved, shouting one thing before he was lost forever ... *Forget me not!*"

He paused and gazed vacantly at the horizon. Persie, understanding his turmoil, finished the narration about the flower and the way she had managed to keep it with her. When she was finished, Michael took her hand and kissed it. He folded the piece of paper and replaced it inside the box, then cupped the box in his palm as if he wished to shield it. He was struggling to maintain his composure. "I'll see you at the port in a short while ... A fisherman friend had a good catch and is expecting us ..."

Michael was already walking away as he said this, possibly to hide his tears. That's when I understood what the title of the portrait meant, the significance of this flower for them. I decided that I would take Persie to see her favorite flower on the island of St. George in Galaxidi the following spring. *Meriza,* Violet had called it, that evening when she had described how her friend liked to sniff them but never cut them when in bloom ...

I watched Michael walk down the steep slope until he disappeared from our view.

"I like how you don't disclose all your secrets, and I want you to keep doing that ..." I told her.

"You can be sure of that," she teased, and snuggled into my arms like a small child.

We fell silent again, but I wanted to share my thoughts with her. "Based on what we know, there is a possibility Michael is your father ... Would you like to know for certain? Did you ever ask him?"

She replied instantly, without too much thought. "I feel like he is the closest thing to family anyhow, so I don't intend to try to prove it. I have had enough of investigations and questions from the past. Whatever was to be revealed has been revealed ..."

"I don't think *everything* has been revealed, do you?" I pointedly asked.

She looked at me, confused.

"You never told me the reason you changed your mind about coming to Galaxidi that evening at the theatre," I explained.

"I see you never forget anything," she said, giving me a playful pinch. She then became serious once again. "You told me something my father used to say, used the exact same words. I did not think it a coincidence. That phrase was mostly what made me change my mind."

"What did I say? It was a difficult evening, as you remember ..."

"You told me 'You were born to do magical things.' That's what my father told me every day, and you can I imagine how I felt when I heard it coming from you ..."

She slowly turned towards me and rested her back against my chest. She lifted her hand and looked at the ring I had given her in Ioannina. I don't think it had left her finger since then. I wrapped my arms around her middle, and, pushing her hair aside, kissed her neck. She turned her face towards me and tenderly touched me. The absolute peace that surrounded us filled our souls.

Unable to contain myself any longer, I decided to ask her about the tattoo. "I saw the pomegranate has now split open ..." I said, stroking her tattoo.

"Yes, it has ..." she replied and turned towards me, wrapping her legs around me so our bodies came face to face.

"What does it mean?"

"I thought you would remember. I told you when and why it would crack open ... Have you forgotten?"

"No, I haven't," I replied, startled. "Are you trying to tell me that ..."

Before I could finish my sentence, her hand covered my mouth and then our lips met. All I could now hear was the soft sea breeze cooling us ...

Kostas Krommydas

# In the beginning ...

The moans of a woman echoing down the staircase struck terror in the heart of Michael. He had never been to a brothel before. His meeting with Melek a few days ago at the police station of Ioannina was the reason behind his sudden presence.

She had tried to run away. Unable to speak each other's language, they had at least managed to understand the basics. Seeing her in such a bad state, he had tried to help her without even knowing why she was there. They had hidden in a closet, could hear the policemen looking for her. Young and inexperienced as he was, he could not understand why she was running away. He had instinctively squeezed in the closet beside her.

He had never been so close to a woman's body before. The only woman to have hugged him until then had been his mother. He had been struck by the beauty of Melek's face, but even more so by the beauty of her eyes. Although she was in a bad state, her looks had entranced him.

When they thought the policemen had given up their search, she had snuck out first. Before Michael could follow her, a policeman lying in ambush had grabbed her, and he had stayed in the dark, alone, shaking with fear and anger that he had not helped her. What could he have done, though? At best, he would have ended up in prison with her.

Later, once he made certain no one was watching him, he had managed to sneak out of a window undetected. He hid, and waited to see what would happen to the magical creature that had crossed his path. He saw her leave the station with a policeman and hurriedly get inside a car. He ran behind them as fast as he could, sprinting down the alleys and following them. He saw them pull up outside a house by the lake, and hid for a while, then hesitatingly approached the house.

When he came nearer, he realized where they had brought her. He had been warned never to come to such places, never to copulate with these monster-women who would fill him with diseases, some of them fatal. He saw the policeman leave the house and spit an unlit cigarette, and realized who it was. The man was new in town, recently transferred, and already rumors were flying about his bullying tactics. As soon as the policeman left, Michael tried to sneak inside, but failed.

It took him to days to earn enough money to be able to come to the brothel. Now he sat outside its door, waiting to see her. He just prayed she was still there.

In front of him, a toothless wreck of a man was curiously observing him. He had tried to slam the door in Michael's face but, once he had seen the money, he let him in. The women's cries could still be heard, a sign that a customer was getting his money's worth. The wait seemed endless to him. Inexperienced, he did not know how he was supposed to behave, and blushed with shame.

A few minutes later, three women slowly came down the stairs and stood before him. They were in their underwear, and as he glanced at them, he did not find the face he was looking for. Melek recognized him, though. Her eyes were sad, but lit up when she saw him. That's when Michael recognized her too, her makeup and clothes in no way resembling the pure, clear face he had seen a few days ago at the police station.

He stood up and firmly pointed at her, telling the disgusting man that she was the one he wanted. He walked up to Michael and stretched out his hand, asking for payment first in his tinny voice. The stench of his clothes filled the air around him. Skeletal, he looked like a specter ready to attack, his sunken eyes two dark holes in his face. Michael handed over the money, and the old man crumpled it up in his fist.

Melek grabbed his hand and pulled him towards the stairs. He squeezed her hand as the other two women watched them climb up the first steps. The sounds of fake pleasure grew louder as they neared the landing.

They entered a room, dimly lit by a flickering oil lamp hanging from a nail above the bed. The smell of cheap perfume burned his nostrils. Awkwardly, Michael approached Melek, and she instantly made to remove her underwear. He stopped her, trying to explain that this was not what he had come for in a low voice. Melek stared at him as it slowly dawned on her that he was not here for her body. The woman's moans in the other room grew louder, foretelling her pretend climax, accompanied by the squeaking bedsprings like a tuneless violin.

Melek looked at him and tried to stifle her laughter as the wooden partition that separated the two rooms shook, threatening to collapse on them. She had heard the noises before in the few days she had been here. It was becoming a monotonous, routine sound to her ears. The older women had shown her how to react when a client picked her, to convince him that he was giving her pleasure. Michael smiled awkwardly, having never found himself in a similar situation before.

After a triumphant crescendo, things seemed to quiet down. Melek took his hand and gestured at him to sit on the bed. In a whisper, she told him her name, and then he spoke his.

"Michael," she repeated slowly, to see if she was pronouncing it correctly.

He repeated her name, too. Introductions over, they both smiled, pleased at their first successful conversation. Her eyes sparkled like emeralds, and he was mesmerized by the crimson waves of her hair. He had never seen a woman who looked like her before. Timidly, he reached out and brushed her hair away from her face. She shifted so he could see her more clearly, face to face. They exchanged an innocent look, like two children that had just met and were examining one another.

Slowly, Melek moved in for a kiss, and he stared at her, unprepared, eyes bulging. As soon as she sensed his awkwardness, she brought her hands to his lips and, holding his face, gave him a swift kiss. When she pulled away, Michael kept his eyes closed, trying to lock the feel of her lips inside his heart. Melek tried to say *kiss* but struggled to find the word, and he slowly enunciated it for her.

They spent some time like this, him saying Greek words and their meaning. Michael pointed at the two of them and tried in vain to get her to say *destiny,* a word she could not pronounce. He did manage to teach her what preoccupied him the most at that moment: *Kiss me.*

When Melek understood the phrase and could say it, she looked him straight in the eyes and spoke the words with feeling. Unused to such things, he started, then came closer. He was clumsy, and she smiled. She motioned for him to say the phrase, and then moved closer, giving him a tender kiss. Everything that was happening was reminiscent of teenage love, rather than two people in a brothel. When they stopped kissing, a sadness came over her features, and she slowly said "I leave," pointing outside the window.

Michael, who had been the witness of her first attempt to escape, understood what she wanted and tried to come to an understanding with her, but failed. All he managed to convey was that he would help her.

The loud knock on the wooden door startled them. The tinny voice of the man rang out again, telling them to hurry up. They both jumped up, realizing the time had come to part. Her eyes brimmed with tears, which then began to flow down her cheeks. Realizing he was running out of time, Michael took a small blue flower from his coat pocket and gave it to her. She smiled through her tears and brought it up to her nose.

"Forget-me-not," he said, and pointed to the blue blossom, trying to teach her the words.

She looked at him intently, then pulled him in for one more kiss. Before opening the door for him, she showed him the flower and struggled to repeat its name. She failed, and Michael hurriedly whispered before the door closed: "Don't forget me!"

# The Letter

*I have started this letter many times over, and every time I read what I wrote, I would tear it up, finding it lacking. I cannot even remember how long it has taken me to complete it, so you can read it today in this, its final form. I am writing the last few words before I enter the hospital again. I have a feeling this will be my last attempt. I have always hoped I would be able to tell you all this in person, but as you are now holding this letter in your hand, I have obviously failed.*

*The few seconds I knew you for, after you left my womb, were enough for you to steal my heart forever. What I would not give to spend another second in your presence, to hold you in my arms for a moment. To feel your heart beat against mine, just like when I had you inside me. I have missed all the simple, everyday things a mother does with her child. To feed you, to scold you, to have you scold me. To see you spread your wings. To rediscover the world through your eyes.*

*I don't know if another mother has written a letter to her unknown child. I want you to know that I never stopped thinking about you. The years would pass, and you would grow up in my thoughts. I pictured you going to school, making friends, finding love, even if I didn't know your sex. As much as I longed for a daughter, I prayed that the child they had snatched from me was a boy, that it may never experience life as I had, as a woman.*

*I don't know what you will have heard about me, but I will try to describe who I am and how things came to be like this. I was born in a village in Armenia. My parents fled our homeland as refugees, and we quickly found ourselves on the Turkish border. I grew up in camps and slums, in cold and dirt. My family was so impoverished that my father decided to sell me to a Turkish traveler. I still remember my young brother's tears, as he cried and begged my father not to give me away.*

*Initially, I thought that if I followed the man my father had given me to, I would be free from our miserable existence. I felt that I would be helping my family and living like a human being ought to. Little did I know that the true nightmare had just begun, that I would soon be yearning for life as I had previously known it. The price of the exchange, as I later found out, had been my virginity ...*

*My real torment began when I arrived in Greece. I thought I would be working as a servant for the man they had sold me to. That is what my father had told me. Later, I ascertained that my virginity had been the good my father had traded. Even as I write these words, I struggle to believe that the man who brought me into this world was aware of the intentions of the buyer. If he did, then he committed the greatest sin there is. This suspicion is the reason I never looked for my parents.*

*After a while, once the man who bought me had fully enjoyed his purchase, he brought me to a cheap brothel close to the lake of Ioannina. I am ashamed, but yes, I did have to work as a prostitute. I had no other choice; I was a prisoner in that house of hell. I was so young, so frightened. There are people who hide a monster behind a mask of kindness—I met many of those in my life.*

*When I tried to run away, I realized that even if I managed to leave the actual house, I would never be able to escape them. Filth, corruption, and depravity can spread their tentacles far and wide. I endured this torture, giving my body to insatiable animals. There is no point in describing what I suffered in any detail. It is too violent, too inhuman, and I wish that the memories burn and vanish with me.*

*Just when I thought all was lost, that I was destined to live a life of bleakness, Michael came into my life. He was the only person who ever truly loved me, who gave me hope. He tried to save me, and paid the price with his own life.*

*I am so sorry you will never get to meet him. He sacrificed himself for me when he could have escaped, and I will never forgive myself for it. I wish I could turn back time and fix everything ... I pray that this unbearable sadness ends with me, that nothing like what I had to live through ever touches your life. The only thing that has kept me alive since my escape has been the hope that I will meet you again someday. That hope is now slowly dying with me. Something tells me that for this meeting to take place, a sacrifice must be made ...*

*Michael and I decided to run away and try to build a better life for ourselves. I felt a defenseless soul growing inside me. I wanted to pull you away from all this darkness, to bring you somewhere bright and sunny where you could flourish like a blossom in spring ...*

*In the months until your birth, my only concern was how to keep you from them, how to run away. I failed. They snatched you, and I never got to see your face, to touch your tiny fingers, to give you your first caress.*

*The lake I hope you now see before you has been my heaven and my hell. There will always be a part of me in its waters. I am not talking of my ashes, but something stronger, something I lived with the only man who loved me, the only man I ever loved. That is the heritage I leave you. Love.*

*The only thing I have of him is inside the letter you have just opened. It is what remains of the flower he once gave me, when he asked me to never forget him. That is the meaning of that tiny flower. That is its name, although it took me a long time to say it. How I managed to keep it with me all these years is nothing short of a miracle ...*

*When they snatched you and Michael away from me, I thought my life was over.*

*I regret everything I did so I could escape. I felt I had no other choice, and the guilt will stay with me forever. The currency I had used to survive until that time was also the currency that saved me. My body kept me alive, against my will.*

*I snuck out of Ioannina, travelled with the gypsies for a while until I found myself in Paris. When I first saw the Eiffel Tower, I thought I was dreaming. Without any papers and with no one to help me, it was not long before I was doing the only thing I knew how to do well. The guilt that plagued me about the harm I had caused never allowed me to believe I could escape my miserable existence. Except that here work conditions were better; I was getting paid. I then set myself a goal—to save as much money as I could, and then come find you.*

*As the years went by, I began to realize that it would be difficult to suddenly appear before you and tell you who I am. Although I no longer needed to work to survive, I continued to sell my body to leave you as much money as I could, fooling myself into believing that it would somehow make up for the time we did not spend together.*

*My only source of comfort has been that you must have gone somewhere better after they snatched you from me, and I hope with all my heart you were raised with peace and love and that they fill your life to this day. Desire and logic fought inside me, logic saying it would be wrong to seek you.*

*I am certain that the disease ravaging my body now is part of my punishment for my past actions. I had a simple choice after everything that had happened: to die, or to live, trying to make peace with my guilt and the suffering that had befallen me. I chose life, and I never regretted it. Even now, when I could be gone at any moment, I choose life. I hope you do the same, for as long as you breathe, every day you watch the sun rise.*

*Maybe all this means nothing to you, and I will not try to take on the role of mother in a letter, a role I hope another woman played in your life in the best possible way. But I do think that, even at this point, you have the right to know who your birth mother was. To know that she loved you dearly, even if she never saw you. I also want everything I own to go to you. It might mean nothing to you, but please accept it. It will give meaning, purpose, to everything I went through and earned ...*

*Believe me when I say it is nothing compared to true happiness. And, because I got to experience it, albeit fleetingly, I want to reassure you that it is out there. I urge you to seek it if you have not found it. And when you find it, I want you to grab it and not let anything stand in its way. Selfishness keeps happiness locked inside a cage. I hope you experience what I didn't have a chance to. I hope you meet a person who makes you feel what I felt for Michael. As you understand, it is hard for me to tell you whether he was your birth father, but it was a role he had taken on, without any thought for himself or the consequences. And that makes him a better father than most.*

*I could write a book about everything I have lived through, but all I want you to understand is that you must live. You must seize every moment that life gives you and add value to it. Life is to be lived now, today, every second that passes never to return, not in postponed wishes that never materialize. To have children and watch them grow and have their own. And when your time comes, to know that you have watched the seeds you planted bloom and continue the perpetual journey of life that you have bequeathed them.*

*I don't know if what I leave you will make your life more comfortable. What I hope is that it makes it more valuable. I wish things had taken a different course. I hope the story of my life goes beyond the discovery of who your birth mother was, and acts as an incentive for you to understand that what you have and love will not last forever. And so, that you must tend to it and fight for it.*

*All I ask, whatever you may think of me, is what my beloved told me when he gave me the flower you now hold. You are the only beautiful thing I manage to live behind, even though I have never seen your face. You are the reason I came into this world, and the only reason I can leave it with some sense of peace. I only beg of you of one thing, so that my life may have been worth the while. My child, forget me not ...*

*M.*

Kostas Krommydas

# About the author

When Kostas Krommydas decided to write his first novel, he took the publishing world of his native Greece by storm. A few years later, he is an award winning author of five bestselling novels, acclaimed actor, teacher and passionate storyteller. His novels have been among the top 10 at the prestigious Public Book Awards (Greece) and his novel "Ouranoessa" has won first place (2017). He has also received the coveted WISH writer's award in 2013 as an emerging author. When not working on his next novel at the family beach house in Athens, you will find him acting on theatre, film, and TV; teaching public speaking; interacting with his numerous fans; and writing guest articles for popular Greek newspapers, magazines, and websites. If you want to find out more about Costas, visit his website, http://kostaskrommydas.gr/ or check out his books on Amazon: Author.to/KostasKrommydas

# More Books

---

## Cave of Silence

### A Love So Strong, It Ripples Through the Ages.

Dimitri, a young actor, is enjoying the lucky break of his life—a part in an international production shot on an idyllic Greek island and a romance with Anita, his beautiful co-star. When his uncle dies, he has one last wish: that Dimitri scatters his ashes on the island of his birthplace. At first, Dimitri welcomes this opportunity to shed some light on his family's history—a history clouded in secrecy. But why does his mother beg him to hide his identity once there?

Dimitri discovers that the past casts long shadows onto the present when his visit sparks a chain of events that gradually reveal the island's dark secrets; secrets kept hidden for far too long. Based on true events, the *Cave Of Silence* moves seamlessly between past and present to spin a tale of love, passion, betrayal, and cruelty. Dimitris and Anita may be done with the past. But is the past done with them?

# More Books

---

## Athora

**A Mystery Romance set on the Greek Islands.**

A tourist is found dead in Istanbul, the victim of what appears to be a ritual killing. An elderly man is murdered in the same manner, in his house by Lake Como. The priest of a small, isolated Greek island lies dead in the sanctuary, his body ritualistically mutilated. Fotini Meliou is visiting her family on the island of Athora for a few days, before starting a new life in the US. She is looking forward to a brief respite and, perhaps, becoming better acquainted with the seductive Gabriel, whom she has just met. It is not the summer vacation she expects it to be. A massive weather bomb is gathering over the Aegean, threatening to unleash the most violent weather the area has ever seen. When the storm breaks out, the struggle begins. A race against the elements and a race against time: the killer is still on the island, claiming yet another victim. Locals, a boatload of newly arrived refugees, foreign residents, and stranded tourists are now trapped on an island that has lost contact with the outside world. As the storm wreaks havoc on the island, how will they manage to survive?

# More Books

---

## Dominion of the Moon

**Award Winner, Public Readers' Choice Awards 2017**

In the final stages of WWII, archaeologist Andreas Stais follows the signs that could lead him to unearth the face of the goddess who has been haunting his dreams for years, all the while searching for the woman who, over a brief encounter, has come to dominate his waking hours. In present day Greece, another Andreas, an Interpol officer, leaves New York and returns to his grandparents' island to bid farewell to his beloved grandmother.

Once there, he will come face to face with long-buried family secrets and the enigmatic Iro.  When gods and demons pull the threads, no one can escape their fate. Pagan rituals under the glare of the full moon and vows of silence tied to a sacred ring, join men and gods in a common path.

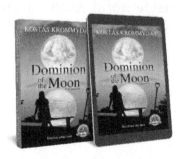

*Very soon, more novels from Kostas Krommydas will be available on Kindle. Sign up to receive our newsletter or follow Kostas on facebook, and we will let you know as soon as they are uploaded!*

Want to contact Kostas? Eager for updates?

Want an e-book autograph?

Follow him on

https://www.linkedin.com/in/kostas-krommydas

https://www.instagram.com/krommydaskostas/

https://www.facebook.com/Krommydascostas/

https://twitter.com/KostasKrommydas

Amazon author page:

Author.to/KostasKrommydas

If you wish to report a typo or have reviewed this book on Amazon please email onioncostas@gmail.com with the word "review" on the subject line, to receive a free 1680x1050 desktop background.

Thank you for taking the time to read *Lake of Memories.* If you enjoyed it, please tell your friends or post a short review. Word of mouth is an author's best friend and much appreciated!

Made in the USA
Las Vegas, NV
23 June 2023

73790123R00243